D1650498

Feminine Wiles

Larry bent Marissa over his desk and pushed her dress up over her back. His other hand trailed slowly down between her smooth buttocks. She felt her sex flutter. He leant over to whisper in her ear: 'You are one wicked lady, Marissa. What we plan to do to Kelly really turns you on, doesn't it?'

Marissa moaned with arousal, her eyes closed, her excitement increasing.

'You know what?' he continued. 'It kind of turns me on, too.'

Marissa laughed softly. 'You are one wicked guy, Larry. How wicked can you get?'

'Let's see,' he said, undoing his zip.

Feminine Wiles
Karina Moore

BLACK LACE

Black Lace books contain sexual fantasies.
In real life, always practise safe sex.

This edition published in 2004 by
Black Lace
Thames Wharf Studios
Rainville Road
London W6 9HA

Originally published 1998

Copyright © Karina Moore 1998

The right of Karina Moore to be identified as the Author of
the Work has been asserted in accordance with the Copyright,
Designs and Patents Act 1988.

Design by Smith & Gilmour, London
Printed and bound by Mackays of Chatham PLC

ISBN 0 352 33874 1

*All characters in this publication are fictitious and any resemblance
to real persons, living or dead, is purely coincidental.*

This book is sold subject to the condition that it shall not, by way
of trade or otherwise, be lent, resold, hired out or otherwise
circulated without the publisher's prior written consent in any form
of binding or cover other than that in which it is published and
without a similar condition including this condition being imposed
on the subsequent purchaser.

1

It was the kind of day that Kelly Aslett loved. Sunny and hot, with the vaguest hint of a breeze. Kelly was thankful for the cooling summer wind as she walked slowly along the street, glancing up at the numbers on each of the fine, dusty, old buildings. In her hand was the torn strip of paper on which, in the middle of the crowded café-bar, he had hastily scribbled down the address. 46 rue Cathédrale. The building opposite was 42. Just a couple more steps and she would be there.

Kelly was feeling slightly giddy. Luc Duras would be famous one day. Kelly knew that instinctively. A modern-day Degas or Manet. His work already had the touch of genius – she had seen it for herself. It was an honour that he wanted her to sit for him. The fact that his eyes had the sparkle of a bottle of Dom Perignon, cool and clear, and as green as a Mediterranean rock pool, was totally beside the point!

A little thrill shot through her as she paused in front of a corner building. Double checking the rather rusty numbers to the side of the door, she assured herself they were a four and a six and then tripped lightly up the steps, pressing the button with a simple 'Luc' scrawled in the space beside it.

'*Oui*?' The voice that responded was crackly, distorted by the intercom.

'It's Kelly.'

'Ah, Kelly. *Entrez*,' said the voice, buzzing her through.

Once inside, she stepped into the lift, an ornamental, cage-like structure built from rusting wrought iron. As the lift groaned into life, rattling skywards with a series of clanks and shudders, Kelly nervously gripped the bars with her fingers.

Luc was there to meet her on the landing at the top. She caught her breath as she saw him, releasing her fingers far too abruptly from their tight grip on the bars, hurling herself backwards in the process. Klutz! she winced to herself, feeling her face burn with embarrassment.

Luc stepped forward. He pulled back the lift's concertinaed railing, his eyes dipping to the five inch gap between the bottom of the lift and the landing floor. With his eyes lowered, his thick, dark eyelashes dusted cheekbones so high and so perfect they could have been sculpted in bronze by Michelangelo.

'*Faites attention.* Careful,' he warned, eyeing her ultra-trendy sandals. 'You do not want to get the heel stuck.'

He helped her out, one very tanned, paint-splattered hand grasping her firmly at the elbow. Kelly felt a frisson of excitement as his fingers made contact with her flesh and when he kissed her on both cheeks by way of a greeting, stepping back so that she could walk in front of him through the open doorway, she wondered if, all things considered, she might not have done better to turn down his invitation to model.

The studio was large and refreshingly airy. Enormous windows covered two of the walls, several of which had been opened slightly, and the muted sounds of the city drifted in. Canvases were all about, stacked against the walls, around the floor. Crayons, charcoal, paints and oils of every conceivable type and colour were crammed on metal wallshelves.

Kelly wandered into the middle of the room, her heels knocking loudly on the hardwood flooring. She glanced around with interest. Strange that his studio should be so modern and well equipped. She had expected something different, older, more like the building's exterior. It was not quite the impoverished artist's garret! Perhaps he had a patron of some kind, she mused, picturing in her mind a tall, gaunt woman dressed in a man's suit, a gravel-voiced, Greta Garbo type figure.

The door clicked shut and Kelly turned. Luc was leaning nonchalantly with his back against the wall, arms crossed on his chest. 'We will begin?' he asked quietly, his voice low and lazy and as smooth as melted chocolate.

'Mmm,' said Kelly, busily shaking off the image of the phantom patron. 'Where shall I –?'

'Over there please, *chérie*.'

Chérie! Kelly knew his use of the endearment was casual but even so it pleased her, and his voice, with its ever-so-slightly accented English, actually made the back of her neck tingle.

She looked over to where he had gestured. Three large white cushions had been arranged in front of a white backdrop. Shafts of sunlight filtered through from the windows, highlighting parts of the whiteness into brilliant, dappled luminescence. The effect was startling.

Kelly, aware of his eyes upon her, walked slowly over and casually dropped her bag.

'Please make yourself comfortable while I mix the palette.' Luc pushed away from the wall. 'It will take me only a little time.'

'OK,' said Kelly, draping herself over the cushions, only too eager to watch him at work. His light-brown hair was slightly wavy, longish, and gently curling as it met the collar of his faded shirt. A tiny gold cross nestled gypsy-like in the lobe of one ear, flashing brightly when he lifted his head to hold the colours to the light. Kelly let her eyes surreptitiously drop, gliding downward to his long, muscled legs, clad in extremely old, extremely faded button-fly Levis which hung very sexily from a lean pair of hips.

Within minutes he was ready and glanced across at her. To her bewilderment, he chuckled. 'You understand how I like to paint you?' he asked, a hint of teasing in his voice.

Kelly, gazing up rather raptly into eyes of liquid emerald, shook her head.

'Perhaps I was not clear,' said Luc. 'You see, I would like for you to undress.'

Undress! She exhaled suddenly in shock. 'Er, d'you mean ... that is ... completely?'

'Uh-huh,' drawled Luc absently, stooping down to sort through some brushes.

Kelly could not seem to move; she felt welded to the cushions. He wanted her to undress. Completely!

'It is OK?' Luc's voice, quiet though it was, made her jump.

Kelly flushed deeply. Naked. In front of him. Lord, why hadn't she realised? He was a painter, wasn't he!

'It is OK?' Luc repeated, his voice now edged with concern. 'We could leave it if you would prefer?'

Heat flared suddenly in the pit of her stomach. Those dark, green eyes gazing at her body. She drew in breath sharply at the thought as the heat spread alarmingly to the tops of her thighs and her pulse began to race haphazardly.

'Oh n-no, that's fine.' She strove for lightness in her tone, shrugging her shoulders and laughing dismissively. 'I'm kind of new to all this. I guess you'll have to lead me through it!'

Luc nodded once. 'OK,' he shrugged, busying himself once more with oils and brushes. The smell of turpentine began to permeate the air.

Kelly braced herself as she got up, fearful her legs

would give way. She turned her back and, with shaky hands, unbuttoned her white muslin shirt, slipping it off her shoulders and folding it carefully to the side. Her breasts, straining against the fine lace of her bra, suddenly felt swollen. Hurriedly she undid the clasp, eager to be free of the fabric's constraint, and immediately her breasts sprang forward, high and full, jiggling deliciously as she threw off the bra.

Slipping off her sandals, she felt for the button of her tight, black jeans. Behind her, she could hear the click-clicking of Luc's paint tray. He sounded impatient. Quickly, she pushed down her jeans, wriggling her hips slightly, easing them down to her ankles and stepping elegantly out of them until she stood barefoot, wearing only a pair of delicate, white briefs.

Hesitating for scarcely a moment, she took a deep breath, then swiftly pulled off the panties, tossing them across to the neat little pile of her clothes.

Standing tall, she stretched imperceptibly, welcoming the sudden freedom of total nudity, letting the warm summer air float over her with sweet, soft caresses. She had her back to Luc, not knowing whether he was looking at her, but knowing that he could be, knowing he could see her legs, her back, her bottom ... Far from unnerving her, the thought sent sparks zipping through her abdomen and she had to clench together her thigh muscles to still the riot of flutters in her groin.

Shaking back her long, tawny hair, she took another deep, fortifying breath, then turned.

But Luc was entirely preoccupied. Chin in hand, one elbow resting on his workbench, he was staring down at a sketch laid out across it. He seemed to have forgotten she was even there.

'Ahem,' she coughed, swallowing a sense of disappointment.

Luc raised his head at the noise and looked at her

intently. Despite her nudity, his cool, calm expression did not alter.

'Please,' he indicated, pointing to the cushions with the open palm of his hand. Then he lowered his eyes again and continued to contemplate the sketch in front of him.

Slightly miffed by his lack of reaction, Kelly sat down, her bottom sinking into the deep, feather-filled comfort of the cushions. She curled her long, slim legs beneath her and modestly rested her hands at the apex of her thighs. The fleecy down on her pubis tickled her palms softly and as she sat, the seconds ticking by, the wisps of air still tracing her body, she found herself longing to push her fingers down, to twine them in her soft, springy triangle of hair, slide them, deeper, further, into the slippery wetness that was gathering. With bated breath, she awaited Luc's instructions.

Without speaking, his face still blank, he walked towards her and crouched down on his haunches in front of her, elbows out as he rested his hands on his knees. He and Kelly were eye level and he looked at her thoughtfully, almost distantly, for what seemed like eternity. He had roughly rolled up the sleeves of his shirt and Kelly stared at his strong, tanned forearms, at the splodges of paint on the backs of his hands. He was only inches from her, so near that she could see the start of a whiskery shadow pepper the smooth, dark skin of his cheeks.

Suddenly he spoke. 'I can show you how I would like you?'

'Yeah, sure,' she answered timidly.

He placed his hands on her shoulders, hands that felt wonderfully cool on her heated flesh. Gently, he straightened her posture and then, with light pressure on her legs, indicated that she should sit in a kneeling position.

'Now lean back,' he said. 'Lean on your arms and tilt your head back also.'

Kelly willingly complied and found in so doing that her breasts were thrust forwards and upwards, their pert, pinky-brown tips almost scraping against the pockets of his shirt. He reached towards her and pushed her hair back so it hung, long and straight, behind her and then he twisted his hands through the shining curtain, scrunching it up into a tousled, tangled mass. Kelly remained motionless, not daring to move.

Seconds later he stood up straight, hands on hips. '*Oui*,' he murmured as if to himself. He nodded decisively as he backed towards his easel and immediately began to work.

Kelly posed and Luc sketched, then painted. Neither of them spoke. Trickles of sunlight filtered through the open windows, warming Kelly's golden body, and a mild, titillating breeze played persistently back and forth across her breasts. Aware her nipples were swelling, Kelly half-closed her eyes, dreamily watching the motion of Luc's arms, the quick, deft movements of his hands. Her breasts began to ache for his touch, for his rough, artist's fingers around them – on them, touching them, teasing them. The image made her sigh out loud.

Startled, she glanced over at Luc, certain he must have heard, but he seemed entirely oblivious, lost in the realms of his art.

Kelly wriggled restlessly. How could he be so cool, so detached? She couldn't believe it. It certainly wasn't something she was used to. Without being vain, neither was she unaware of her charms or the effect she generally had on the opposite sex. She turned heads wherever she went, male arms craned round her in gymnastic contortions as doors miraculously flew open, drinks were bought in abundance when she visited a bar, delivered more often than not with a discreet little cough from a waiter and the rather clichéd spiel, 'Compliments of the gentleman at the bar, miss!'

But here she was, without a stitch on, completely naked – and Luc? Luc obviously couldn't give a damn! He seemed totally indifferent, and in a daze, his face the epitome of studied concentration as he glanced back and forth from his canvas to her.

Gradually, inexorably, his disinterest began to grate and she started to fidget, drumming her fingers impatiently on the cushions.

'*Non!*' Luc shouted angrily.

'W-what?' Kelly swallowed hard, alarmed at the fury in his voice.

'You must be still or how can I paint?'

'I've been sitting still for an hour and a half,' flung back Kelly, her own temper rising. 'My shoulders ache. I need a break.'

Luc was silent. He glared at his canvas as though the fault lay there. Then, with as miraculous a change as night into day, his face softened. Smiling apologetically, he put down his brush. 'Forgive me, *chérie*. I get lost in my work and I forget about my model. I am a tyrant, no?'

'Yes!' muttered Kelly, confused by his sudden switch in tone and expression. She began to stretch her neck with slow, feline grace. Rotating her shoulders one after the other to ease the stiffness, she continued to stretch, enjoying the freedom, the luxury of movement.

Luc was watching her closely. Gradually, his look began to alter. That distant, dispassionate air ebbed away, the objective gaze of the artist receded. Instead, his eyes travelled lazily, openly, down her undulating body and slowly back up towards her face. Keeping his eyes fixed firmly upon her, he reached to the side of his workbench for a cloth.

'I will massage your back,' he said bluntly, wiping his hands on the cloth. 'It will help the ache.'

Kelly was still kneeling, her arms now demurely at her sides. Settling behind her, Luc placed his hands on her shoulders. At his touch, Kelly tremored. Her flesh felt on fire. Slowly he began to massage her, kneading at the knotted tightness in her muscles.

'That's so nice,' she murmured, closing her eyes, leaning backwards slightly, savouring the sensuous feel of his fingers.

His hands moved round to her collarbone, across the smooth skin of her cleavage, down her arms, up the back of her neck, along her shoulders again. Wonderful cool hands, wonderful firm fingers, easing, stroking, stimulating. Finally, it was more than she could stand. Almost feverish, she reached up and ran her own hands over the full, firm globes of her breasts, trailing her middle fingers back and forth across her stiffening nipples.

Behind her, Luc's breathing halted. His short nails dug painfully into her shoulders. Quickly, he released her and, easing his arms through hers, he nudged her hands away and tenderly cupped her swollen breasts. Her flesh spilled into his hands and, lightly, he began to squeeze each breast, teasing the tips with his thumb and forefinger. With each little flick on her nipples, Kelly felt a tug deep between her legs and she moaned involuntarily, pushing her chest out further.

'That feels good, *chérie*?' whispered Luc hoarsely.

'Oh yes,' Kelly sighed, leaning her head back on his shoulder, loving the feeling of hardness in her nipples, the trickles of excitement emanating from them.

Keeping one hand on her breasts, Luc pressed the other into the small of her back. 'Lean forward,' he murmured.

Way beyond inhibitions now, she did as he asked, inclining forward from the waist, resting on her wrists.

9

She trembled as he traced the ridges of her spine, carrying on down over the cleft of her slightly-spread buttocks. With maddening slowness, he moved his fingers back and forth along the silky surface of her bottom crease. She shivered lightly, arching her back, willing his fingers down, inviting him deeper into her warm, sensitive cleft.

Instead, he spread his hand over her behind, firmly pushing her further forward so that her bottom was high, upraised before him. Softly, he tapped the inner flesh of her kneeling thighs, and gratefully she parted them, her excitement surging as she displayed herself to him.

'*Merveilleux!*' he breathed, his voice so husky that Kelly felt almost dizzy with arousal.

Trailing his fingers up her inner thigh, he paused momentarily at the top. She was awash with desire, parting her legs further, desperate for his touch. But still he made her wait, caressing the velvety flesh so exquisitely that she thought she would actually faint.

Then, at last, he felt her, gliding his fingers expertly into the moist pink furrow of her sex.

Using the palm of his hand, he dabbed lightly at her cleft, his other hand still toying with her breasts. Kelly was breathing hard and fast, every nerve in her body sensitised. She could think of nothing other than his hands, teasing her nipples, teasing her sex, brushing lightly against her clitoris till she panted with frustration. She began to press herself downwards, gasping with delight as slowly he started to rotate his palm. Flits of pleasure darted through her. Excitedly, she dipped her head, looking at herself between her own legs, watching his strong, tan hand rubbing her round and round from behind. With two fingers now, he was rhythmically stroking her, the swollen bud of her clitoris hardening, pulling out from her labia like a nubby, rosy ridge. Faster and faster his fingers moved and she writhed joyfully upon them, striving for release. Arching her back and lifting her head, she strained hard against his hand, relishing the ache, the tide of heat spreading steadily outwards from her core until finally, explosively, she came, electricity coursing wonderfully through every nerve in her body.

Weak and gasping, she fell forward on to her forearms. Behind her she felt Luc take her sex in the cup of his magical fingers. With the heel of his hand, he massaged the moist base of her buttocks, stimulating her yet again. He moved to circle her waist and she heard the impassioned thickness in his voice when he spoke. 'Turn over, Kelly,' he urged, already easing her round.

His dark, green eyes were fiery, flashing like glittering stones. Not bothering to unbutton his shirt, he swifly pulled it over his head. Kelly's mouth went dry when she saw the broad expanse of his smooth chest and shoulders. She moistened her lips with her tongue, reaching out to run her hands over the lean, brown muscles, lightly fingering his small dark nipples before moving down urgently to the top of his jeans.

Seeing the long, hard outline of his penis, trapped by denim at the side of his thigh, a white-hot band of desire tightened round her body like a laced-up corset, pulling at her breasts and stomach in unison. She traced her fingers down his crotch, pressing ever more firmly until Luc's breathing was ragged and broken.

Hastily, he tugged at the buttons of his fly but, as she moved to help, breathless herself from renewed excitement, the rude, loud buzzing of the intercom made them both pause.

Chests heaving, they waited.

Again it sounded. Longer, insistent buzzing as though

someone knew for sure that Luc was in. A shadow crossed Luc's face. He glanced down at his watch. '*Merde!*' he cursed.

'What is it, Luc?'

'It will be my agent, *chérie*. I forget. She is arriving here at four o'clock. And look,' he held up his wrist and tapped the face of his watch with his fingernail. The watch showed four exactly.

The intercom buzzed again. Resignedly, Luc stood up. 'A moment, Kelly,' he said, making for the intercom and pressing the button to speak. He spoke rapidly for several seconds, his tone increasingly exasperated, then gestured obscenely at the thing after he had viciously released the button. 'I am sorry, *chérie*. She insists. She is on her way up. Tomorrow I have an exhibition. It is very important for me and there are things she wants to discuss.'

'Great timing,' mumbled Kelly, making a panic-stricken dive for her clothes, then dressing hurriedly.

Outside, she could hear the creaking arrival of the lift and, within seconds, knocking at the door. Grabbing her bag, she rushed towards the door but felt Luc's hand on her shoulder holding her back.

'Hey,' he said, twisting her towards him and tenderly tilting her chin up. 'Not so fast!' He pecked her lightly on the tip of her nose. 'You will come tomorrow, no?' he asked. 'To the exhibition?'

'Mmm,' she answered, catching the sharp, provocative scent of her own dried juices on his hand. Mischievously she rubbed herself against him, chuckling wickedly as she felt the tremendous hardness in his groin.

As Luc groaned quietly at the friction of their hips, another knock sounded at the door, noticeably impatient this time. Luc shrugged helplessly, quickly pulling on his shirt. '*A demain*, till tomorrow,' he whispered, opening the door.

A very attractive brunette, slightly older than Kelly,

was waiting. She looked typically Parisian, dressed smartly in a fashionable Chanel business suit. Her glossy dark hair was cut into a sharp geometric bob, falling bluntly to the top of her shoulders and her face was heavily, but exquisitely made up. She smiled at Kelly, then went on tiptoe to greet Luc, kissing him on both cheeks.

'*Salut, chéri,*' she said against his cheek, her voice a throaty purr.

Completely unruffled, as cool as Kelly was flustered, Luc calmly introduced them. 'Kelly, meet Chantal,' he said, nodding from one to the other.

'*Enchantée.*' Chantal smiled again at Kelly before switching her attention back to Luc. 'We have much to discuss,' she said briskly to him, striding into the room and grabbing him possessively by the hand.

'I was just going anyway,' muttered Kelly, discreetly looking Chantal up and down. So much for the butch, man-suited *patron* she'd imagined! With rising dismay, she took in Chantal's four-inch, patent-leather stilettos adorning shapely, silk-stockinged legs. And then, struggling with a stab of jealousy that Luc should have such an attractive agent, she made her way over to the door.

But she could feel Luc's eyes upon her as she left, and her body was still pleasantly aglow.

Down on the street, Kelly hailed a taxi. 'Just drive around, would you?' she asked the driver, a young Algerian who looked at her uncomprehendingly. Forgetting she had spoken in English, she repeated the phrase in French. Immediately, he grinned and nodded enthusiastically. As he drove, winding out of the narrow streets of Montmartre, he kept glancing at her through his driver's mirror. Kelly ignored him, still light-headed from her encounter with Luc.

'Very nice!' said the driver, tapping his face in the mirror then pointing at Kelly. 'Very pretty lady!'

Kelly smiled at him dreamily, her mind elsewhere, filled with thoughts of Luc.

Dammit! Goddammit! she cursed suddenly to herself, rousing herself from her trance-like euphoria. She didn't want to feel this way. About Luc. About anyone.

Why did she agree to a sitting with Luc? What had she been thinking of? Hadn't her heart just about leapt into her mouth the moment Luc had walked into class four days ago, all clean, soft hair and dark, brooding looks? Hadn't she hung on his every word, his every syllable, as he spoke about the great Impressionists? And hadn't she nearly fallen off her chair to watch him as he flicked nonchalantly through some of his own work, all the while chainsmoking Marlboros and leaning louchely against the blackboard? Yes, yes, yes, to all of that. She'd known she was smitten then and there, and she should have had the willpower to steer well clear!

In all her time in Paris, she'd studiously avoided any sort of involvement. Sure, she'd had dates, boyfriends. Everything purely on her terms. But Luc. Luc was different. He was gorgeous, yes, but it was something more than that. Much, much more. She had never known such shocking, instant desire before. Such intense, raw excitement. And his touch, his hands … stroking her, feeling her, bringing her to …

Stop! she told herself sharply. She was going home in two weeks. For good. One thing she definitely didn't need was this. Getting tangled up with this man would only complicate matters. She'd just have to stay right away. That's it, she resolved, she'd stay right away. Right away! Not go to his exhibition, not see him again, forget what happened. Forget all about Luc Duras!

* * *

Back at the studio, Luc Duras was far from forgetting about Kelly – her flawless face, her firm, ripe body. Of course, he'd known she was a beauty. He wasn't blind. He'd known it the moment he'd seen her in the class, her chin in her hands, long, shining hair falling past her shoulders, huge amber eyes and cheekbones slanting upwards in perfect symmetry. But he'd seen her purely as a subject, a beautiful, glimmering subject, to be painted by him, captured on canvas by *him*.

Then, just now, it had hit him. Out of the blue. As sudden and jarring as a gunshot. Desire. Hard, potent desire; the way she'd moved, the way she'd stretched. Jesus, she'd looked like a golden lynx, her skin gleaming, glistening, catching the glints of sunlight as she'd stirred.

'She is very beautiful, that girl.' Chantal's voice was mild, teasing.

'Yes,' said Luc, moving behind his easel, looking at the outline of his painting of Kelly. He sat down on a small, wooden stool.

'Mmm, quite good,' said Chantal, standing behind Luc, looking at the picture. 'Such bold colours, such strong lines, such definition of light and shadow.' She rested her hands lightly on his shoulders. 'Who is she?' she asked casually.

Luc shrugged. 'An American girl. Jean-Philippe asked me to talk at the Académie. She was there in the class. I think she's been studying here.'

'So you asked her to sit?'

Luc shrugged again. 'I saw her later in a café. I thought she'd be a good study.'

'Ah yes,' whispered Chantal knowingly. 'An excellent study!' Gently she rubbed her fingers against Luc's shoulders, still gazing at the picture of Kelly. Chantal was no fool. When she broke the silence, her voice was little more than a light, wispy breath. 'You will have her, no?'

'Oh yeah,' said Luc quietly.

Chantal twined her fingers in his soft, brown hair. 'You're so arrogant, Luc!' She clucked her tongue against the roof of her mouth.

They carried on staring at Kelly's painting until Chantal sighed, a deep, heavy sigh.

'So,' she exhaled, 'it's back to just business for you and me. You know I do not like to share!'

Luc laughed. 'I suppose so!'

'Such a pity, my love. We have so much fun together.'

Luc glanced up at her. Chantal's voice had been soft, strangely wistful. Not at all like her. Surprisingly, fleetingly, Luc saw sadness in her face. In a second it was gone.

Their business arrangement had suited them both. Chantal was married to a stockbroker, an exceedingly wealthy stockbroker whose sole purpose in life seemed to be to generate money. Fantastically rich, but neglected and bored, Chantal had craved excitement. She had found it in the world of art. Acting as Luc's agent, she had worked wonders for his career and, slowly but surely, success was coming. Generously, she had subsidised his work, keen to encourage his talent, enjoy his success and, more to the point, enjoy him. It had been a passionate affair. Passionate, hot, amazingly creative, but temporary, always temporary. In no time at all, Luc knew she would move on, to protégés and pastures new.

Her hands fluttered delicately through his hair. 'Still,' she said brightly, any trace of sadness gone, 'no harm in a bit of fun now, is there? One for the road sort of thing!' Her eyes shone down at him merrily. 'Before we talk about the exhibition, that is!'

Her fingers wandered down beneath the collar of his shirt, moving slowly forward over his chest. He stirred violently as she lightly raked her long, crimson nails down his front. Still semi-aroused from Kelly, his cock pushed painfully against his jeans, desperately craving freedom.

Slowly, Chantal undid the buttons of his shirt, leaving it open and letting her hands roam freely over his chest, stroking the smooth skin of his pectoral muscles, floating downwards over his hard, flat belly. With each flit of her expert hands, Luc felt his stomach muscles clench and the heavy cloud of her perfume, blending unmistakeably with her own body scent, was intoxicating. Urgently, he swivelled round to face her.

'Take it off,' he said harshly, nodding at her suit.

Chantal smiled widely, her cheeks flushing beneath her make-up. Long fingers moving elegantly, she reached for the top button of her jacket. Quickly, she worked her way down, pushing the jacket off her shoulders and letting it slide to the floor. Her skin was porcelain pale, fragile somehow, completely at odds with her confident persona. She wore a black silk teddy which contrasted beautifully with the whiteness of her skin and beneath it Luc could see the firm outline of her small, unfettered breasts, rising and falling softly in time with her quickened breathing.

Her eyes on Luc's face, she stepped out of her short black skirt. Her hands drifted to the top of her right leg, to the lacy top of a sheer, silk stocking. Slowly, very sensuously, she began to ease the stocking down her thigh.

'Leave it!' Luc ordered abruptly. He stood up sharply and pulled the stocking back in position. Then, taking the bootlace straps of her teddy, he pushed them off her shoulders. The straps slithered down her arms and the slippy undergarment, its support eliminated, collapsed to her waist, baring her upper body.

Roughly, Luc put his thumbs in the crumpled teddy, forcing it down over Chantal's gently flaring hips. She laughed softly as the material began to tear.

'Steady darling,' she whispered, twining her hands in Luc's hair again as he crouched to work the fabric from her body, wresting it downwards until it hung lifelessly round her ankles. Rapidly, she kicked it off, then side-stepped away from her abandoned clothing.

She stood before him, naked but for her silken stockings and high, stiletto-heeled shoes. The sparse items of clothing made her nudity all the more intense and Luc found his eyes glued to her body, each contour already so familiar to him.

Her small breasts jutted jauntily from her chest, the pink tips of her nipples pointed and erect, peeking towards him as though clamouring for his touch. Her tiny waist gave way to curving hips and the dense patch of dark hair nestling between her thighs stood out starkly, enticingly, from her pale, translucent skin. Luc gazed luxuriously at the small curve of her mons. His groin began to throb, his cock so engorged in the prison of his jeans that needles of pain shot outwards.

Hurriedly, he pushed off his shirt and undid the buttons of his fly. His penis leapt up against the thinner cotton of his shorts and Chantal's black eyes dropped covetously towards it, the tip of her tongue darting to the corner of her mouth.

They stood for a moment face to face then Luc pulled her to him, roughly crushing her against his chest, feeling her hard, little nipples press into him. Chantal sighed softly. Stepping back, she brought his hands to her breasts, putting her own hands atop his. Together they massaged her breasts in big, circular motions. Chantal thrust her shoulders back and her chest further forward. 'Harder!' she urged Luc, forcing her own hands down against his as he rubbed her delicious, tiny mounds of flesh.

Easing his hands free, he moved them down the curves of her torso. Lightly, he brushed the backs of his

fingers against her pubic hair, touching almost accidentally the erect little nub protruding from her sex. From
side to side he grazed the nub, Chantal moaning faintly,
then he slid his fingers right into her sex, scissoring her
clitoris, tugging gently. Chantal gasped out loud, her legs
jerking slightly. 'Oh yes, baby, yes,' she murmured, swaying her hips towards him.

Luc lifted her right leg, placing it on the nearby
wooden stool, so that Chantal stood precariously, with
one leg upraised. Her sex was slightly parted now, glistening and swollen, and gently Luc inserted his middle
finger into the tip of her vulva then dragged it back
slowly along her elongated bud. Chantal seemed to trem-
ble as again and again he did this, systematically pushing further inside her, till she clung desperately to his
shoulders, greedily sucking in breath.

'Enough!' she gasped, fiercely curling her fingers into
the waist of his jeans and shorts, wrenching them
together down to his knees. Luc groaned gratefully as his
cock was released and Chantal circled it with her hands,
running her thumbs back and forth over its smooth,
glossy tip.

Unsteadied by his jeans at his knees, Luc slid down to
the floor and Chantal collapsed over him, kneeling
astride his hips. Frantically, she impaled herself upon
him, her insides closing around him like a silken vice.
Together they exhaled in fleeting, momentary relief
before Luc began to move, thrusting upwards, his
momentum slow and deep.

Chantal stayed completely still for a while, hovering
passively as he thrust in from below. He slid up and
down inside her with lubricated ease, then he lessened
his movements as she sank gradually down and began
to move on top of him, the soft cushion of her buttocks
bobbing delightfully against him.

As she rocked eagerly on his penis, Luc gazed fixedly

at her small jigging breasts. Chuckling softly, Chantal leant forwards, pinning his arms to the floor with her hands. Luc played helpless, letting her tease him with her breasts as she dangled them to and fro, brushing them lightly against his face. Raising his head swiftly, he caught one of her nipples in his mouth, pulling at it gently between his teeth. Chantal yelped then moaned joyfully and tried to cram her breast further into his mouth, all the time grinding her hips down hard, bucking wildly upon him.

Sweat streaked their bodies as they raced towards climax, limbs thudding against the hard, wooden floor. Chantal cried out suddenly, sinking her nails painfully into Luc's pinioned arms. Her thighs jerked in spasm as her orgasm shook her. On and on she seemed to go. Luc felt her vaginal muscles contract around his penis, as though sucking his orgasm from him, and with one final thrust, he surrendered, spilling forth and upwards in shattering spirals of relief.

Exhausted and replete, they waited for their breathing to slow. Chantal lay on top of Luc, still kneeling astride him. She rested her head in the crook of his shoulder and neck while he trailed his hands down her sweat-slicked back, absently stroking the soft, pale globes of her buttocks. Chantal sighed contentedly. Sleepily, she raised her head, looking him straight in the eye. 'You're going to be a hard habit to break, Luc,' she said drowsily, before dropping her head back on his shoulder.

2

Kelly leant back in the chair and arranged a cream hessian cushion more comfortably behind her. Her shoulders were a mite stiff from the enforced rigidity of sitting as still as she possibly could for Luc yesterday. In front of her, the double glass doors were open, and instead of gazing out in the general direction of Montmartre as she had been for the last half hour, wondering which particular tiny, glittering pinprick housed Luc's studio, she made a determined effort to focus on the terracotta pots of flowers she'd placed around the terrace. They seemed to be flourishing. Even in the darkness, the colours stood out from the red-slate background of the terrace wall. Beyond, the lights of Paris by night twinkled. If she screwed her eyes up, she could just about make out the dark watery expanse of the Seine and if she swivelled her eyes just a tad to the left, yes, there it was again. Montmartre.

'Here you go.' Angie plonked a large glass of red wine next to Kelly.

'Thanks,' said Kelly, still gazing out of the window.

Angie sat down cross-legged on the floor. They sat for a while in companionable silence, quietly sipping their drinks.

Angie broke the silence. 'I think you're crazy, you know that,' she said softly.

'Hey?' asked Kelly, surprised.

'You know, not going to Luc's exhibition.'

'Oh that!'

'Yes, that! What I wouldn't give for an affair with Luc

Duras,' Angie went on dreamily. 'That face, that body, not to mention that accent –'

'I know,' sighed Kelly.

'Those eyes!' gasped Angie, evidently getting carried away.

'I know.'

'That talent!'

'I know, I know,' breathed Kelly, conjuring up his face behind closed eyelids. 'But –'

'But what?'

Kelly shrugged. How could she explain something to Angie that she couldn't even explain to herself? The plain truth was that she couldn't get Luc out of her mind. 'It's just that when I go back to California, I'll have to stay there a while. And Luc had this crazy effect on me. Sort of like . . .' Kelly's voice trailed off.

'Sort of like?' repeated Angie, clearly not willing to let the matter drop.

'Let's just say, I've got a real strong feeling I could fall for him. Badly. And then I'd have to leave him in two weeks' time. Imagine that!'

Angie nodded slowly. She stared at the carpet, twiddling idly with a loose jute thread, her smooth brow furrowed in silent contemplation. Suddenly, she raised her head, her eyes glittering mischievously. 'Ah yeah, but think of how you could be spending those two weeks!'

Kelly chuckled. Angie had an uncanny knack of reading her mind – they were entirely on the same wavelength. She was really going to miss her when she went back home. Ever since she'd moved into the vacant apartment above Angie's, they'd been the best of friends.

Kelly sipped her wine thoughtfully. She and Angie had so much in common. Both Americans living in Paris, same age, both studying art history at the Académie. They were closer than sisters, confiding in each other, telling each other everything there was to know about the other. Angie was the only person in Paris who knew something about Kelly's reason for returning home.

Nearly four years ago, when Kelly had just turned 21, her wealthy father had died. He had left his estate in trust for Kelly. She was to inherit almost everything on her 25th birthday next month. That was why she had to go back.

'Anyway,' said Angie with the air of having reached a very satisfactory solution, 'say you did fall for Luc Duras, and,' she added with a wink, 'always assuming he fell for you too, there's really nothing to stop you from coming back here – once all that legal stuff has been taken care of.'

''Spose not. Not if everything goes along smoothly.' Kelly's voice was doubtful. 'I'm just worried about my stepmother. She's the bane of my life; the main reason in fact why I've chosen to spend the last four years travelling and studying in Europe. We disliked each other on sight and the thought of having to share the house with her after my dad's death was too much for me. Though dad left me the bulk of his estate, the terms of his will also stipulated that my step-mom could continue to reside at the family home until the time when the property would pass wholly into my hands – on my 25th birthday.'

'Well –' Angie tripped tipsily over to the wine bottle and generously refilled her glass ' – your stepmom will have to leave, once the house is all yours. And then you'll be free as a bird. Free to do whatever. Which leads us back to Luc! If you hurry you know, you could maybe make the end of his exhibition!'

'Nah,' said Kelly. 'Gallery's far too far away.'

'You're making excuses,' sang Angie in a lah-di-dah voice. 'You could do it with time to spare!'

Kelly glanced down at her watch. Could she? If she

really rushed, she could. She could just walk in and see him there and stand around and admire his work. And then later, they could take up where they'd left off yesterday. It had felt so right, his hands all over her, on her breasts, between her legs. His hard, brown body ready to take her. The thought made her breathless, her stomach looping and twisting at the memory. This was just exactly what she was afraid of. 'No!' she said firmly. 'I made up my mind. I need to keep a clear head over the next few weeks. I really, really do. And I definitely *can't* where he's concerned. I'm just going to stay right away from Luc!'

Angie's eyes widened with incredulity. 'What, not even sit for him so that he can finish your painting?'

'Not even that!'

'But, just think, hon. He's going to be famous one day. It'd be an original of you by Luc Duras!'

'Nope.'

'You could be hanging up there in the Louvre.'

'No!' Kelly exploded.

Angie shook her head in disbelief. 'You're going to regret it, Kelly,' she said softly, knocking back the rest of her wine. 'Really going to regret it!'

3

Nestling high in the hills, midway between Santa Ana and the mountains, overlooking the valleys, David Aslett had found the home of his dreams. The view and the location were superb and the house, though fairly modest by Californian standards, was a wonderful, Mexican-style hacienda, with white stucco walls and dark timber shuttering.

David Aslett's young widow, Marissa, was deep in thought as she wandered barefoot along the rear terrace of the house and down the steps towards the swimming pool.

She lay back on a sun lounger, squinting up at the early morning Californian sky, so blue it was almost navy. Within minutes, the heat from the sun was burning her through the fragile cotton of her robe but she was far too preoccupied to move. Instead she reread the note she had in her hand. It was short and to the point and when Marissa had finished, she held it above her in both hands and tore it, with perfect symmetry, down the middle. Then she tore it again and again, letting the scraps of paper flutter gently to the ground.

The note was from her stepdaughter, Kelly, giving the date, time and flight numbers of her intended arrival from Paris. Not for the first time did Marissa curse her late husband for his folly in having a daughter. If it wasn't for Kelly, Marissa would have been set up for life when David went and died on her. She would have inherited everything. As it was, she was hardly destitute – David had left her a very generous lump sum in his last will and testament. But it was by no means enough. No sir. Not nearly enough. Not for a girl like Marissa!

She rested her head back, closing her eyes. What in hell was she going to do? The damn girl was due back soon. No doubt she would sign on the dotted line faster than Marissa could sneeze. And then what?

Marissa opened her eyes suddenly and raised her head to look around her. All this would be Kelly's, she thought, the familiar tide of hatred rising up inside her. She looked at the long, oval swimming pool, the surface of the water sparkling like diamonds; she looked at the lush, low palms dotted haphazardly around the mani-cured gardens, at the magnificent view sweeping down over the valley, at the distant blue of the ocean merging hazily with the skyline. She looked long and hard at it all, unconsciously clenching her fists. She'd be damned if she'd give it all up, just like that. Leastways without a fight. That's one thing Marissa never did, give up with-out a fight! Yes, she'd find a way. Someway, somehow.

Feeling much better, she dropped her head back against the cushion. The brightness made her screw her eyes up again and, ever fearful of wrinkles, she quickly shielded them with her hand. She was only 29, but she'd lived in the sun all her life and there was no way she intended ending up as a Californian prune.

She lay back contentedly, allowing her mind to drift. As she relaxed, a welcome heaviness began to gather, flowing through her body like a strong river current. It seemed that the source was that familiar, desirable ache deep in the pit of her abdomen.

Pity Larry isn't here, she mused, letting her hands wander idly down her body, resting lightly on the tied belt at her waist. Deftly, she undid the knot and opened up her short cotton gown. She was naked beneath.

Slowly, she trailed her hands across her flattened stomach, marvelling at the way it sent shivers through her breasts. It felt good and quiet out here alone. Pushing her gown further open, she spread her legs slightly, running opposite forefingers simultaneously along the tender skin at the edge of her mons and then back up over her hipbones, savouring the little thrills her own touch evoked.

As she stroked herself, writhing gently on the sun lounger, the soft material of her gown beneath her rucked up between her buttock cleft. She wriggled her hips up and down against it, delighting in the gentle friction as it stimulated the little, puckered mouth of her anus. Not wishing to satisfy herself too quickly, she withdrew her hands from her hips and, gripping the sides of the sunbed, she continued to rub her bottom up and down the ruck. She parted her legs a little wider, exposing herself to the hot morning air and pressed her buttocks down harder. Tendrils of excitement ran through them. She could hear the purr of an engine but it seemed so distant, so vague, that she ignored it, rather more concerned with the pleasures of her body.

Suddenly a vehicle door slammed. Unmistakably loud. Unmistakably near.

Quickly, Marissa closed her gown over her, belting it tightly around her middle. A moment later, a young man appeared round the side of the house.

Whistling softly, he strolled towards the pool. He was dressed in a ragged white T-shirt and faded denim cut-offs that ended just above his knees. He didn't seem to notice Marissa.

'Morning, Ray,' she called out.

The young man glanced up, startled. Seeing Marissa reclining on the lounger, he grinned sheepishly. 'Oh, mornin', ma'am. Didn't see you there!'

'I'd forgotten it was pool day,' said Marissa.

'Yep,' grinned Ray. 'Every Thursday. Regular as clockwork.'

Marissa smiled, forming her lips into a silent 'Oh'. She watched as he began his cleaning routine, returning to his van several times to retrieve various pieces of equipment.

He crouched down by the side of the pool, dipping his finger into the water. His muscles moved nicely under his T-shirt and every now and again he smiled up at Marissa, flashing teeth that looked whiter than white against the deep golden-brown of his face. He'd gathered his dark blond hair carelessly into a little ponytail and it rested in the very attractive nape of a very smooth, sun-darkened, blond-fuzzed neck.

Marissa was strangely fascinated. Far from dissipating, her unfulfilled arousal seemed to be leapfrogging. Cute, she thought, moistening her lips. Not at all bad for a pool boy. How come she hadn't noticed that before?

She watched him some more as her mind ticked over.

'Ray,' she called out. 'I'm going in for some juice. D'you want some?'

Ray looked over, surprised. 'Er, yeah, sure. Thanks.'

Marissa sauntered into the house, making sure the thin cotton of her wrap was pulled tight across her buttocks. In the kitchen, she quickly poured some drinks, detouring into the hallway to glance in the mirror. She was startlingly pretty, with a dewy fresh complexion and perfect little button nose. Her big blue eyes stared innocently back at her and ribbons of soft, butter-blonde hair fell in layered waves past the top of her shoulders. She smiled happily at her reflection, briefly primped her hair, then grabbed the drinks and walked back outside.

Setting the tray beside her, she settled back on to the lounger. 'Ray. Juice!' she called.

Ray nodded and wandered over. He looked slightly uncomfortable as Marissa handed him the glass, brushing her hand against his. He stood with his shoulders tensed, silently sipping his drink.

'Sit down, why don't you,' Marissa said softly.

'Uh, um, yeah. OK.' Ray sat on the ground adjacent to Marissa, pointedly staring at the pool.

'Is it cold enough?' asked Marissa.

'W-what?' said Ray, glancing up at her.

'The juice,' she said, flicking her eyes to the glass. 'Is it OK?'

'Oh, yeah, great.'

'That's good,' she said quietly, noticing how perfectly arched his eyebrows were. Casually, she shifted her legs, the smooth skin of her thighs revealed. She watched his face over the top of her glass with the surreptitious gaze of a skilled seductress.

'Rosita's off today,' she murmured, flicking out the tip of her tongue and licking at the frosted moisture round the rim of the glass.

'Yeah?' mumbled Ray, looking directly at her.

'Mmm,' she whispered. 'All day.'

Ray's eyes switched back in front of him. Nervously he licked his lips.

Marissa smiled happily. 'Ooh, it's so hot,' she gasped, stretching up her arms, 'accidentally' tipping up her glass. 'Whoops!' she giggled, as a river of ice-cold, sticky juice trickled down the front of her gown.

Ray's eyes darted back towards her. He looked sort of startled, like a rabbit caught in the beam of a headlamp.

Marissa tugged at the sodden material. 'Darn it! Would you look at this!' she laughed, pulling the clinging fabric ineffectually upwards.

Ray's eyes were now frozen on her body. He seemed to have lost the ability to speak. Marissa shifted a little on the lounger. Then she shifted some more, the robe parting in an upside down V-shape to either side of her hips, still tightly belted at the waist. 'Whoops again!' she giggled, delightedly noting his reaction. He was staring intently at her exposed lower body, seemingly unable to drag his eyes away. He watched mesmerised as she rested her hand on her satiny stomach. 'D'you like what you see, Ray?' she teased.

'Uh ... yeah,' he said, his voice cracking as he spoke.

'I do too,' she whispered, moving her eyes very slowly, very deliberately, down his body.

To her absolute joy, a sweet, faint flush darkened the even, golden skin of his cheeks.

'What're you waiting for, honey?' she purred, stroking the dark-blonde fuzz on her mons. She bent her legs at the knee, letting them fall casually apart, brazenly inviting.

Ray seemed rooted to the ground.

'C'mon, Ray,' she coaxed softly, sliding down the sunbed until she was perched at the end. She spread her legs wide to either side. Her sex was now level with Ray's startled face and Marissa placed her thumbs and forefingers at right-angles at the tops of her thighs, framing the delicate, pink folds of her labia.

Ray flushed even deeper, his breath rasping and uneven.

'You know what I want, don't you Ray,' she crooned, her voice thick and syrupy. She lay back, waiting.

Ray looked incapable of movement. He cleared his throat noisily. 'Um, can I –?' His voice was so croaky he sounded as though a family of frogs had moved in.

'You surely can, baby,' purred Marissa.

Hesitantly, Ray placed his hands on her inner thighs, craning forward. Briefly, he glanced up towards Marissa's face, his own face a blend of delight and disbelief. Then, swiftly, he dipped his head and took her sex in his mouth.

Marissa gasped out loud as he ran his tongue with surprising dexterity down the sides of her clitoris, circling the centre of her pleasure. He started to tease the uppermost tip with little, darting flicks.

'Oh honey!' she gulped, raising her hips up, pushing herself towards him. Gently he licked and sucked her, his confidence growing by the second. Her sex began to darken and swell. She dug her shoulders back into the lounger and raised her feet up on to the sides, sighing breathlessly at the excruciating pleasure he was giving her. Deliriously she fumbled with her belt, undoing the tie and pulling her wrap fully open. She reached for her breasts and fingered her nipples, synchronising her movements with Ray's flicking tongue. A heavy swell began to rise up, spreading sensationally to her knees and chest. Marissa spread her legs even wider, pushing her feet hard against the sides of the lounger, her knees bent outwards. She raised and lowered her hips in a gentle, thrusting motion as Ray started to probe her greedily with his tongue, making it rigid, inserting it inside her.

Marissa closed her eyes, feeling the ripples of pleasure begin. She moaned continuously as he tongued her, lost in her own joyful waves, her body shaking lightly when she climaxed. Ray closed his lips around her clitoris, pressing down hard with his tongue, prolonging the reels of rapture till she dropped her weakened legs to the ground.

Dreamily, she looked at him No trace of shyness now, she saw. He stood up slowly. His eyes were bright, boldly burning, uncertainty long gone. Taking in the curves of her body, he dispensed speedily with his clothing, pulling his T-shirt over his head and dragging off his cut-off jeans. His body was uniformly tanned and Marissa noted with satisfaction the spectacular jutting shaft of his penis, straining out from his hips. She pictured him over her, pushing up deep, deep inside her, filling and stretching her, sating her never-ending hunger. Not yet, she decided. She liked this boy, she wanted to take her time. 'Step over me, Ray,' she instructed.

Willingly, Ray complied, clearly eager for whatever she had in mind. He stood over her supine body, feet firmly planted to either side of the lounger. She took his hands and placed them above her head, so that his bending body was supported, then lightly she pulled his narrow hips towards her chest. Realisation flashed in his eyes, as she grasped each of her breasts and pushed them together, enclosing his penis within.

Excitedly, he dipped his hips back and forth, moving between the rich valley of her breasts, gliding slickly and easily amongst the beads of her perspiration. Marissa rolled her thumbs over her nipples as she pushed her breasts together, delightedly watching Ray's progress. His movements quickened, becoming almost frenzied. Panting unevenly, he thrust his hips back and forth with such long, fast strokes that the tip of his penis jabbed intermittently at the soft underside of her chin. Suddenly, he straightened, groaning loudly as he reached a swift, forcible climax, jaggedly spilling upon her.

Gasping, he stepped away, slipping down exhausted to the ground beside her. Their quick, short breaths seemed amplified in the still quiet of the morning, neither speaking as their bodies recovered.

After a while, Marissa reached down, feeling for Ray's hand. 'Shall we swim?' she asked gaily, shrugging off her gown which hung, fruit-juice stained and limp, from her shoulders.

She walked naked to the edge of the pool, then dropped down on the side and eased herself in. The warm, silky water enveloped her up to her neck and she began a slow, elegant swim across the pool. She felt rather than saw Ray's eyes upon her and smiled to herself. She loved to display her body; loved the effect it had and the power it engendered.

Flipping over on to her back, she started to float, the golden tips of her breasts breaking the surface of the water. Out of the corner of her eye, she saw movement and within seconds Ray was at her side. He began a lazy crawl across the breadth of the pool and back towards her then stood upright next to her. He was chest-high above the water so that little rivulets of moisture ran down his shoulders, drying very quickly in the heat and transforming into glistening droplets. He looked for all the world like a water-soaked Adonis.

Very gently, he placed his hands underneath her buoyant body, palms upward against her submerged back. His touch was enough to inflame her once again and she reached beneath the water, touching and fondling his penis till it stiffened wonderfully in her hand. She eased her fingers between his legs, rubbing the stretched skin of his balls, feeling for his buttocks and then scratching her nails lightly upwards.

He groaned slightly and moved one of his hands responsively down her back, roughly cupping her bottom, kneading and massaging her excited flesh. He pressed her firmly upward until the damp curls of her pubis emerged from the water and Marissa felt the burning torridity of the sun mingle with her own red-hot heat. They continued to stroke and caress each other, murmuring softly. Soon both were gasping with excitement.

Hurriedly Marissa turned and swam to the steps at the side of the pool. She beckoned Ray to follow. Her chest heaving with exhilaration, she positioned herself how she wanted him to take her. Facing the edge of the pool, she grasped the metal poles on either side of the steps, letting her body float back into the water.

Ray stood behind her, pushing her legs apart and moving in between them. Marissa stared steadfastly towards the gardens, trembling with anticipation. She could feel his hands on her buttocks, lifting and separating each rounded cheek then she felt the nub of his penis against her. Wild now for penetration, she rubbed back against him, widening her legs, and all but screamed when she felt him enter. He pushed up deeply inside her, burying his length until she could feel his pubic bone rub on her bottom.

He held her thighs firmly as he began to move, withdrawing entirely at first so that Marissa's vagina contracted in shock, then immediately he thrust straight back in, filling her up once again. Marissa clung tightly to the metal poles, relishing the vigorous intrusion behind her, needles of ecstasy running through her body. She felt weightless in the water, wonderfully at his mercy as he impelled his penis within, gloriously stretching and probing her sex. She never, ever, wanted it to end.

But it had to. All too soon her body betrayed her. A rush of sensation began. Ray was thrusting so wonderfully hard, so wonderfully fast, that she was powerless to delay her orgasm. She closed her eyes tightly as she came, bright, white light flashing behind her eyelids, the throbbing of her sex so sharp that it almost bordered on pain. This was what she loved – lived for. She revelled in the feeling, in the boundless pleasures of her own sensuality. Nothing could compare. Nothing at all.

Behind her, she heard Ray loudly suck in his breath, slapping his hips against her, pressing his fingers hard into her thighs as his own release engulfed him.

Softening her grip on the poles, Marissa relaxed, hazily aware of Ray slipping out of her body. She gently undulated her hips, letting the water seep into her. She felt fabulous, fully sated, and totally at ease – Kelly's return now just a minor blip on an otherwise glorious horizon.

Sighing deeply, she turned to Ray. 'What a wonderful start to the day,' she said, kissing him lightly on the lips. 'Every day should start like this, don't you think?'

'Jesus, yeah!' Ray murmured.

'You're sweet,' she laughed. 'Same time next Thursday?'

'Uh, yeah. I mean, *yeah*. God, yeah! For sure!'

'I'll leave you to get on then,' she said brightly, turning and climbing nimbly out of the pool. She stooped to pick up her discarded gown and, holding it gingerly between two fingers, she wandered fully naked into the house, water still dripping off her body.

Ray got out of the pool, a bemused but elated expression on his face. He shook his head gently, looked disbelievingly towards the house, and shrugged his shoulders. Well, well, who'd have thought it? he grinned to himself.

Then, tunelessly whistling, he dressed very quickly and began to clean the pool.

4

Marissa skipped through the house, leaving a little trail of water droplets behind her. Up in her bedroom, she went to the window and looked down at Ray, now busy working on the pool. She smiled. A long, lazy, satisfied smile.

After several seconds, she twirled away, turning her thoughts to the day, back again to Kelly.

Damn Kelly! Marissa hated to admit it, but the note Kelly had sent had given her a jolt. It made her realise that Kelly would be back home in no time at all. Thoughtfully, Marissa drummed her fingers on the side of her thigh. She would have to think hard and fast of a way to outwit her stepdaughter. Throughout the past four years, ever since David had died, in fact, she'd had Larry look into all the legal manoeuvres. All of which were hopeless. She'd even thought of contesting the will but Larry had laughed at the idea. Of course, Larry was right. Larry was always right. David Aslett may have been considered foolish in marrying a woman half his age, but he hadn't made a fortune out of being foolish and he'd made damn sure he'd protected his assets when he'd married her. The will was watertight – no doubt about that. Larry had combed through it word for word. But there had to be a way for Marissa to get her hands on the house. Had to be! If not a legal way then maybe something else?

Absently, she twirled around her forefinger a tendril of dark-gold hair, still damp from the pool. She glanced across at the clock. Still only 9.40. Plenty of time to drive into town and let Larry take her to lunch.

Unhurriedly she showered, washed and dried her hair and lightly made up her face. Then she stepped into her walk-in closet to decide what to wear.

Scanning the bulging rails, she chose a long, cerise skirt, cut on the bias, that hugged her hips and thighs and flicked out just above her ankles. Teaming it with a very tight, very flattering, black, fine-rib top and black Cuban-heeled boots, she stood in front of the mirror, pleased with what she saw. The tightness of the ribbed cotton emphasised a high, perfect bosom while the skirt showed off the flatness of her toned stomach and the gentle curves of her rounded buttocks.

Throwing her head forward, she pushed her hands through the long, blonde tresses then threw her head back again. Perfect, she thought, pouting at herself as her mass of hair tumbled messily round her shoulders.

Half an hour later, Marissa swung round into the underground carpark at the law offices of Aslett, Barris & Associates. She still had the use of her late husband's carparking space. Though for how long, once Kelly was back, was anybody's guess, she thought tetchily.

She took the lift up to the sixteenth floor and pushed through smoke-grey glass doors into a large, richly furnished reception area. Annie, the receptionist, was almost hidden behind a high, Italian-oak unit, only her head being visible over the top. Her face split into a wide grin when she saw Marissa. Marissa flashed an equally radiant smile back. When she'd married David, Marissa had thought it prudent to win over his staff and she'd been charm itself in all her dealings with them. 'Hello, Annie,' she said brightly. 'How are you?'

'I'm fine, Mrs Aslett. Thank you for asking.'

'I'm here to see Larry,' said Marissa, resting her hand on top of the high ledge. 'Could you check with Justine if he's free?'

Annie nodded eagerly, only too happy to oblige it seemed. She quickly tapped out numbers on a digital switchboard and spoke briefly into the small mouthpiece of the headset she wore. Then she glanced up at Marissa and nodded again. 'Sure, Mrs Aslett, he's free. Go right on through.'

Marissa smiled. 'Thanks, Annie,' she mouthed as she walked off to the left, down a long, beige-carpeted corridor. She turned at the end into an office where huge, sparkling plain-glass windows looked out over the city. A young woman sat behind a desk, her back to the glorious view. She had straight, even features, mostly obscured behind heavy-framed glasses, and her shiny brown hair was arranged in an immaculate French pleat.

'Hello, Justine,' said Marissa briskly. Justine was Larry's assistant and the one member of staff Marissa couldn't quite gauge. Nothing she could pinpoint. Justine was always polite to her, but coldly, distantly so.

'Oh, good morning, Mrs Aslett,' answered Justine coolly. 'I'll just show you in.'

'That's OK. I know the way,' said Marissa, her clipped, icy tone outdoing Justine's cool one. Marissa breezed past her towards the dark wooden door. She tapped lightly, then entered.

Larry had already risen and was halfway round the desk when she went in. 'Marissa,' he said simply, stooping to kiss her on the cheek. He stepped beyond her to shut the door, dipping his head out first. 'Hold my calls, Justine. Mrs Aslett and I have some business to attend to.'

When the door was firmly closed, he put his finger under Marissa's chin, tilting her face upwards, then he kissed her deeply on the mouth. 'Missed you, babe,' he said, pulling back breathlessly.

'Missed you right back,' purred Marissa. In her way, she had. She looked into his handsome face, feeling the little, prickling charges she always got from being with Larry. Larry Barris exuded power and success in the same way his mentor, her late husband, David Aslett, had. Marissa loved it.

She looked around the office, familiar with the opulence. Nothing had been changed since David had occupied the room. His office, sumptuously furnished, original oils adorning the walls, had been his pride and joy, his private haven from where he'd overseen the smooth running of his business. Larry treated it the same way, she knew.

David Aslett had founded the firm, built it up from nothing, honing and refining it into the esteemed law practice it was today. The practice was sleek, successful, independent – precisely the qualities that had drawn a brilliant young lawyer named Larry Barris to seek employment there.

Nine years ago, Larry, newly qualified and third from the top at law school, had approached David for a job, convincing him he needed a new associate. Actually, David hadn't needed a new associate at all but, impressed with the young man's temerity, he'd taken him on anyway. It had proved a wise decision. Larry was as sharp and ambitious as David himself and some time later, David had found himself making Larry an unprecedented offer – a partnership, albeit a junior partnership. Larry had accepted at once.

A year later, David had died. He'd been two points from victory in a game of racquetball when a massive heart attack had killed him. It was the one and only time anything had got the better of David Aslett.

Marissa reached up and ran her hands through Larry's thick, dark hair. He grinned boyishly and she traced the little crinkles that formed at the corners of his eyes. Then she sighed wearily. 'I got a letter from Kelly today,' she said. 'Dates, flight times, that sort of thing.'

Larry nodded, stroking the small of Marissa's back soothingly. 'We knew it was coming, babe.'

'We have to do something, Larry,' Marissa said quietly.

Larry let out a deep breath. 'We've been though all this. There is nothing we can do. David secured everything. All Kelly has to do is sign.'

Marissa stiffened. She grasped his hair tightly in her fingers. 'And when she does,' she hissed, 'she'll be the major shareholder. She'll be your boss. Do you get that? Your boss!'

Larry tensed. A little vein began beating at his temple.

Marissa tossed back her yellow locks, a look of derision on her ravishing face. 'You'll be working for a kid, Larry,' she taunted.

Larry's eyes flashed angrily. She knew the look well. It should have been a warning.

'You'll never have the money to buy her out, Larry. Always be the junior partner –'

'OK. Enough already.' Larry's voice was dangerous and low. 'Enough,' he murmured again, roughly grabbing her wrists and pulling them from his hair.

Marissa glared at him defiantly, her sky-blue eyes like ice. 'We'll find a way to work it,' she said, her teeth clenched together. 'We still got some time, baby.'

Glaring back, Larry held her wrists tightly, moving her arms out to the sides. His eyes glowered back and forth between each of hers. Then his gaze dropped to her full, pink lips, lingering momentarily before moving to the curve of her throat and travelling hungrily down the rest of her body. 'Yeah,' he whispered hoarsely. 'We'll find a way.'

An arc of exultation curved through Marissa's stomach. Then a sudden weakness suffused her limbs. She stared deep into Larry's angry, dark grey eyes, then she curled her fingers back into his hair and drew his head down to her, kissing him so hard on the lips that she scraped his teeth with her own. They pushed urgently against each other, the granite bulge in his groin stabbing painfully into her navel.

He dipped his head to her neck, raining quick, sharp kisses as his hands fumbled at the base of her sweater, trying to pull the clinging fabric upwards. She leant away from him, helping him wrest the skin-tight garment over her head and then they flung it together halfway across the room.

Larry gazed fixedly at her full gleaming cleavage. With each of her short breaths, her breasts threatened to spill out of the delicate half-cups of her bra. Quickly, he pushed his big fingers into the lace, dragging each cup downwards so that Marissa's breasts popped out. He squeezed the reddening nipples with his fingertips, tugging gently till the little cones stiffened and stood out proudly. Marissa groaned blissfully and reached behind her back, deftly unfastening the clasp of her bra and shrugging it off down her arms.

Larry cupped her naked breasts, whispering softly. 'Beautiful,' he murmured, pushing them upwards and then squeezing them together. With the centres of both palms, he brushed lightly at her tips, making her want to thrust them forward and rub them wildly against his shirt. Instead, she tipped her head back, feeling her hair tickle the middle of her naked back as Larry toyed with her breasts, his deliberate, faint grazing of her nipples only exciting her all the more.

As Larry loosened his tie, pulling it over his head, Marissa grabbed at the buttons of his crisp, white shirt, frantically unfastening. He eased it off and she ran her hands over his hard, muscled chest, over the soft, dark covering of hair. Their breath was coming sharp and fast, passion so palpable that it hung in the air like a huge, scorching fireball.

While Marissa fingered his nipples and pressed her

thumbs hard into his lean rib-cage, Larry bent down, reaching beneath her skirt. He trailed his fingers lovingly up her thighs, inadvertently lifting her skirt on his arm as he straightened up, so that half the garment was upraised.

Marissa's flesh tingled at his feather-like caresses on her thighs. Desperately, she sought Larry's mouth again with her own, pushing her tongue hotly against the roof of his mouth, bruising both their lips with the brutality of her kiss. His searching fingers found the thin elastic at the edge of her panties and he eased his hand fully inside, stretching the fragile lace as he cupped the globe of her left buttock, kneading and pinching her satin-smooth skin. Marissa stifled a moan as he moved to her other buttock, gently stroking, steadily inflaming her.

'I want you right now,' said Larry, his voice low, their mouths together.

'Yes,' gasped Marissa urgently. 'Lock the door.'

'No. We'll leave it. No one will come in.'

He swifly pulled up the other side of her skirt, bunching it roughly around her waist. 'Hold that,' he ordered, placing her hands on the ruches of material.

Marissa could scarcely breathe, her excitement multiplied tenfold by the risk of being caught. They were directly in front of the doorway. If someone opened that door ... if Justine came through with an urgent message ... She gasped at the thought, heat searing like a brush-fire through her abdomen.

Larry was dragging her panties down to her knees. He pushed her skirt up higher round her waist and then leant back, drinking in her exposed flesh. Walking leisurely behind her, he paused for several long, thrilling seconds.

'Arch your back for me, babe,' he whispered.

Flushing excitedly, Marissa curved her back, pushing

out her bottom, enjoying every moment of his intense scrutiny.

'Yeah, that's it. Yeah!' he muttered before circling back round to the front. 'Jesus, hon, you're perfect,' he said and, breathing harshly, pushed his hand between her legs, forcing them apart. Then pressing lightly upwards, he probed gently till she felt herself moisten his hand.

'Oh yes, baby,' he murmured as he pulled his hand away, his fingers glistening with her wetness. Marissa was dizzy. She tightened her hands on her bunched-up skirt, counting the knobbles on the sleek column of Larry's spine as he stooped and pulled her panties right off. She was almost naked now. Only her knee-length boots remained, and the scrap of material that was her skirt, bunched up round her waist.

Larry's hands wandered over her hips, round to her bottom, across her mons. She began to sway with weakness till he bent his knees and lifted her, carrying her over to his desk. He placed her upon it, frantically clearing it of papers.

'Now! God, now!' Marissa groaned.

'Uh-huh.' Larry's voice was a croak, barely understandable.

He grabbed her hips, pulling her down to the edge of the desk. Then he pushed her legs up high and wide in the air, sliding his fingers gloriously into her shining sex. With firm, circular motions he stroked her, his other hand unzipping his fly and, as he pulled out his penis, Marissa climaxed, her knees jack-knifing in spasm. Fighting not to cry out, she dug her buttocks into the hard, leather surface of the desk, relishing the cool, clammy pressure on her bottom.

In the middle of her shuddering orgasm, Larry pressed his hands on the tops of her inner thighs, pushing her legs even wider apart. Urgently, he thrust into her, leaning forward at the same time to reach for her breasts. He started to move, filling her up magnificently, completely, stroking her insides with his deep, wondrous technique.

Her first, rippling orgasm had barely begun to subside when she felt another surge of sensation, deeper, more profound than the last. With each thrust of his rock-hard organ, darting jags diffused through her sex and navel and buttocks and very soon she climaxed again, arching her back with the force of it, a long, low moan escaping her lips. Larry pressed his forefinger to her lips, hushing her sounds of pleasure but scarcely had he done so when he ground his hips against her, threw his head back and sucked his breath in sharply, endeavouring to silence a cry of his own. He rotated his hips slowly, gripping Marissa tightly round the waist, releasing himself into her as his body shivered and his cry mutated to a drawn-out hiss.

For some time, they stayed in that position, drained and still, neither wishing nor able to move. Gradually Larry eased away. He placed his hand between Marissa's shaky legs, lovingly massaging the dampness into her small, dark-blonde nest of hair. She closed her eyes in contentment, savouring the soft feel of his fingers soothing the tenderness of her swollen sex.

Groggily she stood, hanging her hands around Larry's neck for support. He pulled her to him. 'The best,' he whispered, a note of wonder in his voice. 'You're the goddamn best!'

'You too!' Marissa leant heavily against him. She felt too weak to move. 'Let's sit down a while,' she whispered and together they moved across to the olive-green, leather sofa.

Marissa sank gratefully into the cushioned softness whilst Larry smoothed the crumpled band of her skirt down over her hips. He wandered around the room, picking up items of their discarded clothing. Then he replaced his shirt and tie and carried Marissa's clothes to her.

'Leave these off,' he murmured, holding aloft a scrap of black lace. 'I want to know you're naked under there.'

'Sure, honey,' Marissa chuckled, grabbing her panties and pushing them into her bag. She delved further into the bag, bringing out a hairbrush, mirror and make-up and held the little mirror up to the light. Her face stared radiantly back at her, eyes clear and sparkling, cheeks slightly aglow. She dabbed at the smears of her lipstick, applied some more and, deciding she liked the even-more tousled state of her hair, didn't bother with the hairbrush.

'There,' she said brightly, carelessly dropping the items back in her bag and hoiking it over her shoulder. 'Ready for some lunch now, lover?'

Larry straightened his own rumpled hair, then reached to the stand for his jacket. Marissa stood before him, wiping her lipstick from his face and brushing fussily at his lapels.

'Let's go,' he grinned, guiding her in front of him and patting her possessively on the bottom.

5

The Café Anognotti was typical of hundreds of Parisian cafés with its small, wood-panelled, smoke-filled, people-packed interior, and an abundance of tables and chairs spilling out across the breadth of the pavement. It was quite a distance from the Académie. Kelly didn't know it at all.

As she decided on an outside table, a balding, sweating waiter with small, piggy eyes and an immense, rotund paunch sidled up. Kelly blinked up at the ghastly apparition, rather taken aback because her mind had been full of green, flashing eyes, brown gleaming skin and long, lean, loose muscles.

She looked intently at the podgy little troll. Despite focusing on the rolls of lard-coloured skin that seemed to strain through each button of the waiter's shirt, Kelly found that she still couldn't fully erase the image of Luc in her mind. Even though it had been a week now. A whole week since she'd seen him, since that glorious afternoon in his studio. A week full of daydreams, frustration, cold showers – the longest week she'd ever known in fact.

'*Vous désirez, mademoiselle?*'

Kelly jumped as the podgy troll spoke, blasting her out of her daydream. He pulled out a pad and a pencil with the determined flourish of a magician.

'Uggh!' Kelly squealed, recoiling in horror as a tongue the colour of liverwurst pâté slithered slug-like out of his mouth. What was he doing?

'*Mademoiselle?*'

'*O, je m'excuse,*' she muttered, sinking back in unmitigated relief as the horrible tongue merely wetted the tip of the pencil. The waiter patiently waited, poised and ready for her order.

Somewhat put off her food, Kelly made do with simply ordering an espresso.

Her coffee arrived within minutes and she settled back for a relaxing break, determined not to think of Luc. She'd piled her long hair up in a loose messy coil and wore faded blue Levis and black biker boots. The clompy boots accentuated her tall, slender frame and, with a plain white shirt knotted above her waist, she looked young, fresh and delectable as she sat sipping her espresso, her nose buried in a book.

A familiar, irritating giggle coming from somewhere nearby suddenly made her look up. A big-boned girl with very dark, unruly bobbed hair and a smile as wide as the Seine, was striding purposefully towards her. Oh no, thought Kelly. Tanya! She just wasn't in the mood for Tanya. Kelly's eyes slid automatically to the sides, scanning possible escape routes. No immediate possibilities presented themselves. People, chairs and tables seemed to block her every exit. Glancing back in front of her, she knew it was too late anyway. Tanya was approaching at speed, homing in on her with radar-like precision, hell bent no doubt on regaling her with all the latest happenings in her life.

'Kell-ee, hi-ee,' gushed Tanya, pulling out a chair and settling herself at Kelly's table. She wasn't the sort of girl who waited for an invitation.

'Oh, hi Tanya.' Kelly managed a sort of twisted smile.

'Listen, I'm glad I've run into you.' Tanya ducked forward across the table. 'I've just got so much to tell.'

'Really.' Kelly nodded blankly. Resigning herself to the inevitable protracted onslaught, she closed her book and prepared herself to look interested.

Smiling smugly and obviously warming up for a very long story, Tanya pushed her thick dark hair behind her ears and swivelled her eyes over the surrounding tables, recce-ing for possible eavesdroppers.

'Well,' she began slowly, milking her gossip for all it was worth.

Suddenly her eyes flew wide open and she stared across Kelly's shoulder into the café. Her hand flew over her gossip-filled mouth. 'Oh, my God. Look who just walked into the bar!'

'Who?' said Kelly wearily, used to Tanya's celeb-spotting. Oh, why didn't she just go away?

'It's that painter guy. You know the one who gave us a talk at the Académie.'

Kelly's shoulders felt like they'd been wrenched up with an iron bar. She sat bolt upright in her chair. Couldn't be. Couldn't be Luc. She'd deliberately chosen a café she'd never been to before. It was miles away from the Académie. What were the odds in a city this size?

'What was his name now?' said Tanya excitedly, still staring across Kelly's shoulder. 'It's on the tip of my tongue. What was it? My God, he's divine. Would you look at that bod! I know!' She snapped her fingers triumphantly. 'Luc, that was it. Luc something.'

'Duras,' finished Kelly quietly.

'Yeah, Duras. That's it. Luc Duras.'

Kelly turned around slowly, trying, though not succeeding, to appear casual.

Sure enough, there, looking very, very cool, and unspeakably handsome, was Luc. He was propping up the bar and deep in conversation with someone or other to his right.

He was dressed in faded blue Levis again. Even from her vantage point of thirty metres or so, Kelly could see the frays at the edges of the pockets and the way those same pockets curved sumptuously around impossibly perfect buttocks. An ancient green T-shirt clung to lean, sinewy muscle and soft brown hair flopped into a brown, gleaming nape. Kelly had to blink twice just to make sure he was real and not that mental picture she'd been floating around in front of her eyes for the past week.

She couldn't drag her eyes away, watching as though hypnotised as he casually raised one heavy black workman's boot, rested it on the panel at the base of the bar and then hoiked himself over the bartop to reach for a packet of Marlboros. She watched every movement as if they were choreographed dance. Lazily, he shook out a cigarette, lighting up with a deft little flick of his thumb on a lighter. He took a long, slow pull, then let the smoke spiral out of his nose and curl up towards the ceiling.

Sitting, staring, watching his every move, Kelly suddenly panicked. Her heart was pounding, her stomach churning. Why, she was throbbing from her head to the soles of her feet! What was happening? This wasn't her. It wasn't! Where was the Kelly she knew, the cool, calm, unshakeable Kelly? The Kelly that called all the shots?

'Hello . . . cooee . . . anyone there?' Tanya gaily waggled her fingers in front of Kelly's face.

Abruptly, Kelly turned back to Tanya. 'Sorry, Tanya. In a bit of a trance, I guess.'

'I'll say,' said Tanya snidely. She jerked her chair back suddenly and stood up. 'Don't blame you though. He is just about the most gorgeous guy in Paris, if not the world! I'm going over to say hi –'

'What? No!'

Too late. Tanya was already heading for the door to the bar with the fixed trajectory of a guided missile. Tanya had the absolute directness of only the truly thick skinned. In no time at all she was next to Luc, tapping his shoulder, greeting him like an old friend.

Then, to Kelly's body-numbing horror, Tanya extended

one long finger straight towards her. Luc's cool, slightly bored-looking, charcoal-lashed eyes dutifully followed that finger.

A deep, dark, penetrating gaze drew Kelly in with the unassailable force of a magnet. Kelly was the first to look away. Like a coward, she dipped her eyes to the table, fiddling miserably with a matchbook. What must he think of her? Not going to his exhibition like she said she would. Not turning up for any more sittings. Must think she's a first-class bitch. God, if only he knew.

Not knowing what to do, she carried on studying the table, concentrating madly on the sachets of sugar in the centre. Ever so slowly and ever so carefully, she raised her eyes upwards. She swallowed hard. Tanya was leading Luc by the hand. Straight towards her table!

Tanya sat down heavily. 'Luc, remember Kelly? From the class.'

Kelly was back counting the sugar sachets. She couldn't bear to look at him.

'Ah *oui*,' said Luc quietly. 'I remember Kelly.' He bent to kiss her on both cheeks. Fleetingly, Kelly caught the smell of him. A faint mixture of cigarettes and paint mingled with the scent of freshly washed clothes. Kelly breathed in deeply, wanting to fill up her lungs and air passages, but all too soon he had drawn away.

As Luc pulled up a chair, Tanya began to prattle, blissfully ignorant of Kelly's discomfort. Luc sat silently. He lit another cigarette, his eyes narrowing as he inhaled. Even his squinting made Kelly's stomach flip.

He must despise me, she thought. He hadn't even mentioned the exhibition, or the sittings she'd just so rudely missed.

Tanya babbled on incessantly. Luc smoked silently. Kelly quaked in her trendy, black boots. He looked so moodily handsome, she was finding it increasingly difficult to drag her gaze back to the sugar sachets. She had to say something. Anything. 'Um, your exhibition. Did it go well?' Her voice came out as a mouse-like squeak.

Luc leant forward and tapped off some ash. 'It was OK, I think. You did not wish to come?'

'No, it's ... I-I couldn't,' Kelly answered lamely.

'Ah, I see.' He nodded slowly and smiled. Amusement, not anger, seemed to glitter in that sea-green gaze.

'Exhibition?' Tanya barked sharply, annoyed that she'd been interrupted mid-flow.

Kelly looked at Luc. Luc looked at Kelly.

'What exhibition?' bleated Tanya. 'No one told me about any exhibition. Where was it? When was it?'

Luc watched Kelly. Kelly watched Luc.

Tanya watched both of them. Like a dimmer switch turned slowly up to full glare, Tanya eventually clicked. Giggles issued forth like spurts from a rusty tap. 'Er, think I've got to be somewhere, people.'

Kelly barely noticed as Tanya slid back her chair and disappeared. But she did notice that her wrist was trembling as she laid her hand on the tabletop. How dare he have this effect on her, she thought hotly, completely unable to slow her galloping pulse or stop the swirling in her tummy.

By infuriating contrast, Luc looked entirely at ease, smoking silently and staring off across the road. She studied the planes of his face, the smooth dark skin, the faint stubble below the sculptured cheekbones. His proximity made her light headed. If she didn't leave soon, she'd be lost.

'Well,' she said abruptly. 'I'd better go.'

Luc looked across at her steadily. 'Do you have to be somewhere, too?' Amusement still flickered in his eyes.

'I ... yes, actually, I do.' Kelly did her best to sound breezy. She did have to be somewhere. Anywhere, away from him. She had to get away. Leave. Right then.

'So, I think you do not wish to sit for me again?' Luc asked.

'Better not.' The mouse's squeak was back with a vengeance.

Slowly, Luc leant forward and stubbed out his cigarette. He reached across the table and gently scraped his finger along her jawline. 'I have time now,' he whispered.

Kelly gulped some air. Then some more. His touch was making her muzzy. She wanted him so much. She musn't. She shouldn't. 'I can't,' she said faintly.

Luc moved his finger to her lips. God, those fingers. How she'd remembered them, touching her, stroking her. Gently, he rubbed his fingerpad along the join. A dagger-like thrill stabbed between her legs and she gasped lightly, drawing the tip of his finger fully into her mouth.

He stood up sharply, grasping her firmly by the elbow. 'Come, *chérie*,' he said softly, throwing down some money for her coffee and guiding her through the maze of tables and chairs.

He held her hand as he led her round the corner. His car was parked up a side street. She followed him meekly. It wasn't any good, she couldn't fight it. Not any longer, not now that she'd seen him again. Desire rampaged through her body like an army of protesters. Just the sound of his voice, the touch of his fingers, his hand clasping hers, made her feel woozy and off-balance.

They got into the car and he drove off quickly, weaving expertly from lane to lane. In next to no time, they reached the rue de Rivoli, driving beyond the Jardins des Tuileries and the Louvre. He turned left down streets she didn't know. Then gradually they became more and more familiar, fine but dilapidated buildings with peeling paintwork and ancient shutters and, as Luc hurtled through the high, winding streets, Kelly found her heart was thumping as manically as the rattling of the car on the cobbles beneath. They were in Montmartre. His studio couldn't be far.

Suddenly Luc shifted down a gear. He pulled to an abrupt, skilful stop outside a building she didn't recognise. Silently he got out of the car, then ducked round to open her door. Taking her by the hand again, he led her towards the building.

Kelly looked around her nonplussed. This wasn't his studio. 'Where are we?' she asked quietly.

'It is my apartment.'

'I thought you wanted to paint me,' she giggled. God, she sounded like a smitten schoolgirl!

'You want me to paint you?' Luc's voice was as fresh and cool and seductive as raspberry juice poured over crushed ice.

'I thought –'

'Right now, you want me to paint you?'

'I –'

Luc smiled. Beautifully. Playfully. He had the sweetest, tiniest chip off one of his incisors, Kelly noticed. If he didn't kiss her soon, she'd die.

They hovered on the step outside the front of the building, bodies not touching at all. Kelly's flesh sizzled where his fingers curled round hers.

'You want me to paint you? Yes or no?' He tugged lightly at her hand for an answer.

Kelly wasn't sure she could stand for much longer, let alone form her mouth around words. Staring at those curving, knowing lips, she tried her very best to speak. A slurry concoction came out. 'Yeah, Iwanyouto –'

His lips covered hers before she could finish. 'I want you, too,' he whispered when he pulled back from the most exciting, earth-shattering, sweet-tasting kiss she'd ever known.

Somehow, they entered the building. Somehow, they climbed the stairs. How many Kelly didn't know.

Vaguely, she saw a door. Next moment they were behind it.

Silently, he leant down to her and brushed his lips dryly against hers, kissing the corners of her mouth. She nibbled urgently at his lower lip, sucking it in, not letting go till he opened his mouth and the incredible doorstep kiss was repeated. Their tongues flicked and duelled together, eyes open, noses rubbing, eyes shut, noses angled.

Their bodies moved closer in a state of slow-motion bliss.

With sudden urgency she tugged his T-shirt up his torso. Luc pulled it quickly over his head.

'Mmmm . . .' she breathed, running her hands over a chest of smooth, shining skin and hard, lean muscle. His skin felt heavenly, like warm, raw silk beneath her fingers and she pressed herself to him, parrying his twirling tongue with her own, moving her hands to the back of his head, twining them in the softness of his hair.

Luc sighed suddenly and eased his head up. He clasped her hand and led her through the apartment and she let her eyes wander down the back of his body, down his dark, bronze-tanned torso, down the contrasting blue of his faded jeans. Around his middle she could just about see the waistband of his undershorts. My God, he was perfect! Amazing. Like a strong, virile Romany. How could she ever have thought to keep away?

They reached the bedroom and a large double bed and collapsed together on to cool, cotton sheets. He leant over and kissed her again and she sucked ravenously on his tongue as he pushed her on to her back.

Running her tongue over the whisker-roughened skin of his chin, she almost yelped with delight when his hand moved to her clothing.

She felt him untie the knot of her shirt, undo the two buttons and twist it off her body. He trailed his hand up her stomach, pausing at the base of her bra. With the practised ease of a man well used to such a task, he located the fastener at the front and, still probing her mouth with his own, he unclipped the bra and freed her breasts.

She held the back of his neck, clinging tightly as his hand covered her naked breasts, roaming carelessly from one to the other.

'You are beautiful, Kelly,' he whispered against her mouth, his hand squeezing lightly, his thumb brushing nipple. 'These are beautiful!'

Moving his lips from hers, he trailed his tongue down the side of her neck, down the side of her chest, and slid in towards her right nipple. Lovingly, deliciously, he skimmed his tongue around the pale pink halo then made his tongue rigid and flicked at the hardened, little centre. Kelly writhed in delight, digging her shoulders back into the bed, pushing her breasts up towards him. Desperately, she dragged her fingers down his back and shoved her hands into his jeans, underneath the cotton of his shorts. His buttocks felt tight and smooth and she clutched at them passionately as he carried on tonguing her breasts.

Yearning to feel every part of him and maddened by the restrictions of his fastened jeans, she verged on brutality as she raked her nails down his bottom cleft, sensing him clench his muscles in response. Luc laughed softly. 'Wildcat,' he whispered, rubbing her nipples between closed lips before flipping over on to his back, trapping her hand underneath him.

Quickly, he kicked off his boots then dispensed with his jeans and shorts. Kelly gasped. His penis was huge, wonderfully engorged, the darkened veiny shaft projecting magnificently from those lean brown hips. She moved her hand round to hold it and could feel its pulsing energy as she squeezed.

Luc began to groan as she worked her fingers to the tip, dabbing lightly with her thumb at a smattering of clear pre-emission, then massaging it seductively along his smooth length. Dipping forward sharply, he undid Kelly's jeans, inching them along with her briefs down to her ankles. He cursed in mock anger as her clompy boots proved a minor hurdle, pulling at them roughly till her clothes could slide easily from her.

They gazed at each other's bodies. Impossibly attracted, unbelievably aroused.

Luc pulled the clip from Kelly's coiled-up hair and a long, lustrous curtain slipped over her shoulders, covering the tops of her breasts. Eyes hooded, heavy with lust, Luc pushed her hair aside, baring her breasts once again.

'*Merde,*' he groaned, staring in awe at her breasts, darting his tongue back to her nipples.

'God,' groaned Kelly at the frenetic pleasure of his flicking tongue. Urgently she pressed her stomach up against his cock, frantic to feel him inside her.

Luc was moving lower now, trailing his fingers over her navel in slow, sensuous s-shapes. Reaching the mound of her mons, he traced the edges of her pubis, tugging softly at the trim, little curls then gloriously, wonderfully, sliding his middle finger downwards.

Kelly sighed deeply as he touched her, rubbing at her sex with delicate, circular strokes. His touch was unbelievable. She didn't think it possible, but it felt more magical even than the time in his studio.

'Oh God!' she quaked as he altered his movements, smoothly vibating his finger now. She moaned and writhed, unbearably stirred, thrills tearing outwards and upwards from her teased, quivering clitoris.

Spreading her legs wide for her and moving his whole

hand on to her sex, he parted her labia with the backs of his fingers and caressed her clitoral nub with his thumb. Simultaneously, he eased his little finger up between her buttocks, stimulating the erogenous skin of her crease. Then he vibrated his thumb and finger in unison.

It was fabulous! Never had she felt so swollen before climax. Her bottom cleft prickled sensationally. She ached for him. She could only moan with desperate, unequalled delight.

Lower body aflame and very close to climax, she reached upwards to encircle his back.

'Luc,' she urged.

'OK, *chérie*.' He manoeuvred himself between her thighs, then she bent her legs up at the knee, stretching herself open as wide as she could for him. With swift, sword-like precision he thrust straight inside, her moist, swollen sex sucking him deep. They gasped in unified joy at the scorching, slippery contact and as Luc lowered his body atop hers she drew his weight on to her, pressing her hands into his back.

Luc gazed down at her face as he began to move and Kelly craned upwards to kiss him. His penis felt hot and gloriously hard, throbbing and enticing, each deep, probing thrust pulsating through her abdomen like a giant, magical wand. She bucked up her hips and clutched at Luc's buttocks then wrapped her legs around him, maximising the pressure within.

Nerves and senses on fire, they ground against each other, panting, moaning, losing control. And their heat and pleasure escalated. As Luc moved faster and faster, Kelly felt the huge sweep of orgasm begin. It rose from her sex, a white-hot ball of sensation, sweeping to her stomach, her bottom, her breasts, steadily gathering force.

She jabbed her nails into Luc's shoulders and looked wide eyed into his smooth bronze face. She knew he knew she was coming and they smiled together in absolute joy. Then it exploded. A momentous, blinding flash. Her body shook, her insides juddered, she grasped out wildly at Luc's back and suddenly felt his body tense. Lifting himself up on his forearms, head back, chest high, he ground his hips against her, panting breathlessly, coming as forcibly as she. Sweat soaked their bodies as they climaxed, stomachs were slippery, sticking together, groins throbbed madly with volcanic intensity.

Bit by bit, the waves eased off. He rested his head by hers on the pillow, his breathing laboured and sharp. She could feel the heavy pounding of his heart on her breasts and her own heart thumped manically back. It was as though their hearts were trying to push through their rib-cages and fuse together as their bodies were still fused. Kelly giggled at the thought.

'*Comment*? What?' Luc lifted his head, looking lazily into her eyes.

'Nothing.' She traced her tongue along his eyelid.

He kissed her lightly on the tip of her nose and slowly made to turn over.

'No,' whispered Kelly. 'Stay like this.' She wrapped her legs and arms around him, imprisoning him on top of her. 'For ever!'

He laughed. 'I am heavy, no?'

'Yes,' she chuckled. 'But stay anyway!' Gently she stroked the back of his shoulders, savouring the feel of him, the sight of him, the smell of him, every tiny little thing about him.

'Ouch!' he winced.

'What d'you mean "ouch"?' she laughed.

Luc examined the back of his shoulder and Kelly followed his gaze. Several angry gouges criss-crossed his flawless skin. 'Oh,' gasped Kelly, realising she must have scratched him with her nails. 'Did I do that? Does it hurt?'

Luc shrugged manfully. 'Just a little.'

'I'm sorry, Luc. I didn't realise, I –,' she stopped as she saw his eyes and that emerald glint of amusement again.

'*Grand bébé*!' she said, slapping his back really hard, making him wince for real this time.

Luc nuzzled her cheek with his own, his light, shadowy stubble scratchy on her skin. Then he looked down deep into her eyes, his gaze truly honest and direct. 'I think perhaps you are worth a bit of pain,' he murmured softly and this time he didn't look as if he was joking.

6

As usual it was dry and hot in Southern California. A gentle breeze blew in from the ocean and tempered the midday heat. Marissa, hair pulled up into a baseball cap, walked alone along a dusty track. She paused on a ridge, adjusted her wraparound sunglasses, and stared out westwards, across to the distant Pacific.

She had been walking for about an hour. She liked to walk when she had some serious thinking to do. It was a kind of therapy for her. Some of her best-laid plans in the past had been formed in valleys or canyons or on long, wild stretches of coastline. But today, for some reason, she couldn't seem to think of anything beyond last night's supper date with Larry.

It had been a pretty normal date at first. Larry had arrived to pick her up around seven and after a lengthy lovemaking session, they'd driven down to the beach, planning to eat at Quingelli's, a small Italian restaurant right on the seafront that was one of Larry's favourites.

As they ate, their appetites heightened by their energetic lovemaking, Marissa had noticed a tall, dark-suited man pass by their table. He glided by, followed closely by two similarly dressed men, their eyes furtively hidden behind inpenetrable, black shades. The man had walked on a couple of paces, paused, glanced back over his shoulder and then done an about-turn back to their table.

'Good to see you, Larry,' the man had said, holding out his hand. Marissa had immediately noticed the man's ring, a beautiful, crested band worn on his middle finger. The man was very soft spoken, his voice husky and low and strangely compelling. It had an almost mesmeric quality.

Larry, staring out at the black ocean, characteristically post-coitally quiet and lost in his own private world, had looked up surprised. Immediately, his face had split into his cute, boyish grin. He stood up sharply and firmly grasped the man's proffered hand. 'Johnny. Didn't know you were in town.'

'Yeah, for a while,' the man – Johnny – said. 'With the boys,' he added, flicking his head back at the two men behind.

Evidently already acquainted with 'the boys', Larry nodded hello to them and then introduced Marissa.

Taking Marissa's hand in a chivalrous, old-fashioned gesture, Johnny had grazed his lips against the backs of her fingers. '*Bella, bella*,' he murmured, black eyes glinting and sliding across to Larry with an appreciative nod. Lips still pressed to her fingers, he whispered, 'Larry always did have exceptional taste.'

That dark, unblinking gaze had held Marissa enthralled. She had found herself staring back in utter fascination. Johnny's complexion was dark and gleaming, as smooth and as swarthy as rich olive oil, entirely unblemished but for a shiny, narrow scar that ran the length of his left cheekbone, ending just below his eye. Smooth black hair was swept back from a high widow's peak. Undeniably, he was handsome. Perfect for the role of the dashing, roguish lead in a '50s Italian film – all white teeth and white shirt and black hair and black suit. Marissa could picture him now, zipping through the streets of Rome in an open-top sports car, cigarette dangling from the corner of his curving mouth.

But there was definitely something else about him, she mused. Something more than looks and glamour. An indefinable quality. There was something vaguely menacing about him.

The man's name was Johnny Casigelli. He had lingered for several moments more, then gripped Larry in a firm, brotherly embrace. 'Come visit me before I leave,' he said, before moving on to the table.

Larry had been silent after that. Marissa had tried to press him for details, who the man was, how did he know him, but Larry hadn't seemed to want to talk about it. Actually, he'd shushed her and rapidly changed the subject. Getting absolutely nowhere with him, Marissa had turned her attention back to her linguini and reluctantly let the matter drop.

What was really sending her mind into overdrive now was Larry's phone call this morning. He'd called from his carphone on his way to the office and said he'd stop by later, that he had an idea he wanted to discuss. He'd said that maybe there was a way to deal with David Aslett's will after all.

There better had be, thought Marissa grimly. Time was fast running out.

She stared out into the blueness, absently tucking a stray piece of hair back into her cap. Then she turned, stepped off the ridge and began the long walk home.

Back at the house, Marissa trailed in through the kitchen. Her maid, Rosita, was there, seated at the big kitchen table cleaning silverware.

Marissa smiled at Rosita's prim, straight-as-a-rod back and immaculate clothing. Her maid wore, by choice, a starched black uniform with a stiff white apron. There was never so much as a spill on that apron. She must have dozens of them, thought Marissa, her mouth twitching with amusement, to keep them so pristine.

Rosita was Mexican, young and very pretty. She always wore her long, black hair tightly plaited down her back. Halfheartedly, Marissa, at David's suggestion, had once told her she that she didn't need to dress in a uniform but Rosita had demurred. It made her feel better, she said, if she dressed properly; she felt more like a real housekeeper. Marissa hadn't argued. Secretly, she rather liked it, the fact that Rosita looked the part. Who would have thought it, that she, Marissa, had her own maid! Certainly not anyone from back home, that was for sure.

Marissa had done her best to reinvent herself, to forget her trailer-trash roots, her lean childhood on the outskirts of Bakersfield, and sometimes it was the odd, small things that pleased her most. The fact she had a maid pleased her a lot.

'Hey, Rosita,' she said, pulling off her baseball cap and tossing it on to the table. The walk had made her perspire and damp tendrils of hair clung to the edges of her face. She tilted back her head, shaking out her hair.

'Hello, Mrs Aslett.' Rosita rubbed vigorously at an already gleaming fork. 'You have a good walk?'

'Mmm,' said Marissa, uncapping a bottle of mineral water. 'Hot though,' she murmured, holding the bottle to her lips and letting the cool liquid bubble into her mouth.

As Marissa drank, Rosita got up from the table. She stood rather tentatively by the sink.

'Something up?' Marissa asked, not really caring.

'Um, Mrs Aslett, I get friend in to see to the broken cupboard. His name is Raoul.'

Marissa raised a beautifully plucked eyebrow. 'Raoul, huh?' She dipped her head round the corner of the large L-shaped kitchen. A dark young man was busy at work on the cupboard, sitting on the floor, a tool bag laid out beside him. Marissa shrugged. 'OK, whatever,' she said, 'so long as it gets fixed.'

She finished off the water and carelessly dropped the bottle on the side then walked out towards the hallway. 'I'm going for a shower and a siesta,' she called back over her shoulder. 'Wake me at five, OK?'

Without waiting for an answer, she tripped lightly up

the stairway, still mulling over Larry's phone call that morning.

Half an hour later, lying in bed with just a sheet drawn over her, Marissa couldn't sleep. She tossed and turned but it wasn't any use – her mind was racing faster than a car at Le Mans. She was bursting to know what Larry had meant that morning. Had he really found a way to deal with the will? If he had, what? Somehow she knew it had to do with his seeing that man, that Johnny Casigelli, in the restaurant. And just who the hell was Johnny Casigelli? The name seemed oddly familiar. Dammit, she'd just have to wait to find out. Larry couldn't get away until later. Dammit, dammit! She just hated having to wait!

Thumping her hands against the mattress in frustration, she sat upright and twisted her legs over the side of the bed. Perhaps she'd sleep if she ate something. She'd get Rosita to make her some lunch.

Pulling on a short towelling robe, she made her way downstairs.

The kitchen was empty. Unusually so. Rosita was always in the kitchen at this time, preparing lunch or even dinner. Sighing heavily because she'd have to make some lunch for herself and not at all pleased at the prospect, Marissa wrenched open the refrigerator door. Something on the floor nearby caught the corner of her eye. She looked closer. A toolbag, with hammers and chisels spilling out messily on to the tiles. Weird, thought Marissa, mildly intrigued. She inspected the cupboard and saw that the repair work had been abandoned halfway through. Typical workman, she muttered, kicking the toolbag lightly with her bare foot. Where was Rosita? She'd have to tell her to get someone decent in.

Annoyed now as well as hungry, Marissa left the kitchen in search of Rosita. She walked down the hallway to Rosita's room at the rear of the house. The door was closed. The room was ominously silent. Actually, the whole house was ominously silent. Probably fast asleep, cursed Marissa, doubly irritated because her own siesta had eluded her. Ready to spit venom, she raised her hand to knock.

Suddenly, she heard a noise. Muffled and indistinct, but definitely a noise. Hand poised mid-air, she paused. Instead of knocking, she pressed her ear to the door. Another, shorter noise. Sounding like a moan. And gentle, coaxing voices. Slowly, Marissa's lips curved into a smile.

Annoyance petering away, she felt for the knob of the door and carefully twisted it. The well-oiled spring moved easily and the door slipped silently ajar. Holding her breath, Marissa peeked through the opened space.

The room was in semi-darkness. Rosita had drawn the blinds but sunlight filtered unchecked through the edges. After a moment, Marissa's eyes adjusted to the darkness and she could see as clearly as though it were daylight.

Her eyes opened gleefully at what she saw.

Rosita's handyman, Raoul, was lying on his back on the floor, slightly at an angle, his head nearest to Marissa. Rosita was straddling him on all fours, her hips positioned above Raoul's head, face towards his groin. Both were entirely naked.

Marissa stared in astonishment at Rosita's nudity. Her body, usually hidden by the frumpy, black dress, seemed surprisingly slim and toned and her berry-brown skin gleamed in the filtered sunlight. Rosita's thick plait hung like a latticed snake along her back, the end curling on to the knobbly base of her spine. Her firm, fleshy behind, poised tantalisingly above Raoul's head, just about faced Marissa.

In opening the door, Marissa had been as silent and

adept as a cat burglar. Consequently, the couple appeared entirely unaware that she was there. Her pulse quickened as she looked on.

Rosita was dipping her head down into Raoul's groin. He'd spread his legs wide and bent them up at the knee. Marissa craned her neck to look further but her view was obscured by Rosita's lowered head. Disappointed, Marissa clucked her tongue silently against the roof of her mouth, then contented herself with what she could easily see, watching as Raoul circled Rosita's thighs with his hands. Stretching his neck, he lifted his head right up in between. Marissa fleetingly saw the flash of his long, pink tongue as he jabbed it upwards, into Rosita's sex. His straight, blue-black hair began to brush the base of Rosita's buttocks as he slowly moved his head, back and forth, from side to side.

Meanwhile, Rosita's head, buried between Raoul's thighs, was also moving leisurely up and down. The sight of the couple, dark, supple and loose limbed, was so unashamedly erotic that Marissa drew in her breath. Her eyes devoured the scene, arousal smarting deep in the pit of her belly.

Rosita was moaning softly now, swaying her hips gently. Raoul moved his hands from her thighs and placed them squarely on her bottom. Continuing to tongue her sex, he began to squeeze her smooth-skinned buttocks. Rosita arched her back responsively, pushing her bottom up higher, so high that Raoul seemed to have to stretch his neck to the limit to reach her.

Suddenly he dropped his head back against the floor, groaning loudly at Rosita's urgent, ongoing ministrations to his groin, pumping his narrow hips rhythmically up and down. His breathing was sharp, cutting the air like a blade as he carried on touching Rosita's buttocks, squeezing more and more vigorously until he was actually lifting and separating the globes. Marissa watched excitedly as Rosita's most intimate, sexual parts were exposed, the long, reddened canyon of her buttock crease, the plump, deep-pink mound of her sex hanging wet and heavy between her legs.

Stifling more groans, Raoul opened his mouth wide and strained his head upwards. As though taking a bite from soft, fleshy fruit, he sank his mouth round Rosita's slippery core. Rosita let out a little squeal. Raising her head up high, she began to move her hips more forcibly, lifting them, lowering them, rocking them from side to side. Raoul clutched passionately at her, pushing up his face still further.

Plunging her head back between Raoul's thighs, Rosita's movements quickened. Frantically, they both moved their hips, sighs and moans mixing with the soft, slippy sounds of sex. Within moments, Rosita jerked her body, throwing back her head, rounding her back, narrow shoulders shuddering lightly.

Marissa clung tightly to the door knob, resting her body against the outside frame. She was hot and weakened by excitement, torn between wanting to watch more and leaving to assuage her own need.

Inside the room, Raoul had scrambled up on to his knees. Rosita was crouching before him whilst he clung tightly to her shoulders. Marissa caught sight of a flicker of white teeth as Rosita opened her mouth and closed her lips round the end of Raoul's penis. It stood extended, splendidly engorged. Rosita shut her eyes, clearly in transport as she sucked and flicked at the tip, now and then running her tongue up and down the rigid shaft.

Raoul's buttock muscles clenched and relaxed, clenched and relaxed. Soon he began to push himself further into Rosita's mouth, panting furiously as Rosita worked her cheeks and tongue, simultaneously squeezing the base of his penis between both her hands. Marissa gazed avidly at his long, hard organ, thirsting for it deep inside her own body. Desperately, she pushed her hand into her gown and cupped one of her breasts and, as Raoul's brown buttocks flexed, faster, faster, Marissa pulled at her nipple, inciting herself to a fever. With a sob, Raoul climaxed. His torso juddered spectacularly as he gripped frantically at Rosita's shoulders, the end of his penis still buried in her mouth.

Marissa's body was aflame. She watched a moment longer, as the couple clung breathlessly together, then drew her head back and quietly closed the door. Noiselessly, she glided along the hallway and climbed the stairs back to her bedroom.

Once inside, she urgently shrugged off her gown, letting it crumple in a heap on the floor. Her bare feet sank into the luxurious ivory-coloured carpet as she walked across to stand in front of her full-length mirror. Full, high breasts swelled magnificently from the top of her slender rib-cage, the nipples dark and pointed with arousal. Between her thighs, the trim dark-gold patch of hair nestled innocently, belying the hot bubbling pulsations beneath.

Swiftly, Marissa moved her legs shoulder-width apart. She could see her little pink clitoris peeking out from the hood of her sex, already glistening with moisture. Enraptured by her body, she didn't hear the footseps on the landing nor the soft tapping at the door. She didn't even hear the door nudged open. Only a harsh intake of air alerted her. Hastily, she twisted around.

'Larry!' she gasped.

'Yeah, babe.'

He walked up to her and turned her back to face the mirror. Standing behind her, circling her waist with his arms, he looked at her reflection over her shoulder. Gratefully she leant back against him, immediately feeling his hardness through the rich fabric of his trousers, pressing searchingly into the cushion of her naked buttocks.

'Thought you couldn't get here till later,' she mumbled.

'Couldn't wait. Had to let myself in though. Rosita wasn't around.'

Marissa laughed softly. 'No, I think she's ah . . . otherwise engaged.'

'Huh?'

'Nothing,' she whispered throatily.

'Jesus, you're beautiful.' Larry stroked her stomach and hips. He pushed his fingers down between her slightly spread legs. 'And hot,' he murmured. 'Red-hot.'

Lightly, he rubbed her clitoris, his fingers moving slickly in her moisture. He scissored the hardened nub gently between two fingers, coaxing it carefully outwards from the succulent, pink folds of skin. From behind, with his other hand, he fingered the rosy flesh of her vulva. Marissa half-closed her eyes.

'Mmm, that's so good, baby,' she breathed, stepping wider apart, willing his fingers inside her, so urgent, so great, was her need.

Larry swirled his fingers round her damp, tumid orifice. Gradually, softly, he eased upwards. Gently, he pushed two fingers inside her, methodically rubbing her stiff, tingling bud with his other hand.

Breathing raggedly, close to release, Marissa watched herself in the mirror and frenziedly reached for her breasts. She pulled hard on her nipples.

'Yeah, baby,' coaxed Larry huskily. 'I love it when you do that.'

Within seconds she came, her knees bending and buckling. Larry opened his big, strong hand out flat between her legs and supported her weakening body. She let herself drop on to his palm, welcoming the pressure on her throbbing sex.

As he pressed up hard with the heel of his hand, stopping her from falling, sharp needles of pleasure serrated the tops of her thighs. Heavy-lidded, she glanced in the mirror at her reflection. Her feet were still little more than shoulder-width apart, but she'd spread her bended knees outwards and could see Larry's supportive hand in between. In spite of her climax, her fervour increased.

'Larry, honey. Take me!' She turned around and kissed him on the lips, rubbing her moist, nude body against the expensive material of his suit.

Suddenly peeling away, she sauntered over to the bed, lying on top of the sheets. Larry grinned as he watched her stretching out, displaying her luscious body for him. Quickly he pulled off his clothing.

Marissa kept her eyes glued to him as layer after layer was discarded. Dark navy suit, grey silk tie, crisp white shirt, and finally he was naked. His broad, well-muscled chest tapered to lean hips and tight, rounded buttocks. She glanced greedily at his crotch. His penis, thick and rigid, rose magnificently from the glossy dense vee of dark hair and, as though easing the weight of it, he held it in his hand as he walked towards her.

He lay down beside her on the huge double bed, dipping his head immediately to hers to kiss her roughly on the lips. Marissa opened her mouth hungrily, darting her tongue gratefully on to his. He sucked on her tongue, sending thrills the length of her body. With a sigh, she drew away and pushed him on to his back.

She flicked her tongue over his chest, licking his small, flat nipples, trailing her tongue down each serried rib, watching his stomach muscles clench as she did so.

Gradually, Larry eased himself up the bed till his back was against the bedrest. He leant forward, grasping Marissa round the waist and pulling her up on to his lap. Eagerly she positioned herself on him, leaning her back into his chest, stretching her legs out on top of his. His penis was probing any entry to her body and she pressed herself down against it, enclosing it in the long gully of her seated buttocks. Larry groaned delightedly as she writhed back and forth on him, stimulating his trapped penis as well as her own bottom. He grabbed unsighted for her jiggling breasts, cupping and squeezing them excitedly, tweaking her sore, sensitised nipples with his fingers.

Gladly, she thrust her chest into his hands. Locking her arms to either side of Larry's hips to support herself, she continued to slide her bottom along his cock, savouring the smart, slightly burning sensation arising in her crease.

Soon the stimulus was too much for both of them. Again Larry grasped Marissa's waist. Glancing below, she saw how his large hands met round the slenderness of her middle. She felt light as a feather as he lifted her and brought her back down, impaling her on to his upright penis. Opening her legs wide to either side of his, she sank her hips down as far as she could, relishing the fullness, the swelling tumescence of him pushing up inside.

His length entirely encased, Marissa wriggled on his lap, rubbing her buttocks excitedly against his pubic bone. With an ecstatic groan, Larry began to raise her slowly up and down. Marissa made herself relax, letting Larry lift and lower her systematically, his huge penis whetting the tight, slick walls of her vagina.

As he bounced her more and more quickly, he bent his knees up between Marissa's legs. Urgently, she leant forward, clasping his knees for support, squashing her teased, aching breasts into the solid, bunched muscles of his thighs.

Larry's fingers tightened round her waist as he thrust and bounced her rapidly. Marissa's sex felt on fire, the nerves red-hot. Sweat broke out on her skin, pearling between her breasts, down her back, in her armpits. She closed her eyes, succumbing to the sensations rocking her body. 'Harder, yes baby, faster,' she moaned to Larry, clinging tightly to his knees.

Behind her, Larry cried out suddenly, propelling his hips high in the air, bucking her up along with him. Feverishly she glanced back over her shoulder, watching his face as he spilled scorchingly into her. His eyes were glazed and half closed, his face bathed in sweat. As she took in his euphoria, her own orgasm began, rampaging jaggedly through her body. She ground her hips down hard and reached for the slippery, swollen bud of her clitoris, pressing her finger urgently against it.

Spasm after spasm shook her till, weak and exhausted and totally spent, she collapsed back gratefully against Larry's chest.

She awoke to the sound of sharp, persistent knocking at the door. Larry was asleep on his stomach, the side of his face pressed into the pillow. His heavy forearm rested on Marissa's navel. With an effort, she slipped out from under it and trooped over to the door. She opened it slightly. 'Yes?' she snapped irritably, finding Rosita outside.

'It is five o'clock, Mrs Aslett,' said Rosita quietly. 'You ask for me to wake you.'

'Mmm, so I did.' Marissa rubbed her eyes sleepily. She peered at Rosita, clad once again in her habitual black and white uniform. A quick picture flashed in Marissa's mind, of Rosita poised naked over Raoul, Raoul kneading Rosita's soft, fleshy buttocks. Marissa's lips curled upwards in a sly, knowing smile. What a sight that had been. What entertainment! Quite a show the two of them had put on for her, albeit unwittingly. She suddenly felt uncharacteristically magnanimous. 'Take the evening off, Rosita,' she said, starting to close the door.

Seeing the look of surprise on Rosita's face, she couldn't resist adding softly. 'You must be tired, sweetie. I know I am!'

Larry stirred in the bed and raised a sleepy eyelid. 'Come back to bed,' he murmured, patting the space she'd vacated. Wide awake now, Marissa slipped back under the sheet, replacing Larry's arm over her.

'Larry?'

'Hmm?' He prized his eyes open.

'Larry, we've got to talk.'

'Yeah,' he muttered quietly. He turned over on to his back and crooked out an arm, resting his knuckles on his forehead. He sighed deeply. 'Thing is, that idea I mentioned; it could be risky!'

'Tell me anyway.'

'Well, that guy we met last night, Johnny Casigelli. He's a major player. Got a lot of clout. Owns companies, hotels, casinos. Mostly legit.'

'Only mostly?' chipped in Marissa.

Larry nodded. 'You got it.'

'So?'

'So, Johnny owes me a favour.'

'What kind of a favour?'

'A big, big favour. A few of his tax accounts weren't as slick as they should be. The IRS started probing, then the Feds started sniffing around. Johnny was looking at being indicted. I sorted it for him.'

'You what –?'

Larry shrugged. 'I sorted it,' he said, enunciating carefully.

'I thought the firm wouldn't act for mobsters? That's what David always told me.'

Larry chuckled. 'Babe, he's not a mobster. He's just a guy with money and influence who happens to owe me big time. He puts a lot of stock in repaying favours does Johnny.'

Marissa was silent. Her pulse had quickened dramatically.

'Besides,' Larry went on, leaning over and lazily stroking her navel, 'David's no longer with us, is he? And who's been running the firm since he died?'

'You, honey.' Marissa's voice was a purr. She traced her fingernail across Larry's dark, tapering eyebrow. She looked at him, saucer eyed, falsely innocent. 'How's this Johnny going to help our situation?'

'That,' replied Larry, 'is something I got to talk to him about. I want total control of the firm, right? Without Kelly breathing down my neck. You want this spread –,' he gestured round the room with his arm.

'And the only thing in our way is Kelly,' whispered Marissa. A searing surge of adrenalin coursed through her body.

Larry gripped her shoulders roughly and forced them down against the bed. He looked searchingly into her eyes and his face began to darken. The small vein pulsated in his temple. 'Nothing,' he said quietly, 'I mean nothing bad is going to happen to Kelly. That's not the way it's going to be.'

Marissa's eyes glittered. 'What then?'

'Leave it to me, babe,' said Larry, easing the pressure on her shoulders. 'Kelly trusts me. I'll make it work!'

Marissa's chest was heaving with excitement. She saw his eyes move downwards and felt his cock dig suddenly into her thigh. He let go of her shoulders and ran his hand voraciously over her breasts. She traced her fingernail down the centre of his torso, twirled her fingertip through the thickening coils of hair below his navel, then reached down and caressed his penis. 'Make it work for me, Larry,' she murmured softly. 'Make it work for both of us!'

7

Luc stepped out of the shower and left Kelly there still washing her hair. He dried and dressed himself quickly, pulling on fresh jeans and an old, blue workshirt. Then, grabbing his wallet, he popped his head round the bathroom door. 'Kelly, I go down for some croissants and some milk.'

'OK,' shouted Kelly, her voice muffled by the sound of drumming water.

Luc unlocked the apartment door, tripped energetically down the five flights of stairs and walked out on to the street. It was eight o'clock in the morning and the street was already bustling, harried workers glancing at watches, early shoppers hurrying to and fro.

Luc ambled down the shaded pavement, stopping at a newstand on the corner to buy a paper. He paused for a moment to skim over the headlines and was mildly aware of being stared at. Flicking his eyes up over the top of the paper, he saw two, pretty, very fashionable girls nudging each other and giggling. Luc winked at them and grinned, watching in amusement as their giggles gathered force. Then he yawned lazily and turned back to his paper.

'Shit, Duras. What's it like to have women fall at your feet?'

Luc rummaged idly in his back pocket for a pack of cigarettes before remembering he was wearing a clean pair of jeans. He glanced at the news vendor who had spoken. Bertrand was ensconced as ever in his wooden chair, avidly watching the world go by. 'It's not a problem, Bertrand,' Luc shrugged. 'But right now, there's only one woman I want at my feet.'

Bertrand grinned, showing a number of unhealthy tobacco-stained teeth. 'Yeh? Who would that be then?'

'A goddess. Truly,' laughed Luc, detouring over to the *tabac* for his brand of Marlboros.

Cigarettes bought, Luc carried on down the road towards the *boulangerie*, pausing yet again as a toothless, old woman approached. She carried a bag with two long baguettes sticking out of the top. The woman stopped and peered myopically at him. Her chin was covered with a heavy growth of hair.

'*Salut*, Ghislaine,' said Luc cheerfully.

The old woman peered closer. 'Ah, Luc, it is you. Where have you been? We have not seen you at the café for days. I have missed cleaning round your chair while you sit like a lump with Pierre and Louis!'

Luc chuckled. 'You're a grouch, Ghislaine. You grumble when I'm there, you grumble when I'm not.'

Ghislaine cackled, pink gums glistening and bristly jowls shaking as she threw back her head. 'I suppose you're not such a bad boy really,' she said, patting his cheek affectionately with a dry, calloused hand. 'You will be coming in today?'

'Maybe,' laughed Luc.

Ghislaine nodded and walked on a pace. She stopped suddenly and called back over her shoulder. 'And bring that pretty young thing with you. The one I saw you taking into your apartment on Tuesday.' She winked mischievously and resumed her waddling journey.

Luc shook his head gently. Pretending she couldn't see indeed. The old woman had eyes like a hawk. It was worse than living in a glasshouse. Everybody here saw everything.

Reaching the *boulangerie*, he bought breakfast, fending off more questions about his recent activities from

Thérèse behind the counter. Then he strolled back to his apartment building.

His apartment, like his nearby studio, was at the top of the building. Kelly was out on the roof terrace when he entered. She'd wrapped a fluffy white bathtowel around her and stood with her elbows resting on the top of the stone wall, staring out at the city.

Luc walked outside to join her, dropping the food on top of the wooden bench table. 'Breakfast, *chérie*,' he said quietly.

Kelly turned. Her hair was still damp from the shower and she'd combed it back off her face. It looked slick and darker than its usual tawny brown. Her face, scrubbed clean of make-up, was radiant nonetheless, the natural golden hues of her complexion gleaming in the gentle morning sunlight. She was beautiful.

The towel looked big and bunched round her body and her long, slender arms, holding it in place, glistened with droplets of water from her hair.

'I've struck gold, I think!' She smiled happily across at him.

'Gold? *Comment*?' Luc was confused. His English was good and it was rare that he didn't understand a phrase.

'You're gorgeous,' laughed Kelly, 'fabulous in bed. And on top of that, you get breakfast too!'

Luc scowled, feigning machismo. 'Just for today, girl. And after you have eaten, you clean the apartment, no?'

Kelly giggled, reaching for a croissant. 'So that's what you wanted me for – my cleaning skills!'

She bit into the crescent-shaped pastry, then broke a piece off and fed it to Luc.

He chewed it thoughtfully. 'I should go to the studio today.'

'D'you have to?' Kelly tried hard not to sound whiny.

Luc nodded. 'I should. It is two days since I have been. I am behind.'

Kelly stepped closer and held another piece of croissant out to him. 'I never did that before you know,' she whispered.

'What?' Luc was still thinking about the studio.

'Spent two entire days and two entire nights in bed with someone I hardly know.'

Luc winked. 'Ah,' he said. 'But now we know each other quite well I think.'

'Not well enough,' murmured Kelly huskily. She brushed a crumb off his lips and he kissed the tips of her fingers.

'I should go.' He didn't sound at all as though he wanted to.

Kelly stuck out her bottom lip, pouting prettily. 'I thought you wanted to paint me?'

'Not at the moment,' Luc mumbled incoherently. He looked pained.

'What? Why?'

'Not now.'

'Why not?'

'Because. Look!' He gestured down to his groin. His erection was huge, pushing uncomfortably against the front of his jeans.

'Aahh,' Kelly giggled. Keeping her eyes on his face, she swiftly undid the top three buttons of his fly and pushed her hand into his jeans. Her fingers probed gently and, moving beneath his undershorts, closed gratifyingly round the thick shaft of his penis. With her other hand, she unbuttoned his shirt and pushed it off his body and, while steadily fondling his penis, she slid her tongue wetly across his chest. 'Go to the studio later,' she whispered, gliding her tongue up his neck and underneath the curve of his throat.

Luc groaned. Two days and two nights non-stop and he still couldn't get enough of her. He gazed down at her. Her hair was drying at the edges now. It was exactly the same shade of light brown as the smattering of freckles on her nose, he noticed. The towel, wrapped precariously around her bosom, suddenly looked flimsy rather than fluffy and, with each movement of her hand in his groin, her breasts threatened to spill out. Roughly, he grasped the front of the towel and yanked it away from her body.

Kelly gasped with delight, flicking her hair back over her shoulders, pushing her chest out spontaneously towards him. Luc loved her lack of inhibition, the total ease with which she went naked for him. Straightaway he reached for her breasts, letting them sit for a moment on the flat of his hands. He marvelled at the full, firm globes, how weighty they felt on his hands, yet how pert and upright they were from the top of her rib-cage. As he began to fondle and lift them, Kelly sighed softly, squeezing his penis harder in response.

He played his thumb-pads idly to and fro across her nipples and then let his hands wander lazily up and down the sides of her slender torso and thighs, her skin satin-smooth beneath his fingers. Meanwhile, her fingers were working their magic in his groin but, with an enormous effort at willpower, he lifted her hand from his jeans.

'Studio,' he mumbled.

'Bed!' she countered.

'Stu –'

The word strangled in his throat as she pressed against him, pushing her bare hips on to his groin. Her breasts were crushed against his chest and, standing on tiptoe, crossing her wrists behind his neck, she drew back slightly so that she could brush her nipples against his. Their nipples hardened simultaneously and Luc lowered his eyes to watch her sway subtly from side to side, grazing her stiffened tips against him.

Tenderly, he gathered her damp hair behind her in a

bunch. Water moistened his hands and he wiped them down the small of her sun-warmed back, on to the sweet, rounded curves of her buttocks. Lovingly, he cupped her bottom. Kelly arched her back, pushing herself into his hands and he massaged her buttock cheeks slowly, still gazing down at the tops of her gleaming breasts.

'Bed!' urged Kelly breathlessly.

'OK, OK. Bed.' Flames of desire tore through his belly. All thoughts of work evaporated. 'Definitely bed,' he said quietly, kissing her forehead, eyelids and nose.

Mute with passion, they made their way silently back to the bedroom, touching and holding each other as they walked, not wanting to be parted even for a moment.

Luc perched on the edge of the bed, pulling off his boots and the remainder of his clothes whilst Kelly knelt behind him, trailing her hands down his spine. He jerked involuntarily as her fingers wandered over his belly, pinching lightly at the fine line of hair that tapered up from his crotch.

As soon as he was naked, they rolled together to the centre of the bed, bodies moulding perfectly as they found each other's mouths. They kissed deeply, slowly, luxuriously.

Gradually, Luc eased Kelly on to her back. Her hair fanned out across the pillow, dark against the pure whiteness of the plain cotton slip. She raised her head up slightly, watching him closely as he manoeuvred slowly down the bed.

He positioned himself between her long golden legs, firmly pushing them apart. The trim tawny hair on her mons nestled in a tiny, perfect vee-shape and he gently twined his fingers through it, fluffing up the soft little curls. The hair petered out to a feathery down between her legs and the sight of her smooth pink sex made his groin ache with longing.

Dipping down, he drew his tongue delicately along the length of her clitoris.

'Oh, yes,' sighed Kelly, pulling in her stomach muscles responsively, catching her breath as he touched her.

With the tip of his tongue, he flicked at her small, soft nub, enticing it gently outwards until it peeped delicately from its protective, silken surroundings. Luc gazed raptly at the core of her, at the essence of her sexual pleasure. Her sex bud was hard and rosy now, swollen with arousal, and he twirled his tongue luxuriously round it, tasting the sugared flavour of her juices. As he licked, his nose brushing lightly across her pubis, he could smell the sweet fragrance of her body blending with the spicy scent of her arousal and he pushed his mouth hard against her, craving more of the taste and smell of her.

Kelly was moaning softly. She had dropped her head back against the pillow and spreadeagled her arms to the sides. The twin cones of her nipples rose perfectly from the centres of her flattened breasts. They had darkened to a deep shade of pink and as he glanced at them, Luc felt a smart stab of excitement rip through his rear.

Stifling a groan, he bent back towards her sex. He placed his hands on the backs of her thighs and pushed her legs up high in the air. Then he brought her feet together and crossed them at her ankles. Kelly bent her knees out automatically, her legs forming an open oval in the air. Because of the position, the folds of her sex closed in a long, glistening line, leading deliciously down to the exposed furrow of her bottom cleft. Tenderly, Luc nudged his tongue right down on to the lowest tip of her spine and into the top of her crease. He trailed his tongue up slowly over the tiny roseate mouth of her anus, upwards along the moist seam of her sex. Kelly was gasping out loud and as he continued, deliberately, precisely, tracing his tongue back and forth, her gasps turned to low, throaty, desperate moans.

She pulled her legs further up towards her body and Luc, making his tongue rigid, pushed it quickly in, out and around the glossy damp slit of her vulva. Kelly was frantic, lifting her hips even higher, mouthing words Luc couldn't decipher. He teased and stimulated relentlessly, his own abdomen burning with arousal.

As soon as he sensed her orgasm was near, he swiftly dragged his tongue downwards and inserted it deftly into the tight, starry mouth of her bottom. Kelly went wild. 'Oh God, oh Jesus,' she moaned, thrashing her hands against the sheets, uncrossing her ankles and stretching her legs out mid-air. Luc expertly tongued her, keen to prolong her euphoria. She tasted so good, like honey and vanilla and soap and sex and hungrily he pushed in further, her taut little orifice contracting rhythmically round his tongue.

He placed his hands on the backs of her knees and gratefully she dropped her legs against them, helpless, sweating and weak, and lost in her own vortex of ecstasy. Only when she raised her head up and reached for his hands, did Luc withdraw his tongue and let her lower her buttocks to the bed.

'Jeez!' she breathed shakily, pulling him up alongside her and drawing him into a deep, succulent kiss.

Running her hands feverishly over his burning body, she climbed nimbly over him, straddling him with her knees, hovering above his swollen cock. She looked down at it, circling it lovingly with both of her hands, stroking it lightly. Gradually she began to nudge the tip back and forth along her engorged bud. Luc pushed his head back into the pillow, agonised by the soft, tender teasing of his penis. When he glanced up, he briefly saw his tip glistening with moisture from Kelly's excited sex, then his tip disappeared as she eased it back between her labia.

With a groan, he dropped his head back again, reaching behind with his arms and tightly clasping the brass poles of the headrest. Very, very slowly Kelly was guiding him inside her, her small moist opening welcoming him gloriously.

As she sank down on to him, her body closing around him in hot, blessed, long-awaited relief, he swallowed hard and lifted his hips, penetrating up as far as he possibly could.

'Mmm. Oh yes,' Kelly softly moaned. She leant backwards, locking her arms to the sides of his knees and began to ride his penis, rubbing the bulb of her buttocks deliciously against his balls. Her lush young body rocked upon him, breasts out-thrust and quivering with her movements. She tilted back her head, moaning, sighing, and Luc could only do the same, closing his eyes as the sensations began to build, spreading from his groin and buttocks, climbing and monopolising every nerve in his body until he gave in totally, surrendering to a racing, searing, liquid rush.

Kelly was snuggled up close, lying with one smooth, silken leg bent across his knees. Trying not to wake her, Luc leant gently towards the side table, reaching one handed for a cigarette.

'What you doing?' whispered Kelly, her face buried in his armpit.

'Cigarette,' mumbled Luc, the Marlboro dangling from the corner of his mouth. He lit up and took a drag and looked across at the clock. 1.15. Hell! 1.15! The studio. He should go. He had commissions to finish that were already overdue. Not to mention his exhibits. Chantal would slice him up and throw away the pieces if he wasn't ready for his next exhibition.

Kelly wriggled next to him and raised her head up. Her hair was tousled round her face and shoulders and her cheeks were slightly flushed, glowing and dewy from their sex. She looked and smelled so good. Incredibly he felt himself stir again and, to distract himself, he took another pull on the cigarette.

'Now, I go to work.' He made his voice sound as decisive as possible.

'Oh, I s'pose so,' said Kelly grudgingly. 'And I should go home and make a start packing up.'

'*Comment*? What?' Luc was sure he'd misheard or misunderstood. 'Packing up? What do you mean?'

Kelly had blushed slightly. She looked at him warily. 'I didn't tell you yet, did I?'

'Tell me? *De quoi parles-tu*? Tell me what?'

Her voice was faint, more than a little wobbly. 'In five days, I have to go back to the States...'

Luc leant over to the side and flicked his ash into the saucer which served as an ashtray. 'I see,' he said quietly.

'That's why I didn't come to your exhibition. And missed the other sittings.' Kelly was talking very fast, almost babbling. 'I-I didn't want to start anything, you see, because I'm going home so soon.'

Luc was silent. He carried on smoking.

'I have to sign some papers over there,' went on Kelly. 'That's the reason I'm going back.'

'Papers? What papers?'

'Er ... legal stuff. My dad died four years ago. It's to do with his will. I have to sign some stuff on my 25th birthday.'

'Ah,' said Luc. 'And you must be with your family, no?'

Kelly looked away from him, dropping her head back on his chest. 'There is no family. There's only me. And my stepmom.'

'She is not family?'

'No!' Kelly laughed scornfully. 'Far from it. She hates my guts. And, I have to admit, the feeling's entirely mutual.'

'How is it possible anyone can hate you?' Luc said quietly, holding his cigarette down to her lips.

Kelly took a quick puff. 'Believe me, she does!' Her lovely amber eyes suddenly looked very serious. 'We never did take to each other. She was half my dad's age and I always thought she was after his money. Still, she seemed to make him happy so I suppose you could say we tolerated each other. But when dad died, he left the house and his business shares to me. Marissa – that's my stepmom – she couldn't believe it. She thought she had my dad so wrapped up in her that he would leave everything to her. I mean, they were married under six months when he died. Did she really think he would cut off his only daughter.'

Luc stroked Kelly's back thoughtfully. 'If you have no family, who sorts these affairs for you?'

'Larry, my dad's partner. He's a lawyer – a brilliant one dad always said – so it's the easiest way to handle things.'

Luc didn't answer. She looked up into his face expectantly, apparently awaiting his reaction. He dropped a kiss on the top of her head. 'So, *chérie*,' he said softly. 'You will come back to Paris after?'

Kelly's face brightened. She smiled widely. 'I don't know. What for?'

Luc smiled back and turned to the chipped saucer on the side table, grinding out his half-smoked cigarette. He pushed his hand beneath the sheet. 'For this,' he whispered, trailing his hand down the side of her thigh.

'What's that?' teased Kelly quietly.

He stroked the delicate skin at the top of her inner thigh and bent his lips to hers. 'This,' he murmured against her mouth, his fingers exploring further.

Kelly kissed him hungrily, spreading her legs to accommodate his hand. 'Ah that,' she breathed between kisses. And then pushed her body against him.

8

Marissa paced nervously round the living room, a white cordless telephone pressed to her ear. 'Justine,' she said, fighting to keep her voice even. 'Why don't you just tell me where Larry went?'

'Mrs Aslett, I don't know where he went,' answered Justine, sounding equally exasperated. 'He just told me he had to go out to a business meeting.'

'And that's all he said?'

'That's all, Mrs Aslett.'

'OK. Sorry to trouble you, Justine.' Marissa ended the conversation abruptly and cut Justine off. It was like trying to get blood from a stone, talking to Justine, she thought irritably. She'd have words with Larry about him getting a new assistant. Justine's days at Aslett & Barris were most definitely numbered.

Marissa threw the telephone disdainfully down on the sofa and moved across to the big picture window. Gazing absently out at the pool, she nibbled on an immaculately manicured fingernail. Damn, she was getting high strung! Larry often went out to business meetings and he certainly didn't keep her informed of each and every one of them. Still, there were only five more days until Kelly got home and they seemed no nearer to working out a solution than they had been before. She was beginning to wonder if Larry really was working on a solution at all. If she hadn't seen him with her own eyes, she might just think Johnny Casigelli was a figment of Larry's imagination.

Wandering restlessly up to her bedroom, she roamed

around the room, picking up costly ornaments, tossing them idly in her hands then distractedly replacing them. Well, she thought, squaring her shoulders decisively, she couldn't just hang around the house all day, waiting for Larry to show up or get in touch with some news. Better to go out. After all, didn't Larry say leave it all up to him?

Slipping out of her jeans and cropped T-shirt, she yanked a tiny yellow halterdress out of the closet and stepped into it, tying it up round her neck. She thrust her bare feet into a pair of low-heeled black mules, then grabbed a brush from her dresser and pulled it energetically through her mass of blonde hair, which she then deftly tied back in a loose, low ponytail. Tendrils of hair escaped and framed the edges of her face, enhancing her pretty, fresh features. Lightly, she glossed her lips to a clear, pale-pink sheen then stepped in front of her full-length mirror to appraise the result.

The bottom of the dress just about skimmed the tops of her sleek brown thighs. Even with low-heeled shoes, her legs looked endless. She did a twirl, cheekily flicking the dress up over her pert, firm bottom to check she'd remembered to put panties on. Larry so often insisted she left them off, it was beginning to be rather a habit these days. Not today however. A lacy pair of briefs was flimsily in place.

Entirely satisfied, she turned on her heel and began to fill a large, leather bag before running jauntily down the stairs.

'Rosita!' she called from the hallway.

'Yes, Mrs Aslett.' Rosita appeared instantly.

'I'm driving into LA to shop. Probably be gone most of the afternoon. If Larry calls, tell him to stop by later.'

Rosita nodded and pulled open the heavy oak front door.

Marissa got into her black convertible and started the engine. She pushed a pair of sunglasses on to the top of her head and began to back quickly down the long straight driveway. Rosita, turning in the doorway, made to close the door.

'Be sure and tell Larry to stop by,' called out Marissa from the road, before speeding off in the direction of the freeway.

She drove fast, covering the 40 or so miles in well under an hour. She visited several of her favourite shops, quickly acquiring a number of packages, lingerie mostly, expensive, scant and lacy. Larry's favourites.

Two hours later, she was bored with shopping and decided to head back home.

Speeding out of LA, she rapidly punched in numbers on the carphone. 'Justine,' she barked. 'Marissa. Larry in yet?'

Justine sighed audibly at the other end. 'No, Mrs Aslett,' she answered languidly.

'Did he call in?' snapped Marissa.

'No-o.' Justine sounded suspiciously as though she were swallowing a yawn.

Not bothering with goodbye, Marissa irritably clicked the phone off. Larry sure as hell better have come up with the goods by tonight, she thought, pressing her foot down hard on the pedal. The car instantly accelerated and she raced along the freeway, filtering off to take the coastal route back.

As she drove, the wind coursed through her loosely tied hair, a welcome relief from the beating rays of the afternoon sun and she kept her foot pressed close to the floor, relishing the breakneck speed.

In awe, Marissa dipped her eyes far over to the right, to the precipitous drops to the ocean. As she looked down at the deep, blue, swirling water, her car so perilously close to the edge, a massive surge of adrenalin assailed her and she gripped the wheel tightly, her knuckles whitening with the force of it.

Without slowing, she rounded a corner, clinging expertly to her lane.

Up ahead, seemingly from nowhere, a vehicle pottered ponderously in front of her. Marissa cursed silently and slammed on her brakes, slowing only just in time to avoid hurtling into its rear. She hovered impatiently behind the car. It crawled along like a silver snail, refusing to be hurried by her irascible tailgating. Another bend suddenly loomed into view. Marissa clung dangerously close to the snail's rear bumper, blasting her horn in irritation. The car stuck steadfastly to its torpid pace.

Infuriated, Marissa pulled out. She sped past the car, overtaking blindly on the curve of the bend. Accelerating hard, she drove round the corner, gasping out loud as she careered straight towards an oncoming jeep. Wrenching the wheel to the right, she veered abruptly back into lane, cutting in sharply in front of the snail. The other cars swerved jerkily to the roadside. Horns blaring, they pulled to a standstill.

Excitedly, Marissa drove on, exhilarated by her manoeuvre. Through her driver's mirror, she looked back and saw people out of their cars, shaking their heads, waving fiercely at her swiftly vanishing car. She threw back her head and laughed and laughed. How hilarious! Leaving a trail of havoc and fury in her wake! Her body felt hot and vibrant and alive and she wriggled in her seat as she drove, a strange flush of arousal rising between her legs. Breathing hard, she accelerated more.

Suddenly she heard a siren. She glanced in her mirror again. A black and white police car was approaching at speed, red and blue lights flashing, garish in the sunlight.

Damn, muttered Marissa softly, lifting her foot immediately and letting her car automatically slow its pace. The car appeared alongside her, gliding up smoothly like a long sleek predator. Marissa turned towards it.

The lights were still illuminated, swirling lazily now, the siren sounding in a slow, distorted, drawn-out pitch. Marissa caught a glimpse of a black-clad figure, arm extended towards her. A gloved finger pointed authoritatively to the side, ordering her to pull over. Meekly, Marissa complied.

Her tyres crunched on the gravelled surface as she drew up to the right, into a widened area close to the roadside. The black and white followed, stopping some 10 yards behind. Marissa dutifully stayed in her seat, lightly tapping her fingers on the steering wheel. She was still breathing quickly, still exhilarated by the speed and risk of her driving.

Behind her, a car door slammed. Slow, deliberate footsteps ground against the stones, halting suddenly near her car door. Marissa turned her head slightly and fixed her gaze on the thick black buckle of a belt. Tentatively, she slid her eyes up over a black, uniformed shirt.

'Can I help you, officer?' she asked sweetly, opening her pretty, blue eyes innocently wide.

For a moment the police officer didn't respond. He stared stern-faced down at Marissa, his eyes masked by dark, mirrored shades.

'Ma'am,' he began, 'do you happen to know what speed you were doing?' His voice was cold, without inflection.

'I'm afraid I don't, officer,' said Marissa quietly. 'A-a little fast, I guess.'

'Way, way too fast. Twice the speed limit as a matter of fact!'

Marissa fluttered her fingers to her lips. She dropped her gaze in a look of embarrassment. 'Oh, officer, is that so? I'm terribly sorry. I'm not used to driving long stretches. I guess I just got carried away.'

'You also ran two red lights on the state highway,' he

said in a monotone. 'Not to mention that little episode back there. You could have caused a major incident.'

Marissa gasped, biting her lower lip. 'Did I really do all that, officer? It just sounds so awful!'

'You sure did.' The policeman pulled out a notebook from his breastpocket. 'Afraid I'm going to have to write you up, ma'am,' he said, shaking open the book.

'Do you really have to?' Marissa added a slight quaver to her voice.

The officer nodded curtly, his mirrored shades glinting eerily in the sunlight. Marissa looked up at him, trying to see his eyes behind the glasses. His hair was blond and short cropped, she could see that much. And his skin looked smoothly tanned across the forehead and cheeks, but it was difficult to gauge his age and looks with the glasses covering his face.

'Could you at least remove your sunshades if you're going to arrest me, officer?' she asked softly.

She thought she saw a glimmer of a smile. 'Ma'am,' he said, 'I'm not going to arrest you. Just a ticket. On this occasion.'

'Still,' Marissa persisted. 'It'd be polite to take them off.'

This time there was a definite smile. Marissa noted the white evenness of his teeth.

He shrugged almost imperceptibly. 'I guess it would at that,' he answered quietly, pulling off the shades.

Marissa smiled sweetly. His cornflower-blue eyes almost matched the colour of her own though tiny lines were forming at the corners of his. He looked 35 or thereabouts. Around the same age as Larry. Good-looking man, she mused, glancing down at his physique. He was tall and broad shouldered and his uniform was sculpted to his body like a thick, second skin, the shirt moulding the contours of his muscles, trousers tight round his hips. His gun holster rested menacingly on one hip and Marissa noticed that the thick, black belt round his waist held his baton to his side within easy reach. Mmm, yum, she thought, armed and dangerous!

'That's better,' she murmured. 'So much more polite.'

She watched him closely as he began to write out the ticket, casually resting her hands in her lap. Raising her arm to the side of her door, she subtly inched her dress higher up her thigh.

'Just a few questions, ma'am. Can I see your licence and registration, please?' The officer glanced up from his pad. His eyes shot immediately to her thighs. Tanned and sleek and utterly exposed. Marissa leant back in her seat, stretching out like a cat. 'Is a ticket absolutely necessary, officer?' Her voice was no more than a whisper.

His face was deadpan and he reverted to his mono-tone. 'Yes it is, ma'am.'

Marissa moistened her lips with the tip of her tongue. 'I know I was a bad girl, officer.'

'Yes, ma'am.'

'And I know you should punish me.'

'Yes, ma'am.' His eyes flickered away and he jabbed the nib of his pen down hard on the pad.

'But couldn't you –,' Marissa paused and rubbed her hands languorously over the golden skin of her thighs. 'Couldn't you do it some other way?' Her voice was soft and breathy.

The policeman shifted his weight from one foot to the other. He cleared his throat noisily. 'I'm sure I don't know what you mean, ma'am,' he said gruffly. 'This is correct procedure.'

Marissa popped the end of her forefinger between her lips. She let the tip of her tongue flick over her nail while she lowered her eyelids coquettishly.

'Big strong man like you,' she murmured slowly. 'Surely you could teach me a lesson!'

The officer watched as she licked at the tip of her finger. His eyes darted back to her exposed thighs. It seemed an effort for him to drag his gaze away. His Adam's apple bobbed in his throat as he swallowed uneasily.

'Ma'am, if you would just answer some questions.' He focused on his notepad again.

'Big strong hands too,' whispered Marissa, tracing the back of his hand as it clutched the notebook. 'Bet you could punish me much more with those than with that little ol' ticket book.'

'I –,' began the officer then stopped. He stared at the ticket book then he stared at Marissa. His eyes lingered on Marissa.

Marissa nibbled innocently on her fingernail. She spoke in a sort of a sigh. 'Bet you could spank me so hard with those big strong hands; so hard that I never run another red light . . .'

His deadpan expression didn't alter. But his eyes still rested on Marissa.

A moment later, he flicked the book shut. 'Follow me,' he said tersely, striding purposefully back to his car.

He pulled back on to the road and Marissa obediently followed, tailing his slow-moving vehicle along the highway. A short distance further on, he turned right on to a narrow, unmade track. They drove for a minute or two, down towards the ocean. Then the track drew up abruptly to a secluded dead end and the officer parked his vehicle parallel to the sea. Marissa pulled up on the inside. She sat in her seat, flushed with excitement.

Silently, he came round to her door, taking her by the hand and leading her back to his car. As they walked, the sun glittered off the water and Marissa had to shield her eyes from the brightness. She lowered her eyes to the ground, concentrating on the officer's heavy black boots.

Opening his car door, the officer seated himself in the

passenger seat. His eyes shone brilliantly as he looked at her. 'So,' he said softly. 'You want me to teach you a lesson?'

'Yes!' breathed Marissa.

'Come here then.' He patted his lap gently.

Marissa lingered in the open car doorway. 'How?' she whispered.

'Over my lap.'

She smiled widely. Slowly she leant down and bent forwards over his lap, resting her arms on the driver's seat. She could feel the slight roughness of his trousers on the tender skin at the front of her thighs. The feeling wasn't unpleasant and Marissa pressed her legs down as she lay across him, weakened by anticipation.

He placed his hand on the back of her thigh, stroking her silky skin. Then, very softly, very faintly, he moved upwards. Tendrils of excitement trickled through her. Through the thin viscose of her dress, he shaped his hand over the curving mounds of her buttocks.

'Fantastic,' he mumbled. Lightly, almost indiscernibly, he patted her. He did it again. Then once more. Too, too gently. Marissa squirmed, brushing her thighs against the thick fabric of his trousers. She clenched her internal muscles tightly, wanting him to undress her, feel her, openly explore her.

The only sounds were the gulls overhead, the lapping of the ocean, the distant hum of the traffic on the highway. His lazy voice joined in.

'It's quite serious what you did,' he said slowly. 'Running red lights, breaking the speed limit, reckless driving –'

Marissa glanced back at him, breathing rapidly. 'I know.'

'I think it warrants quite a punishment, don't you?'

Marissa nodded, her cheeks aflame. 'Yes,' she gasped hurriedly.

His fingers curled at the base of her dress. With one nifty movement, he flicked her dress up to her waist. Marissa heard his intake of breath as he laid his hand back on her behind, those skimpy briefs all that separated her flesh from his.

Leisurely, he moved his forefinger to the waistband of the panties and drew them slowly over her rounded buttocks, pulling them down to the middle of her thighs, baring her bottom completely.

She heard his breath catch again. His fingers lingered in the sliver of white lace now round her thighs. For several seconds, he stared down at her, not touching nor feeling. Marissa's heart knocked excitedly against her rib-cage and she arched her back just a little, displaying herself like a tease.

Suddenly he removed his hand from her panties, raised it up high, and brought it down flat in the centre of her buttocks. 'Ouch!' Marissa yelped delightedly. Her buttock cheeks quivered wonderfully with the impact.

Again, he raised his hand and brought it back down. Then again and again, each crisp, hard slap eliciting a tiny sigh from Marissa. Her buttocks tingled vibrantly. She began to push them up to meet his hand. And as he spanked her harder, the tingles soon grew into a burning sensation, making her insides blaze with arousal.

She wriggled slightly on his lap and could feel beneath her, digging into the fluttering base of her stomach, the huge, hard swell of him. He spanked her faster, Marissa groaning jubilantly at the sharp, stinging contact, and then he began to slow, pausing after each hard slap to squeeze her buttocks together. The keen stinging followed by the vigorous squeezing inflamed her further and she pressed her mons down heavily on to him, feeling his body heat mingle with her own.

As she glanced excitedly behind her again, at the

upraised golden mound of her bottom, now heightened to a deep shade of pink, the officer slid his hand smoothly between the furrow of her legs. He tugged lightly at the soft blonde fur of her pubis. With each little pull, Marissa's breath strangled in her throat. She opened her legs as far as her pulled-down panties would permit and closed her eyes gratefully as his finger found her clitoral bud. Back and forth, with long, slow, dextrous strokes, he rubbed her. She arched her back to coax him on, her breasts beginning to strain within the tight confines of her dress.

'Please,' she prompted. 'My dress!'

No further explanation was needed. Still fingering her sex, he reached for the tie of her halter with his free hand and, with one brief pull, he untied it, eased the dress over her shoulders and head, and tossed it carelessly into the back of the car. She sighed with joy as he fondled her breasts beneath her, and stroked her bud from behind her, and soon she was lost in a world of her own, a world of rich, sensual, carnal delight.

As his fingers swirled in her sex, she could feel her moisture seep to the inside of her thighs. He began to work it upwards, over her buttock cheeks, coating the tender skin with her own intimate secretions. Then he began to spank her again, cupping her sore, glistening cheeks after each swift, hard clap. Beneath, his other hand roamed from her breasts to her stomach to her tiny triangle of hair, magically moving downwards, pressing her sex as he continued to spank her.

Marissa writhed over him, enraptured by the stimuli.

Energised yet breathless, she swayed her breasts lightly to and fro, stimulating her nipples on the imitation leather of the driver's seat. She dipped her hips up and down, lifting her head high, consumed by the pleasure he was giving her. She could hear his breathing, quick and rasping, intermingle with the smart, clapping sounds of each incisive slap on her bottom.

For several glorious moments, she was poised on the edge of her peak, curving her back, tensing her muscles, pushing out her bottom. Suddenly it swept over her, releasing her in a gigantic, flashing tide, making her cry out with the depth of it.

As she lay panting across him, the officer ran his hands freely over her body. He tenderly stroked her slender back and, moving to her thighs, he began to edge her panties down her legs, manoeuvring them over her shoes and then tossing them alongside her dress, into the rear of his car.

Marissa let him lift her up. Facing him, entirely nude now, she knelt astride his lap, leaning back against the dash of the car. He cupped her out-thrust breasts, eyes glazed. He was murmuring softly as though awestruck. Swiftly, he reached down to his trousers. Marissa held her breath as he pulled slowly at his zipper.

Suddenly, from nowhere, came a voice. Startled, Marissa jumped. She glanced nervously around her.

There it was again.

'Radio to 714. Radio to 714.'

'Goddammit!' cursed the officer.

Marissa chuckled. Only a radio. The police radio!

'Respond 714. Suspected robbery in progress on Hermosa Boulevard. Request immediate assistance. Repeat, request immediate back-up.'

The officer swore softly under his breath and didn't move.

The radio crackled again. 'Come in 714. Respond 714.'

He groaned, rubbing his hand longingly over Marissa's gently curving navel. 'Excuse me, sweetheart,' he said, leaning forward to pick up the handset. '714 receiving. Attending crime in progress.'

He hurriedly clicked off. 'Sorry about this, sweetheart,' he groaned.

Marissa shrugged. 'It happens, sugar.' She reached in the back for her clothes.

Still running his hands hungrily over her, he helped her dress. Then he walked her back to her car. Opening her car door for her to step in, he gazed at her, his eyes glassy with desire. He groaned again. 'Goddamn robbery! Goddamn criminals!' he muttered.

Marissa smiled. She tugged him down to her and pecked him softly on the lips. 'Thanks for the lesson, officer.'

'Any time,' he said hoarsely. 'I mean that.'

He tailed her back till she was safely on the highway, drawing up briefly alongside. She blew him a kiss and he grinned. A very cute, Larry-type grin. Then he reached into his shirt pocket, replaced his mirrored shades and sped off in a whirl of sirens and lights.

Marissa let herself in quietly. Aware she must look slightly ruffled, she intended going straight to her bedroom. She slipped off her shoes and, holding them in her hand, tiptoed lightly across the tiled vestibule and started up the stairs.

'Oh, Mrs Aslett. I did not hear you come back.'

Marissa turned. 'Hey, Rosita. Yeah, just got in.'

Rosita's eyes flicked to Marissa's hair, tumbling out of its ponytail, hopelessly disarrayed. 'Um, is everything OK, Mrs Aslett?' she asked uncertainly.

Marissa chuckled. 'Sure,' she said. 'Everything's just fine. I had a flat, that's all, and got in a bit of a mess trying to change it. Some nice police officer gave me a helping hand. What would we do without them, huh?'

'Oh, that is good,' said Rosita, tapping her chest with relief. 'I was worried. You look so, so –,'

'Dishevelled is the word you're looking for,' laughed Marissa.

'Dish-ev-elled?' said Rosita, repeating each syllable.

'It means untidy, messy.'

'Ah,' said Rosita, nodding and repeating the word to herself, obviously filing it away for future usage.

Marissa carried on up the stairs. 'Oh, did Larry call?' she asked from the landing.

'No, Mrs Aslett.'

Marissa glanced down at her watch. Seven o'clock already. Where in hell was he? She shrugged her shoulders with a nonchalance she certainly didn't feel. 'OK, thanks, Rosita.'

She ran a bath, pouring in scented oils of rose and verbena and then eased herself into the tub. The warm, silky water was heaven, soothing her pleasantly tender buttocks. But, try as she might, she couldn't seem to relax. Insidious little thoughts kept darting through her mind. What if Larry didn't come through? What if he buckled and decided just to go along with David's will? Hell, she hadn't seen him in two days. What if he was avoiding her altogether? What if? What if? she muttered silently. It wouldn't happen. Not with Larry. Her Larry. Her handsome, smart, powerful Larry.

She scissored her legs in the bathtub, letting the water slip back and forth over her, her mind drifting back to the first time she'd met him.

It had been just a short while before she and David were married. She'd gone to meet David for lunch. David had been with a client and asked her to wait and so she'd wandered around the impressive offices, ultimately finding herself in the library. She walked up and down the aisles, packed to the hilt with rich, leatherbound volumes. Law this, Judgement that, United States Stat-utes the other. Didn't anyone round there believe in a little light reading, she remembered chuckling to herself.

'Well, hello there!'

Marissa glanced round. He was seated at the end of the aisle, at a long, rectangular reading table. She was surprised. Not because she thought she was alone but because of the way he was seated. Far from the usual, proper, head-down-in-the-library way of sitting, he had his feet propped up on the table, a large, red-leather book open on his lap. His tie was loosened at his neck and his shirtsleeves rolled up to the elbow.

'Hello there,' he repeated with a wide, boyish grin.

'Hello there yourself.' Marissa smiled.

Rocking his chair back on two legs and lacing his fingers behind his head, he let his dark, grey eyes meander almost lasciviously down her body. Marissa was stunned by an immense and immediate bolt of desire. It sliced like a sickle through the edges of her tummy.

'And who might you be?' he asked in that inimitable, faintly teasing, part-lawyerly, part-boyish tone of voice.

'I might ask the same thing!' Marissa challenged, matching him tease for tease.

He smiled. 'Well, whoever you might be, wow!' He whistled softly.

They looked at each other from 10 yards apart, a heat so intense radiating between them, that they would have taken each other right there and then. In spite of the risk. Right there and then, in the middle of the library, in the middle of the offices, in the middle of the day.

If it hadn't been for David, that is, who appeared behind her precisely at that moment.

Marissa started as she felt a hand on her shoulder.

'I see you've met the boy wonder,' David said quietly.

He took her by the hand and led her over. 'Marissa, this is Larry Barris, my newly appointed junior partner. Careful, he's sharp as a barracuda and twice as deadly!'

Larry grinned and stood up quickly.

'Larry, meet my fiancée, Marissa,' said David.

Larry's eyes danced wickedly as he shook her by the hand, his grip smooth and dry and firm. 'So that's who you are,' he said softly, letting his eyes linger just a little too long ...

No, thought Marissa, lifting her right leg gracefully out of the water and watching the water trickle off it, she and Larry were soul mates. Two of a kind. Ambitious, sensual beings. Made for each other. There was no way Larry would back off.

As she rose up out of the bath and swathed herself in a fluffy, buttercup towel, someone tapped lightly at the bathroom door.

'Come in,' she said gaily, dabbing at her arms and legs with the corners of the towel.

Rosita entered. 'Mrs Aslett. I thought I must tell you right away.'

'What's that, honey?'

'Mr Barris just called. He is on his way over right now.'

Marissa watched from the open doorway as Larry's silver Ferrari pulled up, parking nose to bumper behind her Mercedes. He stepped out of his car and walked casually up the driveway, tossing his car keys in his hand.

When he reached the doorway, he placed his hand in the small of her back and jerked her harshly towards him. 'Jeez, have I missed you,' he murmured, stooping to kiss her on the mouth.

His mouth tasted sweet and mintily fresh. Marissa ran her tongue slowly over his smooth, even teeth, half closing her eyes as they kissed, automatically encircling the back of his neck. As they twirled their tongues together, he ran his fingers hungrily up and down her back. She moved her hands to the front of his shoulders. Suddenly, breathlessly, she pushed him away.

'Not so fast, Larry.'

Larry looked startled. 'Hey, what's this, babe?'

'Don't "babe" me! We don't see each other for two days. You don't call me all day. I don't like it. Not at all. You're leaving me in the dark here, Larry.'

Larry grinned. 'No way, honey. I like you best in the light!' He dipped his head to her neck. 'In the light, where I can see you,' he murmured, nibbling her throat. 'All of you. Every last bit of you.'

Roughly, she pushed him away. 'I mean it, Larry. I want to know what's happening.'

'Hey?' He raised a quizzical eyebrow. 'You trust me, don't you?'

'Yeah, but –'

'Hush then and come here.' He pulled her back to him.

She leant against him, resting her head under his chin. He was shower fresh. She could smell his expensive cologne lingering on the line of his jaw. 'Were you with Johnny Casigelli?' she asked softly.

'Uh-huh.'

'And?'

'And, we talked.'

Marissa felt her stomach leap. She pushed her body against him, tilting her chin up to look at him.

Larry glanced down at her. He smiled slowly. 'We worked something out.'

She kissed him softly underneath his chin. 'I knew you would,' she murmured. 'Tell me.'

'It's all done, baby. Just a few final wrinkles to iron out. Johnny came along just at the right time!' He dropped a kiss on the tip of her nose. 'Johnny invited us along to his house tomorrow night. He's throwing some kind of a party. We'll deal with the fine points then.'

Marissa wriggled excitedly against him. 'Tell me all about it, honey.'

'Later.' Larry's voice was suddenly gruff. 'It's been two days, remember!'

He scooped down and lifted her easily. Cradling her in his arms, he manoeuvred through the doorway, shutting the heavy oak door with a swift back-kick. Marissa rested her head meekly on his shoulder. She loved it when he went all macho and domineering on her. She felt light as an air bubble as he mounted the stairs and carried her up to her bedroom.

'I've got something to show you.' She nuzzled into his neck.

'Yeah?' said Larry hoarsely.

'Yeah. I went shopping today.'

'Did you now. What did you get?'

'I'm wearing it, baby,' she whispered.

'Not for long,' grinned Larry, kicking open the bedroom door.

9

Kelly lay in her bed. At least she thought it was her bed. It certainly felt like her bed.

She stretched contentedly, flexing her limbs like a sleek, golden panther. She was still in that blurry, tranquil interlude between sleep and wakefulness and her mind was pleasantly fuzzy. She blinked twice, pointing her toes as she stretched again, letting the light topsheet caress her.

Gradually coming to, she gazed out to the side. Cobalt-blue sky filled the broad expanse of the windowpane; an occasional cottonwool cloud crept by. Another fine day, she mused, flipping over towards Luc. Except that Luc didn't appear to be there. She shook her head lightly, shaking off the remnants of sleep, then looked again. Luc definitely wasn't there.

'Hey Kelly. A razor is where?'

Kelly smiled happily. Luc *was* there!

Rolling over on to her stomach, she wrapped the sheet round her and gazed sidewards.

He was standing in the bathroom doorway, shouldering the frame. He wandered over and patted her sheet-swathed rump. 'Lazy girl,' he whispered fondly.

Kelly plopped her cheek back against the pillow. 'Cabinet,' she murmured drowsily. 'Razor's in the cabinet.'

He dropped a kiss on the top of her shoulder and went back into the bathroom. Sleepily raising her head again, she watched him through the open doorway. God, he was sexy! That sleep-rumpled wavy hair and that teensy gold cross in his ear that looked so right on him, so gypsy like, so sexy. Dress him up in a black frock-coat and black knee-boots and she'd have Emily Brontë's Heathcliff in her bathroom. Only better!

He stood in front of the basin, his back to her, a towel slung carelessly round his hips. She watched the way his gleaming shoulder muscles moved as he tried his best to shave with soap and water and one of her lady's razors. He whistled softly whilst he soaped his face, endeavouring for some time to work up enough of a lather. When his face was half covered in soap suds, he caught her eye in the mirror and winked. A wicked, devilish, dirty wink. Kelly's stomach flipped. She stifled a sigh, pressing her face into the pillow. No man had the right to be so sexy.

'Luc, what you doing up so early?' she called out.

'You forget, *chérie*.'

'What?'

'We came back here last night. To pack up your things?'

Kelly giggled. 'Oh yes,' she said, remembering. They hadn't got around to the packing at all.

Luc was still fighting with the soap suds. '*Merde*, it is impossible!' he cursed, tossing her razor dismissively into the basin.

Quietly, Kelly eased out of bed and wandered naked into the bathroom. She circled his narrow waist and rested her head against his back. 'I like you either way,' she murmured. 'With stubble or without.'

She pressed herself against him, crushing her breasts into his back. Trailing her hands down his hard, flat belly, she reached down into the towel wrapped at his waist. Immediately the towel slipped off.

She glanced in the long oval mirror above the basin. Luc's brown torso gleamed back at her and as she caressed his hips and the tops of his thighs, his long penis responded magnificently. She didn't touch it, eyeing the thickened, engorged shaft almost with reverence as she twined her fingers softly in the vee of hair surrounding it, and then ran her hands back up his stomach and chest. Luc's stomach muscles flinched visibly at her light, fluttery strokes.

'*Viens ici, ma belle.*' He reached behind to pull her closer against him.

Kelly stretched up, pressing her hips into his tight, muscled buttocks. She swayed gently from side to side, sighing softly as she rubbed her mons against his cheeks.

'Oh yeah,' Luc breathed huskily when Kelly started to move up and down, brushing his buttock cleft with her tiny nest of hair.

Gradually, insistently, she nudged at his chest, making it clear she wanted him to turn around. Luc quickly obliged, resting his hands back against the basin. Kelly gazed at him. His dark eyes were heavy with lust, his breathing short and sharp. Swiftly, she sank down before him, kneeling submissively. She placed her hands on his long, muscled thighs. Almost teasingly, she stuck out the tip of her tongue to flick at the head of his hard, jutting penis then delicately she traced the delicious slit. Luc groaned, tilting back his head, tightening his grip on the basin.

Kelly circled his swollen length with both hands and tenderly closed her lips around its head. She sucked on the hot, rounded end, savouring the taste of him, opening her mouth hungrily to take in more of him.

Luc groaned louder as she worked her lips and tongue and as she darted her tongue to his testes, licking and sucking with slow, exquisite finesse. He jammed his buttocks back hard against the basin and moved his legs further apart.

Kelly felt as if her mouth was filled with him. Gloriously, deliciously filled. He smelt so wonderful, so clean and fresh, with his own special man-smell that it actually made her senses reel. Fingering the skin beneath the base of his penis, she watched in muzzy fascination at his body's jerky, excited response.

Sweat began to bead his washboard stomach. Her own breasts and armpits prickled with heat as she slid her mouth frantically around him. Suddenly, whilst she steadied his thighs, he came, crying out her name urgently. Madly she sucked in her cheeks, tasting, savouring, milking him greedily, darting out the tip of her tongue to catch each drop of the rich viscous cream as it bubbled to the corners of her mouth.

'*Dieu!*' gasped Luc shakily. 'My knees. They are weak!'

He dropped down to the carpet beside her, stroking her hair as he recovered his breath.

Seconds later, he rose. Silently taking her hand, he led her into the shower.

Kelly was flushed, fully awake now but woozy with passion instead. Pinpricks of heat jabbed at her and the almondy taste of him inside her mouth, the fresh, intimate scent of him clinging to her nose and lips, made her heady with lust.

Luc turned the shower on full. Hard jets of water streamed down, drumming wonderfully against their burning skin.

Kelly slicked her hair back off her face, then reached for the soap and began to lather Luc down. When she'd finished, he did the same for her, covering her body and legs in a mass of scented foam. He massaged the froth round and round her breasts until her nipples stiffened, peeking jauntily through the suds like two lustrous, dark pink pearls. Luc gazed at them so raptly, so steadily, that she dipped her eyes excitedly to look at them, amazed at how hard and erect they were, and as Luc began to tease them with his thumbs, she thought she would climax right then.

She moaned as he tugged a little harder, corresponding pangs twinging in her groin. Flicking, teasing, gently tugging, concentrating solely on her nipples, Luc inflamed her so much, she was in danger of collapse.

'Luc, it's so good.' She thrust back her shoulders and head. 'So good . . . it's too much!'

'Ssh,' he whispered, still toying with her breasts. Her nipples began to ache, almost too sensitised, and yet she wanted more, needed more, needed him to carry on petting.

Suddenly he stopped. She gasped with anguish, momentarily bereft. Then, as he reached down, cupping her pubic mound in his fingers, she eased out her breath on a grateful sigh.

He'd poured more soap into his hand and gently worked the soap between her legs, massaging her sex till she could feel herself swell. Gradually he eased the froth up between her buttocks. Her crease became slippery with rich, lathered soap and, using the wedge of his hand, Luc rubbed gently up and down her groove sending hot little thrills shooting through her bottom.

'You feel so good,' he murmured against her ear.

'Mmm,' was all Kelly managed to respond. She hung her arms around his neck, supporting herself as his hand rubbed and probed, thrilling her, inciting her.

Minutes later, Luc stretched up for the shower attachment above them. Kelly watched him mistily, dazed with arousal.

'Move your legs apart, *chérie*.'

Still clinging to his neck, Kelly moved a step apart, her pulse accelerating madly.

'Wider,' Luc murmured.

Thrilled with expectancy, she stepped even wider, positioning her feet at the very edges of the tiled shower floor, where the walls met with the floor.

'Yeah,' he said hoarsely, bringing down the shower-head and moving it in between her wide-apart legs.

Deftly, he switched it face up. Kelly convulsed delightedly as the hard, streaming jets shot up against her sex.

'Oh, yes!' she gulped, as a hundred watery rods massaged her. Luc directed the showerhead rhythmically back and forth, one moment she could feel the pressure on her clitoris, the next the water seemed to gush up deep inside her body.

An electrifying tightness gathered in her mons. Standing right up on tiptoe, she rocked her hips back and forth, moaning in clouds of ecstasy as the jets jabbed at her soft swollen skin.

She came very forcibly, jerking her hips towards Luc, bending her knees so suddenly that her sex dropped right down on to the showerhead. Swiftly, Luc wrenched the showerhead away and pulled her close, holding her orgasmic, rag-doll body tightly against him.

Kelly rested her head on his water-slick chest. As her breath began to even out, he tilted her chin up with his forefinger. 'You are beautiful,' he murmured.

Kelly gazed up at him. 'So are you. How in the world am I going to stand being away from you?'

Luc smiled. 'It will not be for long, *chérie*.'

Any time is too long, she thought.

Three large packing crates were lined up neatly against the wall. All the bits and pieces of furniture, all the knick-knacks acquired from four years' travelling, were safely ensconced in the boxes.

Kelly stood, hands on hips, in the centre of the room. She pushed out her bottom lip and blew a wisp of hair out of her eyes.

'There, all done,' she said, swivelling her eyes round the room. 'Looks really strange without all my stuff. Kind of sad.'

Luc moved behind her, looping his arms through hers

and resting his hands on her navel. 'Why you don't leave it here? For when you come back.'

Kelly shook her head. 'Nah, the lease is up anyway.'

'At my apartment, then?'

'Your apartment's too small for all that lot.' She gestured over to the crates. 'You'd curse me!'

'So, we will get a bigger one.'

'No, I'll have my father's house soon. Might as well ship it all there for the moment.'

Luc shrugged OK. He started to move his hands over her stomach in slow, sensual semicircles.

Kelly sighed and leant back into him. 'Tomorrow's Saturday,' she said. 'I fly back on Tuesday morning. That means we only have three more days together.'

'We make the most of it then.' Luc's voice was tender. He twirled his fingers round a long, tawny strand of her hair. For several moments neither of them spoke.

Kelly broke the silence. 'Luc?'

'Oui, chérie?'

'I –,'

'What?'

'Um, I have . . . um, I have an idea.'

Luc's fingers were busy at her front. 'Me too,' he said softly, steadily undoing the buttons of her jeans.

Kelly chuckled. 'No, not that.'

'What?' He was easing her jeans down her legs.

His fingers played over her thighs, settling on the tendons at the edges of her groin. He pushed his middle fingers confidently into the gusset of her panties.

'Luc,' groaned Kelly, totally losing her train of thought.

'Mmm?' He was pulling the lacy gusset to one side now, easing his finger along the soft, peachy lips of her sex.

Kelly could feel his penis dig into the base of her spine. 'It's nothing.' Her voice was slurred, she leant back heavily, pushing all her weight against him. He was hooking his thumbs into the edges of her panties now, dragging them slowly down her thighs. 'Nothing,' she repeated. 'Tell you later.'

Later turned out to be that evening.

Back at Luc's apartment, Kelly sat thoughtfully in the bedroom toying idly with the bangles round her wrist. She was going to do it, she decided. She had absolutely made up her mind. The last four days with Luc had been the most fantastic, overwhelming, fulfilling four days of her life and she couldn't bear the thought of leaving him, for however short a time.

She'd do it before they went out. They'd arranged to meet Angie at the Bar Mistrai, then they were all going on to meet up with some of Luc's artist friends. Yes, she'd get dressed first and ask him then.

Excited by her decision, she rummaged in her suitcase, flinging out tops, trousers, dresses, till she found what she wanted: a plain black Calvin Klein mini-dress and a pair of black strappy wedges.

She left her hair down, parted in the centre, and made up her face with painstaking care – base, powder, eyeliner, shadow, mascara, blusher. A bright-red lipstick completed the look. Then, feeling slinky and glamorous and trendy – and sexy enough to ask him – she went in search of Luc.

He was in the living room, lounging nonchalantly on the sofa, leafing through a copy of *Le Monde*. He looked effortlessly gorgeous. His soft brown hair waved gently to the collar of a casual, white cotton shirt, top button open at his smooth brown throat and shirtsleeves, as ever, rolled up to his elbows.

'Hi,' whispered Kelly.

Luc flicked his head towards her. His eyes opened wide and he whistled softly. '*Merde*!'

'You like me?' she smiled.

'*Oui*, yeah, you look –' he kissed his fingers to his lips, '– *fantastique!*'

She winked one perfectly painted eye. 'Just a little something I threw on,' she joked, nudging beside him on the couch.

He rested his hand on her knee and she traced her nail over his knuckles, scratching absently at a stubborn, dry spot of paint. 'Er Luc, you know before, back at my apartment. I said I had an idea.'

'*Oui.*' He looked at her curiously.

'Well –'

Across the room, the phone rang suddenly. After five rings, Luc's answer machine clicked on. The person rang off without leaving a message.

'Go on, Kelly,' Luc prompted.

'It's ... I –'

The phone rang again. Kelly eyed it nervously. 'Someone's desperate to speak with you.' She laughed. A little flustered laugh.

Luc shrugged, unconcerned. 'The machine will pick it up.'

Third ring. Fourth ring. Kelly stared at it. 'Answer it, Luc. They'll only keep on calling.'

He rolled off the sofa and walked over to pick up the receiver. '*Allô*,' he said. 'Luc ...'

He spoke very rapidly in French. Far too quickly for Kelly to understand. She fidgeted with the edge of the newspaper, glancing up now and again at him, all the while rehearsing her planned speech in her head. The phone conversation, with whomever, seemed to be going on and on. Wandering over to the window, she nibbled absently on a fingernail, listening to the low, steady stream of Luc's voice in the background.

At long last, he put the phone down.

She turned around.

'That was Chantal,' he muttered.

Kelly mouthed a silent, distracted 'Oh,' and prepared herself to launch into her speech.

Meanwhile, Luc bent to the coffee table and pulled a cigarette from the pack. Kelly, somewhat preoccupied how best to broach her subject, didn't notice that he seemed rather tense.

Cupping his fingers round a match, he lit up and inhaled deeply. 'She is not happy,' he said, speaking and exhaling a gush of smoke simultaneously.

'Hey?' asked Kelly, knocked off course again. Would she ever get this darned speech out?

'Chantal. She is not happy I have not worked since Tuesday. She says I will not be ready to exhibit.'

Kelly wandered over to him and placed her head on his shoulder. 'You'll be ready, won't you?'

'*Non, chérie,*' he said softly. 'Not unless I work.' He took another long pull on his Marlboro, sucking in bronze cheeks. 'Kelly, tomorrow I must go to the studio.'

Kelly felt her stomach jolt. 'But –' she paused, swallowing a massive lump in her throat. 'You said you wouldn't work. We agreed to spend the whole time together. Till I have to leave. You said, Luc! You promised!'

Luc stroked her hair gently. 'I know, but you understand, Kelly. I have no choice.'

'No choice! Sure you have a choice.'

'*Non*, no, I do not. My work. It is important to me.'

'More important than me?'

'*Non, non.* Of course not, but –,' he gestured helplessly with his hands, his cigarette waving a curl of smoke in the air.

'But what?' challenged Kelly, suddenly feeling her speech slipping sadly away in her head.

'I have worked very hard to get to this point,' said Luc softly. 'I do not wish to throw it all away.'

She jerked herself harshly away from him. 'So that's

what "you and me" is? Throwing it all away? Funny, I thought there was more to it than that!'

Luc took a step toward her. 'No, I do not mean that. You mix up my words.'

She deliberately backed away and strode over to the window. Her insides were churning, her stomach curdling like soured cream. She had to hold on to the window ledge just to steady herself. 'How can you –' she paused as her voice cracked. She took a deep, calming breath before continuing. 'How can you even think of work when we only have three more days until I go back?'

'*Chérie*, I must think of work!'

'Why? Is your work more important than me, then?' Kelly glared at him, knowing she was sounding hopelessly melodramatic but daring him to answer anyway.

Luc bent down and tapped ash irritably into the ashtray with his thumb. 'You are being crazy. It is not more important than you. It is just … work is work. *Eh bien voilà! C'est simple!*'

They stared at each other in a shocked, angry silence. An argument! Their first!

Seconds ticked by. Long, tense, silent seconds. The distance between them suddenly seemed far greater than merely the width of the room.

Kelly's voice, when she eventually spoke, came out as a whisper. 'So, I take it you'll be off to work in the morning?'

Luc nodded slowly.

'I see,' she said quietly. She looked across at him. He looked straight back, holding her gaze, his dark, green eyes unblinking. A new, unlit cigarette dangled from the corner of his mouth and he stood very still, twirling a red plastic lighter in his fingers. The smooth handsome features were the same, she thought, the eyes, the nose were the same, the mouth that she had kissed so many times – they were all just exactly the same. But, looking across, she almost felt she was looking at a stranger. And yet he was so compelling that she couldn't drag her eyes away, so absurdly good-looking that, despite herself and her disillusionment, the familiar knot of her desire for him tightened in her groin.

'*Eh bien*,' he said, breaking the second silence. 'What is it you want to ask me?'

Her little speech and burning question had dwindled into sorry inconsequence. 'Nothing,' she whispered, striding past him into the bedroom.

She began to wander round the room, picking up the clothes she'd gaily tossed around earlier and furiously throwing them back into her suitcase. Gathering cosmetics from the shelf in the bathroom, where she'd laid them out just an hour before, she dumped them all carelessly into her make-up case.

'Kelly, what are you doing?'

She wheeled round. He was leaning in the doorway, his shoulder to the frame.

She turned back to her packing, ramming in T-shirts, underwear, jeans. Clothes that before, neatly folded, fitted snugly into the case, now spilled out wildly from the edges, victims of her frenzied repacking. She leant on top of the case, pushing down on the lid with all her rather sapped strength.

'I-I need to be away from you right now,' she said breathlessly. 'I'm going back to my apartment.'

Luc walked behind her, touching her lightly. 'This is stupid,' he said softly.

'I don't think so!' Clicking the locks on her suitcase shut, she heaved it off the bed. Then, with make-up case in one hand, suitcase in the other, she glanced quickly round the room and hobbled off, unsteady on her wedges, towards the front door.

'Kelly!' Luc moved to take the cases from her.

She brushed past him and out of the door.

'Kelly, I come to your apartment later. You will feel better then.'

'Don't bother!' she shouted, without looking back. Biting her lip to stop herself crying, she dragged her suitcase down the stairways, scarcely noticing it bang against her shins with each plunk, plunk, plunk down the stairs.

The Bar Mistrai was teeming with after-work drinkers and lively young things eager to start their Friday night revelry. Standing space at the bar was at a premium and a seat was by now a virtually unattainable luxury.

However, knowing the bar well, Angie had arrived early and had successfully jostled and elbowed her way to a single, spare table she'd spotted in the corner. Now on her second glass of white wine and dangerously nearing the end of that, she glanced yet again at her watch. Where was Kelly? She was sure she had said seven. Kelly was now over half an hour late and irritation was beginning to kick in. Probably got sidetracked with dreamboat Luc, tutted Angie, tipping back her head and draining the contents of her glass.

Just when she was mulling over whether to bother with a third and eyeing up a very scrumptious man leaning against the bar, she caught sight of Kelly making her way over. Far from having to fight her way through, the crowds seemed to step aside for Kelly, rather like a religious parting of the waves, lines of male heads craning appreciatively round and following her progress towards Angie.

About to burst forth in a tirade of 'where were yous', instead Angie bit her lip at the sight of her friend. Dressed to kill, hair and make-up exquisite, Kelly looked as eye catching and model-like as ever but, knowing her friend as well as she did, Angie immediately gleaned that all wasn't well.

'What's up, Kelly?' she asked gently.

Kelly sat down shakily. 'Oh Angie!' she gulped.

Angie clasped Kelly's fingers across the table. 'What is it honey? Tell me.'

Kelly raised up her big amber eyes. 'It's Luc!'

'What? Where's Luc? Is he hurt?'

'No.' Kelly shook her head. 'No, he's not hurt. We had a row. Oh, Angie. I think it's over!'

'Aw honey,' Angie said softly. 'Everybody rows. It's in the rules. Be a boring old world if we never rowed.'

'No.' Kelly blinked back the huge tears that were welling in the corners of her eyes. 'Wasn't even a proper row. It was worse. Much worse.'

She picked up a napkin from the centre of the table and dabbed at the threatening tears. Then she told Angie all about what had happened: Chantal's phone call out of the blue and Luc insisting he had to work, despite the promise he had made her.

Angie almost laughed out loud with relief. Was that all? Kelly wasn't usually given to being dramatic but in this case Angie sensed she'd over-reacted. 'Kelly, honey, that hardly means it's over. It means you had a row, that's all.'

Kelly's eyes went liquid again, this time a tear escaped and ran a river down her beautifully made-up cheek. 'Don't you see, Angie?'

'See what?'

'See, if he puts his work before me now, when I'm off to the States on Tuesday, when he might not see me again for God knows how long, it just proves he doesn't feel the same way I do. I would have put him before anything if he'd asked me!' She threw the napkin down on the table, a sob bubbling up to the surface. 'And everything was so fantastic, I really thought he was the one, Angie. I really did.'

Streaks of running mascara joined in the desecration of Kelly's make-up. Angie's heart went out to her friend. She'd never seen her so distressed.

'And another thing,' went on Kelly, stifling another sob. 'I was actually going to ask him to come with me to the States. Can you believe it? Had a little speech prepared and everything!'

Angie bumped her chair round the table and threw her arm round Kelly's shoulders. 'Look honey,' she began, desperate to console her. 'He's a painter. You know what painters are like. Hell, you've studied art long enough! Their work is their life and all that baloney. Most likely, he thought you were the one being unreasonable.'

Angie looked on in horror as her words brought on a full-scale cry. That wasn't at all the reaction she'd intended. People from the bar began to glance curiously across at the weeping beauty.

'Tell you what –' Angie picked up the discarded napkin from the middle of the table and dabbed gently at Kelly's tears. 'He said he'd come by your apartment later, did he? Well, we'll go there now and wait and when he comes by, I'll disappear. You can both sort it out then.'

'D'you think so, Angie?'

'Course I do, honey.'

'But,' whispered Kelly. 'I told him not to bother . . .'

'Don't worry,' assured Angie, sending a quick prayer skywards on her friend's behalf. 'He'll come!'

Five hours and two bottles of red wine later, there was still no sign of Luc. Angie and Kelly sat in Kelly's empty, echoing apartment, curled up at each end of the sofa like a pair of sombre bookends.

Kelly was dry eyed and calmer now. She glanced at

her watch and turned towards Angie. 'It's past one, Angie. He's not going to come.'

Angie didn't know what to say. She couldn't believe he hadn't turned up.

Kelly unfurled her long, brown legs off the sofa and stood up. 'Well,' she said, her voice small. 'Better I found out sooner that later, I guess.'

'Found out what, hon?'

'That he doesn't love me! Not like I love him.'

Angie looked up at her friend. Kelly had washed off her make-up and tears and, despite the fact that it was the middle of the night and that Kelly had polished off most of the wine all by herself, her face still looked fresh and remarkably serene. Angie knew it was a front. Kelly had fallen really badly for Luc and, by all accounts, he'd fallen just as badly for her. 'Maybe he thought it might be better to come by tomorrow,' ventured Angie. 'You know, let things cool a while. After all, you did say not to call tonight.'

Kelly squared her shoulders. 'No, if he loved me – really loved me – he would have come tonight. I remember my mom always said true lovers don't go to bed on an argument. Well, we had an argument, we didn't sort it, and now I'm going to bed. I guess that means we weren't true lovers after all.'

Angie shook her head. 'If ever two people were in love, it was you and Luc.'

Kelly tossed back her hair and tried to look hard, but a tear trickling down the side of her nose gave her away. 'I thought so too,' she whispered. 'Seems I was wrong.'

10

Johnny Casigelli's Californian home wasn't far from Santa Barbara, tucked away from the beach in a crescent of lush, semitropical land with the rich jade slopes of the Santa Ynez Mountains rising idyllically to the north.

Larry drove up the sweeping driveway and pulled up in what looked to be an English-type courtyard in front of the house. Marissa's eyes widened appreciatively when she saw the house. Oh, brother! she thought, taking in the turrets and the ivy-mantled brickwork. It looked just like a mini-castle.

Larry caught her eye and grinned. 'Quite something, huh babe.'

Marissa flashed a smile back. 'Not bad.'

'And this,' smirked Larry, leaning over and placing his hand on her thigh, 'is only his weekend place.' He trailed his fingers slowly up the inside of her thigh. 'Mmm ... can't wait to get you inside.' His fingers moved up under her skirt.

For once, Marissa slapped his hand away. She chuckled softly. 'Stop that, Larry,' she whispered, as a very proper-looking manservant appeared in the large, arched doorway.

Larry tutted and winked. 'Later then, hon.' He leapt out of the car and with a little mock-bow, he opened her door for her. 'Come, madam. The butler awaits.'

Marissa giggled, taking his hand, and they crunched up the gravelled courtyard towards the waiting manservant.

'Good afternoon. Sir, madam,' said the manservant,

dipping his head a fraction to each of them. 'Are your bags in the car? I'll have them sent up.'

'Good man,' said Larry, putting on a very hammy English accent. 'Here you go.' He tossed the manservant the keys to his Ferrari. 'Lock the car when you've finished, would you, old chap!'

Not altering his deadpan visage, the manservant caught the keys niftily in one hand and then pivoted round on his heel. 'Follow me please, sir, madam. I'll show you to your room.'

Larry nudged Marissa as they followed the butler across the huge, Persian-carpeted vestibule. 'Johnny has quite a sense of humour, babe,' he said in a stage-whisper. 'Likes his staff to complement his homes. This is his "English-stately-home-cum-castle" home.'

'Yeah right,' giggled Marissa. 'In Santa Barbara.'

Chortling in tandem, they started to mount the sweeping staircase.

'Larry, Marissa.'

They turned simultaneously, giggles dying out at once.

Johnny Casigelli had appeared in a double-fronted doorway to the left of the hallway. He was wearing a white, billowing shirt, tight black matador-style trousers and knee-length black leather boots. Marissa did a double-take, wondering for a split second whether he was in fancy dress. Then she noticed a fencing mask pulled down over his chest and a long rapier sword propped up in the doorway.

Johnny strode towards them. 'Forgive the outfit. I was fencing. I like to fence when I'm here,' he laughed with a flash of very white teeth. 'Kind of goes with the territory.' He looked directly at Marissa and shrugged a self-deprecating shrug. 'Boys will be boys and play with their toys,' he said.

Marissa smiled, eyeing discreetly the very long gleaming blade of steel propped in the doorway. It looked far from toy-like to her.

'But welcome,' Johnny continued, opening his arms wide, the generous shirtsleeves billowing out so that he looked for all the world like an olden-day Hollywood swashbuckler. 'Welcome to my humble abode.'

All this was uttered in the same soft, compelling, authoritative voice that Marissa remembered from the restaurant. She regarded his handsome profile silently as he and Larry shared a joke. Marissa had always thought that she was a force to be reckoned with. Somehow in life, by fair means or foul – usually foul – she got what she wanted. But in Johnny Casigelli she sensed something more that a kindred spirit. Dashing and charming he may be, handsome without a doubt, but one thing Marissa was suddenly very sure of: Johnny Casigelli was dangerous. Very dangerous indeed.

'Wow, baby!' Larry whistled softly as Marissa smoothed down the gold sheath dress she'd brought along to wear for Johnny's party.

She did a little twirl. 'Like it, honey?'

Larry was perched on the edge of the antique, carved four-poster and she paraded slowly in front of him then wandered over to the mirror to check her appearance. The lustrous silk moulded to the contours of her body like a film of oiled water, falling in a perfect haute-couture finish to just above her ankles. Fine spaghetti straps left her slender gleaming shoulders all but naked and she'd piled her hair into shining blonde coils on top of her head, tendrils left trailing round her face and neck.

'The words "beautiful" and "mermaid" spring to mind.' Larry stood behind and dropped a kiss on her shoulder.

She slid her eyes round to him. 'Not too bad yourself, lawyer-man,' she murmured, dipping her finger into the waistband of his trousers and pulling him towards her. In fact, Marissa mused, Larry looked a whole lot better than not bad. He looked out and out gorgeous. The black dinner-suit was extremely debonair. His thick dark hair had one tiny streak of silver at the temple and his bright silver-grey eyes glittered with what must have been a mixture of excitement and anticipation. He looked more like a raffish James Bond than a bigshot corporate lawyer.

Larry thrived on success, Marissa knew that. This whole thing, coming to Johnny's party, making the final adjustments to their scheme with Kelly and the will – it was all just one more deal to Larry, another chance to win at something. And he needed to win the same way she needed to win. After all, that was why they were so good together. She just wished they could have done it on their own – without the help of Johnny Casigelli.

Still, she reasoned, so long as they sorted it, so long as they fixed things so that she got the house and most of the money, and Larry got control of the firm, what did it matter that Johnny was involved?

Besides, she really was in the mood for a party.

Crooking out his arm, Larry linked her arm through his. 'Ready to go down, Mrs Aslett?' he said jauntily.

'Yes, I think so, Mr Barris. I'm ready.'

Marissa helped herself to another glass flute of champagne from a passing waiter and sipped it quickly. Mmm, Moët & Chandon. But she really ought to slow it down. She was already feeling a little giddy.

Wandering over to the long buffet table, she checked her reflection in the side of an ice cooler before scanning the delicious array of foodstuffs – imported caviars, pâtés, mousses, terrines, gargantuan salmons marinated in honey, lobster, duck, venison. The choice was gloriously endless.

Shame she was wasn't very hungry, she thought, dismissing anything substantial and picking up a canapé. Then, wondering how much longer Larry was going to be in conference with Johnny Casigelli, she walked out on to the terrace.

It really was very beautiful, with the huge lawns and sculpted hedges veiled in deep silver moonlight. Just like an English stately home, Marissa mused. Johnny had even had a maze put in, over by the ornamental pool. Only the heat, the mountain view, and the night-time sounds of the cicadas, gave away the fact that it was Californian heartland.

Surprisingly, the terrace was empty. Not that Marissa minded. Johnny's party seemed primarily a 'business' affair and the party guests ranged from middle-aged, paunchy Italian types smoking fat cigars to middle-aged, silver-haired congressmen types talking politics. Neither type appealed and, despite the number of other beautiful women present, she'd had to do more than her share of fending off uninvited attentions whilst Larry wasn't at her side. It was a welcome respite to be alone on the terrace, sipping her wine, thinking her silent thoughts. Most of which revolved around Larry and the four-poster upstairs.

'Are you with Larry?'

Marissa turned at the sound of a soft, feline voice. 'Pardon?'

'I asked if you were with Larry?'

Without responding, Marissa looked the questioner slowly up and down. She appeared mid-twenties, tall and slender like herself, with long, dark hair and bewitching violet eyes. An emerald-green dress shimmered in the moonlight and clung to her body like scales to a fish.

'I'm here with Larry, yes,' Marissa nodded curtly.

'Good!' The questioner's voice was like a purr. She seemed to wrap her tongue round the word as though licking cream from the top of a gateau.

Marissa was intrigued. She held her glass to her lips and eyed her inquisitor over the rim. 'Why is that good, may I ask?'

'I know Larry quite well. Very well, in fact.' The bewitching eyes flickered just a little.

'Really?' Marissa was even more intrigued.

'Mmm,' purred the young woman. 'Though it's a while ago now since we – since I saw him.'

'I see.' Marissa sipped her drink slowly, waiting.

The young woman blinked her violet eyes languidly. 'I saw you walk in together. You and Larry. He's looking good.'

'Yeah. He is.' Marissa wasn't sure where this slinky, sinuous girl was heading.

'So are you,' she murmured, dropping her gaze down Marissa's body. 'Looking good, I mean.'

Marissa let the champagne bubbles fizz on her tongue. She looked at the girl evenly, taking in the smooth skin, the amazing eyes, the perfect high-arched brows. Larry had good taste, she'd give him that.

The girl reached across and trailed a short French-polished nail lightly down Marissa's arm. 'Where is Larry?' she asked softly. The nail rested on Marissa's elbow.

'Over here!'

They both glanced sideways.

Larry was framed in the light of the open French doors. He held his champagne glass nonchalantly by the stem, a hint of a smile playing across his lips. Slowly, he walked across.

'Hello, Verity.' His voice was low and steady.

The young woman turned those limpid eyes towards

Larry. 'Hello, Larry,' she said huskily. Her nail brushed Marissa's elbow in small, ticklish circles. 'Been a long time.'

Larry nodded, the smile still hovering on his lips. He shot his eyes to her nail, now softly scratching Marissa's forearm. 'Didn't know you knew Johnny,' he said.

Verity kept her eyes on Larry's. 'Yes,' she chuckled softly. 'I know Johnny.'

Marissa didn't speak, calmly absorbing the interplay. She didn't respond to Verity's caresses. But she didn't pull away either.

Larry moved his glass to his lips and jerked back the contents with one hefty swig. 'Marissa,' he began. 'Meet Verity. We knew each other way back.'

'She told me already.' Marissa spoke softy. Verity's fingers were sending shivers rather pleasantly up her arm.

Verity was still gazing up at Larry, whilst her nails played upon Marissa's wrist. 'Marissa,' she repeated, swirling the name round and round her tongue. 'Marissa, Marissa. Beautiful name for a beautiful girl.'

'Mmm.' Larry cast his gaze over to Marissa for a moment, moved it down to the fingers on her arm, then moved it lazily up the length of Verity's dress.

Verity watched him smoothly like an exquisite cat. She cupped his chin gently with her free hand. 'Beautiful Marissa, beautiful you, beautiful me!'

Larry grinned widely. His cute, boyish grin. He glanced aside to Marissa. 'Honey, would you like Verity to join us for a nightcap?'

Marissa took in the girl once again. Curving smile, gleaming hair. The fingers felt good on her arm. 'Yes,' she said throatily, without hesitation.

'Me too,' murmured Larry. 'There's a vintage on ice in the room,' he said softly, lifting Marissa's glass from her hand and placing it along with his own on the top of the stone terrace wall.

Then, pressing his hands into the small of both women's backs, he guided them in front of him, through the French doors, through the milling party-goers, up the sweeping staircases towards the second landing.

Marissa's and Larry's room was large, beautifully carpeted in white with rich oak-panelling to the walls and huge, north-facing sash windows, now obscured by the drawn velvet curtains.

Larry popped the champagne cork expertly and generously filled three glasses. He wandered over to the two white sofas, placing the glasses on the carved oak coffee table in between.

'Champagne, ladies,' he said softly, sitting down on one of the sofas and leaning back gratefully into the down-filled cushions. He had been feeling exhausted. The finer points of the plan had taken Johnny and him much longer to work through than anticipated and he hadn't really got the chance to join the party, which had annoyed him a little. There were a number of useful contacts he could have made there. A touch of networking would not have gone amiss.

Now, however, he was feeling euphoric. Not only did he think there was a real chance they could pull this thing with Kelly off, but he had the two most delectable females sitting opposite, both of whom he was extremely fond, one of whom was like a drug to him. Actually not true, he mused, they were like drugs to each other, he and Marissa. Each completely addicted to the wayward other.

As for Verity, he thought, glancing down at the long expanse of sleek brown leg showing through the side-split in her dress, Verity was something else too. She knew what she wanted and she went for it. Like Marissa. Like himself.

Loosening his tie, he pulled it off over his head then undid the top two buttons of his shirt, running his forefinger round the inside of his collar. 'Champagne,' he repeated as the glasses remained untouched on the table.

Casually, Marissa reached forward. She barely wetted her lips with the wine. Over the top of her glass, she fixed her eyes firmly on Larry.

'Don't mind if I do,' purred Verity, leaning forward too and reaching for the champagne. Instead of sipping it however, she dipped her finger in the sparkling liquid and drew it lightly across Marissa's all but naked shoulder, then lowered her head and, with the tip of a very pink tongue, licked gently along the moistened trail.

Larry smiled. Marissa shivered almost imperceptibly. Her eyes were ice cool but he knew that inside she would be burning with excitement. Time for him to take charge. He took another small sip of champagne. 'Take off Marissa's dress,' he commanded.

Verity's glossed lips curved upwards. 'Honey, I intend to,' she murmured.

Her fingers toyed idly with the tongue of Marissa's zip. Marissa eased forward slightly. Down came the zip, slowly, sensuously. Like peeling paintwork, the dress was pared from her body, dropping to her handspan waist. Marissa rose, easing it over her hips, letting hundreds of dollars worth of designer creation crumple ignominiously to the floor. Silently, she sat back down.

Larry played his eyes lazily up and down Marissa's body. He noticed Verity do the same. Marissa's glorious breasts were uplifted by an ivory, strapless, balconette bra. A waist-high matching G-string clung like sprayed-on silk to her stomach and her long, golden legs were demurely together, feet so close that the ankle straps of her golden shoes seemed joined like a pair of footcuffs.

'Now her brassière,' he ordered.

Marissa's eyes flashed excitedly. Verity's fingers found the clasp. Marissa's breasts were bared in an instant.

'Mmm, how nice.' Verity's voice purred like a whirl-pool. She reached forward again, dipped her finger in her champagne again, trailed the dripping finger over Marissa's shoulder again. As she curled her tongue over the droplets, her hand moved sinuously on Marissa's stomach, rising slowly, steadily up towards her breasts.

Suddenly, her hand closed round Marissa's full left breast. Marissa sighed softly, lowering her eyes to watch as Verity cupped and squeezed at her smooth flesh.

'Wonderful,' breathed Marissa.

On the opposite sofa, Larry gazed raptly. The pink tip of Verity's tongue was flicking softly at Marissa's shoulder. Verity's violet irises drooped leisurely over the shoulder she was licking, watching her own hand fondling Marissa's breasts.

Larry's voice was low and steady. 'Verity, now you.'

Quickly, Verity obeyed. Standing like Venus rising, she turned to face him, a smile on her face as she stepped from her shimmering dress.

She was bra-less. Her breasts were small and rounded, smooth and gleaming like two perfect, caramelised half-apples. Her lithe, olive-toned torso was slender, her legs endlessly sleek.

'Yeah, beautiful!' Larry muttered as she sank back on to the sofa, ever more feline as she settled next to Marissa, stretching her legs out in front of her. She reached for Marissa's breasts again, fondling and squeez-ing, purring deep down in her throat.

Marissa was sighing too now, resting her head back, half-closing her sapphire eyes. From beneath lowered lashes, her eyes roamed Verity's naked upper-body.

Gently, she tapped Verity's smooth brown nipples. They stiffened at once, as instantly erect as soldiers standing to attention.

Larry was silent as Marissa and Verity fondled each other, stroking and caressing firm flawless flesh, teasing and tweaking hard, pointed nipples. Pink tongues darted from lipsticked lips and frolicked playfully together. Small, breathy sighs hung like fine, summer mist in the air.

Larry's eyes were locked on the glorious display, on the curving lips and painted eyes and polished nails pinching at excited nipples. He shifted in his seat, adjusting his position as his cock strained uncomfortably against his shorts. As he did so, Marissa and Verity eased apart, gliding silently to him.

Marissa settled to his left, Verity to his right, both kneeling with legs curled beneath them.

'Need some help, baby?' whispered Marissa, blowing softly in his ear. Her fingers were undoing his shirt. Verity was busy at his waistband, opening up the buttons, pulling down his zip. His cock leapt up through the gap in his undershorts.

'Now, that I remember!' cooed Verity, closing her fingers round it.

Larry tilted back his head for a moment, letting Marissa stroke his chest as she eased off his shirt, letting Verity tug softly at his penis.

Marissa was kneeling upright next to him, softly running her tongue round the edge of his ear. He moved his hands to circle her waist, then, accompanied by an excited inhalation from Verity, he slowly pulled Marissa's G-string down.

Marissa lifted each knee one after the other so he could slip the stringy garment off. 'That's better, honey,' she breathed into his ear. 'Thank you!'

'Stand up, darling,' he urged, nudging her upright in

front of his knees. He took in each line and curve as she stood quietly before him. He'd never tire of her, he thought, eyeing the sweet curve of her navel and the fuzzy, trimmed triangle below. Reaching up to cup her breasts, he felt Verity ease off the couch and move behind Marissa. She trailed her thumb down Marissa's spine, letting her hand fall naturally to the rounded curves of Marissa's smooth buttocks.

Marissa stood between them, still as a statue, the epitome of excited acquiescence. Larry grazed the backs of his fingers over her hard, pink nipples, inclining his head round just a fraction, to watch Verity gently stroking Marissa's bottom. Softly, tentatively, Verity began to pat.

'Yeah, she likes to be spanked.' Larry's voice was as thick as Mississippi mud.

'Good.' Verity's voice was equally thick.

She began to pat a little harder. Marissa stifled a gleeful groan. So did Larry. Marissa's buttock cheeks were quivering deliciously and she was arching her back, pushing her breasts towards Larry, thrusting her bottom back to Verity.

As Verity spanked Marissa, the soft, slapping sounds ringing in the air, her own little breasts were jiggling beautifully. Quickly, Larry moved behind her, cupped her breasts briefly, then dragged off her black lacy briefs to cup and squeeze the satin cheeks of her rump.

His legs began to weaken with arousal. Urgently, he tore off the rest of his clothes. Marissa glanced round at him, her face glazed and gleaming with excitement, her blushed bottom still being delicately spanked. Larry nodded authoritatively towards the big four-poster.

He lay at the edge on his side, resting his head on his bent-up hand. Marissa lay on her back next to him.

Her elaborate, coiled-up hairstyle was coming loose and idly Larry removed the clips, looping each long, butter-blonde tendril round his finger, dragging them down so they spread across the antique lace pillowslip. Verity, lying next to Marissa, violet eyes shining with lust, was coiling her fingers in much shorter, butter-blonde curls.

Crawling down the mattress like a stalking lioness, she pushed Marissa's legs widely apart and swiftly knelt in between. The darting pink tongue slowly followed an invisible trail up the inside of Marissa's thigh, flicking softly at the stretched tendons at the edges of her groin.

Suddenly, like pouncing on its prey, the dark, shining head pushed in between Marissa's wide-apart legs, long straight tresses falling forward over Marissa's thighs. Verity stimulated hungrily. Marissa gasped happily. Larry looked on lazily, like the Lion King of the pride.

Marissa's stomach muscles were now pulled in sharply, her slender neck stretched as she tilted her head back into the pillow. Larry ran his forefinger up her throat, feeling the vibrations of her voice box as she sighed. He traced his fingerpad leisurely back and forth across her full lower lip, drinking in the scene below all the while.

All of a sudden, Verity raised her head. Placing her hands round Marissa's taut waist, she began to ease her round on to her stomach, subtly nudging her towards the top of the bed until Marissa was positioned on all fours. Verity, purring the ever-present purr, settled behind her. Putting her hands on each of Marissa's buttocks, she inched forward, lowered her head and began, once again, to tongue Marissa's sex.

The sight was like a punch to Larry's groin. Marissa – perfect golden body tensed with excitement, hair cascading in buttercup rivers down her back, buttocks high, pertly poised like two glossy hillocks. Verity – behind her, lithe sleek limbs coiled like a beautiful snake, shining dark hair swaying across her back as she moved her head to and fro.

Marissa started to moan. Arching her back, she swung her hips gently from side to side in the air, spurring Verity on. Verity's hands on her buttocks tightened, kneading the sweet firm flesh as she moved her head methodically to and fro. Marissa's moans became louder and louder, seemingly in time with the rhythmic movements of Verity's shining head.

Larry stretched round to Marissa's face and kissed her deeply, swallowing each of her loud moans of pleasure. They carried on kissing, Marissa increasingly frantic, probing his mouth, sucking on his tongue, feverishly gripped in a sexual stupor. Larry pulled away precisely as she climaxed, watching excitedly as she closed her eyes and threw back her head, locked her forearms and pushed her bottom back, pressing her sex on to Verity's eager mouth.

Moments later, Verity sank back on her heels, her face gleaming with Marissa's sugary fluids. Butterwort eyes, full of excitement, darted to Larry and she eased up the bed, sliding slickly between he and Marissa. Trailing her finger up his side as she moved, she rolled over on to her back, resting her head on the pillow. Larry closed his hand round one slender shoulder, then dipped his head to her chest and rubbed gently on a nipple with closed lips.

After several moments, he was vaguely aware of soft blonde hair spilling over Verity's stomach. Looking up, he saw Marissa, circling Verity's other nipple with the tip of her tongue. Without speaking he ducked back and they gently teased Verity's breasts in unison, Verity gasping softly with delight.

Retiring from that, Marissa traced her fingers in elaborate figure of eights over Verity's flat stomach, twining them lightly in the tiny dark triangle lower down. Larry lifted his head too, to gaze at Marissa's oval, crimson-painted nails brushing at Verity's soft fine hairs. As Marissa pushed her middle finger downwards, Verity immediately jerked her head up.

'Mmm, oh yes,' she murmured as Marissa swirled her finger round and round, up and down, from side to side.

Deliberately, Marissa moved Verity's legs wide open, skilfully stroking in between, teasing Verity's clitoral nub until it poked, hard and swollen, from the shiny, pink lips. She dragged her finger briefly back over Verity's stomach, leaving a slippery, silvery trail over the smooth, olive-hued skin.

As Marissa continued to stimulate her in leisurely fashion, Verity writhed in excitement. She began to ease herself slightly on to one side and lifted her right leg high in the air. Throwing her arm back across Larry's torso, she pulled him against her, glancing back at him in lusty appeal.

Larry, aroused almost beyond endurance, pushed reciprocally against her, exhaling with relief as her hand closed round his penis. She worked his tip lightly between her buttocks, coaxing it gradually towards the plump, rose flesh of her vulva. Larry couldn't stand it. With a groan, he moved down the bed, then slid himself up into her, hoiking her upraised leg into the crook of his arm.

Buried deep in moist, tight heat, Larry sighed joyfully and began to move slowly, luxuriously, inside Verity's body.

Marissa, eyes shining, lower lip sucked in, continued to swirl her fingers round the front of Verity's sex, gazing on raptly as Verity moved her body, her leg still high, bent up by Larry's arm.

Larry began to move more quickly, plunging harder, rubbing up against Verity's firm, bulbed buttock cheeks.

She sighed euphorically, jerking her lower body forwards towards Marissa's fingers, and then back against Larry's hips. As she reached a shuddering climax, she slammed back hard against him, drawing him up so deep inside her that his own orgasm instantly began. Boiling arrows of intensity shot from the backs of his knees, his heart knocked in his chest, his head reeled in a colour-filled spin.

Savouring the glorious aftermath, he lay beside Verity, panting into the back of her fragrant shoulder.

Opening one eye an exhausted moment later, he saw that Verity and Marissa had stretched out on their backs, gathering their breath. Both looked glorious, literally glowing with sexual energy. Almost in despair, he felt his stomach tighten, blood already coursing back towards his groin like a Red Army charge. With Samsonite strength, he reached over for Marissa. He hauled her over Verity's recovering body and drew her to him and, as he positioned her over his recharged crotch, he caught the glimpse of pure delight in her beautiful, sparkling, cornflower-blue eyes.

Late next morning, driving home, Larry glanced across at Marissa. Her newly washed hair was scrunched back in a haphazard bunch and her unmade-up face was lovelier than ever. She couldn't have had more than two hours sleep yet she looked as fresh and as sparkling as a summer dewdrop. He shook his head lightly.

'You look gorgeous, honey,' he chuckled. 'Don't know how you do it.'

Marissa flicked very clear eyes towards him and chuckled back. She shrugged. 'Good diet, great sex, lots of it! And –' she flashed a wicked little smile '– the thought of a big, nasty surprise in store for darling Kelly.'

'Hmm,' Larry grimaced. He was certainly up for the first two, but he didn't feel quite so euphoric about the 'surprise in store for Kelly' bit. He had nothing personal against Kelly. He was actually very fond of her. But – and it was a big but – he did want control of the firm and he wanted it now. And if this was the only way to make that happen, then, so be it. Business was business after all. No room for sentiment in business. No room for lawbreakers either, sang a nagging little voice at the back of his mind. Grimly, Larry pushed it away. No two ways about it. He wanted control of the firm!

11

It was Saturday afternoon and it was gloriously sunny. Again. Luc looked gloomily out of the window. Why did it have to be sunny? It should be raining. At least if it was raining, he could pretend it was the weather making him feel this down. He flicked the brush miserably on the canvas and played last night over in his mind. Again.

Kelly's reaction had stunned him. How could she act like that? So spoilt and selfish, treating his work as though it were a rival? Didn't she realise he had to work on his exhibits, that he had to be ready to show? He could easily have worked in the day and spent the nights with her. But no – she hadn't given him a chance to try and explain. His English always seemed to suffer when he was under pressure and he'd been groping around for the right words. Meanwhile, she'd waltzed off like some sort of prima donna, telling him she needed to be on her own, telling him not to bother calling round. It made his blood boil. It made him furious. He scraped his brush roughly over the canvas.

He'd been right not to go round last night. He wasn't going to act like some lovesick puppy. No way. He attacked the canvas savagely. Who was she anyhow? Just some rich American student, playing at studying art. She was stroppy. And demanding. And beautiful, he thought with a groan. And gorgeous and funny and amazingly sexy and . . .

'Luc, you're going to ruin that canvas if you're not careful!'

'Huh?' Luc looked up blankly, brush poised in mid-air.

'The canvas. You've been bashing it as though it were a punch bag.'

Chantal unwound herself from a high chrome stool and walked over to him, pin-prick heels clicking loudly on the wooden floor of the studio.

'Told you,' she tutted, looking at the picture.

Luc looked too. A garish unfathomable mess glared back. Jesus, had he painted that? It was like a two-year-old's finger painting.

'Shit!' he muttered, wrenching the canvas from his easel and tossing it angrily into a corner. 'Sorry, Chantal. Having a bad day, I suppose.'

Chantal stared stonily at him. 'Bad day, hey?' She raised a sceptical eyebrow.

'Yep.' Luc shrugged carelessly and lit a cigarette.

Chantal tapped a fingernail impatiently on the wooden workbench. 'It's worse than a bad day if you ask me. You've wasted all morning on that.' Her lip curled derisively as she gestured to the discarded canvas. 'You might as well not have come to work at all ... like the rest of the week.'

Luc squinted at her moodily through his cigarette smoke. 'I'll be ready to exhibit, Chantal. Don't worry.'

'Oh, but I do worry, Luc. I worry very much. I worry that you're going to try and pass off rubbish like that as priceless art.'

Luc's eyes flashed angrily. 'Rubbish, huh!'

'Yes. But even that's better than just abandoning your work altogether, like this week. Where were you anyway? You still haven't told me.'

Luc dragged slowly on his cigarette. He looked at her coolly, not bothering to respond.

'Well?' barked Chantal, sounding rather like an irate schoolmistress.

'Busy. I was busy, OK.' He looked off distantly through the massive windows.

Chantal regarded him thoughtfully. She hadn't seen Luc like this before. Unconcerned about his work. Slapdash even. Something was definitely wrong. She watched him closely. His eyes had moved down from the window and settled on something against the wall. Quickly, she followed his gaze.

'Ah,' she breathed, completely enlightened.

There, leaning against the wall, was Luc's painting of Kelly.

Chantal blinked from the painting back to Luc's rapt gaze, then back to the painting again. It was glorious, only half finished, it was true, but a triumph. It had the undeniable makings of a masterpiece.

Chantal's voice was much softer this time. 'Is it her, Luc? Is that why you didn't work?'

Luc looked at her miserably and nodded.

'But why so gloomy then, baby?' She cupped his cheek affectionately. 'You did want her, after all?'

Luc sucked hard on his cigarette. 'We argued,' he muttered, exhaling smoke at the same time.

'So? Arguments never bothered you before.'

'This one did.'

'But why, what was it about?'

Luc looked at her cryptically, then turned away to stub out his cigarette end.

Chantal twigged like a shot. 'Oh, I see. About working today?'

'Uh-huh. She's leaving for America on Tuesday. We were going to spend the time together before she left.'

'What!' Chantal attempted to bite back her amazement. She didn't quite manage it. 'You. Give up all your time. For a girl. Never!'

Shrugging slightly, Luc glanced away. Was there a hint of embarrassment there? mused Chantal, narrowing her kohl-rimmed eyes in contemplation, mind ticking speedily over.

Suddenly she laughed out loud, embracing Luc in a swift, tight hug. 'My God, Luc. Oh, you poor darling. Oh well, it had to happen one day.'

'Huh. What?'

'What? Darling, you're in love, that's what. Well and truly, I'd say. No wonder you can't work.'

Luc scowled. 'I can work. Kelly's just a spoilt little rich girl who doesn't understand.' He pulled another cigarette from the pack so ferociously that it broke into two, shreds of tobacco sprinkling over his fingers.

Cursing loudly, he threw the two pieces to the floor.

Oh dear, winced Chantal, it's worse than I thought. 'Do you want to tell me about it?' she asked softly.

'Not really.' Luc fumbled for another cigarette, found the packet empty and squashed it furiously in his fist. He cast round frantically for a new one, jaw tensed, dark eyes lowered. Even when he's angry and messed up, he's magnificent, thought Chantal, wondering if this Kelly knew just what she had when she had Luc. 'Here,' she whispered, offering him a Gauloise from her handbag.

'Thanks,' Luc mumbled, managing a weary half smile. He touched her hand fondly. 'Actually,' he began apologetically, 'yes I do want to tell you.'

Chantal listened carefully as he spoke, absorbing it all like a wise old owl.

'I see,' she gasped when he'd finished. 'So, if I understand correctly, you think Kelly acted spoilt because she wanted to spend time with you? A few precious days before she went away.'

Luc's smooth forehead creased with confusion. 'Yes. No. Not exactly. I dunno!'

'Awful, selfish girl,' Chantal went on softly. 'Wanting to be with the man she loves. How dare she!'

Luc was stung by her sarcasm. Stung and surprised. He would never, never, have expected Chantal to side with Kelly. Especially where work and exhibitions and deadlines were involved.

He paced over to Kelly's painting and stared at it for a while before whispering, more to himself than to Chantal, 'Because she left – just like that. Walked out.'

Chantal heard his whisper. Hard-bitten business-woman on the outside, Chantal had a very well-hidden soft, gooey centre. Just a few select things penetrated her hard outer shell. Luc happened to be one of those things.

'Why didn't you just tell me this over the phone last night?' she asked gently. 'I could have postponed your exhibition. After all,' she paused with a wink, 'it's not every day Luc Duras falls in love.'

Luc gestured hopelessly in the air. 'I thought she would have understood.'

Chantal clicked across to him and, stretching up slightly, gave him a sisterly peck on the cheek. 'You know, Luc, you're too arrogant and too proud for your own damn good. Not everyone thinks that the world revolves around your work. And, when a girl's in love, she doesn't think about being rational, that's for sure. Go round there this minute and make up.'

'But, the exhibition –?'

Chantal waved her hand around airily. 'I'll postpone it, darling. Just like I would have if you'd –'

But he'd already gone. Pressing his lips to her cheek, he'd murmured a sexy 'thanks sweetheart' and disappeared from the studio in a flash.

'– told me all this in the first place,' finished Chantal softly.

Angie was enjoying a quiet snooze on her sun-drenched terrace. The remains of her lunch were scattered on the floor next to her, brie melting to its proper runny consistency, bread turning into granite, rosé wine bubbling in the heat.

At first she thought she was dreaming.

Then gradually she realised the knocking at her door wasn't the result of her wine-soaked, sun-induced nap.

It was real.

With a weary sigh, she rolled off her sunbed, one bare foot landing plum in the centre of the runny cheese.

'Damn!' she cursed, trying to wipe off the warm, squelchy mess, stamping her foot on the ground like a mad bull preparing to charge.

The door knocker was very persistent.

'Coming,' she shouted, making her wobbly way over, leaving a trail of brie-enhanced footprints in her wake.

'Yes?' she said, opening the front door a crack. She rubbed her eyes blearily and took another look. Now she really was dreaming!

He was devastatingly attractive up close. She'd never seen him this close before. His whole face consisted of perfect lines and angles, wonderful smooth, dark skin peppered with day-old stubble, eyes that she couldn't look away from.

'It is Angie, no? I am Luc. I took a class at the Académie, you remember?'

Reluctantly, Angie dragged her eyes from his and fought for some composure. It wasn't really all that hard. She only had to think of him letting Kelly down the way that he had and she found her temper rising.

'I know who you are,' she snapped tightly, adding nothing more.

Luc nodded and scratched the side of his nose. 'Uh, I know you are Kelly's good friend. She speaks about you a lot. Kelly and me, we –'

'I know about you and Kelly!' Her voice lashed out like a whip.

Luc looked at her without comprehension. Her coldness had obviously registered.

'Where is Kelly?' he asked softly. 'I knocked and knocked at her apartment but there is no answer.'

Angie shook her head vehemently. Oh no, he wasn't going to get it out of her. He may be gorgeous but the nerve of the guy. Priceless.

Angie shook her head once again for good measure and made to shut the door. Luc was too quick. He'd lodged a black-booted foot in the doorway.

Angie looked up at him furiously. 'Move your foot please.'

'Angie, please. You must tell me where she is. We had an argument over something very stupid. I have to talk with her.'

His eyes were locked on hers in desperate appeal. Inexplicably, Angie found herself weakening. 'Why didn't you call by last night?' she blurted out, despite her former resolve. 'Kelly waited up half the night for you?'

Looking distinctly uncomfortable, Luc scratched his nose again but he kept his foot firmly planted in the doorway. 'She told me not to,' he replied weakly.

Angie snorted loudly. 'That's a pretty feeble excuse. Always do what you're told, do you?'

'No,' he answered quietly.

'Huh!' scoffed Angie, fiercely loyal to her friend. 'But you do break promises, don't you?'

'*Oui*. Yes, I know.'

'Hmm.' She narrowed her eyes, watching him closely, weighing him up. He was acting all wrong. He was acting ... well, contrite. Where was all the selfish arrogance? The nothing-must-come-between-me-and-my-work attitude?

Suddenly Luc's face brightened. 'But why she did not come back to me last night? If she waited half the night!'

Angie snorted again. Careful, she thought. With all this snorting, she was beginning to sound rather pig-like.

'Because,' she began slowly, 'she thinks you don't love her. You chose your work over her, after all.'

Luc scraped his hand roughly along his jawline. 'Please Angie. Tell me where she is.'

Looking hard into his emerald eyes, Angie found her resolve whipped away altogether, as though zapped by a magic wand. He looked so sad, so desperate. 'You'd better come in, Luc,' she said finally, easing open the door.

He stepped into her apartment. 'Thank you,' he muttered.

Angie moved to close the door. Out of the corner of her eye, she couldn't help but notice his physique. It was as perfect as his face – and his hair! It made you long to run your fingers through it. It was becoming increasingly impossible to retain the horned devil image of him she'd managed to concoct last night during all those long hours she'd sat waiting with Kelly. He was just so goddamn gorgeous.

Guiltily averting her eyes, she gestured over to the sofa, following closely behind him. As she sat, she noticed Luc was staring at her feet in bemusement.

'Why do you have melted cheese on your foot?' he asked.

Boy, was he direct, thought Angie. She liked that. Fact was, she liked everything. If he wasn't Kelly's boyfriend and therefore strictly out of bounds, she didn't think she'd be able to keep her hands off him.

'Can't a girl wear cheese on her foot if she wants?' she joked lightly, flinching even as she said it. Her attempt at humour was woefully mistimed and misplaced. The atmosphere was tense to say the least. And Luc was looking hopelessly disconsolate. But still he made a stab at a smile. Bless him, thought Angie, her heart suddenly going out to him, just as it had to Kelly last night. Why oh why, did lovers cause each other so much unhappiness?

'So, will you tell me where she is, Angie?' Luc looked up hopefully.

There wasn't any easy way to tell him. 'She's gone, Luc.'

'Gone? How gone?'

'Just gone. Back-to-America gone.'

He stared at her incredulously. '*Non!*' He shook his head as though befuddled. 'No, she goes on Tuesday, not today! Today is Saturday, *non*?'

'She thought you didn't want her, Luc,' Angie whispered. 'She didn't see any point in waiting. She convinced herself last night was a sort of test, you see. If you loved her, you'd turn up kind of thing.'

Luc was silent.

'You didn't turn up,' she explained softly, her voice barely audible. 'So, there was the proof – you didn't love her! I went with her to the airport this morning.'

'Gone!' Luc repeated.

Angie nodded mutely, feeling a lump rise in her throat. She knew she was a softie – it wasn't her mess after all, no reason for her to be on the verge of tears. But how awful. What an awful, awful mess. Luc was looking so stricken, he must be in love with her. And Kelly had gone off, thinking he couldn't give a hoot. Oh, what an awful, awful, awful mess.

Luc was fumbling in his back pocket. 'Do you mind?' he mumbled absently as he pulled out a crushed pack of cigarettes.

'Not at all, honey,' she answered. 'Fact, I'll join you.'

They smoked together in a long, gloomy silence. Then Angie had a bright idea. She glanced excitedly at her watch and began frantically working out the time difference between Paris and LA.

Hours later, a world away, on another continent, Kelly wilted in the back seat of a taxi. She was exhausted. Not just from the flight. She was emotionally exhausted too. No matter how she tried she couldn't get Luc out of her mind. She knew he didn't really love her, he'd made that clear enough, but that didn't stop her mind playing tricks. He was there in every thought, every blink, every sight, every movement.

Why had she bolted like that? Don't be so stupid, she told herself, she knew exactly why. Because she couldn't bear the thought that he was in the same city, within easy reach. Because she knew that if she'd stayed in Paris for one moment more, she'd have gone running back to him like some weak, little lapdog, eagerly clinging to any scrap of himself he was willing to throw at her, knowing full well it was his work that he truly loved. Not her.

Misty eyed, she stared out of the taxi window, seeing nothing. The concrete jungle of LA could have been the parched jungle of the Serengeti for all she saw. All she saw was Luc.

It had all happened so fast. One moment they were in love, so she thought. Next moment – whoosh! He'd acted as cool and distant as that very first moment in his studio. An arrogant pig. That's what he was.

'An arrogant, artistic pig!' she blurted out loud.

Through his rear-view mirror, the taxi driver eyed her warily.

And yet, she mused, the past week had been the best of her life. How could he have made love to her the way he did and not love her? She rested her head back on the cheap, black plastic seating, her mind drifting back to yesterday, before the argument, before her world crashed.

They'd packed up all her stuff, she remembered, and she'd been about to ask him to come back with her. Then he started to make love to her and she'd got hopelessly sidetracked.

He'd stripped her naked in the empty flat and taken her on the sitting room floor. It was a swift, gymnastic, spectacular screw! Luc had been all strong masculinity and heaving testosterone. Then afterwards, they'd fallen back into bed and Luc had made love to her for hours and hours and hours. She'd thought she was in heaven. Luc-filled, pleasure-filled heaven.

'I love him!' she cried out in an anguished wail.

The cab driver eyed her again. He shook his head slightly.

He pressed his foot on the accelerator, as if anxious to be rid of the crazy, beautiful, nervy girl and at home with his plain, placid, wonderful wife.

The cab driver deposited her bags at the door, thanked her for the generous tip and disappeared at sonic speed.

Kelly, putting her key in the lock, was surprised when it actually turned. She'd half expected Marissa to have had the locks changed.

The hallway was empty. The house was quiet. Welcome home, she told herself sadly before remembering she wasn't actually supposed to be arriving until Tuesday night.

She wandered through the silent house and out on to the terrace, stopping dead in her tracks when she saw the two lovers, locked in a passionate, body-moulding kiss.

'Hi,' she said loudly.

Two sets of eyes opened lazily and turned towards her. Immediately, the lovers sprang apart.

'Kelly!' exclaimed Larry. He stood rigidly for a moment then, seeming to collect himself, strode towards her and kissed her lightly on the cheek. 'Honey, what you doing here? We didn't expect you till Tuesday!'

Obviously, thought Kelly. 'I came early,' was all she said.

Larry smiled. Same cute grin, Kelly noticed. Same crinkly, grey eyes. Same athletic build. At one time, she'd had quite a crush on Larry. Long, long time ago.

'Well, hey,' said Larry, swinging out his hands. 'Welcome home, honey.' He kissed her cheek again.

'Thanks,' Kelly answered.

Larry turned towards Marissa who was hovering by the terrace wall. A glassy smile seemed to be pasted on her face. 'Marissa, aren't you going to welcome Kelly home?' Larry's voice was tight. It almost appeared to be an order.

Unhurriedly, Marissa sauntered over. 'Welcome home, Kelly,' she said.

You could skate on that voice, it's so icy, thought Kelly. 'Thanks,' she replied quietly. She looked at her stepmother. Damn, she looks pretty, she thought. Why didn't she look like some gnarled old hag like fairy-tale stepmothers?

Marissa looked back at her stepdaughter. Damn, she looks beautiful, she thought. Why wasn't she fat and frumpy and full of pimples?

Kelly glanced back at Larry. 'Didn't know you two were together,' she said lightly.

Larry coughed and then cleared his throat. 'Uh, yeah. We've grown kind of close. You OK with that?'

'Fine,' she replied, with a listless smile. What did it matter to her? What did anything matter to her ... without Luc? 'D'you mind if I go straight to bed?' she added. 'Been a long flight and a long day.'

'Sure,' said Larry. 'No problem.'

'Your room's just the way you left it,' purred Marissa.

'I'll bet, thought Kelly. Ten to one, Marissa had sold all her valuables.

12

Whilst Kelly slept, Larry and Marissa stayed on the terrace, talking softly together through the late afternoon and into early evening. Marissa watched absently as shadows grew across the wide, lush lawns, drawing the pool and poolhouse into muted shade. Elsewhere, outside the shadows, the sun still dazzled, touching every leaf and flower, every slope and valley.

'Why do you think she's come back early?' Marissa asked Larry for the fourth time.

Larry pressed his thumb and forefinger to his eyes. 'I tell you I don't know, honey. Doesn't matter though.'

'But everything was arranged around her arriving on Tuesday.'

Larry flashed her a wide, white grin. 'So we improvise, baby. We improvise.'

Marissa's stomach flipped over. Larry was so cool, so in control. She adored it, really adored it. Desire rifled through her, darting from her groin to her thighs to her stomach back to her groin, like a barrage of ricocheting bullets. She wanted him badly. 'Come here baby,' she said urgently, pressing her knees to his underneath the table.

'Uh-uh.' Larry shook his head. 'Not now, especially not here. We've got to play this right. Kelly said she was OK about you and me, but you never know. If we're too open, she might just decide to up and stay in a hotel.' He kissed the tip of Marissa's button nose. 'And we don't want that, do we babe?'

'Suppose you're right,' she begrudged, wanting him all the more.

Larry's cool, grey eyes rested on her lips. 'What I want to do to you though, babe!' he muttered huskily.

'Do it,' whispered Marissa.

Larry's eyes darted to the silent house. 'Yeah, maybe.' He bumped back his chair quietly.

Marissa knew it was foolish but she wanted him there, not in the privacy of her bedroom. There, on the terrace, with the waning sun on their writhing, naked bodies.

Suddenly, inside the house, the telephone rang again.

Damn! cursed Marissa. She rolled her eyes impatiently as Larry jerked his towards the sound.

'Quick, hon. Answer it. Before Kelly hears it, or Rosita come to that.' He nudged her in the direction of the phone.

Marissa scraped back her chair irritably and ran into the house. She snatched up the receiver, spoke tersely for several seconds then clanked the phone down rudely.

'That Angie girl again, for Kelly,' she muttered, rejoining Larry on the terrace. 'That's the third time she's phoned already. Jeez, it must be the early hours in Paris. Don't they ever sleep over there?'

'She say what she wanted?' asked Larry, an edge of concern to his voice.

'Some garbled message about someone called Luc. I told her Kelly's going to be jet-lagged tomorrow and to call back in a couple of days.'

'Good girl.' Larry nodded pensively.

Marissa nibbled doubtfully at a fingertip. 'I don't think she listened though, Larry. I told her the same thing twice before when she phoned.'

Larry furrowed his brow slightly. 'Hmm! Could complicate things if Kelly gets to speak to her. She might be wanting to invite her out here.'

Marissa tugged gently at Larry's sleeve. 'What do we do, baby?'

'I think,' he said, absently patting her hand, 'I think, we move things forward a tad. Like to Monday.'

Marissa's eyes glittered with excitement. 'Monday? You sure?'

'Yeah. And I'll need to change tack slightly. We better go to the office now, phone Johnny from there, and collect the papers.'

'Right,' murmured Marissa, clenching together her thighs. She felt so hot she thought she could be feverish. About to waylay Larry for a quickie before they went, she saw that his mind had moved elsewhere. He was already heading on into the house, car keys jangling.

'Tell Rosita we're going for a drive,' he said, glancing back at her. 'Oh, and switch off all the phones. We don't want Kelly talking to anyone.'

Because it was a Saturday and 8.30 at night, the offices were empty. It was oddly restful being there without all the bustle of business going on around them, mused Marissa, sitting quietly whilst Larry took a file of papers from the wall safe and placed it carefully in his burgundy attaché case.

She watched his every move as he clicked the case shut, as he relocked the wall safe, as he picked up the phone and punched in the number of Johnny's private line. She listened, without really hearing, to his every soft-spoken word. Larry's cool, controlled voice was smooth and unhurried – she wanted him hot, sweating, breathless. His disciplined stance as he stood there calmly altering their plan, made her insides constrict – she wanted him dishevelled, horny, wild. It was desire reaching fever-pitch. It was desire at fever-pitch, laced with wicked, wicked excitement.

As Larry spoke into the mouthpiece, Marissa reached underneath her red and yellow gingham sundress and eased her panties down her legs. Larry, deep in conversation and staring off into space, didn't appear to have noticed.

Standing up quietly, Marissa stepped out of the cerise-coloured panties. She stood for a moment, letting the air drift luxuriously underneath her dress, then she glided over to Larry.

He was standing to the side of his desk. As she laid her head on his shoulder, he stroked her hair absent-mindedly. His soft, distracted caresses ran shivers right down her body. Silently, she undid a middle button on his shirt and pushed her hand inside, running her nails over his lean, hard rib-cage. By way of response, Larry dropped a brief, perfunctory kiss on the top of her head.

Marissa tensed with frustration. She was feverish with wanting him. She manoeuvred herself to the side of his hip and began to rub her abdomen gently against him. The friction of her movements warmed through to her belly. Her whole lower body felt tight and tremulous.

Larry's voice lowered. Instead of softly stroking, his hand now began to grip her hair, but still the phone conversation continued.

Biting her lip to keep silent, Marissa pulled her dress up to her middle. Larry's eyes darted downwards. With a taunting smile, she slowly grazed her knuckles across the soft, fresh curls of her pubis. Larry knitted together his eyebrows and deliberately turned to gaze out of the window. She began to brush her naked hips against him. He moistened his lips with his tongue. She pressed a little harder. He gripped the phone tighter. He spoke for several moments more. He became increasingly mono-syllabic. Finally, sweat beading his upper lip, he uttered a harassed goodbye.

'Just what the hell do you think you're doing?' he hissed at Marissa. 'You know I was speaking to Johnny.'

'So?' hissed Marissa back, glad that Larry's eyes were glued to her bare, undulating hips.

'If you'd worked me up any more, Johnny would have sensed it!'

'So?'

'So ... you don't show disrespect to a man like Johnny Casigelli.'

Marissa tilted back her head, eyes blazing with arousal. 'Show me disrespect, Larry. Right now!'

Larry groaned, anger flooding out, desire flooding in. Roughly, he turned her round and bent her over the edge of his desk, pushing her dress right up her back. He scrunched her dress up in his fist, pressing the same hand between her shoulderblades and pinning her down to the desktop.

The fingers of his other hand trailed slowly down the hollow of her spine.

Marissa sighed softly.

The fingers moved down, down over her bottom, down between her sweet, smooth buttock cleft. She felt her sex flitter excitedly.

A strong finger touched her anus. A fingerpad dabbed softly, gently, deliciously.

She moaned with long-awaited delight, stretching her arms out in front of her, pushing her buttocks up towards the enchanting teasing.

Larry bent his head close to hers. Easing away the hand that was in between her shoulderblades, he reached up and tucked her hair behind her ear. 'You are one wicked lady,' he murmured, his lips so close that his breath caressed her inner-ear. 'The idea of scamming Kelly really turns you on, doesn't it?'

'Mmm, yeah baby,' purred Marissa, closing her eyes. His finger now circled her rosy rear-orifice, teasing, tantalising.

'You know what?' Larry breathed huskily.

'What?' she gulped. What he was doing to her bottom was divine!

'It kind of turns me on as well.'

Marissa laughed softly. 'You are one wicked guy, Larry Barris. How wicked can you get?'

'Let's see, shall we?' he said, voice thick as treacle.

He opened up his zipper and pulled out his rigid penis, tracing the bulbous, slightly moist tip up and down the line of her bent-over buttocks. Marissa sighed again, pressing her fluttering stomach into the cool leather of the desk. The tender teasing of her bottom crease was making her head blurry, her body weak. Somewhat dazed, she noticed it was growing dark outside. A dull, pewter veil was swiftly descending over the city.

Suddenly, Larry clicked on the green desk lamp. 'All the better to see you with,' he murmured in his best big-bad-wolf voice.

Marissa couldn't chuckle, couldn't answer. Her insides felt so tight, she thought she would burst. Gulping with pleasure, she focused on the muted, green light.

Larry moved down to her vulva, nudging his rock-hard tip round and round her soft swollen skin. When he gradually eased up inside her, appeasing the tightness, stretching her wonderfully, she gripped the far side of the desk in relief.

'Oh baby!' she gasped, her body welcoming him like he was part of her.

Clutching her tightly round the waist, Larry began to move slowly, rocking his trousered hips gently against her bare buttocks.

'Faster,' she urged in desperation.

'No, baby,' answered Larry. 'Nice and slow.'

Slowly, slowly, slowly he stroked her insides. Gliding once, twice, thrice. Marissa ground back with frantic arousal.

Suddenly Larry withdrew.

'Larry!' she cried out. 'What are you doing?'

Larry hoiked her up quickly and spun her round to face him. 'Ssh,' he whispered, pressing his finger to her lips. He cocked his head and listened. 'Did you hear that?' he breathed in her ear.

Marissa hadn't heard a thing. But she could taste the spicy, aphrodisiac taste of herself on his fingertip and her head simply reeled with her body's arousal. 'Hear what?' she forced out.

'That noise. Like a scrape.'

Marissa drew his finger into her mouth. 'It's nothin', sugar.' She licked his fingertip gently. 'Don't go getting spooked on me now.'

'Yeah right,' grinned Larry, looking handsomely sheepish, dipping his eyes to her body once again.

Her dress had fallen, creased and bunched, back over her hips and, with an urgent swipe, he pulled it up and over her head, running big, strong hands over every inch of her feverish, nerve-enhanced nakedness.

He shed his own clothes in a second and sank back into the leather deskchair. Spinning her round again so that her back was to him, he pulled her down on to his lap, impaling her immediately on to his massive erection.

'God, yes!' she breathed in elation. She leant her back against his chest, and stretched her arms up high, reaching behind to twine her fingers in his hair.

Brushing her shining tresses aside, he dipped his mouth to her neck and nibbled vampire-like at the sweet skin between the curve of her neck and shoulder. His hands moved under her extended arms to cup her drawn-up breasts. As he began to play with her stretched, velvet-pink nipples, he bucked up slightly underneath her, the simple thrust enough to ripple right through her excited abdomen. Teasing fingers on her breasts and gentle thrusts up inside her made the ripples converge somewhere in the region of her rib-cage and then diffuse back through her body, like hundreds of stones skimming across water.

'Larry,' she moaned softly, utterly moved by the sensations. She wanted him everywhere, touching every part of her, loving every intimate inch of her.

His chest heaved against her shoulderblades, his skin burning into hers, damp flesh clinging to damp flesh.

'Larry,' she moaned again, grinding her head back against his collarbone. She opened her legs wide to either side of his. Her untouched clitoris was hot and shining, pushing stiffly out from her deep-pink labia. The penile vibrations deep inside her heightened the needle-sharp flutters in her sex and she opened her legs even wider, straining so wide that the tendons in her groin felt stretched to capacity and muscles along her thighs and calves burned beneath her skin.

'Oh God, Larry,' she begged as his hips bumped up underneath her. 'Touch me.'

'Yeah baby,' he murmured, sliding a hand from one of her breasts down to her straining sex. His coveted touch on her erect little bud was as light and sweet as the kiss of a breeze. He touched a little harder, then harder, then harder, then harder still, until he was pressing the length of his finger against it.

'There, sweetheart, how's that?' he muttered breathlessly against the shell of her ear. He began to rub just a little.

At once, Marissa's body arched. Her leg muscles tensed. She dug her painted toenails into the carpet. She couldn't even cry out. Rack after rack of orgasmic contractions shook her whilst Larry, still huge and hard inside her, moved up and down beneath her.

When finally she melted back against him, sweat glistened on her skin like a lustrous oil slick, hair framed her face in soaking tendrils.

With a growl like an angry bear, Larry withdrew yet again. He lifted her under her arms and tumbled her face down on the floor. Swiftly, he dropped down behind her and, hoiking up her hips until her bottom was raised high, he eased her legs apart with his knees. Marissa was weak from her orgasms but, as Larry parted her legs, the sudden shock of air on her wet, excited sex made her senses flicker and ignite and when he pushed in again, she moaned with delirious pleasure.

Larry began moving with quick-fire thrusts, pummelling his hips against her buttocks. Gripping her thighs with iron-like fingers, he pumped up and down, panting like a madman, until his breathing suddenly caught and he collapsed over her slender back. Marissa sighed with joy as his semen spilled into her. With each convulsive jag, he was yanking up her hips against his and yet another climax soon claimed her, weaker and less sustained than before but, even so, draining her of her last vestige of strength. She couldn't even raise her head from where her cheek was pressed uncomfortably to the carpet.

In the far corner of her darkened office, Justine drew back further into shadow. She was still able to gaze through the open doorway into Larry's semi-lit office; still able to see Larry's gleaming, muscled torso, slick with sweat, lying over Marissa's prone body.

As soon as she'd seen them in there, she knew she should have left. But she hadn't. She knew she shouldn't have watched them. But she had. The sight of their passionate, torrid, abandoned lovemaking had left her breathless with excitement. Putting her hand against her cheek, she felt her skin burning with arousal. She had to admit that Marissa, dislike her though she definitely did, had an amazing body. No wonder Larry was smitten, Justine thought enviously, looking longingly at Larry's muscled back and thighs and hard, rounded buttocks. No wonder he'd never seen her as anything more than his super-efficient secretary.

She chewed on her bottom lip thoughtfully, still gazing at the exhausted lovers. At first she'd been frightened when she heard voices in the offices. She'd thought she was bound to be found out. Unbeknownst to Larry and the rest of the firm, she was studying law at nightschool. She wanted it kept secret, she didn't want the expensively educated Ivy League lawyers laughing at her evening class efforts. But one day . . . one day she was going to be a brilliant lawyer, just like Larry.

She'd been coming in on Saturday nights for a while now. The firm's library made a fantastic, ready-stocked study centre and she'd been using all sorts of materials for reading and research. Only thing was, as Larry's permission hadn't been asked, she wasn't at all sure he would appreciate finding her there.

The voices had alarmed her. She'd recognised Larry's low, sexy, confident drawl straight away and she'd crept through to her office, ready with the perfectly plausible excuse of catching up on work if she'd been caught. But she hadn't been caught, and she'd known she should have counted her blessings then and there, and left right away. But she hadn't. Couldn't. The illuminated spectacle in Larry's office had been far, far too compelling.

She crept out slowly from her hiding place, checking that the lovers were still occupied. Larry had now rolled off Marissa and she'd flopped across him, resting her cheek on his chest, one long, golden thigh thrown across both of his. He was softly stroking her back, talking in muted tones. Pillowtalk, thought Justine jealously. About to leave, something made her pause and prick up her ears attentively. She tutted at herself as she now added eavesdropping to her evening's voyeuristic activities – but this made for interesting listening.

As she crept from the room and tiptoed down the long, beige corridor, she mulled over what she had just heard. Whatever did Marissa's stepdaughter, Kelly Aslett, have to do with a man like Johnny Casigelli? Justine wondered. And just where exactly did Ensenada fit in?

She eased herself carefully between the smoke-glass doors, relocking them after her, and decided to take the stairs down – long and laborious thought it would be, it was safer than risking any noise from the lift.

Interesting, she reflected as she tripped silently downwards. Very interesting. What was it she'd just read in the library tonight – knowledge is power. Well, maybe on Monday morning, she'd dig out the Johnny Casigelli file for herself and do a little unauthorised research and gain a little power of her own.

Her time-clock upside down, Kelly awoke at 1 a.m. She lay in bed, completely disoriented and for one brief, blissful moment, felt for Luc's warm, sleeping body beside her. Her fingers curled sadly round the cool, empty sheet as she remembered.

She sat up slowly, long, silky hair falling forward as she rested her head against her drawn-up knees. How easy it was to get used to something, she thought mistily, when it was something good. How hard was it going to be to get over it? She hadn't even spent a whole week with Luc but being with him had seemed as natural as breathing. She knew every inch of his glorious body and he hers. Now, sleeping alone, there was a huge, empty space next to her, and she felt as if her world had been ripped apart.

She swung her legs off the side of the bed, then padded over to the window. It looked out to the front of the house. She gazed down the long, dark driveway to the tops of the surrounding houses, shining in the silvery pools of the streetlamps. Each affluent house was individual and stood in its own large, impressive gardens. Luxury cars were parked in each driveway. So different from Paris, she mused, pressing her forehead to the cool pane of the window. This was home, and yet already she longed for her tiny apartment, for her view over the beautiful city, for her wine-sozzled gossips with Angie, for Luc. Most of all she longed for Luc.

Down at the bottom of the driveway, a Ferrari glided smoothly into view, crawling up the drive and parking outside the house. Larry got out first, then Marissa.

Marissa's mussed-up hair shone like spun gold in the light from the streetlamps, her expensive gingham sundress was a mass of twisted creases. She was barefoot, carrying her shoes in her hand. Larry, arm thrown carelessly round Marissa's shoulders, was nuzzling her neck as they walked towards the doorway. Marissa's girlish giggles filtered up through the window. It didn't take Einstein to work out what they'd been up to, thought Kelly, staring wistfully down at them. They looked good together though, she'd give them that, the lustrous dark head bent close to the shining blonde one. So did we, she said softly to herself, drifting back in her mind again, picturing the way her own long hair had looked, spread over Luc's brown chest.

Still at his large house near Santa Barbara, Johnny Casigelli was hosting a dinner party. The party was dragging on. It was the middle of the night and his guests, several minor politicians and their wives, were showing no signs of tiredness. Johnny, on the other hand, was quite tired. The party he'd thrown last night had gone on well into the early hours and tonight's much more modest affair seemed to be similarly fated.

Johnny watched silently as his male guests smoked his Cuban cigars and guzzled bottle after bottle of his Château Lafite, their red, sweating faces growing redder and sweatier with each glass they knocked back. Naturally, the conversation revolved around politics – liberally interspersed with ribald anecdotes. So, not only was he tired, Johnny was also bored. The only politics that interested Johnny were the ones that favoured his own activities and since all these politicians were already on his payroll, he wondered why he was bothering to wine and dine them at all. Keep the old codgers sweet, he supposed. Not that they'd dare be anything else.

'Eh, whaddaya say, Johnny? I sure told 'em, eh, Johnny, whaddaya say?'

Johnny slid his eyes over to the speaker. A bulbous wine-soaked face, chin thrust towards him, was obviously awaiting a response to an unlistened-to story. Johnny flashed his brilliant white smile. 'You sure did, Samuel,' he replied, shaking his head and creasing his eyes indulgently. 'You sure did!' I should have been an actor, he thought, hiding his contempt by filling up the old fool's glass.

Swirling cognac round the bottom of his own glass, he thought about Larry's phone call earlier on in the evening. It was irksome, this matter for Larry – Johnny had much bigger fish to fry. But he owed Larry. Bigtime. And if this was going to make Larry and that stunning woman of his happy, then what the hell.

He shrugged his shoulders and threw back the snifter of brandy. He wasn't remotely surprised when he felt a slender hand rest lightly on his thigh. He'd been expecting it.

He was seated at the head of the table and he turned slowly to the person seated to his left. Soft, auburn hair framed clear, pretty features, and fell in autumnal clouds to perfect, porcelain shoulders. Beautifully painted, pale blue eyes looked directly into his.

He smiled as the hand moved upwards in small sensuous semicircles.

'You just shrugged,' breathed a girlish voice, through pouting scarlet lips. 'Why's that?'

Still smiling, not answering, Johnny shrugged again.

He leant back in his chair, listening to the cacophony of drunken voices in the room, waiting for the hand to go higher. It did.

'That's very nice,' smiled Johnny, his voice perfectly audible. 'But won't your husband mind?'

The pale blue eyes darted panic stricken to the far end of the table, rested briefly on a portly senator in the midst of a heated discussion, then slid nonchalantly back up the table to Johnny. 'Oh, I don't think so,' whispered the voice through the shining red lips. 'After all, you did just provide him with the most marvellous dinner.

'Fine,' laughed Johnny, black eyes glittering. Nothing like taking another man's willing wife, he mused. Tiredness and boredom drained away fast. 'I'll meet you in the library.'

'Fine,' breathed the soft voice back.

With a rustle of russet silk, she rose from her seat and glided to the opposite end of the table. Johnny noted with satisfaction the long, willowy figure, the dress dipping right down the flawless white back. She stooped to kiss her husband goodnight. Not turning his head from his heated discussion, the husband harrumphed an irritable response. As she swept back past Johnny, en route to the library, she winked a heavily mascara-ed, glinting eyelid.

On the tabletop, Johnny drummed his fingers casually to the count of five hundred, idly focusing on the white-gold, crested band he wore on his middle finger. At five hundred and one, he pushed back his chair and rose.

'Well, ladies, gentlemen,' he announced, smiling benevolently at his beet-faced audience. 'I think I'll say goodnight.'

As he turned to leave, a discordant chorus of voices

and shuffling chairs followed him. Johnny stopped dead. Without turning back, he held up his hand, his ring glinting in the light from the crystal chandelier. 'No, please,' his voice rang out authoritatively. 'You are my guests. Stay at my table. Enjoy my hospitality. I insist.'

With a distinct lack of reluctance, the dinner guests settled happily back at the table, resuming arguments, refilling glasses, murmuring drunken accolades to their host's boundless generosity.

Whistling softly, Johnny left the dining room and strolled across the enormous oak-panelled lobby to the library.

She was seated in a deep, winged armchair over by the window. Silently, Johnny closed the door. He leant back against it for a moment. Watching. She was certainly very attractive. Young as well. Far too young and pretty for that old goat in there. Idly, Johnny rested his forefinger above his top lip, then walked over.

She leant round the chair as he approached. A tentative smile played upon her scarlet lips. She didn't seem quite so sure of herself now that she was alone with him. Johnny was used to that. In fact, he expected it. He smiled reassuringly back. 'Hello,' he said softly.

Her fingers fidgeted nervously with the beaded purse in her lap. 'Hello,' she whispered, dropping her eyes demurely to the purse.

Ah, acting shy now, he thought. This was going to be better than he'd anticipated.

Standing beside her chair, he reached beneath her auburn waves and softly traced his knuckle down the back of her neck. Gently coiling his finger in the fine wisps of hair at her hairline, he saw a trail of goosebumps rise along her upper arms. She shivered delightedly and lifted her head, pastel eyes now raised towards him. Johnny noticed them flick momentarily to the long scar just below his left cheekbone.

He grinned widely and angled his cheekbone towards her. 'Nasty, huh?'

'No,' she breathed. 'It's kind of sexy.'

'Sexy, hmm.' Nothing sexy about the way I got this, honey, thought Johnny, remembering the cold steel on his skin, the shocking warmth of his own spilt blood. Still, he'd made sure his wasn't the only blood that was spilled that night. He played his fingers softly across the top of her milky shoulders. She tilted back her head, half-closing her eyes.

Johnny stooped to her ear and pulled off a diamond earring. Very, very gently, he bit at her tiny earlobe. She sighed sweetly and reached up towards his face, tracing the back of her forefinger beneath his scar. 'Very sexy, she murmured.

He blew softly in her ear. 'You like to play with fire, honey?'

'I'd like to ... oh!' Johnny's tongue circled the inside of her ear. 'I'd like to play with you, Johnny.'

Johnny chuckled. Abruptly he lifted his head and hands from her body and strolled to an armchair opposite. Casually he sat down, brushing at nothing on his dinner suit trousers. 'Honey, no one plays with me! I'm the one does the playing. You got that?' His voice was very low and his smile flickered constantly as he spoke.

He waited while she nodded, raw excitement glazing her pretty, doll-like features.

Johnny tapped his forefinger thoughtfully against his front teeth. 'Would you like to undress for me, sweetheart?'

Her hands twiddled faster with the beads on her purse whilst her eyes shone brightly. Her silk-swathed chest fluttered with each tiny, short breath. 'Yes please, Johnny,' she said meekly.

Leaning back in the chair, he rested his hands on each of the arms and nodded. 'Go right ahead.'

Biting the lipstick off her lower lip, she eased forward, placing her beaded purse at her feet. Her hands moved to the straps of her high, criss-cross evening shoes.

'Leave the shoes.'

She looked up, surprised.

Johnny shrugged. 'I like them,' he said softly.

She stood up in front of him and pulled down the side zip of the russet, silk dress. Shrugging the straps down her arms, she stepped from the garment.

Johnny whistled softly. 'I'll bet you're just murder on the senator's blood pressure. You trying to finish him off, honey?'

It was her turn to shrug and chuckle.

Johnny took his time letting his eyes run over her. 'I like that you don't wear panties,' he whispered, staring at the expanse of exposed, white flesh. Tiny, nubby breasts peeked jauntily down at him and a smooth, straight torso led to long, long thighs. Her small, red-gold patch of pubic hair nestled tantalisingly at his eye level.

Cocking his head on one side, Johnny rested his temple pensively against his extended forefinger. His companion stood uncertainly in front of him.

'Get me a drink, would you honey,' Johnny asked softly.

'Huh?' She nibbled at her lipstick again.

'A drink, please.'

She looked at him nervously. Excitement gilded the nerves, he could see that. He could read exactly what was going on in that doll-like head – she was envisaging having to walk through to the dining room, naked like she was, just to please him. He wondered whether she'd risk displeasing him. Somehow he didn't think so. She wavered giddily.

Johnny chortled, enjoying her mix of confusion and excitement. He toyed idly with the idea of sending her through. She wouldn't dare disobey him, whatever the marital consequences. Nah, he decided, he wasn't in the mood for histrionic husbands. A moment later, he nodded to a drinks tray in the corner.

'Oh!' she said, 'I thought you meant –' She shook her head lightly and turned.

Johnny watched her walk over. Her long, coltish legs moved surprisingly elegantly, given that her shoes were almost four inches high. Rich auburn hair swayed across her shoulderblades and her narrow white back looked almost ethereal. Little fleshy buttocks arched deliciously outwards. 'Scotch,' he called over.

She nodded, carrying his drink back to him.

'Thanks honey.' Unhurriedly he took a sip. 'Good,' he murmured as his teeth clanked against ice. 'You added the rocks.'

Her knee brushed purposefully against his leg. 'I saw you drinking it earlier, Johnny.'

'Did you now, well, well.' She was a good girl, this senator's wife. Eager to please. He liked that. 'Let's see if we can find you a reward!'

Deftly he fished out a piece of ice. As he took another sip, he eyed her smooth, naked hips. Nonchalantly, he ran the ice cube over her pale skin. She jerked and gasped excitedly.

'Eew, that's cold, Johnny.'

'You don't say,' he answered, brushing the ice across her mons, watching the minute droplets of melting water glisten on the neat coils of hair. When he moved lower, rubbing it lightly between her legs, she tensed immediately, staring down in startled fascination. Back and forth he rubbed, the ice wetting her labia and gradually melting in his fingers. As she hissed a blend of shock and pleasure, he ran the melting cube over her stomach and up over the tips of her tiny breasts. Her nipples tightened to rosy ball bearings.

As she gasped at his touch, she swayed a little, slightly unsteady on her narrow heels.

Johnny reached upwards and lazily fingered her damp, straining nipples.

'Oh God, Johnny,' she breathed, shivering lightly. 'I'm so excited!'

'Let's hope hubby doesn't decide to take up reading,' Johnny muttered.

'W-what?' She looked down at him, dense with passion and arousal.

'Joke, honey,' he whispered, nudging her legs apart with his knees. 'We're in the library, remember.'

'Oh yeah,' she said dully, 'Oh yeah!' she moaned as he eased his hand on to her watery sex. She stood precariously as he massaged her sex with the flat of his hand. He could feel the honeyed moistness of her excitement mix with the melted ice and soon she was bending her knees, pushing them out to either side, dipping herself to and fro across the flat of his hand.

'Yeah, that's good,' Johnny said, his voice low and gutteral. 'Move yourself, angel ... rock those pretty little hips.'

His words made her frantic. She bent her knees out further, swaying her sex wildly over his hand, rubbing the base of her firm buttocks against his fingers.

'Touch your breasts,' he suddenly ordered brusquely.

Eyes dancing deliriously, she cupped her own small breasts and tweaked at her tips, simultaneously brushing her sex frantically against Johnny's hand. Her smooth, slender hips rocked towards him, her knees now bent so far outwards that Johnny was amazed she could keep her balance. Her sex was heavily engorged and she was gasping, perspiring, pressing her straining clitoris down urgently.

'OK, honey,' he whispered, suddenly moving his hand very fast, moving the fluff-covered skin of her mons with his palm, moving her sex with his fingers. She climaxed within seconds, soaking his hand, shuddering lightly.

'Oh Johnny!' she gulped delightedly between laboured breaths.

'Lie down,' he ordered quickly, scarcely giving her time to recover.

She obeyed at once.

'Good girl,' he muttered, standing over her, loosening his diamond cufflinks.

Delicate blue eyes, drunk with passion, followed his every move. Quickly he took off his clothes, then positioned himself between the wonderful widespread thighs.

'After the ice, comes the fire,' he murmured softly, easing inside her welcoming body.

At her flat in Paris, Angie replaced the receiver and looked across at Luc. She shook her head gently.

'Still there is no answer?' Luc asked.

'No answer, no dial tone,' replied Angie. 'I think there's a problem with the phones.'

Luc raked his fingers through his rumpled hair. His eyes were bleary from lack of sleep and his stubble was more peppery than ever. But oh my, he's handsome, thought Angie, rubbing at her own weary eyelids.

'Don't worry, Luc,' she said softly. 'We'll get through. We'll keep on trying till we do.'

13

Kelly belted her ankle-length, white cotton robe tightly around her middle and wandered barefoot down to the kitchen. Rosita was standing to the side of the sink, busily juicing fresh oranges.

'Good morning, Miss Aslett,' Rosita sang gaily.

'Morning, Rosita. And it's Kelly, not Miss Aslett!' Kelly rolled her eyes in mock frustration. 'How many times did I tell you that?'

Chuckling brightly, Rosita peeled another orange and placed it inside the juicer. 'Welcome home, Kell-ee!'

'Thanks,' Kelly replied, pilfering an orange segment. 'You sound very bubbly today. What's up?'

Rosita giggled and, wiping her hands for once on her pristine, white apron, she proudly displayed the tiny, cluster ring on her wedding finger. 'I engaged, Miss Aslett-oops, I mean, Kelly. Yesterday.'

Lord, must be something in the air, thought Kelly. First Larry and Marissa acting like a pair of love bugs. Now Rosita. She pinched her arm sharply, ashamed at herself and her reaction. It's just sour grapes, she winced. Just because things didn't work out between her and Luc.

Rushing over to Rosita, she gave her a hug. 'I'm so pleased for you, honey,' she said. 'Really I am. Who's the lucky man?'

Rosita giggled shyly and blushed. 'His name is Raoul.'

'Oh no, not Raoul, the handyman?' A soft voice came from the direction of the doorway.

Kelly turned to see Marissa, daisy fresh, glide into the kitchen.

'Really Rosita,' continued Marissa smoothly. 'You could do so much better than a handyman.'

Rosita blinked rapidly at Marissa then cast her eyes down to the floor. Her eyes seemed suspiciously watery.

Kelly stared furiously at her smiling stepmother. What a bitch. Obviously the love of Larry hadn't changed her at all. Turning back to Rosita, Kelly hugged her tightly again. 'I'm sure he's absolutely gorgeous, Rosita.'

'Oh, he's gorgeous all right,' Marissa purred knowingly. 'Gorgeous – but poor! No Rosita, you should be setting your sights way higher, like on a dentist or a doctor or even –,' she paused and and looked pointedly at Kelly '– a lawyer.'

'There speaks the voice of experience,' muttered Kelly.

'That's right,' quipped Marissa gaily. 'Twice over. First the senior partner, now the junior partner. Both I can highly recommend.' Casually she poured herself a glass of juice and leant back against the onyx-marble surface of the kitchen unit. She sipped her juice slowly, looking Rosita up and down. 'My God, Rosita, look at your apron. Things are going downhill already and you're not even married to him yet.' With a loud tut and sarcastic smile at Kelly, she waltzed off out of the room.

Rosita stared down at the orange stains on her apron and promptly burst into tears.

'Come on honey,' comforted Kelly. 'Don't let the wicked, wicked stepmom upset you.'

Rosita's trembling lower lip slowly stopped trembling.

'There, that's better,' whispered Kelly softly.

Rosita managed a tearful smile.

Kelly smiled mischievously back. 'Now then. How about you tell me all about this gorgeous Raoul.'

After breakfast Kelly decided on a swim. She was genuinely very pleased for Rosita, but somehow Rosita's obvious happiness seemed to twist the knife further into her own abject misery. A swim would take her mind off things. If only for a little while.

She swam hard for twenty minutes or so, then eased up out of the water to gather her breath. Resting her elbows on the side of the pool, she closed her eyes against the brilliant sunlight. When she opened them, an attractive pair of muscular male legs were planted firmly in front of her. She let her eyes wander up to the sleek black swimming trunks and broad, muscled chest.

'Hey Larry,' she said, dipping her head back into the water then slicking her damp hair back off her face.

'Hi darling.' Larry crouched down on his haunches, resting his hands on his outspread knees. 'Good swim?'

'Yes. You?'

'Yeah, I was in earlier.'

Kelly nodded. She was disturbingly on a level with Larry's crotch and a sudden need for Luc suffused through her. She tried to look away but Larry was so near, she could have counted the hairs on the inside of his thighs.

Pressing her hands into the stone flags on the pool-side, she made to hoist herself out of the water.

'Here, darling.' Larry thrust forward a hand and pulled her effortlessly out.

'Thanks,' gasped Kelly, suddenly finding herself upright on the side of the pool.

He dipped to the side and presented her with a towel.

'Thanks again,' laughed Kelly.

'*De nada*,' he answered, chucking her fondly under the chin. 'Paris agrees with you, honey,' he said lightly. 'You're beautiful!'

'Not too bad yourself.' She pinched hard muscle on his stomach playfully. Larry was a bit like the older brother she never had, she mused. The days of her crush on him were well and truly over. Now she just liked him, respected him, trusted him – the same way her father had trusted him. His taste in women was a bit dubious though, she thought, catching sight of a sullen Marissa watching them from her bedroom window. But then, her father had fallen for Marissa too. What was it about Marissa and lawyers?

'Er, Kelly?' Larry had moved over to lounge on a sunchair.

She glanced across at him. Unlike Luc's, Larry's hair was short and dark. Luc's hair was longer and light brown. Unlike Luc's, Larry's chest had a generous coating of hair. Luc's chest hair was much lighter. But something about the broad, lean muscles and the insouciant way Larry was lolling on the chair reminded her unbearably of Luc. Her body tangibly ached for Luc. Was that possible? Was it possible to love someone so much, so quickly? Was it even possible to love someone so much when she knew he didn't love her back?

'Kelly?' Larry repeated, louder.

'Mmm?' She dragged her thoughts away from Luc and dabbed her arms and legs with the towel, then lay down on a lounger next to Larry.

'We have to talk,' Larry continued. 'You know about signing those papers for the will.'

Kelly closed her eyes. The papers! She hadn't even thought about that in the past few days. Before it had seemed so important. Even more important than starting something with Luc, she remembered hollowly. God, that was only a matter of days ago – it seemed like a lifetime. Now, she'd give it all up in a flash, if she could just have Luc love her again. 'Yes,' she muttered listlessly. 'I know. I have to sign them on Wednesday, right? On my birthday?'

'That's right, hon. Actually –'

'What about Marissa?' Kelly butted in suddenly. She raised her head and shielded her eyes towards Larry. 'Did she buy another house to move into yet? Or is she moving in with you?'

'Don't worry about Marissa,' Larry said softly.

'I don't worry about her. I just wondered, that's all.'

Larry looked at her evenly. He seemed to be about to say something then evidently changed his mind. 'Anyway, about the signing,' he went on. 'It's a big responsibility, what's going to be happening to you. More the business side of things than the house.'

'I know,' Kelly mumbled. 'And I know you can't be crazy about suddenly acquiring me as a silent partner but it's what dad wanted.'

'Yeah,' said Larry brusquely. 'Well, anyway, like I said, a big responsibility. So, what I'd like for you to do is to start getting a feel for things right away.'

Kelly raised an eyebrow at him. 'A feel?'

'Yeah. Like you say, it's what David wanted – you involved in the business to some degree.'

'Well, what d'you mean by a feel?'

'First off, there's someone I'd like you to talk to. A client of mine. I'm travelling down to see him first thing tomorrow. I'd like for you to come along.'

She stared at him in surprise. 'But Larry, why? I'm no lawyer. You are. Why would I need to speak to a client?'

'I think it would do you good, give you an insight into the business, the way we work.'

Kelly lay back and closed her eyes again. 'But why? You run the business, Larry. You have ever since dad died. Why do you want me to come along to a client?'

Larry didn't respond. He got up silently.

Kelly's eyes flew open as a shadow suddenly fell over her. Larry was staring down at her, his body silhouetted against the sun.

'I'd like you to come along, Kelly,' he said softly. 'Trust me – it'll do you good.'

Kelly looked up at his darkened features and thought for a moment. She had no other plans until Wednesday and maybe, just maybe, it would stop her thinking about Luc. Besides, if it kept her away from Marissa, that had to be a good thing. 'OK,' she said. 'Where are we going?'

Larry smiled, his teeth very white in his shadowed face. 'Just down past the border. Ensenada.'

'Mexico?' Kelly asked, wide eyed with surprise. 'You have clients in Mexico?'

'Sweetheart, I have clients all over. See what I mean, you should learn something about a business you're going to be a part of. In whatever capacity.'

She nodded. 'OK,' she said. 'But we'll be back by Wednesday to sign?'

'Course,' answered Larry lightly, stooping to plant a kiss on her forehead. 'Back by Wednesday. Oh, and keep the fact of the trip to yourself, hon, my client's a very private man. Enjoy the sunshine now, darlin'.'

Kelly watched him absently as he walked back toward the house. That's so weird, she thought. Larry wanting her to learn about the business. He'd been positively paranoid about keeping his business dealings from her over the past few years. Telling her not to worry her pretty head about such things. She shrugged non-chalantly. What did it matter? After Wednesday, she'd have the house and an income from the business and then she'd have to think about what to do with the rest of her life. Somehow the thought did nothing to cheer her up.

Larry didn't look back at Kelly as he strode into the house. He didn't dare lest he gave something away. He didn't feel that great about what he was doing to the girl – but he didn't feel that bad either.

Wandering up to Marissa's bedroom, he found her still standing by the window. She'd evidently been watching his whole conversation with Kelly.

'Well?' she said quietly.

Larry licked his fingertip and painted a triumphant strike in the air. 'No problem. Like leading a stray dog to food,' he grinned.

'Or Little Red Riding Hood to the Big Bad Wolf!' cracked Marissa.

'Yeah, whatever,' whispered Larry. 'The new angle worked. Phase One complete. Kelly and I'll be heading off in the morning.'

Marissa pulled in her lower lip pensively. She breathed out a long, low sigh then walked behind him to the door. She made much of turning the key in the lock. 'In that case,' she whispered, leaning back against the door knob. 'Let's not waste any more of today.'

Her hair was still coiled high from the swim they'd taken together earlier and the high-leg, one-piece swimsuit clung damply to her golden curves. Reaching up, she deftly uncoiled her hair, letting it tumble past her shoulders.

Moving behind him, she eased her arms through his, running her hands hungrily over his chest. She circled his small, flat nipples, whilst trailing her tongue across the broad breadth of his back. Larry felt himself harden uncomfortably in the tight, black bathing shorts.

'My thoughts entirely,' he mumbled back hoarsely.

Behind him, Marissa planted butterfly kisses down his spine. She pulled her hand from his chest and pushed it into the back of his shorts, trailing her nail softly down the cleft of his buttocks.

Larry flinched delightedly. 'Jesus, Marissa,' he whispered at her delicious downward strokes.

Pushing her other hand into his trunks, she began vigorously to massage his hard, muscled cheeks, murmuring deep in her throat. Larry clenched his buttock muscles in response to her invigorating touch. The action of her movements pulled the material of his bathers tight at the front, stretching them vice-like across his straining cock.

Larry groaned loudly and wrenched the shorts down, breathing a shaky sigh of relief as his genitals were freed.

Chuckling softly, Marissa eased her hand between his legs, fingering his balls, gently separating them in their enclosed sac and cupping from one to the other. 'How's that?' she murmured.

'Heaven!' he gasped.

Stooping down behind him, she kissed his buttocks lightly whilst working the bathing trunks down his legs. Kneeling at his ankles, she tugged at his hand for him to lie down. Gratefully he knelt beside her, letting her push him on to his back. She bent up his knees and spread his legs wide apart.

'Larry, Larry, Larry,' she giggled, cupping his swollen balls in her hand again. 'You are such a big, big boy!'

Larry closed his eyes and groaned again. She was teasing his testes with knowing fingers, alternately squeezing and stroking. 'Come on, baby,' he moaned urgently. 'Come on.'

She settled down between his legs and moved towards him. Circling his penis with both her hands, she poised her mouth teasingly over it. Larry waited, his crotch a riot of frenzied arousal. Leaning down, she dipped beneath his penis and darted her tongue to his balls.

'Oh yeah,' he sighed.

Seconds later, she drew back.

'Come on, babe,' he urged again.

Marissa moved her beautiful mouth closer.

Larry pulled his stomach in sharply, his groin burning. He raised himself up on his elbows, and could see Marissa's dipped head, her shining hair spilling forward, her hands clasping his rigid penis tightly. She eased the tip of her tongue between her full lips and flicked her eyes wickedly up to him.

'Stop messing, honey,' he gasped. 'Come on. What you waiting for?'

Marissa ran her tongue between her smiling lips. 'Just one thing, baby. Can I trust you?'

Larry tensed his whole body, tightening his muscles into bunched knotted masses. She looked so beautiful crouched between his legs, knowing exactly what she was doing to him. 'What d'you mean by that?' he mumbled.

'I mean, can I trust you ... with Kelly?'

Larry, deep in the fog of arousal, gazed at her, completely baffled. 'What the hell are you talking about?' he hissed impatiently.

'I saw the way you were looking at her out there,' Marissa snarled back quickly.

Stretching back his head, closing his eyes tightly, cartwheels of light formed behind his eyelids. 'What?' he gasped, bewildered.

'Can I trust you with Kelly, Larry?' Marissa repeated, softer now, her eyes flickering with ill-disguised doubt.

Jeez, he realised with a jolt, she's jealous! Beautiful, hard-hearted Marissa was actually jealous! Larry felt a sudden weird warmth that was far from sexual. He eased himself forward and ran his finger down the side of Marissa's fresh face. 'Honey,' he whispered tenderly. 'I have to admit it – Kelly's a beauty.'

Marissa looked aghast.

'But you're *my* beauty. There's no one in this world but you. You're my one and only, you know that.'

'Sure I know that.' Marissa flashed a sardonic smile, almost – though not quite – hiding the glimmer of relief. Quickly, she flicked her tongue along the end of his penis.

He fell back down as she moved her mouth on to him. 'Come on now, baby,' he urged again, stretching his legs wider apart. His groin ached furiously.

'OK, lover,' she murmured as she closed her coral lips around him and sucked a swift, shattering orgasm from him.

14

Kelly and Larry left for Ensenada at around ten o'clock next morning. Larry had been exceptionally vague about the length of their stay. 'Take enough stuff for a couple of days,' was about all she could get out of him. So, Kelly had done just that – packed enough to see her through until Wednesday morning at the latest.

They travelled a good deal of the way in companionable silence. Early on in the journey Larry had made a few half-hearted attempts at conversation, asking her about Paris, about art school, about why she'd come home early. Kelly really hadn't wanted to get into it, and after a few evasive answers from her, Larry had got the hint and shut up. It didn't seem to bother him.

Despite making a concerted effort to cheer up, Kelly was feeling worse than ever. After Paris, California no longer seemed to hold any charm for her. True, there was the ceaseless sunshine, the beautiful scenery, the undoubted luxury of her home but, regardless of it all, everything seemed empty – bland almost.

She'd got one thing right, she reflected, as they sped along the coastal highway. At least she hadn't managed to ask Luc to come with her. He would have hated it. Luc out of Paris was about as incongruous as cocoa without chocolate. It just wouldn't work and, if you tried it, it would lose all its flavour.

She shook her head lightly, annoyed at herself again. Boy, was she turning bitter. First she reacted like a sour old puss when Rosita said she was getting married. Now she was comparing Luc ... *Luc* ... to chocolate. She groaned miserably.

'OK, honey?' asked Larry, evidently mistaking her groan for discomfort.

'Oh, yeah, fine,' answered Kelly, flustered. She really had to get hold of herself.

'Not far now.' Larry winked at her reassuringly.

'Sure, no problem.' She forced a smile.

'You know,' said Larry, patting her knee fondly. 'You're going to find this visit interesting. I guarantee that.'

'Sure, no problem,' she repeated absently, then wondered why Larry was looking at her nonplussed and gently shaking his head.

By lunchtime, they'd journeyed well beyond the border. The combined lull from being driven and travelling in silence had sent Kelly into a deep, dreamless sleep. She awoke abruptly when the smooth running of the Ferrari suddenly became bumpy.

Kelly glanced round her. A dusty desert landscape stretched endlessly, interspersed with giant cactus, odd-shaped elephant wood, dried-up yucca. Distant mountain ranges rose unusually from the plateau, their peaks cutting sharply into acres and acres of brilliant, blue sky.

Kelly lifted her sunglasses and did a double-take out of the car window. 'We're here? We're across the border?'

'Uh-huh.'

'But, didn't you need to wake me at the border?'

'Nah,' Larry grinned. 'Border guard took one look at you and fell in love. His eyes crossed he was so smitten. He certainly didn't want to disturb "*la hermosura*" by waking her.'

'Oh. Was he handsome?' Kelly joked lightly.

'Yeah. In a kind of pot-bellied, droopy moustached kind of way.'

Kelly surprised herself by giggling. She hadn't giggled

a true giggle since before the argument with Luc. Maybe Larry was right, maybe this trip would do her good.

She glanced round her again. They seemed to be following an unmade-up, stony trail deep into undeveloped desert land.

'He doesn't actually live in Ensenada, then? This client of yours?' She looked sideways at Larry.

'No. No, he doesn't.' Larry cleared his throat noisily. 'He lives outside of Ensenada. Inland.'

'Who is he?' she asked, intrigued by the location. What sort of corporate client of Larry's would live way out here?

'He's a businessman,' replied Larry quickly. 'You'll meet him soon enough. Look, that's where we're heading.'

Larry pointed to a sprawling development, barely discernible on the horizon.

Kelly squinted to see. 'Sure likes out of the way places!'

'Mmm,' Larry answered softly.

He sped along the track, kicking up a trail of dust behind them. Bit by bit the development came into focus. Kelly caught her breath. It was enormous. As they drew closer, she could see that it was a huge, high-walled compound.

'Wow!' she whispered, awestruck.

Pulling up in front of ornate, wrought-iron gates, Larry vaulted athletically out of the car and spoke into an intercom, inlaid into the white stone wall. He returned to the car. Seconds later, the gates opened and Larry drove through into the compound.

Inside was a revelation. Lush, rolling lawns, dotted liberally with water sprinklers, replaced the arid, dusty terrain of outside. Potted palms and assorted tropical plants lined the curving driveway, which seemed to wind and bend endlessly as Larry drove. Finally they reached a house.

Kelly found herself speechless. It was far too grandiose to be termed merely 'a house'. It was a white-walled mix of Southern plantation mansion and handsome Mexican hacienda. A profusion of trailing plants weaved round the edges of a huge, arched, terracotta-tiled doorway. Everywhere she looked, the brilliant colours of flowers in bloom dazzled her eyes. It was like stumbling on a haven in a land of hostility.

'I suppose this is what they mean by finding an oasis in the middle of a desert,' she joked in wonder.

'Yeah,' said Larry, quietly.

They were let into the house by a petite Mexican maid who reminded Kelly of Rosita. She showed them through to an outside patio at the edge of an oval swimming pool.

'Please sit down,' said the maid. 'Señor Casigelli will be arriving at any time.'

'Thank you.' Larry pulled a chair out from the table and gestured for Kelly to be seated. He followed suit.

'He isn't even here?' Kelly mouthed to Larry in astonishment.

Larry pressed his finger to his lips. 'Shoosh, darlin'. He'll be here soon enough.'

Even as he spoke, a breeze began to gather, followed by the sound of a low distant rumble. The water of the pool began to ripple as the breeze picked up and the sound got louder. Kelly turned, her hair slapping sharply against her face. 'What the –'

There, touching down in the centre of the lawn, blades spinning furiously, was a helicopter. Hefty gusts of air whipped up the pool water, choppy waves splashing out on to the patio.

As Kelly struggled with her hair, bunching it back to

keep it in check, she saw the helicopter door open. A man got out, his face obscured as he ducked low to avoid the swirling blades. Immediately out of the blades' vicinity, he straightened and, seemingly impervious to the violent gusts, he strolled casually towards them.

Face to face with him, Kelly swallowed hard. Her vision blurred slightly in the wind as she took in gleaming, jet black hair, and smooth olive-hued skin interrupted by a narrow fissure of scar-tissue running the length of a cheekbone.

Flashing black eyes flicked briefly towards her, then turned almost immediately to Larry. The man gripped Larry in a demonstrative embrace.

'Larry,' he grinned. '*Benvenuto*. Welcome.'

Larry smiled, returning the embrace. Kelly stared. There was something slightly uncomfortable about the situation. They were greeting each other like brothers, not like a lawyer and his client.

Larry stepped back. Placing his hand in the small of Kelly's back, he nudged her forward. 'Johnny, this is Kelly.'

Johnny glanced briefly back at her. He nodded once, his black eyes cold and unreadable. Then, he turned abruptly to Larry again. 'Come on inside. I'll have Conchita show you your rooms. You can freshen up before lunch.' He threw his hand loosely on Larry's shoulder and they began to walk towards the house.

Kelly, not knowing what else to do, followed meekly.

Some time later, Kelly flopped down on the huge double bed in her room. One of her heels caught in the stitching of the exquisite antique lace coverlet and she kicked her sandals off hurriedly, watching with satisfaction as they spiralled in the air and clonked against the front of an equally exquisite dresser. Lying back, she gazed up at the ornate coved ceiling. Her room was magnificent, situated on the upper floor of a corner wing. She couldn't have asked for more comfort or luxury.

What am I doing here? she wondered dismally, spreadeagling her arms and legs across the bed. The whole day so far had been utterly bizarre. Lunch had set the precedent. Johnny Casigelli had all but ignored her, talking to Larry in hushed tones about legal matters that went totally over Kelly's head. Neither of them had made any attempt to include her in the conversation. Her few attempts to join in had been met with a blank stare from Johnny and a response from Larry phrased in such complicated legal jargon that she wished she'd never asked in the first place. To cap it all, she found herself fascinated by Johnny. His good looks would capture anybody's eye, but it wasn't that – Lord knows, she was no stranger to good-looking men. No, there was something indefinable about him that fascinated her, some kind of strange, enigmatic charisma.

The afternoon had been just as odd. Johnny and Larry had continued their discussions over coffee out on the patio, both apparently oblivious, or worse, indifferent to Kelly's exclusion. Bored and restless, she'd taken herself off for a walk round the grounds. She'd been astonished by the number of people about the place, all men, all wearing dark suits and dark glasses, all exceedingly courteous. Just who was Johnny Casigelli? she'd found herself wondering again. And why had Larry been so keen for her to come along if they were both intent on ignoring her the whole time?

Wandering back towards the patio, she'd realised one thing. Her mind had been so taken up with questions, that she hadn't once thought about Luc. Realising that, a bleak emptiness had welled up inside her. What would he be doing now? she mused, picturing his face, his curving mouth, his smooth dark skin. Lost in her dreamy thoughts, she'd been flustered to find Johnny Casigelli staring at her as she approached the patio. For a fleeting moment, his black eyes had locked on to hers then swiftly he'd turned back to Larry.

Kelly shook her head lightly on the pillow. What was this trip all about? It certainly hadn't given her any insight into the business so far. She could go along to Larry's room and ask him but she had no idea where his room was, and the idea of wandering around this huge house aimlessly searching for Larry's room seemed rather futile. Perhaps dinner tonight would be better.

Moving across to her case, she pulled out an ankle-length, black, halter-neck dress. She held it in front of her as she stood in front of the mirror. Perfect to make an impression, she decided, flinging the dress down on the bed and heading on into the shower.

But dinner turned out to be no different from lunch.

She'd dallied over her hair and make-up, not really knowing why she was taking the trouble. She may as well not have bothered. She could have been dressed in sackcloth for all the attention she got at dinner.

Trying to corner Larry for an explanation had been hopeless. If the idea weren't so ridiculous, she might have thought that Larry was avoiding her on purpose. She hadn't wanted to embarrass Larry by demanding to know why she was there in front of Johnny. After all, Johnny was supposed to be a very important client. So, she'd sat miserably through dinner, being ignored, chewing on the exquisite food as though it were cardboard. Finally, wearied by it all, feeling like a piece of the furniture, she'd excused herself and wished them goodnight.

A dip of the head from Johnny and a subdued smile from Larry had been her only response. Baffled to the point of fatigue, she'd sunk gratefully into the comfort of her luxurious bed and immediately fallen asleep.

Someone was stroking her face.

'Luc,' she muttered dreamily.

'Señorita, is morning.'

Kelly dragged herself awake.

'Señorita, señorita. Is morning time.'

Kelly fluttered her eyes open. A pretty, vaguely familiar face was staring down at her. It was Conchita, Johnny Casigelli's maid. 'Oh hello,' Kelly smiled and, stretching gracefully, eased up to a sitting position. 'What time is it?'

'Is morning, señorita. Eight o'clock. I have brought you some breakfast.' Conchita turned to a nearby table and lifted a huge, silver breakfast tray towards Kelly.

'You didn't need to bother,' Kelly said as the tray was laid across her lap. 'I would have come down for breakfast.'

Conchita shook her head vigorously. 'No, no, Señor Casigelli say for you to have breakfast brought to your room.' She smiled prettily.

Kelly mouthed 'oh' in astonishment. Judging from the way she'd been treated yesterday, she was amazed he even remembered she was there, never mind ordered her breakfast to be sent up. 'Thanks, it looks delicious,' she said to Conchita who was busily fussing round the room, hanging up the dress Kelly had hurriedly discarded last night, drawing back the curtains to let the morning sun flood the room in a sea of white-gold.

Lifting the heavy white breakfast cup, Kelly leant back into the pillows and took a sip of the rich, hot coffee. 'Mmm, yum,' she muttered softly.

Conchita smiled across at her, obviously pleased that she was pleased.

'Er Conchita?' Kelly took another sip. 'Did you take Larry his breakfast already?'

Conchita's eyes darted nervously towards her, then she bustled towards one of Kelly's sandals that she appeared to have spotted on the floor by the dresser. She picked up the shoe and headed for the cupboard.

'Conchita?'

'No, señorita,' mumbled Conchita. She walked quickly towards the door.

'Oh, is he up then?' asked Kelly brightly. This might be her chance to get Larry on his own and ask him what the hell was going on.

Conchita speeded up. She suddenly seemed anxious to be away. 'I no know, señorita,' she said softly, easing through the doorway. 'I go now. Thank you.' And she was gone.

This place is so weird, thought Kelly, munching on a piece of lightly buttered wholewheat toast. The sooner she got up and got dressed, the better. Then she'd find Larry for herself.

At precisely that moment, Larry was letting himself quietly into Kelly's home near Santa Ana. He'd journeyed back through the night, leaving Mexico in the early hours of the morning, after first making sure Kelly was sound asleep.

The house was quiet. There were a few vague sounds coming from the rear end of the hallway. Rosita getting up, assumed Larry. He tiptoed silently to the staircase, climbing each stair with the light-footed stealth of a cougar. He certainly didn't want to alert Rosita just yet, and have her ask any awkward questions. Marissa would be dealing with that later on this morning.

Noiselessly, he padded across the large landing and twisted the knob to Marissa's room. Unlocked, good. He'd surprise her.

The room was steeped in a silvery light, early-morning sun penetrating the frothy, ivory fabric of the drawn drapes. Larry could smell Marissa's faint, fruity perfume the moment he entered. He took a deep breath, his tense muscles relaxing as he inhaled the fragrance. Almost immediately, he felt a stirring in his groin. The citrus smell, redolent of Marissa, never failed to excite him.

From where he stood inside the doorway, he could see Marissa in the huge double bed. She was lying across the bed at an angle, a crisp, white cotton sheet pulled over her. She was on her stomach, her cheek pressed into the pillow. She was sleeping.

Dropping his clothes, item by item, where he stood, Larry walked naked over to the bed. Already his hard-on was huge. Relief that things appeared to be moving along smoothly, and excitement at Marissa's sleeping body, had his own body in a state of intense arousal.

He stood by the side of the bed. Picking up the top edge of the sheet between his thumb and forefinger, he gently eased it down Marissa's back. She was wearing an ivory, lace and silk baby-doll nightdress, one that he'd bought her last month. As he drew down the sheet, he could see the short nightie ruched around her body, skimming the very tops of her thighs. With a deft movement, he flicked the sheet to her ankles, staring at her long, golden legs flung across the bed. The sudden loss of the sheet appeared to make her stir. Shifting her legs slightly, she groped back unsighted for the sheet, then raised her head curiously off the pillow. Her eyes opened sleepily.

'Hey baby,' she murmured. 'You're back already.'

'Yeah,' he replied, rubbing his fingerpad gently along the back of her knee.

Marissa flickered her thick eyelashes, opening her sapphire eyes wider. 'You OK, baby?'

Larry nodded.

'And ...' Marissa raised her head higher. 'Everything go off all right?'

'So far,' he grinned. He drew his gaze down her body. 'I want you bad, hon,' he whispered.

Marissa reached for his hand. 'You can have anything at all that you want, sweetie.'

Larry found his voice thickening. 'I want you.'

Smiling wickedly, Marissa tugged him down on to the bed. 'You got me, anyway, anyhow,' she whispered, trailing the tip of her nail slowly across the back of his hand.

Sliding into bed beside her, Larry noticed Marissa's sleep-dazed eyes sparkle. 'My, my,' she chuckled softly, brushing the flat of her hand round and round the end of his engorged penis. 'A welcome home present?'

He grinned broadly. 'I'm the one's been away. Where's mine?'

'Here!' Marissa swept her hand theatrically down the length of her body.

'That'll do for starters,' he said fondly. He coiled tendrils of her hair round his forefinger, tucking it behind her ear. Dipping towards her, he kissed her tenderly on the bony base of her skull behind her ear. Softly moving her hair to the side, he placed a line of kisses down the hollow of her neck then trailed the tip of his tongue slowly across the top of her flawless back.

'Mmm,' breathed Marissa. 'That's good.' Moving her hand from his penis, she first stroked the base of his taut, flickering belly then moved her hand beneath his jutting cock, gently tickling his balls.

'So is that,' murmured Larry, kissing the top of her shoulder. With his teeth, he tugged the ribbon strap of her nightdress down her arm and then nudged her up on to her side, facing him. The lacy bodice of the nightdress, along with the strap, slipped down on her uppermost side. One perfect golden breast was revealed.

Larry, also propped up on his side, stared at her breast. The smooth pink nipple, as yet untouched by him, centred the circular mound like a velveteen button. Lightly, he ran his forefinger along the crease between her full breast and her rib-cage. Marissa kept her eyes riveted to his face.

'Beautiful baby,' he murmured, passing his thumb over her nipple, eliciting a tiny, euphoric sigh from her. Back and forth he rolled his thumb, watching the tip of her breast pucker and harden. Marissa wriggled slightly on the bed, moving her own hand up to his chest, twining her fingers in his dark chest hair.

Satisfied with the stiffness of her nipple, Larry began to squeeze the rounded flesh of the same breast. Marissa moaned lightly, closing her eyes. She made to bare her other breast.

'No.' Larry caught hold of her hand. He moved her hand to the breast he'd recently been squeezing. 'Touch yourself,' he whispered, closing her hand round her own breast. Marissa flicked her eyes lazily open and began to fondle herself, pulling lightly at her nipple as Larry watched closely.

Larry's groin blazed furiously but, despite his state of arousal, he wanted to wait. He gazed avidly at Marissa's hand. She was breathing heavily now, exciting herself, her flesh glowing with arousal. Stooping to her mouth, to her full, parted lips, he kissed her roughly, forcing his tongue deep inside her warm, soft mouth. They kissed for a while, passionately, roughly, bodies not touching, until Larry suddenly drew back. He watched for a moment more as she circled her pebbled nipple with her fingernail, then he pulled her back on to her stomach.

Tracing his hand down her lace-clad back, he leant forward to whisper in her ear, 'Are you wearing panties?'

'No.' Marissa's voice was husky.

'Are you sure?' Larry's hand was trailing down her back. 'I'll be mad if you are!'

'I'm not,' she whispered, excitement making her voice catch.

Larry moved his hand down the back of a silken thigh, then slowly eased it up underneath the nightie. 'Good girl,' he breathed as his hand skimmed a naked, sateen cheek. He inched the nightie up to her waist. Marissa sighed gently, letting her flushed cheekbone drop back against the pillow. Casually, Larry stroked her smooth bared buttocks. He followed the line of their join with his forefinger, tracing delicately up and down.

'I'd die for this ass,' he chuckled.

Marissa giggled back. 'You don't have to. It's yours.'

'Yeah.' His fingers tickled the knobbly base of her spine. 'You know what I feel like?'

'What's that?'

'Feel like playing,' he mumbled, twisting back to reach into the drawer of the nightstand where he knew Marissa kept one of their favourite toys.

'Mmm, yes please, sugar.' She lifted her head in excitement, barely able to contain herself.

Finding what he wanted, Larry turned back to her. Eyes dancing, Marissa moistened her lips with her tongue. Swiftly, she moved both her hands up on to the pillow.

Shifting down the bed, Larry wedged his hand underneath her stomach and lifted her on to her knees. Pushing her nightie far up her back, he followed the curve of her spine with his knuckles. Marissa shivered lightly, locking her forearms so that she was positioned on all fours. She twisted her head round to Larry. 'Play with me, Larry,' she moaned urgently.

'Sure babe.' He sank on to his heels behind her. Gently, he eased his hand between her legs. He reached underneath her, feeling and cupping the sweet, soft fur on her mons. Marissa wriggled slightly, pressing her sex into his hand. Slowly, he drew his fingers backwards and then rubbed back and forth along the slick furrow. His fingers slid deliciously in her piquant juices. She moaned in delight as he circled her hardening clitoris but he was careful not to make her climax. Instead, he assiduously worked her moisture up between the cleft of her buttocks until her dark-pink, silky crease glistened invitingly in front of him. Scorching nerve wires pulled at his crotch.

Darting his eyes up to hers, he saw her waiting expectantly, her face awash with anticipation.

He held up the slender item he'd taken from her side table. 'Ready?'

'Uh-huh,' she gasped. 'Now honey.'

Larry opened up the case. He took out the silvery string of tiny, spherical love beads. Easing her buttocks further apart, very slowly, very gently, he inserted the beaded string into Marissa's moistened bottom.

'Oh yes,' she gulped, thrilled. 'Yes! More, baby, more.'

Carefully he pushed the stringed beads inside, charges of searing excitement careering round his body as he watched her tiny, rose-petal orifice swallow each of the beads.

Swaying her hips slightly, Marissa turned her head forward. As she stretched her neck back, her thick blonde tresses tumbled wantonly round her shoulders, with one ribboned strap still hanging down one arm.

Moving her hand underneath her, she began to rub lightly on her clitoral bud. She fluttered her fingers across herself, breathing rapidly, eyes half shut.

As Larry watched avidly, he began to tug on the silvery string.

Marissa moaned with delight. 'Oh baby,' she purred deliriously.

Larry tugged again, lost in his own heavy fog of arousal. One silver bead popped out, shiny and warm.

Marissa squealed blissfully. Her fingers swirled faster between her legs.

'Again,' she gasped.

Another silver bead appeared, and then another and another. Larry felt fevered with excitement.

Marissa parted her kneeling legs wider. She arched her back. Larry could see the sheen of sweat glaze her golden skin and the glimmering beaded string dangle tantalisingly from in between her upraised buttocks. Her fingers moved rapidly between her legs as she sighed and moaned, now and again twisting round to look at him.

As her eyes locked on to his, she parted her lips in suspended wonder. Her fingers were suddenly still and she pressed the heel of her hand against her sex, her body muscles tense. Simultaneously Larry tugged on the string. The final silver bead began to appear in her rosy anus. Larry held it in place to prolong her climax, gazing raptly at her spectacular, bucking body, listening to her gasps of pure ecstasy.

When it was over, Larry pulled the final bead clear. He stretched out alongside her, his abdomen taut and aflame.

Marissa had collapsed on to her stomach, looking joyfully weak. Once again, she had pressed her cheek into the pillow. He nudged her exposed cheek with his nose, loving the damp, flushed feel of her skin.

'Amazing,' she murmured.

'Yeah,' he agreed croakily, pulling her crumpled night-dress up to her shoulders and over her head. 'I need you now, babe. Right now!'

Marissa nodded eagerly. Flipping over on to her back, she pulled Larry towards her. He knelt between her thighs, pushing them wide apart, flat against the bed.

Reaching into her exposed sex, he fondled her slippery labia. Her clitoral bud clung to his fingers, swollen and succulent, heightening his already blistering excitement. Holding his penis in his hand, he guided it inside her, the warm folds of her body making him cry out with absolute joy.

'It's OK, honey,' Marissa soothed. 'Oh yes, that's it, more, baby, more.' Tugging him down, his chest on to hers, she wrapped her arms around him, hugging him tightly. As he reached full penetration, she spread her legs wider, still keeping them flat against the mattress.

'Larry,' she sighed blissfully, rubbing her mons urgently up against his pubic bone.

He made love to her quickly, desperately, his mind a blur of intense dizzy arousal. Pinning her arms back to the pillow, he pumped his hips furiously, hazily aware of her climaxing beneath him. His own orgasm shook him to the core, hurling his body into a reeling, spinning mass of sensation.

Dropping his head by hers on the pillow, he felt her twining her fingers gently in his hair.

'It gets better and better,' she whispered eventually.

Larry moved over on to his back. 'You're not wrong,' he gasped.

Their fingers clasped lightly together as they each lay spreadeagled on their backs, sprawling out with exhausted abandon across the huge mattress, letting their sweat dry and their pulses slow.

Larry felt his eyelids grow heavy. The combination of no sleep last night and immense sexual satisfaction was proving a heavy force to counter. He let himself drift towards sleep.

Beside him, Marissa stirred. Rolling over into the crook of his arm, she tapped lightly on his chest. 'Hey, lover,' she said softly.

Larry prized his eyes open. 'Mmm?'

She kissed his damp chest and, faking a strong

Southern belle accent, said 'Don't think you can come here and have your way with me, sir – and then fall asleep.'

Larry smiled sleepily. 'I do apologise, ma'am. I just cannot stay awake one moment longer.'

Marissa bit him playfully. 'Men!' she said. 'You'all just want your way with me.'

'A very nice way it is too.' he mumbled, closing his heavy eyelids again.

Suddenly, downstairs, the door chimes sounded. Larry and Marissa both started, Larry instantly awake. He had an awful vision of Kelly somehow having appeared at the door. Impossible! he told himself. Anyway, Kelly wouldn't ring the chimes – she had her key.

All the same, he sat bolt upright. 'Expecting anyone?'

Marissa shook her head, biting her lower lip nervously. She eased herself up on her elbows.

The door chimes sounded again.

They listened hard. Rosita's lilting, melodic voice was now faintly audible downstairs.

Marissa began to relax. A chuckle bubbled out. She pulled Larry back down to her, rubbing her hand soothingly along his collarbone. 'Relax baby. I know who it'll be. Rosita's fiancé.'

Larry arched a thick, tapering eyebrow. 'Fiancé?'

Marissa's chuckle got louder. 'Yeah. She only went and got herself engaged – to a handyman! He's always turning up. She pretends she has these little jobs for him, I'm sure she breaks things on purpose so she can have him come over and fix them.'

Larry rubbed his knuckles over his eyes, visibly relieved. 'Oh,' he said simply. 'Listen honey, I've got to get some sleep. Getting strung out over someone at the door!' He shrugged helplessly.

'Sure,' said Marissa. She threw one of her legs over his

and snuggled up close. 'Sleep now. And then tell me all about everything.'

Larry, sound asleep, didn't answer.

At the law offices in town, Justine printed off the final letter. She placed it triumphantly along with a pile of others into Larry's signature book, ready for signing when he returned to the office tomorrow. Leaning back in her chair, she straightened a leather blotter on her desk, aligning it with the leather signature book. She was now completely up to date with correspondence, phone calls and filing. There wasn't any work to do until Larry came back in.

She pushed her glasses needlessly back up on her nose. It was a nervous habit she had been trying in vain to break. Standing up, she walked to the doorway, glancing furtively up and down the corridor. Then, satisfied she had a moment to herself, she stalked into Larry's office, being sure to close the door behind her.

She headed straight for the wall safe. Larry didn't know it, but she had watched him open up the safe before now and memorised the combination. Easy peasy, she chuckled as the safe door dutifully clicked open. A quick flick through turned up the file that she wanted. There, printed in the corner of the grey-blue cover, was the name – CASIGELLI J.

Pulling it swiftly from the safe, she relocked the door and returned to her office. Her heart was beating furiously. First thing yesterday morning, when Larry had phoned in to say he would be out of the office until Wednesday, she had looked for Johnny Casigelli's file, mindful of the conversation she had overheard between Larry and Marissa on Saturday night. She knew Larry had acted for Johnny Casigelli in the past, although, oddly enough, Larry had done all that work personally – she had never even seen the file.

Her curiosity had been further piqued when she couldn't find the file in the filing system. She had searched high and low. Finally, she had hit upon the only place it could be – Larry's wall safe.

Now, setting the file out in front of her, she hesitated. She stared for a moment at the cover. Her thumb and forefinger lingered in the bottom right-hand corner. If Larry ever found out she was doing this, she would be fired on the spot. Still, something was going on, thought Justine and, with the instinct of the lawyer that she hoped one day to be, she wanted to find out exactly what.

Without further delay, she flicked open the file. Resting her elbows on the desk, she pushed back her glasses and began to read.

An hour later, she was well versed in Johnny Casigelli's assets, both the expertly hidden assets and those actually declared to the tax office. Wow, she thought, how could one man be so incredibly rich? Closing the file, she blew out a deep breath of dissatisfaction. She was hardly much wiser – other than finding out that Johnny Casigelli had a compound near, of all places, Ensenada.

Justine stared off at nothing. She had to train herself to think like a lawyer. Think, girl. Think. When Larry had been talking to Marissa on Saturday night, he had definitely linked Kelly Aslett with Johnny Casigelli. And Larry had definitely mentioned Ensenada. Did that mean Kelly was having an affair with Johnny and they were meeting in Ensenada? Justine shook her head to herself. Nah, Kelly was in Paris. Wasn't she?

A sudden bleep of the phone startled her. Composing herself, she picked up. 'Justine,' she said calmly.

It was Annie, the receptionist. 'Someone here for you.'

'Who is it?' asked Justine, hurriedly stuffing the file in a drawer.

Annie giggled. 'Someone you'll want to see.'

'A name?'

'Er . . .' The receiver crackled as Annie evidently sought to get a name.

Justine tutted impatiently to herself. What was wrong with Annie? She wasn't usually so disorganised.

'Annie?'

'Yes,' replied Annie dreamily. 'Just one moment –'

'Oh never mind,' sighed Justine. 'Just tell the "someone" to come on through.'

Marissa woke up feeling lively and sexy. She lifted her head off Larry's fuzzy chest to gaze up at him. His breathing had the soft, even regularity of somebody in a deep, sound sleep. Poor lamb's exhausted, she thought, nuzzling his shoulder. Wanting to make love again, she wondered briefly whether to rouse him but he looked so sleepy she decided against it.

She lay back, eyes wide open, thinking. She was feeling very contented. Kelly was out of the house – for good. Soon it would all be hers. She smiled a smug little smile.

In fact, she mused, she felt so content that she wanted to do something wicked.

Suddenly, remembering the door chimes earlier, she chuckled mischievously. She flung her legs over the side of the bed, then padded over to her dressing table. There, she dusted a covering of rose-pink blusher over her nipples, making them sparkle deliciously in the centre of each perfect breast. She twisted round to her full-length mirror to look at herself. She was gorgeous, she knew it. Her golden body glowed, her face was still flushed from sex and sleep, and her eyes danced merrily at the thought of causing trouble. Running her fingers through her tangled, blonde tresses, she chuckled again, then turned and silently made her way downstairs.

As she went down, her toes curling round each carpeted stair-edge, excitement licked at the base of her belly. She pictured the look on Rosita's face when she walked into the kitchen and paraded herself naked in front of Raoul. The mere thought of it made her woozy.

Gliding into the kitchen, she saw Rosita seated at the table. Marissa smiled at Rosita's shocked expression.

'Morning, Rosita,' she smirked. She feigned a sleepy yawn and stretched with exaggerated slowness, showing off her magnificent body.

Rosita gazed at her.

'Lordy,' giggled Marissa, glancing down at herself. 'I'm so tired I forgot to put on my robe. Silly me!'

Rosita cast her eyes quickly down to the table. 'Good morning, Mrs Aslett,' she mumbled uncomfortably.

Marissa brushed past her and wandered in a leisurely way round the room, wondering which little task Rosita had made up for Raoul today. She couldn't wait to flaunt herself in front of him. It would be such fun! She slowly walked the length of the kitchen, round the L-shaped corner, and back again. Raoul wasn't there.

'Raoul not here today?' she asked casually.

Rosita didn't look up. 'No, Mrs Aslett.'

Damn! cursed Marissa, stomping back towards Rosita. He must have left already. She stared in annoyance at Rosita. Rosita's tactfully bowed head was irritating her. She wanted to show herself off, dammit! 'Rosita?' she snapped.

'Yes, Mrs Aslett?'

'Set a brunch tray for me and Larry,' she ordered rudely. 'And bring it up to us.'

Rosita nodded.

That's better, thought Marissa, considerably cheered all of a sudden. She'd make sure Rosita caught her and Larry *in flagrante* – that should add a little extra something to what she had in mind for her and Larry.

Hurrying out of the door, she stopped dead. Lord, she'd almost forgotten! 'By the way, Rosita. Kelly went back to Paris yesterday.'

For the first time, Rosita looked up, her dark eyes confused. 'But yesterday, she drive off with Mr Barris?'

'Yes,' replied Marissa, not missing a beat. 'That's right. Larry drove her to the airport.'

Before Rosita could ask her anything more, Marissa drifted out towards the stairway. 'Bring up the tray in a half hour or so,' she called back, flutters of excitement darting through her thighs – that should give her time to wake Larry up well and truly! 'Oh, and don't bother to knock,' she added as though it were a helpful afterthought.

Marissa tripped happily up the stairs, busily thinking up something ultra steamy for Rosita to walk in on. She had thoroughly enjoyed the little sexual display she'd witnessed between Rosita and Raoul a while back. It was about time she repaid the compliment.

Larry, however, was already wide awake when she re-entered the bedroom. Lying on his back with his fingers laced behind his head, he clearly had ideas of his own.

'Get that pretty lil' butt over here,' he grinned.

She walked over, crawling slowly up the bed then kneeling astride his waist. His hands moved to her torso, stroking the toned flesh of her navel.

'I just told Rosita that Kelly went back to Paris,' she whispered.

'Atta-girl,' said Larry. His hands travelled up to her breasts, squeezing lightly. She dipped her eyes to watch, thrusting back her shoulders. He began to graze her nipples with the flats of his hands. Round and round, making them stiffen, and she arched her back even more, pushing her chest out as far as she could, relishing the teasing on her tips.

Thrills shot through her chest. She closed her eyes and

tipped back her head, her hair spilling down her back. Gently, as Larry continued to toy with her breasts, she began to press herself down on Larry's stomach, desperate for pressure between her legs.

'Here, honey,' he said, hoiking her up suddenly under her arms and lifting her towards him. Eagerly, Marissa got herself in position, knowing exactly what he wanted. Placing her hands on the headrest, she knelt over his face. Swiftly, he lowered her down far enough so that he could reach and then began to nibble at her sex. She gripped the headrest in delight, feeling him lick and suck at her roseflesh and tug lightly on her fluttering clitoris. As he moved to her vulva, stimulating wonderfully, she dropped down a little further, brushing her glistening clitoral nub rhythmically back and forth against his nose.

Warmth and pleasure swept through her abdomen and she clutched wildly at the headrest, systematically lifting herself off Larry's wonderful mouth in an effort to forestall her orgasm. With a sudden groan, Larry heaved her backwards so that she was lying on her back with her head over the end of the bed. Preventing her sliding totally to the floor, Larry gripped tightly on to her thighs, kneeling in between. She opened her legs as wide as she could, squealing with delight when she felt his massive organ prod at her, steadily pushing inside.

Holding her round her waist, Larry thrust easily up and down, now and again moving his thumb to her clitoris and teasing gently.

Marissa was in heaven, her penetrated body stretched gloriously, moving in tempo with the force of Larry's thrusts.

She was dizzy. With her head off the end of the bed, everything was upside down and, all the while, the sharp darts of pleasure were razoring through her abdomen.

Suddenly, very close to climax, she noticed the upside down door open and Rosita wander in with the brunch tray. She watched muzzily as Rosita froze in the doorway and gasped out loud with shock. Marissa smiled feverishly. Then she gasped out loud herself as a shuddering, spinning orgasm took hold.

15

Kelly ate her breakfast quickly, then showered and dressed and made her way downstairs in search of Larry. Yesterday, despite Larry's assurances, she had learnt nothing at all about the way the business was run and if today was going to be a repeat performance then she couldn't see the point in staying on. And that's exactly what she was going to tell Larry!

She couldn't find him anywhere however. She wandered from sumptuous room to sumptuous room. No Larry. Come to think of it, no Johnny. The only people she did see were the endless dark-suited, dark-shaded men around the place – and Conchita, who seemed to dart from one room to another the moment she saw Kelly. Kelly, running after her only to find her and then have her dart to another room, felt as if she was involved in a game of tag. Eventually, she doubled back and surprised Conchita crouching behind the doorway of a large reception room.

'Conchita!' she gasped, out of breath. 'Why do you keep running away from me like that?'

Conchita wheeled round, startled. She could obviously see there was no escape this time – Kelly was just inches from her. 'I not know anything, señorita,' she whispered.

Kelly looked at her curiously. 'Know anything about what, Conchita?'

'Not know anything, señorita,' Conchita said again. She grasped the doorframe nervously.

Kelly could see the anxiety on the maid's face. Something was definitely wrong here, but she didn't want to upset Conchita any further. 'Conchita,' she explained softly. 'I was only looking for my friend, Larry. That's all. I'm sorry if I startled you.'

'I not know anything, señorita.' Conchita looked up uneasily, her hands still gripping the timber doorframe.

Kelly could see she would get nothing from Conchita. Not that she was sure what there was to get. She held up both her hands in mock surrender.

'OK, OK,' she said softly.

Conchita blinked furiously. 'Please, señorita. I have the work to do.'

Kelly nodded mutely, watching Conchita scuttle off through the doorway. She banged her fist against the side of her thigh in frustration. Where was Larry? She wanted to get the hell out of this nut-house – and fast.

She sank down on to a nearby brocade couch and closed her eyes wearily. This was the last thing she needed at this time. On top of her heartache over Luc, she was now stuck in a house with men who ignored her and a maid who treated her like she was some sort of mad axe-woman.

'Kelly?'

Kelly opened her eyes, surprised at the sound of the low, masculine voice. Standing over on the far side of the room, his hand resting lightly on a heavy, Spanish dresser was Johnny.

It was Kelly's turn to blink furiously. Something about the man made her incredibly nervous. 'Yes?' she said timidly.

Johnny gazed at her silently for a long, long time. Kelly shrank under that intense black stare. He's not ignoring me now, she suddenly thought hysterically.

'Kelly,' he repeated eventually. 'Kelly, I have to tell you that Larry is gone.' His voice was so soft, so compelling, so intoxicating, that Kelly involuntarily felt a tingle in her spine.

'Gone?' Kelly laughed abruptly. 'Is he coming back?' she joked.

Johnny didn't laugh with her. 'No,' he said quietly.

She stared into Johnny's face, the laughter dying on her lips. She tried to speak but found that her throat was tight.

He walked slowly towards her and sat down next to her, resting one highly polished shoe across the opposite knee. 'Larry left here last night.'

Kelly struggled to find her voice. 'But why?' she asked. 'Was there an emergency? An accident? Why didn't he wake me?'

Johnny brushed casually at his trousered thighs. His crested ring caught her eye for some reason. 'There wasn't any emergency,' he said simply.

She shook her head foggily, not understanding this at all. 'But, if he's already gone, how will I get home?'

Johnny curved his mouth into a slow, sinister, very white smile. 'I will make sure you get away safely.'

She tried to smile back but her lips felt frozen. Something about the way he was looking at her was making her insides curdle.

Reaching to her face, Johnny traced his finger lightly under the line of her jaw. She recoiled slightly, shocked at the intimacy of his touch. Was this the same man who'd all but ignored her yesterday?

'I will make sure you get away safely,' he repeated. 'Just as soon as I am ready.'

'W-what?' Kelly tried another smile, sure he must be joking.

Johnny said again, 'Just as soon as I am ready.'

'I-I don't understand.' She blinked nervously.

He drew his hand away from her face. Placing his arm on the armrest of the couch, he cocked his head and rested his temple against his extended forefinger. He glanced sideways at her. 'No reason why you should –

understand, that is.' He chuckled softly. 'But I can assure you, just as soon as you have pleased me, I will take you home.'

Kelly swallowed hard. Pleased him? Whatever did he mean? This wasn't happening, couldn't be happening! She stared dumbstruck at the scar on his handsome profile, trying vainly to get hold of her situation.

Johnny turned full face. His hand went back to her jawline, cupping her chin tenderly. 'Don't worry, Kelly.' His voice was gentle, like a lover's almost. 'It'll be very easy to please me.'

'W-what –' She stopped as she struggled with the waver in her voice. In spite of his hand still clasping her chin, she took a lungful of air and forced herself to speak. 'What is it that I have to do?'

Letting go of her, Johnny gazed into her eyes intently. 'It's very simple, Kelly. I have some papers I would like you to sign.'

'Papers? What sort of papers?'

'Come,' he said. 'I'll show you.'

He stood up sharply and began to walk. Kelly, confused and startled, stared after him. She was trying desperately to think, a part of her still telling herself this was all a practical joke. Larry would turn up any moment now. 'Got you!' he'd say, grinning his boyish grin.

Johnny halted mid-stride. 'Come, Kelly,' he said, beckoning her to follow. He started to walk off again.

Standing up on very shaky legs, Kelly then walked after him.

He led her to a large study. It was light and airy, much like the rest of the house. Three large sash windows gave out over the grounds. A huge, dark-oak desk dominated the room.

Johnny strode directly to the desk, then took out a burgundy attaché case from a deep side drawer. Balancing the slimline case on the desktop, he then clicked the lid open and lifted out a set of papers. He set them out on the desk.

'The papers,' he said quietly. Pulling out the chair from under the desk, he gestured at Kelly to sit down.

Dazed and bewildered, she did so.

Johnny placed a pen in front of her. 'Sign the papers, Kelly.' His soft, authoritative tone raised the hair on the back of her neck. Despite the warmth of the weather, she shivered. She looked down at the papers. Black, typed lettering leapt out from the pages, blurring into nonsense before it reached her eyes. She blinked twice, forcing herself to concentrate. Slowly, she started to read.

As she moved down the pages, digesting the contents, just about managing to decipher the complicated legalese, her nervousness began to recede. A heavy flush of anger rose up inside her. When she'd finished, she glanced towards Johnny, amber eyes ablaze. 'The hell I'll sign these,' she snarled.

Johnny coolly lent his buttocks against the edge of the desk and folded his arms across his chest. 'Sign the papers, Kelly,' he said patiently.

Jerking her chair back, Kelly stood up. She tossed her hair back defiantly. Suddenly everything was clear as crystal. This whole trip was just a ruse, a twisted ploy to kidnap her, to get her to sign some ludicrous documents, to get her to waive her rights to her father's business, to her father's home. Suddenly, she felt very weak. How could Larry do this to her? She trusted him. Her father had trusted him. For God's sake, her father had been like a father to him!

She leant against the desk edge to steady herself. 'I will not sign these papers.'

Johnny, a bored expression on his face, flicked his eyes to her then flicked them towards the window. He stared out at the view. 'Sign them,' he ordered quietly.

'No way!'

'Sign them.'

'No!'

'Kelly, if you know what's good for you, sign them!'

She looked at him evenly, her fury vanquishing the nervousness she'd felt before. 'Give my father's house to that bitch, Marissa, and his business to that double-crossing louse, Larry?' She shook her head vehemently. 'Never!'

Johnny sighed. He shrugged his shoulders with an air of indifference. 'You can sign now or you can sign later, but one thing I can tell you Kelly – you *will* sign. And, when you do, I will take you home.'

She scoffed. 'If I sign them, I won't have a home.'

'Larry has found you an apartment and, as you can see, you will still receive a considerable part of your inheritance. It is primarily the business and the property in Santa Ana we are concerned with. Now, sign!'

She didn't answer. By way of response, she picked up the papers and slowly tore them through the centre.

Johnny laughed softly and shrugged again. 'I have copies,' he smiled.

Shaking her head lightly, trying to come to terms with Larry's betrayal and make some sense of it all, she whispered, 'Why are you doing this? I don't even know you. Why would you do this for them?'

He walked behind her and ran the back of his finger-nail lightly down her bare upper arm. 'That,' he murmured, 'is none of your business.'

She could feel his breath fall gently on her shoulder. For some unfathomable reason, she felt a sexual tug in her groin.

'Now,' continued Johnny smoothly. 'I will get another set of papers out and, you will sign them.'

'Go to hell!' she said tightly.

In a flash, his fingers moved from her arm to her neck.

He stroked her throat menacingly. 'Never, never, say that to me again,' he murmured. 'Do you understand?'

Kelly swallowed hard, nervous again but still defiant. 'I won't sign,' she whispered.

'Yes you will!' Johnny took his fingers from her throat. 'I guarantee that.'

He walked off out of the room, pausing in the doorway and twisting his head round to her. 'You know why? Because if you ever want to leave here, Kelly, you'll sign!'

Striding out on to the patio, Johnny crooked his finger at a dark-suited man leaning against a wall.

'Giuseppe,' he said to his chief bodyguard. 'The girl has the run of the place, OK. But watch her closely. If she tries to leave the compound, tell me.'

Giuseppe nodded. 'Yeah boss. But if she leaves, she won't last long in the desert!'

Johnny's dark eyes flashed angrily. He raised his hand and softly smacked Giuseppe's cheek. 'If she tries to leave, tell me,' he repeated, a quiet menace in his voice. 'And remember, Giuseppe, anything happens to the girl I didn't order to happen, I hold you responsible! You got that?'

Giuseppe's Adam's apple bobbed nervously. 'Sure thing, boss,' he mumbled. 'I got that. No problem.'

Johnny nodded and waved his bodyguard away. He sank down in a patio chair. Suddenly, he laughed out loud. Damn, he liked the girl's spirit! And her loyalty to her father. That was one thing Johnny admired above all else – loyalty.

He tapped his front teeth pensively. By God, that wasn't all he liked. He thought of those defiant amber eyes, that smooth, flawless skin, the lush, golden body. Larry had warned him she was a beauty but, Jesus, he hadn't felt this turned on since … since … he couldn't remember when. Maybe this little favour he was doing Larry wasn't going to be quite as irksome as he'd thought.

Still laughing softly, he sprang from the chair and wandered into the house.

In the study, Kelly sat back down at the desk. She swiped viciously at the torn papers on the desktop, sending them flying. Anger was still bubbling furiously inside her. How could they do this to her, how could Larry do this to her? Did they honestly think they would get away with it?

Pressing her fingertips wearily to her eyes, she tried to assess her situation. She was somewhere in the middle of nowhere in Mexico. Where? Where was she? Oh, why didn't she take more notice? Why did she go and fall asleep on the way here?

Glancing helplessly out of one of the windows, she caught sight of Johnny out on the patio. He was talking to one of his men. Kelly looked at Johnny's tall, athletic physique with absolute loathing. Businessman! she whispered to herself. Some businessman! Oh yes, it had all clicked into place now. This compound, the men stationed all over the place, Johnny's masterful demeanour. Johnny wasn't any businessman, any client ... Johnny was a member of the Mob. Saying it out loud to herself suddenly made it seem more scary. Flames of anxiety leapt up in her stomach.

It didn't matter, she told herself, swallowing the bitter taste of rising alarm. Whoever he was, she still wouldn't sign those stupid papers.

Watching closely, she saw that Johnny was softly slapping the other man's face. The man looked cowed, intimidated. Johnny must be awfully powerful, she mused. Why wasn't she as frightened as she should be? He was sitting back in a chair now, laughing softly to himself. Bastard! she cursed, but even as she said it, a

sharp sensation stabbed between her legs. She was hor-
rified, shocked into panic as fluttery warmth spread to
her thighs and stomach. This was a level of arousal she
had only ever felt for one man. For Luc.

She held her head despairingly in her hands. What
the hell is wrong with me? she thought, squeezing
together her thighs in an effort to still the sensation.
First, she'd fallen for Luc who'd let her down desperately
– and now? Now she was being turned on by a Mafiosi,
not only that – a Mafiosi holding her prisoner. Some
judgement she had!

Suddenly she jumped up. She had to do something.
She couldn't just sit around and be made a fool of.

A telephone! That was it, she needed a telephone. If
she found a phone, she could call the police. She cast her
eyes frantically round the room. No phone.

Darting from the study, she ran through the house,
urgently scanning the rooms for a phone. Not a phone in
sight. She ran up the wide-stepped staircase, pushing
open door after door along the landings. Still nothing.
Finally, she reached an imposing double-fronted doorway. Twisting the golden knob, she thanked the Lord it
was open, and entered. Her startled eyes met equally
startled eyes.

Conchita rushed towards her. 'Sēnorita. What you do
here? This Señor Casigelli's bedroom.'

Kelly, breathless from running, felt the sweat prickle
in her armpits.

'Conchita, please,' she pleaded urgently. 'I need a
telephone!'

Conchita stood still. Her kind brown eyes darted from
Kelly to the open doorway. She appeared to take stock of
the situation, then quickly she took Kelly's hand and
tugged her into the room. Pressing her forefinger to her
lips in a hushing gesture, she pointed to a white telephone on a mahogany side table next to the bed.

'Thank you,' gasped Kelly, racing to the phone.

Conchita smiled nervously. 'Hurry, señorita,' she whispered, before fleeing the room.

Kelly lifted the receiver. She stalled for a moment, unsure of the emergency number in Mexico. Her trembling fingers tried 911. She could feel the sweat running in rivulets down her body now, pooling between the cups of her bra. 'Come on, come on,' she urged. 'Answer, dammit, answer.' Suddenly she realised the dial tone was off. She touched the cut-off button and frantically pressed redial. Her knuckles whitened as she grasped the receiver, willing an operator to pick up.

Without warning, a strong hand closed over hers. Kelly stared down at it, dazed. The white-gold crested band dug painfully into her fingers.

'The phones in the house are all coded, sweetheart.'

Kelly looked up dully. Johnny, staring down at her, deliberately unfurled her clasped fingers from around the receiver and replaced the receiver in its cradle.

'No use even trying,' he said softly, stroking her cheek with his bended forefinger.

The air seemed to stagnate in her windpipe. Her shoulders sagged wearily.

'Now,' Johnny went on, almost whispering. 'I knew you'd come to my bedroom – my bed – sooner or later. I'm so glad it's sooner!'

Kelly stared at him open mouthed. He was stroking the tender skin beneath her earlobe now, looking down at her in a knowing way. 'Come to your bedroom!' she cried out, suddenly energised. 'I, I'd rather rot in hell for all eternity than climb into your bed!'

Johnny chuckled. Then abruptly he walked off. Without looking back, he said loudly to her, 'Sweetheart, don't you know it yet? You *are* in hell! And you will – as you put it – rot here for all eternity ... unless you sign those papers.'

Left sitting forlornly on the side of her captor's bed, Kelly stifled a rising sob. She mustn't cry, she told herself weakly. She wouldn't give them all that satisfaction. She mustn't give in. There had to be a way out of there.

Flopping heavily back against the mattress, she began to acknowledge how her body had just betrayed her. As Johnny had stood over her, his fingers soothing her cheek, his black eyes laughing down at her, she had known in that instant that he wanted her. Even before he had said what he'd said, she had known.

But as she lay there, on his bed, in his palatial bedroom, a prisoner in his luxurious home, she couldn't push away the brutal, awful fact. The fact that she had wanted him back.

Johnny strode purposefully along the landing, away from his bedroom. His face was set. He was furious with himself, furious that he'd let her see how much he wanted her.

At the top of the stairway, he stopped. Roughly, he cracked his knuckles against the flat of his other hand, his jaw tensed. No one got the upper hand with Johnny Casigelli. Ever!

Wheeling around abruptly, he then walked back to his bedroom, pushing violently against the doorjambs of the double-fronted doors. The doors swung inwards, leaving him framed in the open doorway.

She was half-sitting, half-lying on his bed. Her clear, amber eyes flicked fearlessly towards him.

He walked silently over to her, then heaved her fully on the bed. The skirt of her dress rode up her thighs. In the split-second that he stood there, Johnny drank in the expanse of exposed satin skin. As he eased himself down on top of her, pinning her forearms to her sides, he couldn't fail to notice she hadn't uttered a single sound. No cry. No protestation.

Straight away he kissed her, parting her full, unlipsticked mouth urgently with his own. He darted his tongue on to hers, savouring the fresh taste of her mouth, licking each of her smooth, even teeth.

His cock pressed painfully against her pubic bone as he lay across her. Pulling back swiftly, he stood up. She looked flushed, glowing, glorious – with her eyes heavy, her lips rosied from his kiss, her chest fluttering rapidly. She still hadn't made a sound or uttered a word.

'Sign the papers, Kelly,' he muttered, before walking away yet again.

Out on the landing, he felt much better. Despite the painful, unsatisfied throbbing in his groin, he felt much, much better. This favour for Larry was actually becoming quite interesting. One thing Johnny had now decided for sure – before he left Mexico to tend to his businesses, he would have Kelly Aslett as his own.

16

Marissa was on a natural high. Everything was working out beautifully. Kelly was out of her life, at last. She didn't reckon on her stepdaughter holding out for very long before signing those papers – not with a man like Johnny involved. Kelly would sign for sure within a couple of days. Then Larry would have the business. She would have the house. Beautiful!

She raised herself up, resting back on her elbows, and shaded her eyes to the shoreline. Blue, blue water stretched endlessly before her. High, riding waves broke on to the sand, spewing white froth up the beach. Larry emerged from the water, short dark hair slicked back, brown, water-soaked muscles gleaming as he moved. He flopped down next to her on the towel.

'Water's fantastic,' he gasped, water droplets pearling all over his torso. 'You should come in!'

Marissa shuddered. Swimming off Laguna made her scared – the waves further on crashing up against rocks, the deep, oily swell of the water. 'No thanks,' she muttered.

Larry laughed. 'For such a wicked babe, you're a real scaredy-cat, you know that!'

'Yeah?'

'Yeah,' grinned Larry, rolling on to his back and creasing his eyes against the sun. He rested his forearm casually across his eyelids.

Reaching out to the side, Marissa scooped up a handful of sand. She leant over to Larry and, fisting her hand, released it slowly into his navel.

'Ouch!' Larry flashed open his eyes, flinching as the boiling sand hit his water-cooled skin.

'You like it when I'm wicked though, don't you?' cooed Marissa, brushing the sand off his stomach. She casually pushed her hand down into his damp bathing shorts. 'After all, if we weren't both as wicked as each other, Kelly wouldn't be locked away in Mexico right now, would she?'

Larry grunted.

Unperturbed, Marissa closed her hand round his soft penis. Her simple touch was enough. She could feel it grow and harden in her hand. With a soft chuckle, she started to pull his shorts down his thighs.

Larry jerked up his head, looking round the beach in alarm. 'What are you doing?'

'What do you think, lover?' she purred, glancing round at the scattering of people in the cove. She left his shorts at mid-thigh. Then easing up on to her side, she gazed down at his awakening crotch. His soft dark coils of hair were dusted with sand from her fingers. Moving her hand beneath his penis, she gently cupped his swelling testes, softly squeezing from one to the other.

'Marissa, baby,' Larry groaned. 'We'll get arrested.'

'Now what they going to arrest us for?' She slid her finger up his buttock cleft, loving the feel of pushing between his tight, muscled cheeks. 'Making love?' She rubbed lightly up and down.

'Ah!' gasped Larry, involuntarily pressing down on her finger. 'Ah Jeez, stop that!'

Marissa giggled. 'Go on, tell me. What will they arrest us for, lawyer-man?'

Larry gritted his teeth. 'Lewd conduct in a public place for starters,' he gulped.

She leant over to blow in his ear. 'Lewd conduct, huh? So long as it isn't conspiracy to kidnap!'

Larry caught her wrist as she began to work her hand

up and down his hardened shaft. 'Might as well be, baby. If I'm arrested for lewd conduct, my reputation as a lawyer goes down the toilet.'

'Now who's a scaredy-cat?' she cooed. But all the same, she withdrew her hand and whisked his shorts back up. The summery cotton fabric bulged obscenely. Quickly, Larry flipped over on to his stomach.

Marissa stared at him. She wasn't through teasing him yet, she decided. Pouting prettily, she ran her finger lightly over the top of her chest. Larry was watching her. Moving systematically down, she graduated to the edging of her bikini top, tracing the periphery of the bright-yellow bra-cup, then, locking eyes with him, she pushed her finger down.

She gasped lightly as she touched her nipple, parting her glossed lips mostly for Larry's benefit. Back and forth across her nipple she moved her fingerpad, stretching the bikini top until her breast was all but showing.

However reluctantly, Larry's eyes were glued to her.

She took her finger out of her top and dragged it down her gleaming stomach. Then, slowly, she moved it up to her mouth, running the tip of her tongue along it, tasting sun cream and a hint of Larry's more intimate taste. Her eyes flickered longingly at him as she licked, then, still slowly, she eased her finger down into the front of her bikini bottoms.

Without meaning to, she sighed at the slippery feel of herself. Scarcely moving, she began to tickle her clitoris.

Larry, still lying on his stomach, was breathing heavily. A sheen of sweat varnished his upper lip. Glancing up round the beach again, he moistened his lips with his tongue. Marissa allowed herself a coy smile, revelling in his discomfort. His eyes shot back towards her.

'Larry,' she breathed. 'This feels so good.'

He closed his eyes and took a deep breath.

'So good, Larry. Don't you want to know how good –'

'Right!' Larry said tightly. He sprang up sharply, wrenching the towel out from under her. Marissa rolled clumsily on to the sand. Holding the towel in front of his jutting groin, he grabbed her by the wrist, hauling her to her feet. Without another word, he dragged her off up the beach, seemingly mindless of the interested stares from the other people on the beach.

Marissa, half-running, half-stumbling behind him, gazed at his long smooth back. The leaden warmth of arousal hung in her belly. She smiled feverishly at the thought of what was coming: a frantic, energetic session of lovemaking. Lifting her feet high off the hot sand after each stride, as if she was running on burning coals, she clung tightly to his hand.

He pulled her round a facing of stone, making her climb over jagged, slanting rocks. Jerking her under a rocky overhang, Marissa suddenly felt the softness of sand beneath her feet again. A tiny plip-plop of water sounded, dropping from the stony overhang into a sea-green rockpool. She looked around her. Perfect, she thought, heart beating frantically as she surveyed the inlet.

Larry was still pulling her around – roughly. She loved it. His face was suffused with rampant arousal. He was glancing wildly round at the rocks. Evidently finding nothing that suited his intentions, he sank to his knees directly in the centre of the sandy inlet, dragging Marissa down with him.

Holding her wrist painfully, he said softly, 'I told you "no", didn't I?'

'Yes baby,' she whispered.

He wagged his forefinger. 'Bad, bad girl.'

'Yes Larry.'

'Come here,' he grinned, patting his lap.

Slowly, Marissa leant forward over his lap. He always knew what she wanted, she thought with pleasure. She could feel his penis digging into the curve of her stomach and she wriggled lightly against it.

Larry looked around him, checking they were alone. A sheer rockface rose up behind him, smaller jagged rocks enclosed them on either side. Yards in front of him was the endless, dark blue expanse of the ocean. He took a long, deep breath. His balls ached with arousal and Marissa's soft wriggling stomach on his cock was more hell than heaven. Gazing down at her glorious body, lying over his lap, he felt sweat break out on his torso.

Swiftly, he pulled down her bikini bottoms, leaving them just below her buttock cheeks like a tight yellow band.

'You know,' he said, tracing his finger down her spine, stopping short of her bared bottom. 'You were very bad back there, and –' he paused to smile as he thought of that morning, '– you were very, very bad having Rosita walk in on us this morning.'

Marissa chuckled, wriggling restlessly.

Larry bunched his hand round the banded bikini bottoms, inching them down her legs, down her ankles, then throwing them off so that they splatted against the rocks. 'We know what happens to bad girls,' he whispered, 'don't we?'

She was waiting for him, her firm, trim bottom rounded. He brought his hand down hard, slapping her dead in the centre of her buttocks. The golden flesh quivered and a flushed imprint immediately appeared.

She squealed delightedly, arching her buttocks upwards.

'You like that, babe?' he asked softly.

Twisting her head up to him, eyes shining, she nodded.

He spanked her again. And then again and again.

Her sighs grew so loud that Larry was fearful somebody would hear and climb over. After all, the peopled beach was just seconds away. He glanced nervously towards the rocks. Nothing. He relaxed – as much as he could relax with excitement tearing at his belly.

Marissa lay fully stretched out across him, wearing only the top of her bikini. Her naked thighs and buttocks were raised up by his knees. She would drive any man to distraction thought Larry, raking his eyes over her beautiful body.

Next time he spanked her, he kept his hand on her bottom.

'Spread your legs, honey,' he said, voice tight with excitement.

As she moved to comply, parting her stretched-out legs, he could feel the muscles in her bottom flex and he massaged her smooth flesh harshly, making her gasp with pleasure. Moving from her bottom, he began to stroke the insides of her long, tanned thighs, progressing slowly upwards. When he slid his hand to her sex, both he and Marissa groaned.

'Yeah, oh yeah, sugar,' she gasped.

'Mmm, baby, you're so ready!' He dropped a kiss in the hollow of her back whilst burrowing his fingers in her sex. Delicately he stroked her outer lips, then her slippery inner lips, then the nubby flesh of her clitoris, then he inched underneath her and rubbed his fingers through the trim little coils on her mons.

Marissa stretched her arms out in front of her. 'Oh, I'm ready,' she moaned. 'Hurry, baby!'

Larry, enduring the riot of arousal in his groin, bent his head round. He looked from the satin cheeks of Marissa's slightly upraised bottom down to her stretched-out sex. Her sex was smooth, shining with wetness, plump with excitement. Her clitoral bud poked like a rigid tongue from the deep-pink labia and the tight, dark slit of her vulva made him weak with longing.

Marissa was lying very still, head craned round to watch him. She liked him to look at her, he knew that. And boy, did he like to look!

Taking his time, he carefully eased his middle finger into her. Buried up to the knuckle, he softly began to stimulate. His movements made her buttock cheeks quiver.

Marissa was no longer still. She waggled her hips across his lap, writhing as he vibrated his finger inside her. She parted her legs even wider and raised herself up on her forearms so that her hips pressed down against him.

Larry was pouring with sweat. The spectacular sight of her writhing body had him dizzy. He drew out his finger, silvery, glistening and tangy from her body's juices. Marissa, flushed with arousal, scrabbled off his lap and tugged at his shorts, wresting them off him. His cock, purpled, vibrant, enormous, sprang free.

Quickly, she turned around to face the sea, knelt down and rested her locked arms between her parted knees. Larry knelt upright behind her. Hoiking up her bottom, he eased apart her buttock cheeks, and pushed up inside her, her moist vulva dilating sweetly for his entry.

She felt like heaven. Tight and long and enclosing him entirely. He paused for a moment, entranced in limbo, and then began to thrust gently. Placing the flats of his hands round on to her stomach, he stroked inside her with slow, glorious movements, all the while massaging her buttocks with his hips.

As he moved faster, she bobbed energetically in front of him, panting more with passion than exertion. 'Love me hard, Larry,' she moaned quietly. 'Oh yes, love me, baby. Love me.'

Her softly spoken words inflamed him. He punched his hips against her, relishing the sharp, scorching tugs deep inside his abdomen. Blindly, he moved his hands from her stomach, groping for her breasts. Finding them covered, he wrenched at her bikini top, pushing it up roughly. Her freed breasts spilled into his hands and he squeezed them hungrily, thrusting up frenziedly inside her, hitting her bottom with his hips.

Marissa started to lean forward, gasping, moaning. Suddenly, she turned her face round to him. 'Let's hope a cop –' she paused for breath '– doesn't decide to swim by!'

'Uh?' he gasped, mind numbed, body almost out of control.

With a sly, passion-glazed smile, Marissa rushed her words out. 'This baby, this is just about as lewd conduct as you can get!'

With a great slap of his hips against her, riding on a huge arc of pleasure, Larry climaxed.

Marissa, flopping forwards, arching her back, pushing her bottom back against him, sighed with ecstasy and came too.

17

Kelly lay back on the white quilted coverlet, her mind blank. She rubbed her lips together dreamily, running her hands absently down her body.

Suddenly reality kicked in. He had kissed her. *He* had kissed her!

She shot to her feet, wiping her lips furiously with the back of her hand. How dare he kiss her. How dare he hold her prisoner here. How dare he try and force her to give away her father's home, her father's business. How dare he kiss her?

Fury made her blood boil, her temperature soar.

She rushed from the room and ran along the galleried landing. Looking down the wide-stepped staircase, she could see him strolling casually across the lobby. Sonofabitch looked like he hadn't a care in the world.

Gripping the oak balustrade, she tore down the stairs.

'H-how dare you!' she spluttered.

Johnny, heading for a doorway, stopped. He turned around slowly.

'Sorry?' A jet eyebrow was raised quizzically.

Kelly stood still for a moment, endeavouring to compose herself. Taking a deep breath, she walked towards him. 'I said, how dare you!'

'How dare I what?' A smile played upon his lips. She could see he was taunting her.

'How dare you keep me here, make me sign things!' She snapped back a ribbon of hair. 'How dare you kiss me!'

Johnny tapped his front teeth nonchalantly, his black eyes dancing with mirth. 'Oh,' was all he said.

Kelly, hand on hip, was incensed. 'Oh? Is that all, oh?'

'Er, let me see now.' He ran his eyes slowly down her body before taking a step towards her. He played his eyes between each of hers, then dipped them to her lips. 'Did you enjoy it?' he asked quietly.

Kelly dropped her jaw, incredulous. She tried not to stare at his smiling mouth, tried not to think of how it had felt upon hers.

'Did you enjoy it, Kelly?' he repeated.

She looked up at him, focusing on his scar, the one imperfection in that dashing, swarthy face. Fighting a rising weakness, she forced herself to speak. 'No!'

His smile grew wider. 'Oh, so you wouldn't like me to kiss you again?'

'No!'

He shrugged his shoulders carelessly. 'Pity, I rather enjoyed it.'

Turning on his heel, he made to walk through the doorway.

She stood rooted to the spot, anger ripping through her. 'Well, *I* didn't! You repulse me,' she cried after him. 'I hate you. You're an animal!'

She bit her lip as he whirled around and grabbed her wrist.

'I can be an animal,' he purred. 'Perhaps you'd like that. Would you like that, Kelly?'

He gazed mercilessly down at her. He was so close, just inches away. Sensations rocked her, slicing, arcing, through her body. Sensations of what? Fury, desire, arousal? What? She trembled as she stared at his white, white teeth.

Without thinking, she drew back her free hand and slapped his face with all her strength.

A muscle flickered in his smooth cheek. His own hand went to his cheek, rubbing it softly. His eyes were so black, his gaze so intense, that her knees buckled with fear.

'Well, well,' he murmured, still rubbing his cheek. 'It seems we're a little feisty, sweetheart.'

He was still holding her wrist. He was so strong. And so angry. Suddenly, incredibly, she wanted to collapse against him.

Slowly dipping his head, he moved his lips to hers. She parted her mouth in readiness.

He was so near she could feel his angry breath.

When he licked along her bottom lip, she heard herself sigh.

'Sign the papers,' he whispered as he kissed the corners of her mouth. And with that he released her and stalked off abruptly.

By nightfall, Kelly was exhausted. After Johnny had left her standing alone like an idiot in the lobby, she'd run up to her room – and stayed there.

Later, Conchita, eyes cast sorrowfully downwards, had brought her up a tray of supper. But Kelly had no appetite. The food lay untouched in the corner of the room.

Despite the exhaustion, she simply couldn't sleep. Her mind raced frenziedly. Images of Larry and Marissa danced inside her head. She could see them laughing together, celebrating together, clinking glasses gleefully and making love, while she languished here. She pictured Luc, miles away, at work in his studio, handsome face a mask of absorption. Probably forgotten her already, she thought bitterly, cursing at the pangs of emptiness that griped in her stomach. She thought of Johnny, somewhere in this house, playing with her as a cat played with a defenceless mouse, toying with her, confusing her.

Suddenly, white glaring light filled the darkened front window of her bedroom.

Startled, she slipped back the bedcovers and wandered over. Tentatively, she peeked out. She had to blink furiously against the brightness but, as her eyes adjusted, her breath caught in her throat. She stood up straight in her darkened room, smiling shakily. Suddenly, there was a chance. Suddenly, there was hope!

For there on the lawn, like a giant, shiny black beetle, was the helicopter and there, climbing inside, dashing in dinner suit and tie, was Johnny.

Kelly watched transfixed as the door slammed shut and the chopper took off, rising up into the navy, star-speckled sky, then flying off into oblivion. All that remained of its presence were the ripples in the lit-up pool.

She nibbled on her lower lip pensively. If Johnny had gone off somewhere, that meant that she was alone in the house – or as good as. Conchita scuttled away from her like a frightened rabbit each time she saw her and the mysterious dark-shaded men seemed remarkably relaxed around her, only watching her closely when she ventured out into the grounds. Certainly they didn't seem to watch her in the house.

Leaving her room, she crept barefoot along the dark landing, feeling her way by the oak-galleried railings.

Before long, she recognised the distinctive outline of the double-fronted doorway to Johnny's bedroom. Now or never, she thought, twisting the doorknob. Damn – the door stayed shut. She twisted again. It was locked, well and truly!

Backing silently away, she racked her brains. Where had she seen another phone? Where, where? Feeling her way back along the landing, she then made her way downstairs, padding quietly through the darkness, thinking all the while. She pictured each room that she knew, trying frantically to visualise the layout, trying to place another phone. In a flash it came to her. She darted through the rooms, stopping only when she reached a small, low-ceilinged reception room just off the patio. Sure enough, on a table in the corner, like a silent offering from above, there was a phone.

Slumping down to her knees, she delicately lifted the receiver, holding it gingerly between her thumb and forefinger. Here goes, she muttered, haphazardly punching in numbers. She'd decode the damn thing if it took her all night!

Half an hour later, she still hadn't made a connection.

Wearily trying another combination, she could sense the glimmer of hope fading. Sapped of adrenal energy, it was almost a relief when the lightswitch flicked on and bathed her in a golden glow.

When the man – tall, dark-suited – walked over and held out his hand, she took it, letting him lift her to her feet. He stooped to the abandoned receiver, replacing it without a word.

He guided her back to her room, nudging her firmly inside. As he took the key from the inside lock, he said quietly, 'Goodnight, miss.'

Kelly ignored him. She climbed into bed, totally drained, and didn't even flinch when she heard him outside her door, loudly turning the key.

When she heard a lock scrape, she wasn't sure she wasn't dreaming.

When she sensed a shadow over her, she thought that perhaps she wasn't.

When she felt a finger tracing lightly down her arm, and a crested ring glinted in the darkness, she knew for sure that she wasn't.

'Kelly?' His voice, as ever, was low.

She feigned sleep, in spite of the gooseflesh rising on her arms at his touch.

'Kelly?' he whispered again. 'I hear you played with the phones while I was gone. What did I say about playing with the phones?'

She didn't answer. Breathe deep, she told herself, concentrate, one, two, one, two.

He stood over her silently. His finger moved up to her face, delicately stroking her cheek.

She held her breath, heart rapping against her ribcage. She could smell cologne, a wonderful, fresh smell. She tried not to think of it, tried desperately not to inhale, tried not to think, not to think ... oh Lord, was he going to come into her bed?

She felt his lips on her temple and that rush of sensation swooped down her body again. Damn him. Damn him for having this hold on her. Mustering all her willpower, she still feigned sleep.

'Honey-sweet,' he was murmuring, close to her ear. 'Sign those papers for me tomorrow. Sign them, sweetheart. Give Bonnie and Clyde what they want.' He drew away silently.

When he'd gone, she flicked her eyes wide open and stared up into the darkness. Her hands moved restlessly down her body, touching where she yearned for his shameful touch.

18

Next day, Kelly woke very early. She slipped her white cotton robe around her, and tentatively twisted the door-knob, unsure whether she was locked in again. She wasn't. Strange as it seemed, Johnny hadn't relocked the door.

Wandering barefoot through the silent rooms, she emptied her mind of everything. Of the papers, of Larry and Marissa, even of Luc. Instead, the presence of Johnny somewhere in the mansion seemed to pull relentlessly at her subconscious. She couldn't put it aside, his dark, handsome face, his taunting smile, his cruelty. She could scarcely bear to admit what it was she was feeling, that her sexual feelings for him seemed to be transcending, or worse, heightened by, her fear and loathing of him.

Approaching the rear of the house, she began to hear sounds – thuds, heaving rasping breaths, male laughter. Intrigued, she walked towards the noise and, before too long, found herself standing on a small galleried ledge at the top of an iron spiral staircase. The ledge looked down into a large oak-panelled room. The room was empty of furniture. A huge, rich, crimson rug carpeted the floor.

Two men were down in the room, both dressed entirely in black. Their faces were covered in grey meshed masks and each held a long silver sabre in his hand.

Fascinated, Kelly leant forward. She watched their stances as they fenced, hand on hip, muscular legs bent. As they circled and dipped and jabbed at each other with glinting, razor-sharp blades, she noticed with amazement that they wore no body protection. For some reason that made her feel heady, excited. A rush of energy tore through her, the display of raw masculine competition below unleashing an almost primitive instinct inside her. She felt weak, absurdly feminine – and decidedly turned on.

Suddenly they stopped, throwing down the swords simultaneously. Before she had time to move away, they had pulled down their masks. Johnny's face shone with perspiration as he laughingly shook hands with his opponent and when he swung his face upwards, locking eyes with her, her own body broke instantly into a feverish sweat.

They stared silently at one another, she on the ledge, he down below.

The other man stooped to pick up the swords. Johnny nodded dismissively at him and the man walked away. Then there was just the two of them.

He beckoned her down.

It didn't enter her head that she had a choice, that she could have withdrawn from the ledge and run back to her room. Drawn inexorably down, she followed the winding stairs carefully. The iron steps were cool on her bare feet and, as she stepped on to the warm, deep carpet, she inadvertently smiled at the luxury. She took a few steps away from the staircase, then stood silently, waiting.

He strode towards her, legs encased in tight, black trousers, casting aside his mask as he walked. Words were redundant as he curled his fingers round the belt of her robe and yanked her to him.

She dipped her eyes in bewitched fascination as he undid the tie in the belt and opened up her robe. Deliberately he eased it off her shoulders, pushing it from her body.

'Beautiful,' he breathed, black eyes dropping slowly down.

She felt the tips of her breasts swell with inner heat as his gaze washed over her. Her belly started to flutter.

What am I doing? she thought wildly as she stood naked before him. She loved Luc, so how could she stand before this man and revel in his scrutiny? But revel in it she was doing and, as she gazed up at the swarthy face and saw the pure sexual hunger in his eyes, her own hunger thrashed whip-like in her stomach. She was lost. Powerless and lost.

He grasped each of her wrists, pinning them almost painfully behind her back. Then he jerked her toward him, crushing her breasts against his chest. She felt his hard, lean muscles through the thin sweater that he wore; she caught the faint scent of fresh male sweat from his fencing exercise. Her head reeled and she couldn't stop herself pushing against him, standing up on tiptoe to press her lower abdomen into the rock-like bulge in his groin.

Johnny wrenched her arms further down behind her, forcing her shoulders and head back. The blood was pounding in her veins, and her breasts heaved perspiring and swollen against him. As he held her hands tight and immovable, his wrists pressed into the smooth, soft skin of her naked buttocks. That small touch seemed so intimate, so forbidden, that for one brief moment, amidst the heady fug of arousal, she wriggled to free herself. He held her firm.

'Going somewhere, sweetheart?' he whispered, letting his eyes fall deliberately to the tops of her breasts. He leant away from her slightly until the full swell of her breasts was exposed, no longer pushed and hidden against his chest. His black-eyed gaze was locked upon them and, despite herself, Kelly dipped her eyes also. Her nipples were deep pink, rosied and beautiful. As Johnny looked upon them, not touching at all, Kelly was ashamed to see them stiffen, and all the while his wrists pressed hard into her buttocks. She wriggled again, her breasts jiggling. Johnny smiled. Excitement passed like a power charge through her chest. She wriggled ineffectually once more, scarcely able to breathe with excitement.

'You're hurting me,' she gasped without conviction.

'We can't have that,' he murmured. Still smiling, he eased his grip on her hands but simultaneously jerked her into him again. Before she knew it, his lips were on hers, kissing her roughly, deeply, his mouth parting hers – his mouth so strong and forceful, her mouth responding whilst her head railed against it.

As he kissed her, he pressed his groin harder against her and she lifted herself again, reciprocating, able to feel his trousered cock mould perfectly into the wet softness of her sex. She parted her legs fractionally and he pressed a little further and sharp, scalding darts of pleasure rushed through her mound. A dislocated moan of delight seemed to ring in her head, then she realised with horror that it was she who had uttered it. Johnny pulled back, chuckling lightly.

'I guess you're enjoying yourself, honey,' he murmured.

She stared, passion glazed, into his cruel, laughing face. 'I despise you!' she hissed.

'Sure you do,' he laughed.

'I, I hate you,' she stammered, aware of his hard, jutting penis still pressed magnificently into her.

'Sure you do,' he said against her ear. Still holding her arms fast with one hand, he brought his other hand in front and swiftly cupped her pubic mound. Kelly gasped with a mixture of thrill and mortification.

'That's a sure sign of hate,' he whispered, rubbing his fingers slowly through her rich, heavy dew.

Kelly swallowed hard, shocked, shamed, but weak with lust. He was staring intently at her face as his hand roamed skilfully between her legs. He stroked her clitoris lightly. Thrills erupted in her sex and another low moan began to rise up. Kelly bit her lip to stop it, but not before Johnny had heard it.

'Another sign of hate,' he said softly.

She gazed up at his taunting, dashing face. Lord, she detested him. But God, how she wanted him.

He was still stroking her sex. This Mafiosi. This kidnapper. He was fondling her so confidently, such expertise, such intimacy. She was going to climax right there in front of him, because of him, and there wasn't a single thing she could do about it.

Suddenly he withdrew his hand, then released his other hand from behind her. She stood before him, shakily pre-orgasmic.

'Lie down for me, Kelly,' he ordered.

'I –!' she wavered.

'I won't tell you again,' he said.

She couldn't help but obey, slipping to her knees then lying down, her arms at her sides.

He stood over her, tall, lean and menacing. 'Good girl,' he murmured and, for the first time, Kelly detected the strained thickness of arousal in his voice.

He knelt to the side of her, locking his arms over her shoulders, and brushing her lips dryly with his. As he traced the curve of her throat with his tongue, a shiver ran the length of her spine and she flashed open her eyes, gazing at his smooth jet hair as his head dipped towards her chest. She slid her eyes over his kneeling, black-clothed body, aching to see him naked.

His lips closed around her left nipple, sucking, flicking lightly with the tip of his tongue. Excruciating darts of pleasure spread through her breast. He moved to her other nipple.

233

She stifled a sigh and he lifted up his head. He stared down at her darkened, stiffened nipples.

'Just how I like them,' he purred, dropping his head again and tugging gently at them with his lips. The delicate but relentless pulling on her tips made her moan out loud. She pushed her chest up to his mouth, wildly reaching for his body. Her fingers found the bottom of his black sweater. As she twisted it up his torso, she caught a glimpse of gleaming, olive-hued muscle and a scorching stab of desire tore at her.

Calmly, Johnny removed her hands from his clothing and spread her arms wide to her sides.

'You first, sweetheart,' he whispered.

She looked up at him, dazed, impassioned, confused.

He smiled, seeming to like her confusion. 'Ladies first – always,' he muttered as he circled her nipple with his tongue. 'Then, honey –' He left his words hanging as his strong hands roamed her body. Touching her every-where. From her breasts to her shoulders, from her stomach to her thighs. Every inch of her prickled with arousal. Her arms were spread so wide to the sides that her breasts felt stretched and utterly exposed. The position intensified the sharpness in her nipples and she jerked her chest back up to him.

But he was moving down to her stomach now, then licking the sides of her torso. He traced his tongue down the outsides of her thighs so slowly, so divinely, that her sex began to throb.

Putting his hands on the insides of her thighs, he nudged gently. 'Open up for me, sweetheart,' he murmured.

Hastily she parted her legs.

'Oh no, honey. I mean, really open up for me.'

Jerking her head up excitedly, Kelly spread her legs as wide as she could, as wide as her arms were spread. She gasped with excitement at herself, at her total abandonment. She was helpless. It all felt so glorious, lying naked and vulnerable in the centre of this massive room, arms outstretched and legs spread wide. Completely at his mercy.

He gazed at her smooth, glistening sex. 'Mmm,' he said softly. He licked his finger then ran it along the stretched tendons of her groin. Kelly's leg muscles twitched involuntarily and she moaned with frustration at his teasing touch. He patted her tiny nest of tawny hair before sliding his finger with such skill along the peach-skin of her sex lips that she wanted to clasp her legs together and trap him there, making him touch and stimulate for ever.

She luxuriated in the familiar band of sensation tightening around her groin and buttocks as he circled her stiffening clitoris, circling and circling until it stood out like a swollen red ridge from her sex.

'Just how I like that too,' he breathed.

His voice, his amatory, blatantly sexual words, inflamed her. Her head felt muzzy with excitement now. When he sank his finger into her, she clenched her internal muscles, gripping him tightly. He chuckled softly, easing out then inside her, again and again, until she dropped her head back to the floor.

'I can't stand it,' she moaned.

'Yes, sweetheart, you can stand it.' He pulled out his finger and traced a glistening line up her satiny stomach, then rubbed at her nipples with her own clear moisture. Round and round he rubbed until her tiny, hard tips were shiny with dew.

He slid his drying fingers back into her sex and she writhed mindlessly on the carpet, so very near to a climax. Oh God, she thought, it was too much, the sonofabitch! Too good!

Suddenly he pushed her legs up high into the air and began to stimulate the mouth of her bottom. Wetting that tiny orifice now with her juices, he dabbed so lightly, so wonderfully, that she felt the sensations begin.

As her orgasm started to build, he moved back to her nipples, then down to her sex, then back to her anus, each time stopping just short of her climax. Her whole body tingled with sexual energy, every nerve, every sense screaming out for release, until finally, spectacularly, she came, her back arching, her knees bending almost to her shoulders, her mind swimming in tide after rapturous tide. So strong was her orgasm, she had to sob with relief. She let her legs collapse to the carpet, aware through her hazy stupor of Johnny looking on.

'Do you want more, Kelly?' he murmured.

Nodding deliriously, she watched him kneel between her open legs. He pulled his sweater over his head. A hard, gleaming torso was bared. He moved to the waist of his trousers. She saw the taut, olive skin of his navel. He was going to take her. Oh God, he was going to take her. And, oh God, she couldn't wait!

But a discreet cough from a nearby doorway instantly had Johnny on his feet.

'Er, excuse, boss.' Giuseppe was hovering outside the door.

Johnny walked over. He was curt when he spoke. 'What's up, Giuseppe?'

'I, er, I think we may have a problem, boss.'

'What kind of a problem?'

'We appear to have a visitor, boss.'

Johnny raised a smooth jet eyebrow. 'A visitor?'

'Yeah, some Frenchman, boss.'

Kelly's eyes widened in alarm and she muffled an involuntary cry. Johnny glanced toward her, curiously. She was suddenly aware of herself, of her naked openness. Belatedly she tried to cover herself, sitting up and curling her knees into her chest. Johnny seemed amused by her futile attempt at modesty. He turned back to Giuseppe. 'A Frenchman, you say?'

'Yeah boss. Says he's here for the girl. Says he knows she's here.'

'That a fact?' Johnny looked toward Kelly again. 'Okay, Giuseppe,' he muttered dismissively, still staring at Kelly. He wandered casually back to her, held out his hand, and hauled her to her feet.

'Well, well, sweetheart. What do you know!' He brushed her ear with his lips as he spoke. 'Looks like we got ourselves another houseguest. How about that!'

Kelly was speechless. Johnny hadn't taken his eyes from her. His gleaming chest was heaving, whether from sexual excitement or from anger, she couldn't tell.

'A Frenchman, hey,' said Johnny softly. 'Well, since this Frenchman's come all this way, seems the least I should do is go meet him, don't you think?'

He stepped to the side for his sweater and deftly pulled it over his head. Then he took a pace back to Kelly, raking his eyes down her body. Kelly shivered slightly, the sweat of sex and passion drying now. She eyed her crumpled robe with longing, but didn't dare move to retrieve it. Johnny played his fingers in the hollow of her damp back, rubbing lightly on her spine.

'Go back to your room now, sweetheart.' There was no mistaking the command in his voice. He walked off quickly, pausing in the doorway to look back at her. 'But I will see you later, Kelly,' he promised, his meaning unequivocal.

Kelly's stomach lurched with excitement and she hated herself for it.

19

Luc! Who else could it be but Luc?

Once Johnny had left, Kelly threw on her robe and hurried back to her room. She showered swiftly. Her body felt gloriously, disgustingly vibrant thanks to her time with Johnny, but her mind was racing, filled with jangled, convoluted thoughts.

How could it be Luc? Luc was in Paris. How would he know she was here? Even if he'd turned up at home, Larry and Marissa weren't exactly going to tell him where she was — considering the circumstances. And besides, he wouldn't even give up a few days' work for her so he would hardly be likely to travel thousands of miles to see her. Would he?

Holding her face up to the shower, she let the water drum hypnotically against her skin. She thought of Luc, here in this house.

As she stepped on to the showermat, it struck her belatedly, with the force of a thunderbolt. Luc here in this house! Johnny Casigelli's house! Johnny was so dangerous, so powerful — and he had gone off to 'meet' Luc. Whatever was he going to do to him?

Oh God, oh help! she shrieked wildly to herself, cursing her own stupidity. Lust for Johnny had dulled her senses. She should have held Johnny back, begged him not to hurt Luc, clung to him, anything! She tore out of her bathroom, dragging on jeans over shower-damp thighs and grabbing for a top.

Flicking back her hair, she raced barefoot to the door.

She twisted the doorknob. Oh no, please no. She twisted it again. Nothing happened. The door was locked.

Slumping against the doorpanels, tears began to sting her eyes. The tight hand of panic clutched at her throat. Visions of Luc, battered and bleeding, played horrifically in her mind.

She kicked viciously at the door, succeeding only in bruising her foot. Helpless, she limped to the bed and lay down. As she lay there, locked in, anxiety ridden, and truly, truly scared, she suddenly remembered what day it was. It was Wednesday, her birthday. Happy birthday, Kelly, she murmured ironically.

Ten minutes earlier, Johnny had stood outside Kelly's door. He'd turned the key silently and pulled it from the keyhole.

Leaning against the outer doorframe, he tapped the key pensively on the palm of his hand and thought about his new visitor. A Frenchman. Didn't Larry tell him Kelly had been living in France until recently? And, judging from the look of shock on her face when Giuseppe had mentioned a Frenchman, she had a damn good idea who it would be.

Shit! he cursed, pushing off from the doorframe. Then he dropped Kelly's doorkey into his shirtpocket and began to walk off. Better go and see to this Frenchman, he decided.

Larry straightened his navy silk tie in the mirror then wandered over to the bed.

'Geddup!' he said fondly, smacking Marissa smartly on the rump.

'Ouch!' she murmured, shifting position.

Minutes later she opened her eyes and sat up. 'Where you going, baby?' she asked, voice husky with sleep.

Larry lifted an eyebrow. 'Work, remember?'

Mouthing a silent 'Oh yeah', Marissa leant back into the feather pillows, letting the sheet drop casually to her waist. Larry's eyes flicked automatically to her smooth, bare breasts. 'Do you have to go right now, sugar?' she asked innocently.

With a great deal of trouble, Larry pulled his eyes away. 'Yeah. It's Wednesday. I told Justine I'd be back in today. Better stick with that!'

'OK,' Marissa murmured. She closed her eyes dreamily. Suddenly she shot them open. 'Wednesday! You said it's Wednesday, Larry – Kelly's birthday!'

'Yeah,' Larry grunted.

'If it weren't for you, she'd be throwing me out on my tush today. You're my lifesaver, my sweet baby, baby!'

Grinning, Larry walked over and kissed the tip of her perfect, button nose. 'You wouldn't exactly be penniless. David made sure of that.'

'I know it, Larry, but –'

'I know, babe,' he murmured, hushing her with his mouth. 'Don't mention it. You're welcome!'

'Did you call Johnny already?' She tilted her ravishing, make-up free face to him. Her voice rang with excitement. 'Did you call? Is it all done? Did Kelly sign?'

'I didn't call yet.' Larry sat down on the edge of the bed. He chucked her affectionately under the chin. 'But since you're so cute, I'll do it now.' Reaching for the white phone on the nightstand, he plucked up the receiver and cradled it in the crook of his neck.

She rested her head back, smiling. As Larry punched in numbers, she rubbed her fingers affectionately in the coarse, short hair on the back of his neck, gazing dreamily up at the ceiling, soon to be her ceiling. All hers!

Just as Larry started to speak into the mouthpiece, Marissa heard a tapping at the door. She slipped out of bed and, gathering the Egyptian-cotton sheet round her like a sari, stepped out on to the landing. Rosita was there and began to talk. Marissa shushed her, nudging her to the top of the stairs.

'Hush, Rosita,' she whispered. 'Larry's making an important call. What is it?'

'There is a lady here, Mrs Aslett.'

'Lady, what lady?' Marissa peered down the stairway.

'She say her name is Verity.'

Ah Verity, thought Marissa, tummy flipping deliciously.

Nodding OK to Rosita, she tripped merrily down the stairs, clutching the sheet around her.

Verity was waiting in the living room. She looked as beautiful as ever, Marissa noted gleefully, dark hair shimmering to her shoulders, violet eyes shining. 'Hey Verity,' she said softly.

'Marissa!' replied Verity. She kissed Marissa's cheek, letting her hand linger on Marissa's one exposed shoulder. 'I just stopped by to give you this.' She held her hand out flat. A small, diamond earring sparkled in the centre of her palm.

'My earring!' exclaimed Marissa, delighted. 'I wondered where I'd put it.'

'You left it in bed.' Verity chuckled mischievously. 'At Johnny's houseparty, remember?'

'How could I forget!' They giggled simultaneously as they each recalled the energetic, sex-charged night they had spent there.

'Actually,' began Marissa, 'Larry's here right now. In the bedroom as a matter of fact. You don't have to be someplace, do you?'

Verity's smile grew wider. 'No,' she said softly.

'That's good,' murmured Marissa. She played the tip of her tongue slowly along her top lip. 'What d'you think? Shall we go give Larry a treat?'

'Uh-mmm,' purred Verity, eyes wickedly alight. 'A treat *à trois*?'

'Uh-huh,' giggled Marissa.

'Wonderful,' breathed Verity.

Clasping her hand, Marissa led her from the room and up the staircase, pausing when they reached her bedroom door. Pressing her ear to the door, she listened. No talking. Larry had obviously finished with his call.

Verity was lightly stroking her back. Sighing softly at the lovely sensations, Marissa turned to her. Without speaking, she reached for the zip of Verity's green A-line mini-dress. Verity twisted round obligingly and Marissa began to pull the long zip down. Verity's dress parted to the base of her spine, showing the smooth, olive-hued centre panel of her back. She eased her dress forward off her shoulders, then quickly stepped out.

Biting her lip with excitement, Marissa undid the front clasp of Verity's black lacy bra. Her small breasts jiggled free. Giggling softly, Marissa brushed the backs of her hands over them.

'Mmm,' sighed Verity, lowering her silky eyelashes to watch.

Rising excitement making her hurry, Marissa nudged the bra off before curling her fingers into the edges of Verity's black panties and inching them slowly down her long, svelte legs.

'There!' she gasped as Verity stood magnificently naked before her. She noticed Verity's cheekbones were coloured with a natural flush and her own heart was knocking violently at her ribs.

'Stay here a moment,' she whispered, clutching the sheet round her and making to enter the bedroom. 'I want to surprise Larry.'

Larry was in the far corner of the room, pulling on his suit jacket. He flashed his cute grin at her as she entered. He looked wonderfully handsome and businesslike in the dark navy suit and tie and the crisp white shirt. His skin gleamed healthily from yesterday's afternoon on the beach. Marissa's stomach rolled with lust and arousal.

'Johnny was tied up,' Larry was saying. 'I'll catch him when I get to the office.'

'OK.' Marissa was flippant. 'But you might want to be busy yourself a while first!'

'Uh?' Larry looked at her curiously.

Quickly she stepped to the door and tugged Verity into the room. Larry did a comic double-take as Verity stood, naked and glorious, next to Marissa.

'Hey Larry,' breathed Verity. 'How are you?'

Larry grinned. He looked from Verity to Marissa back to Verity, then jerked his chin up lightheartedly as he asked, 'What you two up to?'

'Nuthin',' pouted Marissa teasingly.

She let the sheet slip from her body, kicking it away with a golden bare foot. 'Sit down, baby,' she said softly to him. 'We're going to give you a treat!'

He wavered for one whole second before he threw up his hands in mock surrender. Taking off his jacket again, he loosened his tie and undid his shirt collar then sank back into a nearby chair. He rested his hands on his widespread knees. 'Go right ahead, girls,' he grinned.

Exchanging glittering glances with Verity, Marissa paraded over to her dressing table, aware that both Larry and Verity were watching her closely. She picked up an exquisite glass perfume bottle, filled with expensive scented oil, and wandered jauntily back to Verity.

'How about I give you a little massage, Verity?' she asked gaily.

Verity's eyes shone brighter. 'That'd be nice.'

Pouring some oil into her hand, Marissa began to smooth it into Verity's toned navel, round and round across the tiny curve of her tummy. Her skin started to shine like lustrous silk. Marissa moved downwards, stroking the fronts of Verity's slender thighs. As her hand roamed lazily over Verity's flesh, Marissa glanced toward Larry. He was, she noted happily, utterly transfixed.

Sucking in her lower lip with excitement, she liberally poured more oil into her hand, the perfumed scent assaulting her nose like a powerful aphrodisiac. Gently, she eased her hand between Verity's thighs, massaging the lubricant sumptuously over Verity's small dark triangle of hair, then down into the intimate, peach-skinned furrow below. Verity stepped apart slightly, enabling Marissa to run her oiled fingerpad along the seam of her smooth sex. The soft, slippery feel of Verity, the sounds of her delighted sighs, the fact that Larry was enthralled – all of it thrilled Marissa to the bone. Dizzily, she whirled Verity around and began to rub the oil over her pert bottom.

Verity gasped. 'Harder, honey,' she urged, curving her back.

Marissa rubbed harder, soon panting from the exertion, her hand sliding hungrily over Verity's greased, scented skin. Suddenly, out of breath, she had to pause. She stood still for a moment, shaky and aroused, then gulped with relief when she felt Verity move to stand behind her. Reaching beneath her arms, Verity was cupping her high, full breasts. With exaggerated movements designed mainly for Larry's benefit, Marissa presumed, Verity began to squeeze and caress. Marissa sighed at the wonderful, light, squeezing touches, automatically pushing out her chest, pressing her breasts into Verity's hands.

Verity was teasing her nipples now, touching lightly with her fingerpads, twisting and pinching, making them rigid. Little corresponding tugs rose deliciously in Marissa's stomach and groin and she pressed herself back against Verity. She was in heaven – Verity's downy mons tickled and titillated her bottom whilst her elegant, expert hands fondled her breasts. Inflamed, Marissa pushed her bottom back.

'Mmm, yes,' she breathed, as Verity brushed her fur lightly against her. Marissa gazed at Larry feverishly. His rapt expression made her tingle all over.

Half-turning, flushed and excited, she nudged Verity round and began to sway her nipples over Verity's. She watched in fascination as Verity's smooth brown tips tightened, stiffening to small, milk-chocolate pearls. Verity moaned softly, placing her forefingers beneath her small breasts and brushing her nipples back against Marissa's.

Verity was moving down now, tracing her tongue down the centre of Marissa's torso. She sank to her knees in front of Marissa. Placing her hands on the insides of each of Marissa's golden thighs, she tilted her head upwards and began to tongue Marissa's sex – delicately, precisely, daintily. Larry could see her glide the tip of her tongue slowly back and forth along Marissa's peeking clitoris, flicking her lust-glazed violet eyes wickedly towards him as she did so.

Marissa was sighing, moaning with pleasure, toying with her own swollen breasts as Verity stimulated below. She tilted back her head, her buttery tresses hanging down her back, and swayed her naked hips gently, back and forth, back and forth, until she reached a climax, straightening her body and legs, nudging her sex against Verity's lovely mouth.

Her release was fleeting. But it was too much for Larry.

He sprang to his feet, shedding his clothes within seconds. A couple of strides and he was upon them, grasping them round their minuscule waists, hauling them caveman-like across the room. They giggled delightedly as he threw them simultaneously face down on to the bed.

Grabbing two of the pillows, he pushed one beneath Marissa's stomach, one beneath Verity's. Two beautiful, firm bottoms were lifted up on the mattress in front of him.

They twisted their necks round to him, faces flushed and eager.

Kneeling behind Marissa, he yanked her legs apart and immediately pushed himself inside her.

'Oh yes, honey,' she moaned, arching her back ecstatically. He guided himself fully inside, as her body swallowed him, her warm, wet opening tight at the base of his penis.

As he began to move, he leant across to Verity, pushing her long legs wide apart. Already, her oiled sex glistened invitingly and as he slid his fingers hungrily around, her lips swelled to roseate plumpness. When he rubbed lightly on her clitoris, now reddened and erect, she moaned as earnestly as Marissa, wriggling her hips excitedly against his teasing fingers.

As he pushed inside Marissa, nudging the bulb of her bottom with his hips, her golden body lifted deliciously; as he stimulated Verity, she rocked her gleaming torso in rhythm. Both had their heads half twisted round to him, their hair tumbling messily across their shoulders, spilling over on to the bed. They were still sighing softly, lips slightly parted, eyes fully closed in obvious rapture.

Definitely paradise! he gasped to himself, keeping his own eyes well and truly open.

20

Johnny was in a very black mood.

He ordered Giuseppe to stay with the damn Frenchman while he made his way back up to Kelly. Glancing at his watch, he saw that almost two hours had passed since he'd locked Kelly in her room. Which meant that it was over two hours since he and Kelly were alone in the fencing room. The thought of how she'd lain there, open like a beautiful flower, her naked body feverish with passion, sent a searing slice of desire through his abdomen. He almost doubled over with the force of it. Goddammit, he wanted that girl!

He tripped swiftly up the staircase, thoughts of Kelly swimming through his mind. As he strode along the landing and his thoughts turned back to the Frenchman, his set jaw tensed even further. Passing by a mahogany display table, he swiped viciously at a Chinese ornamental vase. The vase went flying, crashing against the wall, shattering into a multitude of pieces. Priceless blue-veined Ming scattered the carpet.

'Shit!' he cursed as a shard of the porcelain stuck in the back of his hand. Quickly, he wrenched it out, putting his hand to his mouth as the blood began to spot at the cut.

Temper fouler than ever, he marched on to Kelly's room, unlocked the door and entered.

She was lying curled up on the bed, her silky brown hair strewn across the pillows. Her back was towards him and he saw the way the jeans she was wearing moulded the contours of her perfect behind. He pictured parting those beautiful cheeks, seeing her twist her head back at him as he did so, her eyes an intoxicating mix of passion and loathing. He'd take her right now, he decided. He'd have her every way he damn well pleased!

She turned towards him.

Oh Christ! he thought as he saw the tears. Streaking her golden cheeks they were, falling like silvery dew-drops. Johnny didn't go for tears, not one bit. Tears turned him off entirely. He rubbed, with growing impatience, at his left temple.

Suddenly, Kelly squealed in horror. She looked from his hand to his eyes, despair rising in her face. 'You ... you brute!' she screamed, pointing to the bloodied cut on the back of his hand. 'What did you do to him? Oh God, whatever did you do?'

Johnny frowned at the torn skin on his knuckles from his run-in with the vase.

Kelly was looking decidedly ill, her face blanched, her voice shaking. 'Why hurt him?' she was whispering over and over. 'Why?'

Johnny let out a bored sigh. This whole deal was turning into a regular cartoon. The Frenchman turning up like it was cocktail hour. The girl verging on hysterics. Favour to Larry or not, matters were getting complicated. Oh, to hell with it, he decided. He'd pay back Larry some other way.

Grabbing Kelly's hand, he tugged her off the bed. 'This way, Kelly,' he muttered.

Kelly stumbled after Johnny, trying to free her hand from his strong, vice-like grip. She was a mess, her thoughts full of worry for Luc. The walk seemed to take an eternity.

'Right,' said Johnny at last. He paused outside a double-fronted doorway towards the front of the house.

'OK, Giuseppe,' he said, opening one of the doors and beckoning crisply to his man within.

Giuseppe nodded. The blank expression on the bodyguard's face remained unchanged as he stepped from the room.

'You'll find your friend in there,' said Johnny, nudging Kelly through the doorway into the room. She thought he was following but the door closed silently behind her.

The room was huge, deathly quiet. For a brief, unreal moment, Kelly feared she'd been duped again, that there wasn't really anyone here. Then she heard the flick of a lighter and her eyes darted to the sound.

He was over by a window, his back to her, evidently unaware of her entry. He held his cigarette down by his thigh, the curl of smoke rising sinuously upwards.

'Luc?' she whispered shakily.

He wheeled around at once, those green, green eyes locking on to hers, that handsome, dark face completely unscathed. Luc. It really was Luc!

For one fleeting second, they each stood rooted to the spot, incredulity mirrored on the other's face. Then, with almost synchronised timing, they moved. In a flash they were together, arms wrapped tightly, bodies moulding perfectly.

'Kelly,' Luc was murmuring. '*Chérie!* What is happening? Why are you here, in this place?'

Kelly couldn't speak. She just rested her head snugly on his chest, wanting to hold him, wanting to be held.

Several minutes later, when Johnny entered the room, they were still clinging desperately together.

Johnny's face was set, devoid of expression. He stared intently at Luc.

'You love this woman?' he asked coldly.

Luc stared coolly back, matching Johnny's intensity glare for glare. 'It is your concern?'

Johnny's face darkened. 'Maybe,' he said ominously.

Imperceptibly, Luc pulled Kelly closer. Kelly stole a glance up at him, trying frantically to catch his eye. Say no, Luc, she willed, knowing how much Johnny wanted her, knowing how simply he could remove anything or anyone standing in his way, knowing he could click his fingers at any moment and his men would come running.

'Yes,' Luc answered. 'I love her.'

So much for her powers of telepathy! He'd said it! She almost fainted, slumping, a dead weight, against Luc's chest. It was only by virtue of his strong arms around her that she didn't crumple to the floor. A dull kind of pain throbbed in her head. That was it then. He'd said it. Now God only knew what Johnny would do.

For a while Johnny didn't speak. Suddenly, he smiled, the flash of brilliant white lighting up his features. 'I see,' he said, nodding gently.

He reached very deliberately towards his shirt pocket.

Too late Kelly saw the bulge in his pocket. 'No!' she screamed wildly, picturing the gun he would pull out at any moment. She hurled herself forward, clutching at his arm.

Johnny shot his eyes from Luc to her, outright amusement gilding his features. Despite Kelly's fingers clasped around his forearm, he continued effortlessly to his pocket.

'It's OK, honey,' he said, brandishing an innocent set of carkeys from inside the pocket. 'Car keys are not my preferred choice of weaponry.' He switched back to Luc, 'I apologise for relieving you of these earlier,' he said. 'At the time I thought it was necessary.'

Quickly, he threw the keys to Luc. 'Go start your car,' he muttered. 'Kelly will join you in a moment.'

Luc didn't move.

'You have my word, my friend,' said Johnny quietly.

Luc looked at her doubtfully. 'Kelly?'

'Go on, Luc,' she whispered, not at all sure what was happening.

Luc still seemed dubious. 'Five minutes!' he said tersely to Johnny. 'She must join me in five minutes.'

Kelly almost fainted again. Luc giving orders to Johnny. To her amazement, Johnny merely nodded. 'Five minutes,' he agreed.

Silently, Luc walked off. Kelly watched through the window as he reappeared outside and leant against the side of a car. Johnny, she was acutely aware, was watching her.

She felt him move nearer, felt his body within a hair's breadth of hers.

'Say goodbye to me, Kelly,' he whispered.

'Goodbye?'

'Yes.'

'You . . . you're letting me go?'

He ran his fingerpad delicately up the slender column of her throat. 'Uh-huh. I'm letting you go.'

His warm, fresh breath tickled her neck. He let his finger fall to the neckline of her shirt. 'But I'm going to have to ask you to keep quiet about your little trip out here. You know that, don't you?'

Kelly swallowed, not answering.

Johnny dipped his finger into her shirt, tracing the initial swell of her breasts. 'OK, honey,' he said softly. It wasn't a question.

She nodded nervously.

'I'm glad we understand each other,' he smiled.

He was so close, so goddamn close, and his finger was going lower and goddammit, her stomach was looping. She wheeled abruptly away from him, glaring into his black, flashing eyes, into that dangerous, swarthy face.

'Goodbye, Johnny Casigelli,' she said coldly and, fighting the urge to race from the room, she walked away slowly, with what she hoped would pass for some dignity.

Johnny stood briefly by the window, watching as the rental car sped off down the curving driveway. A final glimpse of shining tawny hair sent that sexual lurch through his groin again. Having Kelly in the house had nearly caused him to lose his mind. He had wanted her so badly he had almost ordered Giuseppe to take her so-called boyfriend for a little drive in the desert and lose him. At the last moment he had stopped himself from getting into some very risky business. He owed Larry; but he didn't owe him so much that he'd risk being charged with murder. No woman was worth that. The last thing he wanted were cops crawling around, involving him in a missing-person enquiry. Temptation had nearly got the better of him but his freedom and his business were more important. Turning on his heel, he strode towards the door and yelled for Giuseppe.

'Yeah boss,' said Giuseppe from just outside the doorway.

'Get the gate opened for those two,' ordered Johnny. 'See they get out OK.'

Get out OK? Guiseppe eyed his boss curiously. The boss was letting them go?

Johnny snapped his fingers irritably. 'Now!' he barked.

Giuseppe jumped to it. It wasn't for him to question the boss. 'Yeah boss. Right away.'

'And then get the chopper down here fast,' said Johnny abruptly. 'I want to get the hell out of this desert.'

Now for Larry, he thought after Giuseppe had hurried off. Snatching up the phone, he dialled through to California. 'Larry,' he said as the familiar confident drawl came on the line. 'Change of plan. I decided to let Kelly go. Yeah, you could say unforeseen circumstances. She's on her way back right now. So anyway, here's the new deal ... how do you feel about heading up a brand new law firm.'

Luc's rental car groaned and grumbled as they sped across the desert. Kelly felt hot, uncomfortable and emotionally exhausted but, as she gazed across at Luc, she could not have been happier.

Luc had hardly spoken, rather more concerned she supposed with getting out of there. There was so much she wanted to ask him! And tell him. Wherever was she going to start?

'Luc?' she began softly.

He turned his head briefly from the dusty track in front of them, a half-smoked Marlboro dangling from the corner of his mouth. '*Oui?*'

She smiled a hint of a smile. 'You're my hero, you know that! You're my knight in shining armour, oops, I mean, my knight in T-shirt and Levi's!'

He smiled back, resting one hand lightly on her knee, steering with the other. He flicked his eyes back to the track.

'And, you know back there, you said you loved me. Well,' murmured Kelly, 'guess what. I love you too!'

Luc stared steadily at the dusty road in front.

She glanced down at his strong, tanned hand on her knee and ran her fingernail lightly over his knuckles. 'In fact, not only do I love you too,' she said softly, 'I love you three, four, five –'

Abruptly, Luc veered off the trail and slammed on the brakes. Tossing his cigarette out of the window, he leant towards her.

'– love you six,' went on Kelly, her voice playful, 'seven, eight –'

'Shuddup,' murmured Luc as his lips touched hers.

Mouths glued together, their hands roamed hungrily, pulling at clothing, frantically unbuttoning, unfastening.

Desperate to unclothe herself for him, Kelly tore off her flimsy white blouse whilst he wrested her jeans down her legs. Naked, her body vibrant and glowing, showing no hint of the stresses of the past few days, she welcomed Luc's hands all over her. Urgently, she tugged his T-shirt over his head.

His lean, brown chest was heaving with excitement.

'I'm sorry for running out on you in Paris,' she murmured as she butterfly-kissed all those smooth, gleaming muscles. 'I thought you didn't want me. I acted so spoilt.'

'Yes,' said Luc hoarsely, kissing the back of her neck. 'You did act spoilt.'

'What?' she drew back. Feverish with passion, nonetheless she felt sudden self-righteousness kick in. 'I wasn't that spoilt!'

Luc's hands closed wonderfully over her full, pert breasts. 'Yeah, you were,' he murmured, voice cracking, 'but then, I was acting selfish.'

'Yeah, you were.' giggled Kelly. 'So we're even.'

'*Oui, chérie.*' Luc's voice was mud-thick. 'Even.'

He ran his thumbs over her pointed nipples and she arched her back away from the seating as darts of pleasure speared her chest. Pulling at the button-fly of his jeans, passion made her clumsy and she had to abandon the task and let him take over. Their furiously panting breaths filled the car as they kissed and caressed, hands and eyes feasting upon the other.

Kelly's pulse rate surged when Luc placed his arm under the backs of her knees and lifted her legs up from the seat. She rested her feet high up on the dashboard in front as he stroked the backs of her long, golden thighs. Catching her breath, she felt him move up delightfully to the exposed bulb of her bottom. With the flat of his hand, he rubbed round and round the base of her smooth buttocks whilst she urgently sought his mouth with her own, sighing and kissing him simultaneously. He hadn't yet touched her sex, but she could feel herself moist and swollen with need for him. Desperately, she moved his hand upwards, pressing his fingers into her damp fur.

'Mmm,' he whispered as he felt her. 'I have missed you so much, *chérie*.'

'Show me, darling,' she breathed, excitement constricting her airways.

'Yes,' he said simply.

His voice was so low and so sexy that Kelly found herself feverish. She pushed her chest out as he leant towards her breasts, flicking his tongue in turn at each of her dark, hardened nipples, making her twist her upper body frantically to his mouth. Below, after fondling her nest of pubic hair, he delicately eased his fingers on to her sex, parting the peach lips to toy, almost idly, with her clitoris. Kelly moaned softly, relishing the flutters along the seam of her sex. She let her knees fall widely apart, displaying herself openly to him. His eyes dropped downwards and his face glazed over with arousal.

'I want to taste you,' he murmured.

'Oh God, yes,' she sighed. 'Hurry.'

Quickly, he stepped out of his door, round to her side of the car. He opened her door and, lifting her out, wrenched open the rear door, placing her along the length of the back seat. Crouching down on his haunches outside the open door, he dragged her hips towards him, parted her legs and balanced them on each of his shoulders.

Excitedly Kelly eased herself up, resting on the backs of her elbows. She watched transfixed as Luc dipped his head between her legs.

'Oh Lord,' she moaned when his tongue touched her sex. With exquisite slowness, he moved the tip along her smooth inner lips, back and forth, forth and back, until she ached to have him touch her centre.

Weak with excitement, she dropped her head back on the seating just as he inserted his rigid tongue inside her. In and out, he poked at her swollen flesh, licking skilfully round the edges of the moistened opening. When he moved up to her clitoral nub, closing his lips around it, sucking deliciously, flicking wondrously with his tongue, she squealed with delight, her pleasures and senses all reeling towards her stimulated sex. Automatically, she began to move her hips, rhythmically raising and lowering, working herself in harmony against Luc's mouth. He pressed his lips harder against her, moving his hands up her flat, fluttering stomach, straining forwards to find her nipples. Teasing her nipples with his fingers, teasing her sex with his mouth, he sent her wild with arousal and desire. She was desperate for him now.

'My darling,' she moaned urgently. 'Luc! Now, my darling. Please!' Hurriedly, she tried to part her legs wider for him but the restrictions of the seating and the doorway made it difficult.

'A moment, *chérie*,' murmured Luc, gruff with passion. He stood upright and pulled her out of the car.

Holding her shaky body steady with one hand, he tugged inside his opened fly. Frantically, she moved to help him, drawing down the waistband of his underpants, releasing his magnificent penis.

As she circled it with both of her hands, savouring its heat, running her thumbs over the smooth, bulbed end, Luc groaned loudly, involuntarily jerking his hips towards her.

Roughly, he lifted her hands from his cock, placing them instead on the tops of the two parallel open car doors. Then, grasping her round her waist, he hoisted her up around his hips, simultaneously easing himself inside her.

'Mmmmm, oh Luc,' she sighed as he penetrated, probing and stretching her, gloriously filling her. She gripped the doors for support, wrapping her legs tightly around his hips, so tight she could feel the buttons of his open fly dig into the base of her bottom cleft. It didn't matter; she pushed hard against him and he clasped her buttocks roughly, beginning to move slowly, beginning to move her along with him.

Stroking deep inside her, Luc bent his knees and hoiked her up higher. The rhythmic movements caused the front of his body to rub against her clitoris. Her mind began to spin along with her body. She closed her eyes as silvery lights danced in her head and sharp blades of pleasure sliced through her sex. As Luc moved faster, each upward thrust rippling through her abdomen, she could think of nothing other than her pure sexual delight.

Luc ground into her faster and harder and began to clutch urgently at her buttocks, kneading and massaging each stimulated cheek. His passionate groping, coupled with their fusion, rocketed her pleasure to another, higher, dimension. Higher and higher she went. And then, to the highest of all. Her orgasm burst throughout her whole being and she jerked herself wildly against him, squeezing her thighs round his hips, savouring his hardness still thrilling her insides.

As her climax tore through her, sapping her of energy, her arms no longer had the strength to hold her up. She threw them round Luc's neck, almost knocking him off balance.

'*Un instant*!' he gulped, swiftly lifting her off him, withdrawing so suddenly that Kelly gasped with shock. Turning her round, he placed her hands on the roof of the car. Immediately understanding his wish, Kelly arched her back, pushing her bottom out towards him.

'*O oui*, oh yeah,' murmured Luc, parting her gleaming buttocks and sliding back inside her.

Feeling him fill her up again, Kelly's body reawoke

and energy began to flood back. Deliciously he moved, nudging his hips against her damp bottom, reaching round beneath her arms to cup and fondle her swollen, jiggling breasts. When she felt him grab her hips and stab more urgently, her body magically responded. She arched her back as much as she could, drawing him in as deep as she could and, as he climaxed, so did she. Again and again and again.

They lay together on the back seat of the car, somewhere in the middle of the hot, arid desert. Gleaming arms and legs entwined. Kelly rested her head contentedly on Luc's chest. She fluttered her eyelids open as he stirred, watching him as he threw out an arm and groped around on the floor of the car. Reaching into his discarded jeans, he pulled out his pack of Marlboros and shook out a cigarette. She snuggled happily against him, not quite believing the love they'd just made, not quite believing he was really there. In fact, not quite believing anything at all about the past few days.

'Are you really here, Luc?' she muttered. As if to check, she ran her fingers lightly along his collarbone. 'Or am I dreaming?'

Luc chuckled wickedly. 'If it is a dream, *chérie*, it is a very dirty one.' At first, she chuckled with him but, after a second or so, she jerked her head up, totally serious. 'But how did you get here? How did you know where to find me?'

Luc winked and smiled. 'No problem!'

'Don't tease me, Luc. Tell me.'

He looked long and hard at her earnest expression. His smile ebbed away. He too turned serious. 'I thought I had lost you, Kelly,' he whispered. 'I went to your apartment the day after we argued and you were gone. I spoke with Angie. She told me you'd gone, why you had gone –'

'It was stupid of me,' murmured Kelly, dropping a kiss in the centre of his chest.

'So we telephoned,' he continued. 'At first, Angie spoke with your stepmother. She would not get you, said you were sleeping or something, and then later we could not get through at all.' He shrugged, pulling deeply on his cigarette. 'So, I thought to myself I have no choice. I decided to come to you.'

'You went to my house? But I still don't understand. If you went there, how did you find out where I was? That I was here?'

'Yesterday morning I called at your house, *oui* – Angie, she gave me the address – and I spoke with the maid. She told me you'd gone off somewhere with Larry. She did not know where so she gave me the directions to Larry's office to speak with his assistant. The maid, she said it was too early to disturb your stepmother to ask her.'

'Thank goodness for that at least,' muttered Kelly. 'God only knows what yarn Marissa would have spun you. So you went to the office?'

Luc nodded, picking up the story. 'The assistant, Justine, is the one we have to thank. She suspected Larry and Marissa were up to something. She didn't know for sure what it was, but she thought this guy, this Johnny, was involved. She had looked out a file and found out he had a property in Mexico, near Ensenada. So, I drove through the night, searching for this place *et voilà* –,' Luc clicked his fingers, '– I am here. *C'est ça!*'

'My proper, proper hero,' whispered Kelly, shifting up him a fraction and nuzzling the crook of his shoulder and neck. 'And I hardly know Justine but I owe her so much.'

'You can thank her soon, *chérie.*'

'Can I thank you now?' Keeping her eyes firmly on his face, she moved her lips down the side of his neck and over his chest.

Luc smiled his gorgeous smile and her insides dissolved into jelly. He tossed his cigarette butt out of the window, then tenderly stroked her hair. 'In a moment,' he murmured. 'But first you tell me what this was all about, no?'

So Kelly told him, the words tumbling forth, the pent-up emotion releasing cathartically. She told him all about the sham visit, Larry and Marissa's betrayal, the papers Johnny wanted her to sign. When she'd finished, she felt drained, depleted. Luc hugged her tightly to him. 'It's OK now,' he whispered, stroking her hair. 'Something like this will never happen again. I'll look after you, Kelly.'

They kissed slowly, totally enraptured, totally in love. Kelly craved his mouth, scraping his teeth with her own, twirling her tongue hungrily around his. She simply couldn't get enough; his sexy, fresh taste made her senses sizzle, her body blaze.

'Luc,' she began, overwhelmed. 'I love you!' She climbed on top of him.

'Love you too!' he gasped back, heaving her over him.

Straddling him, she banged her head on the low car ceiling and they almost slid off the seat as he hauled her roughly to him. Positioned precariously on all fours, she dipped her chest down to him. He tugged urgently at her nipples with his lips.

She could feel his cock, smooth and hard, press against the inside of her thigh.

'Mmm,' she breathed huskily. 'You feel so good.'

Leaning back, she twisted her head round and reached behind her, enclosing his penis in her hand. With long, firm strokes, she began to stimulate, moving her hand rhythmically up and down, now and then stopping to rub lightly on his swollen balls.

Luc arched his hips up, groaning ecstatically. 'Oh yeah Kelly,' he moaned, craning forward himself and sliding his fingers between her legs. Back and forth his fingers glided, deliciously vibrating her fleshy nub, easing up and down inside her.

Together they stimulated, harder, faster, oblivious to their cramped, awkward positions. Muscles tensed, groins on fire, hands moving with urgent, skilful rapidity, they brought each other swiftly to a keen peak of pleasure. They climaxed jerkily, crying out together, hot, gleaming bodies exploding in spectacular unison.

Turning from the large airport window, where she'd been pretending to watch the taxi-ing jets for the past ten minutes, Marissa glanced sideways at Larry. She was still sulking. She knew it wasn't really Larry's fault, but it certainly wasn't hers and, as she'd left everything up to him, surely he should have foreseen something like this. Damn Larry! Damn Johnny Casigelli! Damn whoever the hell that Frenchman was! Most of all, damn Kelly!

As she glanced furtively at him, Larry turned his head slightly. For a split second, she caught his eye. Immediately, she looked back toward the window.

'Come on now, baby,' cajoled Larry. 'Quit sulking.' He covered her hand affectionately with his.

She snatched her hand away irritably. 'Don't tell me what to do. And don't treat me like a child.'

'Well, quit acting like one then.'

Marissa snapped her head back to him. 'Me?' she said furiously. 'Who's the one supposed to be a big-shot lawyer? Who can't even pull one teensy, lousy deal off — even with a wise-guy Mafiosi in on the act?'

'Keep your voice down,' hissed Larry, staring rigidly in front.

Glaring fiercely at his handsome profile, Marissa bit her lip and turned back to the window. She focused on a Boeing 747.

Several angry seconds ticked by.

'Look,' Larry began, his voice gentle again. 'It was a

long-shot, honey. We both knew that. How were we to know Kelly had some Frenchman hooked – and a resourceful one at that? She never said anything to any of us.'

'You're a lawyer. You should have thought of it.'

'Yeah,' sighed Larry. 'You're right, I was sloppy.'

He balled his fist angrily on his thigh. She was right. He had been sloppy. In all his years as a lawyer, he'd never been so sloppy. What he still couldn't work out was how in the world the Frenchman had found out where Kelly was. The only people who knew were Johnny, himself and Marissa.

Wearily, he shrugged his shoulders. 'Hon, it's not so bad. Johnny stemmed the flow. He couldn't risk carrying on with it once the Frenchman turned up. He didn't know how many people the Frenchman had told where he was going.'

'"Johnny stemmed the flow",' mimicked Marissa sarcastically, rocking her head from side to side. 'Johnny, Johnny, Johnny –'

'You got a lot to thank Johnny for,' warned Larry. 'He's going to smooth things over with Kelly while we're gone. And he's going to finance my new law practice.'

'Yeah, your practice. What about me? What do I get?'

'Babe, you know I'll always take care of you.'

'Hmm,' grunted Marissa.

'Honey, it's all about damage limitation now. We just got to make the best of a bad job.'

They both glanced up as the gate opened. As First Class passengers, they strolled to the front of the line, boarding passes at the ready.

'What if I don't want to make the best of a bad job?' muttered Marissa.

'Then I guess that's your choice!' Larry muttered back dismissively.

I'll show him, she thought sourly. Sashaying sexily

down the entry run, into the plane, she knew that his eyes would be glued to her. She smiled beguilingly at a good-looking, dark-haired steward who almost fell over himself to show her to her seat.

Steadfastly ignoring Larry seated next to her, she flirted outrageously with the steward, all through the flight preliminaries and take-off. By the time they were airborne, she had the steward almost panting like a puppy and she was feeling much, much better.

'I think I'm going to enjoy this flight!' she said, stretching out like a sleek blonde cat, revelling in the steward's wide-eyed, lust-sick gaze. Slipping off her shoes, she watched with mild amusement as he immediately knelt before her, placing a cushion beneath her feet.

'That more comfortable, ma'am?' asked the steward eagerly.

'Mmm, yes, thanks,' sighed Marissa, wriggling her toes luxuriously against the rich, velvet fabric. She glanced surreptitiously at Larry. The little vein in his temple was pulsing. A sure sign of anger, she smirked. She knew that if they had been anywhere else and she had flirted like this right in front of him, he would have pulled her away by now, put her roughly over his lap, pulled up her skirt, pulled down her panties and spanked her gloriously! The thought sent shivers right up her spine. She knew it was futile – not even Larry would do that slap bang in the middle of First Class. Still, it was fun to annoy him.

She giggled girlishly as she 'spilt' a drop of champagne and the steward sprang gallantly forward with a cloth.

'Oh, for God's sake!' muttered Larry, snapping off his seatbelt and striding off to a spare row of seats on the other side of the aisle.

Marissa's smirk got wider and she turned the full force of her charms upon the defenceless steward, who seemed to have forgotten he had a job to do and was hanging on her every word, tending to her every need. For ten whole minutes she didn't once look at Larry.

When she decided to glance across, knowing full well that by now he'd be fuming, she almost choked on her champagne.

A tall, willowy brunette had slipped into the seat next to Larry. She was laughing lightly, obviously at something Larry had said. Not only that, her French-polished nails were virtually resting on the sleeve of his jacket. Not only that, her thigh was just inches from his – and moving closer.

Marissa gripped her armrests, alarm bells clanging. 'Run along and get me another drink, would you, sweetie?' she purred to the suddenly annoying steward. Then, slipping her shoes back on, standing tall, and smoothing down her tight, black micro-mini, she marched across the aisle.

'Excuse me,' she said sweetly to the brunette. 'I do believe that you're in my seat.'

The brunette looked up defiantly. 'I don't think so,' she said coolly, smartly switching her attention back to Larry.

'I do think so,' said Marissa, still sugary sweet. With one swift yank, she jerked the brunette straight out of the seat.

'Hey!' gasped the startled woman.

'Beat it!' hissed Marissa. 'He's mine.'

Sliding in beside Larry, Marissa watched the furious brunette slink off, glaring daggers back at her all the while. Satisfied, Marissa leant back comfortably in her appropriated seat. She glanced at Larry.

'You can wipe that smile off your face, lawyer-man,' she murmured.

Larry's grin grew wider. Marissa couldn't resist it. 'Maybe I will make the best of a bad job!' she said, snuggling against his arm, resting her head on his shoulder.

Larry leant close, whispering softly in her ear. 'Soon as we get to Rio, I'm going to have to punish you for your little game just now.'

Marissa gazed up, eyes dancing excitedly. 'I don't think I can wait!'

'Think you're going to have to, babe.'

She looked feverishly around. 'What's behind that curtain over there?'

'Dunno,' grinned Larry with a wink.

Smiling wickedly, she nuzzled his neck. 'Come on, baby,' she breathed, tugging urgently at the wrist of his sleeve. 'Let's go make our own cockpit.'

21

'There!' sang Kelly, dropping the pen on the last of the documents. 'I'm done! Only a day late.'

'Good.' Bill Stern deftly gathered together the papers. He started to check they had all been signed correctly. 'It's all yours now, honey. Just like your dad wanted.'

Kelly beamed across the desk at him. 'Yes,' she agreed.

Bill smiled back. She was a beautiful girl, Kelly, and a very sweet girl too. He was extremely fond of her – she was like one of his own. Still smiling, he pushed his little wire specs up his chubby nose, dipped his eyes and began expertly scanning the documents.

Bill Stern was an excellent attorney. He ran his own, highly successful law practice from the building just across the street from Kelly's father's firm. He'd known Kelly's father well, they'd been the best of rivals in business – and the best of friends out of it.

Bill shuffled through the papers in silence. Satisfied, he reached to the floor for his attaché case. As he locked the papers securely away, he shook his head to himself. Something was a little off the mark about this procedure. Strictly speaking, it should be Larry Barris here today for Kelly, holding her hand so to speak. After all, Larry was the surviving partner in the firm and had handled all Kelly's affairs for her ever since David had died. Not that Bill minded the favour – he just found it curious, that was all.

'Larry can go through things in more depth with you, once he gets back from his trip.' Bill's eyes twinkled merrily. He pulled off his specs, chewing the end of the earpiece absently. 'Er, do you know when he'll be back?'

'No,' Kelly replied softly. 'No, I don't.' Her sunny smile wilted slightly and she suddenly seemed very tense.

Mmm, thought Bill, curiouser and curiouser. Something was very definitely off-kilter here. He'd had an odd feeling ever since Larry had called him up out of the blue yesterday and asked him to act for Kelly in the signing of the documents at her coming of age. Simple enough task, mused Bill. Larry had left everything properly in order on his desk. Still, something just wasn't quite right.

Bill cleared his throat noisily. 'Um, everything OK between you and Larry, Kelly?'

Kelly looked across at him, big amber eyes watery. 'Not really,' she whispered. 'Larry won't be coming back here, Bill.'

'Oh?' replied Bill, shooting up a bushy grey eyebrow. 'Want to tell me about it?'

Kelly smiled shakily. 'No. People fall out. These things happen.'

Bill, with his honed intuition, his years of reading people's true emotions, could see she was putting on a brave face. He closed his chubby hand round hers. 'I'm sorry,' he said gently. 'I know you put a lot of faith in Larry. But, if you ever need a shoulder, you know where to find me.'

'Thanks, Bill,' she said softly. She flicked back her hair and squared her shoulders, before pushing her chair back from the desk. 'Actually,' she said, just a little too brightly. 'I could use your advice right now. About a replacement for Larry. After all, somebody's got to run my dad's firm, haven't they?'

'Sure.' Bill grinned affably. 'Off the top of my head even, I know some people. Leave it to me.'

Relieved it was all over, Kelly wandered out into the long, beige corridor. At the far end, she could see Luc leaning nonchalantly against the reception unit, chatting idly to Justine and Annie. Both girls seemed unusually flustered, giggling and blushing and surreptitiously fluffing their hair when they thought the other wasn't looking. Heavens, Justine had even taken off her glasses and uncoiled her French pleat!

Kelly rolled her eyes goodnaturedly but inside she was bursting with pride and love and unbridled lust. Even now, when she looked at Luc, she could flush to the very roots of her hair. She couldn't blame Justine and Annie for flirting with him. Not one bit!

Luc's eyes flicked up the corridor. As soon as he saw her, his face broke into a grin and he strolled toward her.

'Hey heartbreaker,' she murmured fondly, poking him in the ribs.

'Hey yourself,' he said softly. He kissed the tip of her freckled nose. 'All done?'

'Yeah,' smiled Kelly. 'All done. Hey come on . . . let me show you over the firm.'

Clasping his hand, she danced off down the corridor, proudly showing him this office and that plant and this painting and that computer. Peeling off to the left, she stopped excitedly. 'And here's the library!' she announced grandly, pushing him through the heavy oak doors.

Luc looked suitably impressed. He whistled softly, letting her lead him by the hand round the room.

'Look at this,' she panted excitedly. 'No one bothers with it, but there's a whole section here on art.' Reaching up amongst the leather-bound books, she paused at one particularly lustrous-looking volume.

Heaving down the book, she lugged it over to a nearby table. Leaning over the table, she began to flick through the glossy pages, pouring over the illustrious works of art. 'Luc,' she enthused. 'Come and look at this!'

'I am looking!' insisted Luc.

His voice was so low and croaky that Kelly glanced round sharply. His eyes were fixed firmly on her bottom.

'Not that,' she giggled. 'This!' She jabbed her finger down at the book.

Luc moved behind her, looking down over her shoulder. She gazed up at him as he studied a rich reproduction of Gauguin's *L'esprit Veille*.

'One day you're going to be in a book like this,' she said softly. 'I know it.'

'Yeah,' he muttered, sounding oddly disinterested.

'What's up?' she began. Then she realised what was up as he pressed his denim-clad penis against her.

Quickly, he slipped his hand under her dress and down the back of her white lace panties.

'Luc!' she protested. 'We can't. Not here!'

'Why not?' he murmured. 'It is your firm now, no?'

He slid his middle finger into her buttock cleft, gliding magically up and down, pressing his fingertip into her bottom. She sighed with delight.

'You like that, *chérie*?'

'No,' she whispered, grinding back her hips for more. 'It's very boring!'

'Boring, huh?' chuckled Luc, still teasing her intimate, sensitive flesh. 'I had better stop then?'

'No!' she gasped vehemently. 'Only ... mmm oh yes that's so nice ... only kidding!'

She rocked her hips urgently against his probing fingers. Deftly, he flipped up the back of her short, tangerine mini-dress, and eased her white panties down her thighs.

Kelly felt the sudden brush of air on her bared flesh. She knew this behaviour was highly inappropriate – what if one of the associate lawyers walked in? But then, it did feel so good and –

'Oh God,' she moaned as he pushed his hand between her thighs, cupped her sex, and stimulated the whole of her pudenda. Within seconds, she could feel herself coating his hand with her dampness and when he moved back up to her bottom, roughly rubbing her buttocks, glossing each cheek with her sex dew, she was totally, totally lost.

'I give in!' she cried, throwing back her head so that her long, shiny hair cascaded down her back. Closing her eyes, she savoured his touch.

'Good!' murmured Luc, now fingering her nubby clitoris. As he toyed with her stiffening bud, Kelly's sex began to throb and tighten fantastically. She moved her legs wider apart, stretching the sliver of her pulled-down panties so much that they cut into her thighs. With a sharp breath, Luc seized the stretched band of lace, swiftly ripping it through the centre. Breathing a sigh of relief, Kelly giggled a lusty giggle. 'I hope you're going to buy me some new ones!'

'*Non*,' said Luc bluntly, his accent stronger than ever. 'They only get in the way, no?'

'I guess so,' she murmured, distracted once more by his skilful fingers.

Suddenly, he leant his head down to hers. 'Get up on the table,' he whispered.

'I c-can't do that!' she stammered, but even as she said it, her heart was hammering with excitement and her stomach was a riot of zigzags and flutters.

'*Chérie*, get up on the table. I will lock the doors.'

No sooner had he moved away to lock the doors than Kelly had eased herself on to the table, muzzy with lust and anticipation.

Shakily positioned on all fours on the tabletop, her dress flicked up to her waist, her panties torn in half upon the floor, Kelly was feeling very, very wanton. As she glanced sidewards to watch Luc walk back towards her, she felt overwhelmed once again with love and lust. His gorgeous, dark face was tense with desire, his eyes heavy with arousal.

'*Magnifique!*' he gasped, moving behind her and running his hands hungrily down the outsides of her thighs. For a while he stood at the table end, tracing the lines of her lower back and thighs. Kelly was almost gulping for air as his hands moved over her, deliberately avoiding, it seemed, the parts of her body which most craved his touch.

Without warning, he suddenly grasped her thighs, dragging her hips to the table end. Swiftly he sank to his knees and, squeezing together the cheeks of her bottom, began to lick, first tracing lightly along the pushed-together join, then easing his tongue steadily in between. The sensation was fantastic. As he ran his tongue deliberately up and down, now and then pausing to tease and tickle her starry nether-mouth, Kelly's internal muscles jerked in a frenzy. Moaning and shivering as pre-orgasmic pleasures took a hold, she pushed herself back against him.

However, Luc seemed to have other ideas. He stood up sharply. This time, he pushed her forward on to her forearms, her hips positioned very high, her rosy, luscious sex exposed. Excitement tearing at her tummy, Kelly stole a glance behind her. Luc was leaning across the table towards her. Closing his lips around her swollen clitoris. Starting to suck skilfully.

Her orgasm was almost immediate. It seemed to begin at the very top of her head, pervading every nerve in her torso and legs, peaking in a burst of spectacular thrills and, throughout it all, she could feel Luc's lips tugging gloriously at her hot slippery core as though pulling her orgasm through her.

Panting for breath, flushed, dizzy, she felt him lift her round. Sitting up now, her legs dangling off the end of the table, she clawed frantically at his clothes, yanking his T-shirt up his hard, bronze belly, hurting her fingers as she tore at his button-fly, succeeding in opening it by sheer, brute force. She wrenched his jeans and shorts down his long, muscular thighs, rubbing her hand hungrily round his naked groin, cupping his tight, hard buttocks.

Luc was as frantic as she. Their passion was so rampant that nothing – wild horses running riot, an influx of employees – nothing, could have stopped their lovemaking.

Pulling him to her, Kelly lay back on the table. Luc pushed her legs wide apart and lifted them high in the air, so high that she was able to rest her feet over his shoulders. Then, magnificently, he guided himself inside her, pushing so deep so quickly that she could feel him, almost instantly, bob against her cervix.

Their lovemaking was fast and furious. He held her legs against his chest as he bumped against her, rubbing his balls on her bottom cleft, filling and stroking her insides with searing, magical intensity.

Luc came first. Gripping Kelly's knees against his chest, he rotated his naked hips in sexy, grinding movements against her, spilling deep, groaning with climactic ecstasy. Mistily, through half-opened, passion-glazed eyes, Kelly watched him. Deep in the throes of the pleasure he was giving her, the sight of his face, his rapt expression, his bronze skin glowing with sexual fulfilment, provoked a massive surge of sensation within her. Closing her eyes, she threw her arms out wide to the sides and, as lights danced frenziedly inside her head, she surrendered to a glorious, golden, rippling orgasm.

'Not bad,' joked Luc, collapsing over her seconds later, smudging his lips against hers.

Kelly chuckled. 'If we work very hard, you know, practise our technique ten times a day, we might even get quite good at this.'

'What!' said Luc, locking his forearms over her shoulders and gazing down into her face. 'Only ten times! Phh, it is nothing. I think we have to do it more than that – to get it exactly right.'

'Oh, OK,' she quipped playfully. 'Make that fifteen times a day.'

Luc looked thoughtful for a moment. He glanced down at his watch with a mock-worried frown. 'That means we have to fit in nine more times today, no?'

'No wonder I'm getting a bit sore,' she giggled, reaching up and nibbling his lower lip.

He caught her mouth with his and turned her nibbling into a long, delicious, airless kiss. Then, straightening up from the table, he helped Kelly slide to her feet. Casually, they saw to their disarranged clothing. With a slight chuckle, Luc stooped and retrieved the two torn fragments of Kelly's panties from the floor. Stuffing them into his back jeans pocket, he then drew her into the circle of his arms.

'Home?' he asked softly.

'Where's home?' she whispered. Now that she'd signed all the papers and got her inheritance, where was home?

Luc raised a quizzical eyebrow. 'Paris?'

'Er,' Kelly wavered. She thought of her father's beloved business and the beautiful house he had left her. When she and Luc had arrived back there last night to find it miraculously Marissa-free, it had suddenly felt like home again. The house, the business – how horribly close she had come to losing them both...

Luc glanced down at her. 'Here?' he asked tentatively.

'Um,' she stalled. She thought of Luc trying to live here, away from his beloved Paris, away from his studio.

Luc slipped his arm from her shoulder to her waist, and gave her a loving squeeze. 'Both?' he suggested.

Kelly stretched up. Perfect, she thought, as she kissed the corner of his gorgeous mouth. 'Both,' she agreed decisively, snuggling happily against her man.

Epilogue

The ceiling fan was so darn noisy, humming and whirring till her nerves felt raw. In fact, the whole place was so darn noisy she could hardly get her thinking straight. She drew back from the window to stare round at the room. The loud, geometric designs on the drapes filled her with pure revulsion, the mustard-coloured carpet made her sick. But it was the plastic-wood furniture that really got to her. It was disgusting. Hell, she hadn't set foot in a place like this since she was sixteen years old! Before she got wise. Before she realised exactly where her looks could take her.

Turning back to the window, Marissa gazed through the blind at the neon sign flashing in the darkness by the roadside. Blue Tropicana Motel. Boy, oh boy. There was Kelly in the lap of luxury in Santa Ana and where the hell was she? The Blue Tropicana Motel!

Behind her, Larry stopped talking. She looked round again. He sat on the far edge of the unmade bed, his smooth, brown back gleaming in the muted light. Despite her bad mood, she felt the familiar flicker of desire for him. As he replaced the phone and stretched out on the bed, she raised an eyebrow in query.

'No go,' he said.

'No go?' she parroted, her tone deceptively sweet.

'That's what the man said.' Larry shrugged, flicking the remote control at the television.

Marissa glided over to him, curling up beside him on the bed. His short dark hair was slicked back from the shower he'd just taken and his skin felt cool and damp as she traced her finger across his shoulders. 'What do you think, baby?' she said quietly. 'You think Johnny's playing us along? You think maybe he's enjoying that we're holed up in this dump?'

'What I think hon, is that we do what the man says. If he says we've got to hide out a while longer, give him a chance to smooth things over for us with Kelly, then stay here's exactly what we do.'

Marissa kept her voice sweet. 'But why here? In this dump. Why not the Meridian or some other –'

Larry pressed his forefinger to her lips. 'Because we're nobodies here. No one asks any questions. No hassles. Johnny wants us lying low. We can tough it out here a few days more.'

Marissa whined petulantly. 'It's a sty, Larry! I want to go stay someplace nice. I want some action.'

'You got complaints in the action department?' grinned Larry, slipping his hand up her cropped T-shirt and cupping one very full, warm breast.

Marissa closed her eyes, distracted by his hand 'No, baby,' she exhaled. 'No complaints in that department.'

'Good,' murmured Larry.

She let him lift her over on to his lap and she straddled his hips with her knees. He pushed her T-shirt up to her collarbone and she held it up herself whilst he gazed in wonder at her breasts.

'How did you get to be so beautiful?' he said softly as he dipped towards her right nipple. With his tongue flat, he licked the nipple, did the same to the other, then drew back to gaze once again. Marissa arched her back as Larry's hands came forward to squeeze the rich mounds of flesh, then she lowered her eyes to watch excitedly as he pushed her breasts together and flicked his tongue from nipple to nipple. Tendrils of pleasure threaded from their tips, trickling through to the flesh of each breast. She held her T-shirt up higher, pushing her chest toward him even more. 'Feel me all over, Larry,' she breathed, as he cupped and fondled and licked and sucked. Flushed and aroused, she fumbled with the zip of her tight black jeans, scrambling off Larry and flipping over on to her back to facilitate their undoing. As she did so, she caught her arm on a rough edge of the cheap plastic nightstand.

'Dammit!' she cursed, rolling off the sagging mattress and examining the scratch on her forearm.

'What's up?' gasped Larry.

'Goddamn cheap plastic furniture! Look what it did to me!' She thrust out her forearm to show him.

'Aw baby, it's just a scratch. Come here, I'll kiss it better.'

'Sure you can kiss it better ... someplace else. Any place but here.'

Larry patted the bed. 'Come here,' he coaxed, throaty with passion.

Marissa glowered at him. 'You don't care at all, do you? You don't care that I hate it here. I didn't come to Rio to stay cooped up in some crummy motel. I want to go to out. See some nightlife.'

'Sweetheart,' Larry soothed. 'We'll go to Ipanema, we'll do the nightlife. Just as soon as Johnny okays it.'

'Tell you what, Larry,' snapped Marissa, doing up the button on her jeans and slipping on a pair of high, black mules. 'You stay here and be a good boy just like Johnny says.' She wandered casually over to the mirror, fluffed her hair and checked her lipstick.

'What's that supposed to mean?' muttered Larry, watching her.

'Means baby,' she sang, grabbing her bag and waltzing over to the door, 'that you stay here and be good if you want. I'm going out!' With a smirk at Larry's darkening expression, she stepped out of the room making sure to slam the door behind her.

* * *

Marissa sauntered round the edge of the dance floor, happily noting every single pair of male eyes watch her as she passed by. This was more like it! She headed straight for the bar, climbed up on a barstool and ordered a margarita. Within moments, she sensed someone behind her.

'Buy you a drink, pretty lady?'

The voice was Californian in accent, deep and pleasantly husky in tone. It definitely had promise. Marissa discreetly crossed her fingers in her lap, hoping the looks lived up to the voice. 'I just ordered,' she said as she glanced back over her shoulder.

The man was tall, dressed in jeans and a T-shirt. So far so good, she mused as her eyes fell upon a taut flat belly. Her eyes began to sparkle as she took in the broad, lean chest, the strong, deeply tanned arms, surfer's unkempt hair the colour of wheat. As her gaze wandered to his face, sky-blue eyes, strangely familiar, stared back at her. Marissa gulped. Her heart plummeted to the pit of her stomach and she quickly turned back to the bar.

'Hey,' said the man. 'Don't I know you?'

'No.' Marissa concentrated on sipping her margarita.

The man leant on the bar and peered round at her face. 'Yeah. Yeah, I do. Just a moment –'

The man wouldn't stop staring. But she didn't want to cause a scene. She inclined her head away a fraction. 'You don't know me,' she muttered.

'Sure I do,' said the man and his deeply tanned face broke into a grin. He pointed his thumb and forefinger, gun-like, towards her. 'I'd know you anywhere. Even after all these years. It's Marissa, ain't it? Marissa Brant.'

Marissa winced. Brant! Ugly, ugly name! 'No,' she repeated gulping back her drink.

'Hey, come on. It is Marissa, ain't it! It's Sam. Wild Rose trailer park. You can't have forgotten! All them high times we had. All them long, lazy afternoons underneath the covers. Remember them?'

She did remember them. And she remembered Sam all right. Sex at sweet sixteen with twenty-year-old Sam. That had been the one good thing about Wild Rose trailer park. Better than good even. But Sam hadn't figured in her long-term plans. Sam was no rocket scientist – there was no way he was ever going to make it away from Wild Rose. She'd sacrificed Sam and his lovemaking skills without a second thought when she'd headed on out of there. Still, she thought now, evidently he had made it out of there. What in heaven was he doing in Rio? She almost wanted to ask him. Don't blow it, she cautioned herself. Don't blow all you've built up. Not even Larry knew the truth about her background and she fully intended it to stay that way.

'I told you,' she said deliberately. 'You don't know me. I don't know you, OK.'

Sam scratched his chest, confused. 'Hell, I don't know why you're playing so cagey. All I know is you're Marissa and all I got for you is sweet, sweet memories. I know you ran out on me baby but, hell, there's thirteen years gone by since then. Least you could do is be a little friendly, let me buy you a drink!'

Marissa flicked her eyes up toward him. He was certainly a looker. She'd had good taste even way back. A fluttery warmth spread through her stomach as she looked at him. His handsome, weather-darkened face looked steadily back at her and the warmth started to move downwards. She wriggled a little on her barstool, noting the broad lines of his shoulders as he leant against the bar, the perfect backside delineated by his jeans. She was weakening, she knew it. But what harm could a little trip down memory lane do?

'I can be friendly when I want,' she said.

'I don't think I'll ever forget how friendly you can be,' he answered, a slight croak in his voice.

Marissa ran her fingertip round and round the rim of her ice-cold glass. 'Would you by any chance be flirting with me, Sam?' she asked, popping her finger into her mouth and savouring the piquancy of the salt and lime juice on her tongue.

Sam smiled at her, deep laugh lines creasing round his eyes. 'I guess I might be.'

Marissa nodded, enjoying the moment. She tipped her head back and drained the contents of her glass.

Sam inched closer. 'What do you say? You going to let me buy you another?'

She smiled a little. 'Sure, Sam. Why not!'

He ordered quickly, then turned back to her. 'Where were we?' he grinned.

'I think that you were flirting with me, Sam.'

'So I was,' he said, picking up her hand from the bartop. He pressed her palm slowly to his lips.

Mmm, Marissa decided, she liked that. He floated his lips across the inside of her wrist. She liked that too.

'You smell good, Marissa,' he murmured. He lifted her forearm and kissed the inside of her elbow and she liked that even more. If he could make her feel like this just kissing her arm, what the hell could he do for the rest of her?

'Sam,' she pouted, running the back of her fingernail across the gold-brown skin of his forearm. 'You know that I didn't *want* to leave you all those years ago. I had to, you know that?'

Sam smiled. 'I figured on something like that.'

Marissa smiled radiantly back. She always could twist him right round her finger.

'Er,' Sam continued. 'Maybe we could get, you know, kind of reacquainted?'

'Oh gosh, I don't know about that, Sam,' she teased, trying to look shocked.

Sam cleared his throat, embarrassed. 'Oh well, you know, I didn't mean right now of course.'

'Then again,' whispered Marissa, letting her hand wander up the sleeve of his T-shirt to cup a smooth muscle. 'Right now works for me.'

'Yeah?' he asked hoarsely, his eyes dropping to her hand on his arm.

'Uh-huh,' she murmured, finger-walking down to his wrist.

'OK then,' he grinned. Swiftly, he threw back the end of his beer.

'OK then,' she purred, reaching behind to the bar to finish her own drink. She groped back for the glass, still looking sexily at Sam. She groped back a little further. Where in hell was her drink? she cursed to herself, twisting back to the bar.

'This what you're looking for, Marissa?'

She snapped her head back around. Oh God in Heaven! Larry!

He was standing right there, shaking her glass right in front of her nose.

She snatched her hand from Sam's arm, sitting bolt upright on her barstool. 'Oh, er, hi Larry,' she gulped. 'I was just saying hi to an old friend here. Sam. Fancy, we just met up, just like that . . .'

'Old friend, huh,' muttered Larry, one eyebrow sceptically raised.

'That's right,' gabbled Marissa. 'Isn't it, Sam? Sam, isn't it?'

Sam was looking handsomely bewildered. Marissa shot him a look. 'Oh yeah, that's right,' said Sam at last. 'Marissa and me, we grew up together on Wild Rose. We were just catching up on old times –'

'Wild Rose?' interrupted Larry.

'Yeah, uh-huh,' nodded Sam, emphatically. 'Wild Rose trailer park, back in Bakersfield. You know it?'

Marissa slumped forward on the bar, gripping her hair in her hands. Jeez, shut up Sam, she willed. Dumb jerk was running off at the mouth.

'No, I don't know it,' Larry was saying very politely to Sam. Then he turned to Marissa and bent close to her ear as he replaced her glass on the bar. 'A trailer park, huh Marissa?' he whispered. 'Whatever happened to the childhood in Bel Air, huh baby? That before or after the trailer park?'

Marissa didn't answer. She raked her fingers back through her hair, stalling, stalling . . .

'Well, anyway,' Larry was saying to Sam. 'Nice meeting you, Sam.'

'What?' mumbled Sam, nonplussed. 'Uh yeah, nice meeting you too, I guess.' Sam's voice trailed off.

Marissa spun around to see Larry stalking off.

'Thanks a whole bunch,' she hissed to Sam, who was, by now, looking entirely perplexed. She jerked off her stool, striding angrily after Larry, her mind ticking madly over for an explanation to offer up to him. He was walking so fast that she couldn't catch up. Despite her sticky predicament, her tummy gave a little leap. Larry was particularly sexy when he was mad, and he was looking particularly sexy right now. He'd obviously thrown on the first set of clothes he could find to come and look for her – his white shirt rumpled and untucked over his black, Armani trousers. He looked appealingly dishevelled, as if he'd just rolled out of bed – which of course he had.

She could see his tall figure weaving through the sea of nightclubbers. He was approaching the exit, going out of the door now.

'Get out of my goddam way!' she snapped at a poor, unwitting couple who'd dared to stray into her path. She quickened her pace, stepping on to the pavement outside. The heat of the night seemed unbearable as she trailed after him, her heels clacking loudly on the concrete.

Abruptly he stopped and whirled around. 'Quit following me, Marissa,' he said coldly.

Thank God, he'd stopped, she thought, able to catch her breath a little. She slowed down to a sexy saunter and walked up to him.

'You know,' she began, supremely confident in her power to manipulate. 'It wasn't what it looked like back there.'

'Oh really?'

'No, not at all. You see –'

'I know what I saw, Marissa!' He spat out the words.

For a split second, she faltered, surprised by his tone. Her recovery was laudable as she quickly changed tack.

'Larry, baby,' she said in a little-girl voice. 'Don't be mad with me.'

'Honey, you're not worth getting mad over.'

Marissa dropped her jaw, momentarily speechless. Larry had never spoken to her that way before. He really was furious. Truly, truly furious. 'Larry,' she purred. 'Don't be that way. That old friend of mine, Sam, well, he really was an old friend, and what he said about a trailer park ... he was just having a little joke with you, he –'

'Save it, Marissa,' Larry said tightly. He turned round and made to walk on. Dismissing her.

Marissa saw red.

'Don't you turn your back on me, Larry Barris,' she hurled after him. 'OK so what! So what if I grew up on a trailer park!'

Larry stopped again. 'Sure accounts for a lot,' he threw back.

'*What!*' She stamped her foot on the ground. '*What* did you just say?'

Larry walked slowly back toward her. He dipped his head and neck forward. 'Honey,' he said quietly. 'You can take the trash right out of the trailer park, but you can't take the trailer park out of the trash.'

She drew back her head and spat in his face.

'See what I mean,' he chuckled without mirth, wiping his cheek. 'Classy. Very classy.' He shook his head slowly. 'You're really just a tramp, aren't you babe. I mean, I come out to look for you because I'm worried about your sulky little ass and I find you draped all over some long-haired surfie. Old friend indeed.' He snorted with derision.

Marissa was seething, trembling with fury. 'You're a real smartass aren't you!'

'Smarter than you, baby!'

'Oh yeah? You're just a cheap hustler, Larry. You think Johnny's really going to set you up in some fancy law firm?' She laughed nastily. 'You'll end up a dime-store lawyer, see if you don't.'

Larry's vein started beating at his temple. His face darkened. 'I will never be a dime-store lawyer,' he hissed, jaw muscles clenched. 'But you'll always be a trailer-trash whore.'

She flew at him. He caught her by her wrists. They glared at each other, rage and venom aflame in their eyes. Her wrists began to burn as she panted with impotent savagery, twisting and jerking to shake herself free. His eyes dropped suddenly to the curve of her breasts. Her nipples had hardened visibly beneath her T-shirt.

'Goddamn, you're so gorgeous,' he growled.

She looked daggers up at him, at the set of his handsome features, at the anger in his dark grey eyes. 'Pretty goddamn gorgeous yourself,' she snarled.

Roughly, he wheeled round, dragging her by her wrist along the pavement. The neon sign for the Blue Tropicana flickered up ahead, bright and tacky, set back from the roadside. By the time they reached it, Marissa's legs were weak and her heart was crashing at her rib-cage.

He pulled her violently into the motel room, back-kicking the door behind him, then he strode over to the window, flicking the blind so that light from the neon sign just filtered through. She watched him perch on the nearside of the bed.

'Come here,' he drawled.

She tried so hard not to hurry, fighting the urge to rip off her clothes and race over and wrap her legs around his delicious, smartass hips and bang him from here to eternity. Instead, she'd act like a lady. She stepped oh-so-casually out of her black mules, tossed back her soft blonde tresses, then wandered over and stood barefoot in front of him. Immediately his hands went to her jeans. Without speaking, he slowly unfastened them, eased them down her legs, then lifted each of her ankles in turn and kicked her jeans to one side with his foot. He ran his fingertips lightly up the sides of her long, sleek thighs, up over the tiny curve of her stomach and round along the base of her back. He began to play non-chalantly with the waistband of her string-panties, pulling them up high at the back until the string felt tight in the crease of her bottom. Marissa gasped softly as he twirled the waistband around his finger like a tourni-quet, the string of her panties ever tighter, rubbing at her sensitive skin, making her clench her internal muscles in excitement. Casually, he unwound the material from his finger, instantly relieving the pressure. She felt a light sheen of perspiration break out as his finger trailed down her buttocks before hooking into the gusset of her panties. He pulled the gusset to one side and skimmed the fine hairs along the seam of her sex. His touch was so light she could barely feel it, but the flutters it elicited in her sex made her ache with arousal.

Her panties were annoying her now; she wanted them down, off altogether, to be naked and unhampered for his strong, searching hands. He let the gusset drop back and began to feel her through the thin, fragile lace.

'Can't wait, can you baby?' he taunted. He hooked his forefingers into the waistband of her panties and began to drag them down her thighs.

'Sonofabitch,' Marissa hissed at him, sighing with relief as he pulled them down to her ankles. Rapidly, she kicked them off.

Her lower body was nude now, her midriff at Larry's eye level. He circled her minuscule waist and then his hands wandered up beneath her short T-shirt and closed around her moist, perspiring breasts. Larry groaned almost grudgingly as he felt her, cupping each rich, warm globe and dabbing lightly at her nipples with his thumbs. Marissa could barely stand. Yearning for pressure between her legs, she eased herself on to one of his outspread thighs, straddling and pressing down till she could feel his solid muscles through the exquisite fabric of his trousers. Larry put his mouth to hers and kissed her hungrily before lifting her upright in front of him again. He slid down to the floor before her, placing his hands at the inside edges of her thighs. With gentle firmness, he nudged her legs apart. Marissa felt a huge rush of excitement as her angry lover knelt before her. Frantically, she criss-crossed her arms at the base of her T-shirt, tugging it up and over her head. As she lowered her eyes, she saw him glance upwards at the full undersides of her breasts and with his eyes locked upon her, he tore open his shirt, the lean gym-toned muscles in his torso rippling as he twisted the garment from his body.

Her mouth went dry and she ran her tongue between her lips, letting her fingertips dangle on the tops of his shoulders.

He placed his hands on the insides of her knees,

stroking upwards along her inner thighs until he reached the tendons at the top. Whilst rubbing the tendons carefully with his fingers, he began to brush his thumbs across her pubis, gazing intently at the tiny curve of her mons as he did so. Marissa closed her eyes and tilted back her head, sighing happily as he played with her trim nest of hair. After a moment or two, he leant forward and kissed along the edges of her downy triangle – small, floaty kisses. Marissa found herself breathless, her sex fluttering excitedly each time his lips made contact with her skin and when he wandered to her sex, parting her luscious labia with his thumbs, she shivered with anticipatory delight.

'Oh yes!' she cried as he drew his whole tongue from back to front along the length of her clitoris. He licked again, slowly, dipping his tongue into the tip of her vulva and pulling forward across her swelling nub. He licked with his tongue flat as though thirsty for every drop of her sex juice. She moved her hands to his head, twining her fingers through his hair as he pleasured her. He was tonguing her so very slowly and exquisitely that darts of sensation dashed from her core, shooting through her hips and thighs. Each firm, wet drag of his tongue made her heart beat a little faster, her breaths feel a little shorter. Her clitoral bud seemed to keep hardening and swelling until she literally thought she would burst into climax – but Larry was far too skilled for that, moving too slowly, lifting away too frequently. When she thought she could stand it no longer, when she was panting for air and begging for release, he began to move more quickly, flicking from side to side. Marissa's head started to spin. She clung desperately to Larry's hair, nudging her sex against his mouth. She could feel her wetness seep to the insides of her thighs, hear the slick, slippery sounds of Larry's lovemaking, and it was all she could do to stay upright. A superb tightness began to build behind her mons, spreading to her stomach and diaphragm. Automatically she stepped wider apart, losing all sense of herself as Larry sucked hungrily. Her head began to throb and her legs to tingle and colours swirled wildly behind her closed eyelids.

Suddenly, Larry changed position, sitting instead of kneeling, his legs spread in front, his back against the side of the bed. She slipped down to the space between his legs, grappling at the waist and zip of his trousers until his penis was freed, slanting huge and smooth against his flat lower belly. He hoiked her urgently on to his lap, pulling her legs around his hips and, as she held his cock, he eased her down, letting her guide him inside her. It was almost too much for Marissa. The sheer, undiluted pleasure of it! She sank down hard, rubbing herself against the hair-roughened skin of his thighs, feeling him penetrate so deeply within her.

They moved wildly in rhythm, he grasping her hair, she gripping his shoulders. As their urgency mounted, Larry slipped his hands to her bottom, clasping her bobbing buttocks as she moved. Suddenly he grabbed her buttock cheeks roughly and pressed her hard into his crotch. He was bordering on climax, tilting his head back against the mattress, tensing his neck muscles, closing his eyes. As he came, Marissa leant forward, pushing her mouth, her breasts, her sex, against him, relishing his release within her until her own orgasm jarred her to a disjointed peak of blissful delirium.

Still pressed against him minutes later, Marissa licked Larry's salty neck. 'You move me, baby,' she whispered.

Larry tilted his head up from the edge of the mattress.

'Really you do,' she breathed. 'You move my whole world.'

'All part of the service,' mumbled Larry, exhaustion pulling at his eyelids.

'But Larry –'

'What?'

'You're still just a hustler with a law degree.'

'And you, darlin',' Larry said sleepily, 'are still just a two-bit whore.'

Visit the Black Lace website at
www.blacklace-books.co.uk

FIND OUT THE LATEST INFORMATION AND TAKE ADVANTAGE OF OUR FANTASTIC FREE BOOK OFFER! ALSO VISIT THE SITE FOR . . .

- All Black Lace titles currently available and how to order online
- Great new offers
- Writers' guidelines
- Author interviews
- An erotica newsletter
- Features
- Cool links

BLACK LACE – THE LEADING IMPRINT OF WOMEN'S SEXY FICTION

TAKING YOUR EROTIC READING PLEASURE TO NEW HORIZONS

BLACK LACE

LOOK OUT FOR THE ALL-NEW BLACK LACE BOOKS – AVAILABLE NOW!

All books priced £6.99 in the UK. Please note publication dates apply to the UK only. For other territories, please contact your retailer.

WICKED WORDS 9
Various
ISBN 0352 33860 1

Wicked Words collections are the hottest anthologies of women's erotic writing to be found anywhere in the world. With settings and scenarios to suit all tastes, this is fun erotica at the cutting edge from the UK and USA. The diversity of themes and styles reflects the multi-faceted nature of the female sexual imagination. Combining humour, warmth and attitude with imaginative writing, these stories sizzle with horny action. **Another scorching collection of wild fantasies.**

THE AMULET
Lisette Allen
ISBN 0 352 33019 8

Roman Britain, near the end of the second century. Catarina, an orphan adopted by the pagan Celts, has grown into a beautiful young woman with the gift of second sight. When her tribe captures a Roman garrison, she falls in love with their hunky leader, Alexius. Yet he betrays her, stealing her precious amulet. Vowing revenge, Catarina follows Alexius to Rome, but the salacious pagan rituals and endless orgies prove to be a formidable distraction. **Wonderfully decadent fiction from a pioneer of female erotica.**

COMING ROUND THE MOUNTAIN
Tabitha Flyte
ISBN O 352 33873 3

Flighty Lauren is on the top of the world, literally, travelling in the Himalayas to 'find herself'. But while enjoying the rugged landscape she runs into Callum, her first ever boyfriend, and soon *everything* turns rocky. Lauren still loves Callum, Callum still loves Lauren; the problem is that he is on his honeymoon. Then, while trekking, Callum gets altitude sickness. Lauren wants to take care of him and tend to his every need, but what will happen if his new wife finds out? **A jaunty sex comedy for the backpack generation.**

GOING DEEP
Kimberley Dean
ISBN O 352 33876 8

Sporty Brynn Montgomery returns to teach at the college where she used to be a cheerleader but, to her horror, finds that football player Cody Jones, who scandalised her name ten years previously, is now the coach. Soon Brynn is caught up in a clash of pads, a shimmer of pom-poms and the lust of healthy athletes. However, Cody is still a wolfish predator and neither he nor his buddies are going to let Brynn forget what she did that fateful night back in high school. **Rip-roaring, testosterone-fuelled fun set among the jocks and babes of the Ivy League.**

UNHALLOWED RITES
Martine Marquand
ISBN O 352 33222 O

Twenty-year-old Allegra is bored with life in her guardian's Venetian palazzo – until temptation draws her to look at the curious pictures he keeps in his private chamber. Physically awakened to womanhood, she tries to deny her new passion by submitting to life as a nun. But the strange order of the Convent of Santa Clesira provides new tests and temptations, forcing her to perform ritual acts with men and women who inhabit her sheltered world. **A brooding story of art and lust in the cloisters.**

Black Lace Booklist

Information is correct at time of printing. To avoid disappointment check availability before ordering. Go to www.blacklace-books.co.uk. All books are priced £6.99 unless another price is given.

BLACK LACE NON-FICTION

☐ THE BLACK LACE BOOK OF WOMEN'S SEXUAL   ISBN 0 352 33793 1   £6.99
    FANTASIES   Ed. Kerri Sharp

To find out the latest information about Black Lace titles, check out the website: www.blacklace-books.co.uk or send for a booklist with complete synopses by writing to:

    Black Lace Booklist, Virgin Books Ltd
    Thames Wharf Studios
    Rainville Road
    London W6 9HA

Please include an SAE of decent size. Please note only British stamps are valid.

Our privacy policy
We will not disclose information you supply us to any other parties. We will not disclose any information which identifies you personally to any person without your express consent.

From time to time we may send out information about Black Lace books and special offers. Please tick here if you do not wish to receive Black Lace information.   ☐

Please send me the books I have ticked above.

Name ....

Address ....

....

....

....

Post Code ....

Send to: Cash Sales, Black Lace Books, Thames Wharf Studios, Rainville Road, London W6 9HA.

US customers: for prices and details of how to order books for delivery by mail, call 1-800-343-4499.

Please enclose a cheque or postal order, made payable to Virgin Books Ltd, to the value of the books you have ordered plus postage and packing costs as follows:

UK and BFPO – £1.00 for the first book, 50p for each subsequent book.

Overseas (including Republic of Ireland) – £2.00 for the first book, £1.00 for each subsequent book.

If you would prefer to pay by VISA, ACCESS/MASTERCARD, DINERS CLUB, AMEX or SWITCH, please write your card number and expiry date here:

....

Signature ....

Please allow up to 28 days for delivery.